CHEERS FOR *FROST THE FIDDLER*

"An amazing tour de force. . . . Turns the espionage thriller into a magnetic lure which won't let you go even after you have read the last word."
—*New England Review of Books*

"A brash spy novel . . . witty, and sexier than I dare say."
—*Boston Globe*

"High-spirited and engaging . . . Weber's flair for satire is highlighted in her hilarious portrait of a publicist who will stop at nothing to get her clients' names in print."
—*Publishers Weekly*

"Janice Weber is an American concert pianist. . . . On the evidence of *Frost the Fiddler*, she writes as well as she plays. . . . A lively writing style that is spiced with naughty comments."
—*New York Times Book Review*

"A fast-paced thriller."
—*Library Journal*

"A James Bond clutter of frantic antics, sex on the run, memorable last-second escapes, and rub-outs. . . . A virtuoso manipulation of hallmark preposterous super–spy novel elements—and it's very, very funny indeed."
—*Kirkus Reviews*

"Makes James Bond look like a Quaker . . . The web of intrigue is neatly spun, and Frost finds herself caught up in situations she cannot resist, even though she knows they aren't safe."
—*Booklist*

Also by Janice Weber

Customs Violation
The Secret Life of Eva Hathaway
Frost the Fiddler
Devil's Food

HOT TICKET

JANICE WEBER

WARNER BOOKS

A Time Warner Company

WARNER BOOKS EDITION

Copyright © 1998 by Janice Weber
All rights reserved. No part of this book may be reproduced in any form or by any electronic or mechanical means, including information storage and retrieval systems, without permission in writing from the publisher, except by a reviewer who may quote brief passages in a review.

Cover design by Patty Manzone/Design Monsters
Cover photo by Herman Estevez

Warner Books, Inc.
1271 Avenue of the Americas
New York, NY 10020

Visit our Web site at
www.twbookmark.com

 A Time Warner Company

Printed in the United States of America

Originally published in hardcover by Warner Books
First Paperback Printing: January 2000

10 9 8 7 6 5 4 3 2 1

To Ed
with love

With special thanks to Manuel Lluberas, Jessica Papin,
Armand Pohan, and Susan Sandler

HOT TICKET

Chapter One

𝒥N A FEW seconds the president of the United States would begin to snore. I had been watching his eyelids droop for the last quarter hour; too many glasses of Riesling at a state dinner, compounded by the strain of trying to see through my gown, had finally knocked him out. Couldn't take his inattention personally since the man didn't know Brahms from Buxtehude. To him, violins without bluegrass were like Novembers without elections. And the poor sod had been up since six trying to run the country. He had probably blown the morning at the hospital with Jordan Bailey, second in command. He could have visited a mistress on the way back to the White House, then spent the afternoon hallucinating with his spin doctors. After that, another screaming match with wife Paula as he zipped her into that atrocious orange dress. Let him snore, I thought. It was impossible to get mad at Bobby Marvel. He just wasn't a serious president.

Perhaps my East Room recital was meant to help the First Lady score a few points with the German foreign minister, here to apologize again for World War II in exchange for a few billion in trade concessions. The invitation had come to my manager two days ago. "You've got a date at the White House Tuesday night," Curtis had told me.

"Is that so? I thought I had a rehearsal in Munich."

"Canceled."

Ah: my boss Maxine—the Queen—was sending me to Washington. She hadn't called in months. I would have been more flattered had she not kicked things off by making me *über*-dessert at a State Department orgy. "Are you coming along, Curtis?"

"I think it's time you headed out alone."

A great vote of confidence. Admittedly, on my last case Agent Smith had won the battle, lost the war; but the battle had been Maxine's, the war mine. Other people had died, I had lived: she and I would forever interpret that outcome differently. Perhaps the Queen was giving me another chance to even the score in that murky game called espionage.

"What's the deal?" I sighed.

"As far as I know, you eat, play, and leave."

Right.

I had eaten, now I was playing in a cheerful, fairy-tale room with glittering chandeliers and walls the color of lemon mousse. No critics here; perhaps cheered by that fact, my accompanist Duncan Zadinsky opened the Brahms sonata faster than usual. Had the honor of the occasion unnerved him? Duncan was the skittery type and I probably hadn't given him enough time to barf backstage before the concert. I glanced casually toward the piano bench. He didn't look up but he slowed down: I have that effect on certain men. Nestling into my Stradivarius, I began to play, closing my eyes as the old wood vibrated against my shoulder and high, exquisitely pure melody rippled over the room. I had been making sounds like that for twenty-five years and the first fluttery note was always like a kiss from the gods, tempting me to live forever. As music flew from violin to the far wall, my brain ran myriad acoustical calculations and sent correcting data to my fingertips. I half opened my eyes again: other work here.

Paula Marvel wore a dress with a little more bouffant than her hips could gracefully handle. Her rhinestone tiara topped a pageboy that absorbed but did not reflect light; once again, her hairdresser had gone one shade overboard washing away the gray. Deceptively tiny mouth, apple cheeks, everlasting smile ... eyes blue and lethal as prussic acid. As I played, she memorized the scrollwork in the ceiling. Next to her, the president slept. Gold and bow ties dominated the rest of the front row, Bobby and Paula having surrounded themselves with the sycophants, moneybags, and movie stars who had gotten them elected. Not one of these half-assed Machiavellis was listening to Brahms. Neither was the German foreign minister, for that matter: in half an hour he'd be back at the bargaining table, trying to screw everyone he had just been toasting at dinner. Meanwhile, of course, his intended victims sat figuring how to screw him even worse. The violent beta waves charging from three hundred skulls were beginning to undermine my concentration, not to mention patience. Damn Maxine! This little put-down was her way of reminding me that I was agent first, musician second. Human a far third.

Fine. I played my part. Fortunately, President Marvel was about to provide a little side show. I loved loud snoring at black-tie affairs. At best, it came from the husband of the female heavy, a tight-faced woman in the front row whose jewelry should have been fake. Her reaction to that first snort never ceased to amuse me. Aghast, she would raise an eyebrow. If the offender's own stertor didn't wake him after a few seconds, her shoe would creep sideways and slowly *ccrrrush* his until he resuscitated. This was all done while benignly, sadistically, beaming at the sole witness—me. I caressed Brahms, fighting back a smile: Bobby Marvel's left shoe had five seconds to live.

Perhaps the president's electromagnetic field changed. I saw the First Lady's eyes disengage from the ceiling and glide to her husband's too still profile. Reacting with the reptilian calm that still terrified Washington after three-plus years, Paula snuggled into her seat as one gloved hand crept into Bobby's lap. I put Brahms on automatic and watched, entranced, as two of her fingers constricted around the president's testicles. His only response was a slack jaw, prelude to a snore. So Paula squeezed harder, her biceps rising hideously from her upper arm. President Marvel opened an eye and eventually recognized his surroundings. As Paula's hand slithered back to her lap, he took a deep breath and recrossed his legs. The two of them smiled lovingly at each other, as if this concert made them very, very happy. An overblown performance, even by silent film standards: everyone on the planet knew their marriage was radioactive waste.

Brahms ended. I ran Duncan through Ravel then a bunch of Gershwin arrangements, earning us a flurry of applause. Afterward, President Marvel gave me a gummy kiss and Paula, paradigm of hospitality, invited her guests to stay and dance. She spoke in a deliberately somber voice so that everyone would know she was extremely concerned about the vice president's condition but hell, this evening had been planned months before Bailey had gotten himself terminally ill.

I took my accompanist's arm as a few hundred cabalists rose from their seats, smarmy smiles ready for action. "Duncan, let's go."

"Now?! Paula's about to ask me to dance!"

Next he'd want me taking pictures for his mother in Cleveland. I left him near the butler with the most champagne glasses and waded toward the exit. My manager Curtis would howl in frustration: once again I was neglecting the postconcert schmooze, an artistic duty nowadays as indispensable as tuning my violin. But coed grazing appalled me. Always had. I was the one-on-one type, with men who preferred lamps low and conversation soft. Too many capped teeth here and the place was verminous with media. They had had a field day with my private life last spring, after my Grand Guignol in Leipzig. Someday I'd return the kindness. Meanwhile I'd continue playing the role of Leslie Frost, the fiddler who rode Harleys and broke men's hearts . . . if they were lucky.

Maxine had recruited me—and six others like me—almost ten years ago. We called her the Queen not only for her imperial bearing, but for her ability to psychologically decapitate her subjects. First she tried to break us in a boot camp that would have made a marine mush, then she christened us the Seven Sisters. Sanitation Crew would have been more accurate: dancer, archaeologist, or in my case, violinist, we girls roamed the planet eliminating nasty situations for an agency that did not officially exist. Unfortunately, five of us had been eliminated in return. Maxine ran her last survivors Barnard and me—Smith—from Berlin. I suspect the Queen's desire to live close to me derived less from heroine worship than from a lingering apprehension that I would someday blow her whole operation. Performing artists were fundamentally unstable and I had always been the delinquent of the lot. Maybe my death wish was the adjunct of a desire to play the Tchaikovsky concerto perfectly in front of two thousand people. Like the other girls in Maxine's litter, I lived to taunt the gods. So far they hadn't struck me with lightning, but the bolts were dropping ever closer: five people dead last time out, two of them my lovers. All I got in exchange for that carnage was the puny consolation that I had not yet killed anyone on purpose. I had killed by omission, by accident, in self-defense, yes; on purpose, no. Once you crossed that line, you were good as dead. Would this be the assignment that finished me? It had begun innocently enough. But I knew Maxine better than that. And she knew me.

I waded through a wash of executive branch handshakes and shallow smiles, waiting, observing, until a fiftyish woman with shrewd eyes and a shrewd yellow suit blocked my way. Great knees. Primed for cameras, she wore heavy powder and enough hairspray to deflect an F-111. On the tube, she'd look part mom, part CEO; in the flesh, one trembled before a Hun in tweed. At her right stood a lusterless assistant, about my age, in neutral suit and prim linen blouse. At her left stood a smug, possessive man who looked like the only person alive who could handle her.

Assuming I recognized her, the woman bypassed introductions. Daughter had been taking violin lessons. The girl was a genius. I would be thrilled to hear her play, maybe tomorrow. Where was I staying?

Fortunately the foreign minister interrupted. "Help has arrived," he whispered in German, kissing my hand. "You can make it up to me later."

I turned to the woman. "Perhaps you could send your daughter to Berlin. I'm leaving Washington tonight."

Her glare could have melted glass. "Ah."

Folding his arm over mine, the minister led me past a few photographers. We'd be all over *Der* damn *Spiegel* this week. "Who was that?" I whispered.

"You don't know? Don't you read the newspapers, darling?"

"Just the comics. The characters are more believable."

"I see," he lied, smiling at an actor whose career had peaked a decade before his first face lift. Hollywood intoxicated the Marvels. "The woman in question is your next vice president. Aurilla Perle."

Jordan Bailey, the current officeholder, had been stung by the wrong mosquito on his last trip to a rain forest. No cure existed for dengue hemorrhagic fever. Last I heard, red spots covered his lungs and blood was beginning to swamp his brain. He lay ravaged and comatose at Walter Reed, waiting for his heart to collapse. Even so, I would have preferred him to that neutron bomb in the yellow suit. "I thought Bailey was improving."

"Jojo's history. The poor man should have stuck to whales."

"What makes you say Aurilla's going to replace him?"

"It's common knowledge."

Another woman in a suit blocked our path. At least this one I recognized: Vicky Chickering, the First Lady's right arm. They had known each other since eighth grade, which meant they were the same age. Paula looked years younger, but she had gotten a lot of exercise waving to crowds while Vicky was stuffed in the back of the campaign bus with the pizzas and telephones. No problem: a lesbian who viewed the female body as an impediment and torment, Vicky had achieved liberation by becoming a 250-pound hulk with sensible shoes. She had spent the last week testifying to a Senate panel about discrimination against fat persons.

"I enjoyed the performance, Leslie," she said, crushing my hand.

"Thank you." Vicky hadn't heard one note. Each time I had looked at her, she had been scribbling on a little pad that hung from her neck. It was as much a trademark as her Betty Boop hairdo.

Enough of me. Vicky homed in on more pressing business matters. "Minister Klint, the First Lady would like to speak with you."

The minister's perfect smile suggested that the feeling was not mutual. "Aren't we meeting at ten tomorrow?"

"Before the meeting."

My escort reverted to German. "Back to the bloody war. A

drink later?" His lips lingered over my hand. Ace diplomat: hard to say whether he was wooing me or insulting Vicky.

"Some other night." I had almost escaped the East Room when Aurilla Perle's escort caught up. Expensive suit, brazen green eyes flecked with gold. Heavy black curls framed his face. He was probably ten years older, fifty times deadlier, than he appeared. I should have recognized him. "The recital was marvelous," he said, clasping my hand. "My name is Bendix Kaar."

I didn't care if he was Henry VIII. "Hello."

"You're not staying?" Voice cool as granite: I would not want to be this man's enemy.

"I don't dance." Across the room I could see Mr. Godo, president of my record company, shaking hands with Bobby Marvel. Any second now Godo's photographer would be dragging me back inside for a dozen historic shots. "Good night."

I nearly ran to the door, where a marine escorted me to the limo waiting behind the White House. We didn't speak; I was imagining him naked and I suppose he was watching for thugs in the shrubbery. The night was dense and paludal, throbbing with crickets. Ahead of us the Washington Monument rose like a gigantic tack from the cushiony Mall, daring history to sit.

I entered the limousine. The marine handed over my violin. "Good night, ma'am."

Ah, men in uniform: would that he could take a ride, let me peel off those perfect white gloves. It had been a while. "Good night."

The chauffeur's eyes met mine in the rearview mirror. "Scenic route, Miss Frost?"

Any route, as long as it wasn't back to my vacant bed. "I'll tell you when to stop."

We rolled past magnificent buildings, many of which people called home, judging by the slumberous bodies on their front steps. As the limo neared the Capitol, I wondered why Maxine had sent me to Washington. She knew I disliked working in America: too big, too diffuse, unpredictable for all the wrong reasons. I didn't know the movies or the slang and I never wore sneakers. Having lived so many years abroad, isolated from the stunning degeneration of the language, I now spoke a mildly archaic English. Natives knew immediately, from my clothing and voice, that I wasn't one of them. Maxine would be out of her mind to send me here for undercover work. Wasn't America Barnard's territory? She was the agent who could pass for anything from El Paso barmaid to Boston pediatrician.

Lightning needled the hilltops as we crossed the Arlington Bridge. Cornering like a blimp, the limo skirted the Pentagon. I poured myself a Scotch and sank into the seat, listening to the drone of rubber on pavement. I missed my Harley. It was a good companion after concerts, more intoxicating than alcohol, less demanding than a man. After a siege under the spotlights, nothing recharged the batteries like a supersonic zip along the Autobahn, especially when I had the Stradivarius strapped to the rack. Tempting fate kept one humble—and brave. Couldn't happen here, of course, not with a speed limit of sixty-five mph and a radar trap beyond each hill. No wonder everyone had a gun.

As we drifted into Virginia, the phone rang. A mistake—I hoped. "Hello."

"Raoul?" asked Maxine.

I knocked on the partition, playing the hole through. "Is your name Raoul?"

He shook his head. "Mickey."

"You've got the wrong number." Hung up, finished the Scotch. After a while I told Mickey to return to the hotel: Maxine expected me ready for action in an hour. I had to smile as trees became streetlights and the limo fell in with police cars prowling the boulevards. The Queen knew the best time to get me was after a performance, when the ganglia were still smoking and the brain ached for a new riddle, any riddle, to stanch the void. I was suicidally fearless now. Or I used to be . . . the concerts had resumed only three weeks ago. My first few strolls into the spotlight had been frightening. During my sabbatical, a tiny switch that fused brain to finger had turned off; without that switch on, I had no shield against the terror that seized performers seconds before they had to go onstage and string a few thousand notes, beginning to end, flawlessly. Tonight the switch had flicked off only a few times, an encouraging sign, but now I was tired rather than wired. Whatever little errand Maxine had concocted, I hoped it would be easy.

After halting the limo in a brass alcove, Mickey unhanded me to a doorman. I went to my room and changed from flowing white to tight black. As the costume changed, so did my pulse: Maxine was sending me back to the razor's edge, bless her conniving, pitiless heart. I packed my plastic knife, which wouldn't ruffle any metal detectors in this security-mad town, and coiled my hair under a black scarf. Left the room. The doorman who had just helped me from the limousine looked twice as I returned to the lobby: in five minutes I had gone from goddess to buccaneer. Nevertheless, he put a whistle to his mouth. Guests of his hotel did not walk the streets at this—indeed any—hour.

"No cab," I said, sailing past.

Headed toward the White House, where the president's soirée, or a major fire, still raged. Lights from the East Room threw buttery shafts across the lawn. Tourists along Pennsylvania Avenue pressed their faces to the high iron fence, chattering in a stew of tongues as they photographed the distant chandeliers. By now my accompanist Duncan was either tangoing with a princess or puking in LBJ's toilet.

Minister Klint would be in one of those overstuffed reception rooms, sipping champagne as he allowed Paula & co. to think they were getting the better of him. President Marvel? Engaging a cigar or a woman: end result about the same. Hard to believe I had been with them an hour ago.

Found a phone at Pershing Square, called a local number. The line fizzed and clicked. Finally Maxine answered. "Play well?"

"I would have been a bigger hit at Arlington Cemetery."

"Meet anyone interesting?"

"Was I supposed to?"

I could hear her patiently swallowing coffee four thousand miles away. "How's the weather?"

"Stinking hot." Same as two weeks ago, when Maxine had been in town rooting around the NSA computers with her five-star general. Maybe she had been trying to dig up some easy work for me. "Can I come back to Berlin now?"

"Drop in on Barnard first. She's right down the street."

Something wrong. Not once in all these years had one of Maxine's other agents dropped in on me, or I on them. Now that five out of seven of us were dead, perhaps the Queen was relaxing her social policy. "Is she expecting me?"

"She knows you're in town."

"What's she doing here?"

Again I heard a quiet swallowing. "You got me."

Hard to say which was worse, Maxine not knowing what was going on or actually admitting so. She gave us girls a long leash, but we were expected to bark at reasonable intervals. "What do you want me to do?" I asked.

"Just check her out." Maxine told me an address: Watergate.

"Come on, the place is a fortress!"

"You'll see three fountains outside the north lobby. Keys are in the middle one. Apartment 937. Her name's Polly Mason."

Before Maxine could explain how to unlock Barnard's door,

I hung up and joined the tourists cruising the Ellipse. Hard to be invisible in this town: too damn broad and bright, zero foliage cover, and every other pedestrian carried a videocamera. No wonder there were so few assassinations anymore. Crowds, lights, thinned after the Lincoln Memorial. Soon even the sidewalks disappeared. I walked along the Potomac, reacquainting myself with the rhythm and insinuation of shadows as adrenaline began seeping into my blood. It was a heavier mix than my brain had put out for Bobby Marvel's concert a few hours ago; then again, no one killed a violinist for bad intonation. I could feel the rush in my arms and legs. They were already in super shape; during my time off, I had been working out. Smith had never been leaner or stronger. Odd that the less I cared to live, the better care I took of my body.

Cut through the bushes behind the Kennedy Center. Though all was now quiet on the immense back palazzo, tonight's opera would end in fifteen minutes, spewing several thousand witnesses my way. Even now a few spoilsports were scuttling out before the final curtain. Limousines crawled up the ramp, motors rumbling, masking low frequencies; a battalion of taxis would invade any minute. Hurrying, I crossed the street to the Watergate complex, where once upon a time a few cocky amateurs had performed the mother of all botch jobs. Careful, Smith: bad karma here.

Heard water before I saw it. Ahead of me, three oval basins tinkled into each other, exactly as Maxine had described. Three tiny moons danced on their surfaces. I froze, horrified: my last assignment had begun in a fountain in Leipzig. Now Maxine had brought me halfway around the earth to not one fountain, but three. Was this the Queen's way of telling me to get on with it? Worse, a dare: If I couldn't make this first hurdle, she'd know my guts were still soup, my nerves steady as ice in a desert. I'd sink to the bottom of her class, maybe for good.

On a nearby balcony, a woman laughed softly, ecstatically: stopped me dead. She was watching the moon with someone she loved. I had laughed like that once . . . did that woman have any idea what was to come? If so, she laughed anyway. Goaded by her defiance, her hopeless bravery, I stalked to the middle fountain. No fish. Just pennies, pebbles, balls of gum. I had nearly circled the basin when the phantom of a shadow wavered beneath the water. A jellyfish with straight edges? My hand raked the slippery bottom: keys all right. Clear plastic.

Above, I heard another low, maddening chuckle. Up the street, cars began to honk: opera *finita*. I quickly circled the Watergate complex, a hulk of jags, tiers, and curves—half yacht, half Moby-Dick. Like most buildings in Washington, it was a tad too white. Out back, a grove of pines shielded the service entrance. Pulled on my gloves and hid my face in the scarf. Tried one of Maxine's keys. No alarm sounded, but up in security a little beeper had probably gone off; armed guard would be checking in any minute. I trotted down a humid, linty corridor. Behind closed doors, machinery whined so that folks upstairs could coast through four seasons at a comfy seventy-two degrees. I ran up the stairwell to the ninth floor. Barnard would live near the top, of course. Ostentation was the best cover, she always claimed. But Barnard would have stuck out in any crowd. She was a stunning six-foot blonde. Liked her hair in a high chignon and shoes with four-inch spikes: working altitude easily six six. She could do a mile in under four minutes and after a half bottle of gin she could still pick off a chipmunk at two hundred yards. Maxine had scooped her out of med school and somehow convinced her that squashing bad guys was more patriotic than finding a cure for cancer. I think her love life was like mine but with a few hundred more correspondents, thus fewer wrenching finales. What could she be doing in Washington? Rang her doorbell, concocting my spiel. *Hi, remember me? We went to camp together.* After a minute I rang again. Through the peephole, lights burned. I unlocked her door.

"Polly?" No, Ella Fitzgerald crooning from the speakers. I was looking at more art and carpet than Barnard could have afforded after working a century for Maxine. Maybe she still did a little brain surgery on the side. The decor favored beige and olive, the colors of dollar bills. On a sideboard flared an enormous bouquet of purple orchids. Beyond the music, an ominous silence pressed the nerves. My heart began thumping erratically: I was not alone here. Drawing my knife, I entered the bedroom.

Gloriously naked, Barnard sprawled facedown across the bed. A tattoo glowered on her left buttock. From the looks of the rumpled bedding, she had either fought—or fucked— very hard. But no blood. And no pulse in her still warm neck. The faintest scent of grilled pineapple lingered in the air. I was inspecting a puncture near the edge of Barnard's hairline when the phone rang. The answering machine picked up.

"The ice-cream man will see you at midnight." Woman's voice. Contemptuous, biting the *t*'s. "Don't be late."

I pocketed the cassette and rolled Barnard's lush, heavy corpse over. Blue eyes bulged from a blue face. Strangled? No welts on the throat. Pills? Drano? I pried open her jaws. Tough work, since they were beginning to mortise. Her mouth looked pink and healthy except for a dash of white down by the tonsils. Dug my finger in: eh? String? I pulled, felt the resistance, knew, didn't believe but continued to tug, almost gagging when the thick, white head of a tampon loomed like a giant maggot at the base of her mouth. Slow suffocation: what a terrible way to die.

I went to the bedroom, found a safety pin and another tampon. Sorry, friend: stabbed Barnard's neck, near the original puncture. She bled heavily, warmly, still so alive. I was swabbing the last beads of blood when a key slipped into the front door. In a few seconds I'd be at a bad pajama party so I cut to Barnard's plant-clogged balcony. No chance of winging the twenty-foot gap between here and the neighbor's begonias. Nine stories below I saw only trees. Damn! Where were all the swimming pools when you needed them? Looped my scarf around a balcony post and somersaulted over the edge as a figure burst into Barnard's bedroom. Whoever it was stomped onto the balcony, pausing in the moonlight as I swung by the wrists a few inches below. Breathless, we both listened to the wind, to the hum of traffic along the Potomac. Should the intruder look down, should a pedestrian look up, I was finished. But a terse whistle inside the apartment saved me. The footsteps retreated and I was left alone to calculate the number of seconds I could hold on before my grip melted or the scarf tore. Minutes crawled by. My wrists became numb, white hot, numb again as I dangled in the breeze. Diversion necessary so I ran the first movement of the Brahms concerto, note by note, through my head. Curtis had scheduled me to play it in Frankfurt next week. I was almost through when the lights snapped out in Barnard's living room.

Counted to ten, willing strength to my dead arms. Mind gradually won over matter and I began to swing back and forth, finally gaining enough momentum to curl knees to chest, then clamp the ankles around a balcony post. One last pull and I lay gasping, threatening as a squid, behind Barnard's azaleas. Acrid fumes of hundred-fifty-proof sweat rose from every pore, evaporating along with my energy. Eventually I dragged an ear to the sliding door: Ella still sang the blues. I went back inside.

Dim light played evenly over Barnard's bed. Her body was gone. So was the answering machine. In the living room, paintings had been slashed, pillows disemboweled.

Even the oranges in the fruit bowl had been sliced and squeezed into grotesque parabolas. Maximum damage in minimum time, yet they had overlooked the dead weight hanging off the balcony: amateurs? Worse: zealots? I doubted they had found what they were looking for. You had to know Barnard, and Maxine, for that.

Found the crème de menthe at the back of the liquor cabinet, where one would normally keep the more repellent *digestifs*. Although the bottle looked and felt full, few would be tempted to decant the sticky emerald liquid. Just as well, because it wasn't alcohol, and that wasn't really a bottle. Snapped off its neck, took a few scraps of paper from its belly. On the way out I noticed deep, fresh dents in the door frame, paint on the floor: Barnard hadn't been hauled out of here in a rug. Near the Arlington Bridge I got to a phone. "I found her, Maxine."

After ten years reading tone of voice, the Queen didn't even sigh: six of the Seven Sisters confirmed dead, and the violinist had outlived them all. Unbelievable. "How bad?" she asked.

"Naked in bed with a tampon down her throat."

A moment of silence as Maxine considered the mechanics of that. "Barnard could have fought off three men with one hand."

"Puncture on her neck. I got some blood." The second tampon lay stiff as a finger in my pocket. "They took the body away in something big." I sighed: how banal.

"Where were you, hiding behind the shower curtain?"

"No, under the bed with a teddy bear. You would have preferred casualties?"

Her silence shouted *yes*. "Who were they?"

"Couldn't tell you. I was hanging off the balcony. My arms are a lot longer than they were an hour ago." That got no sympathy whatsoever. "I found a theater ticket in her bottle. Show's tomorrow night."

"What's playing?"

"*La Ronde*. The ticket cost a thousand bucks. Fund-raiser for endangered species."

"Bizarre."

So was Schnitzler in English. I felt for my knife as a man in tennis whites sauntered by. When he wandered around the bend, I squinted at the little slip of paper that had been in Barnard's bottle with the ticket. " 'Yvette Tatal. Saint Elizabeth's,' " I read. "Mean anything to you?"

"No." Heavy breathing on Maxine's end. "Why didn't they find you hanging off the balcony?"

"Amateurs in a rush."

"They kill a pro, toss the apartment, take the body, and *miss you?*"

I had never heard the Queen raise her voice before. Her fear galloped through my blood. "Maybe I got lucky."

Maxine only chortled. "Look for me after the play."

I returned to the Watergate complex, circled a few times but saw no large, clunky objects leaving the premises. Nothing emerged but toilers and spoilers, all alive. Each time I passed the triple fountain, I listened for that soft, knowing laughter, proof that another woman, drunk with love, had defied the gods. But the sound had vanished with Barnard. I went back to my hotel. Same doorman: damn, he had seen me go and come. I entered the elevator with a Korean whose eyes crawled torpidly over the curves in my black leather. Left that poor sod on the third floor and unlocked my door. My white concert gown still draped a chair. Bed looked wide and barren as Antarctica, with two silly chocolates on the pillow now. I stashed the bloody tampon, all I had left of Barnard, in the minibar. As I grabbed a beer, the phone rang.

"How'd it go?" Curtis asked.

"Better than last time." I could hear eggs and sausage crackling on my manager's end of the line. Sunshine would just be warming the violets on the kitchen sill. Home, Curtis, safety: all a fantasy now. He listened to "My Night at the White House," aware that the pull in my voice had nothing to do with Brahms. "I might stay here a few days," I said finally.

"What about Duncan?"

"I left him dancing with a few menopausal Cinderellas. He's probably booked for lunch until Thanksgiving."

"Leave yourselves a little time to practice. Carnegie Hall on Saturday, remember."

I'd be lucky if circulation returned to my fingers by Christmas! "Yes, Mother."

Took a bath, thinking about Barnard, whom I had last seen eight years ago. Camp Maxine had just opened for business and the Queen was intent on exterminating the weaklings in the bunch. She'd almost succeeded with me: I was the drinkin', smokin' musician, unused to sleep-outs and twenty-mile hikes before breakfast. Barnard thrived on such abuse. She was also off-the-charts smart, a fatal attribute in a beautiful female—but the perfect requisites for Maxine, who had managed to find seven of us with that peculiar nimiety. Barnard could play Texas bimbo, Swedish hippie, frigid WASP, to perfection. I wondered which persona she had used last. Whatever the pose, Barnard could enslave a man in fifteen seconds. Ordinary women hated her. Sad that she and I had not become closer as our sisters fell. Not smart, but sad just the same. After Wellesley turned up—in two pieces—in Johannesburg, Barnard had called me. "Looks like you and I are holding the fort, Smithy. Care to place your bets?"

"Fifty thousand bucks."

"Son of a bitch! On you or me?"

"I bury you, babe."

"I'll use it for violin lessons," Barnard had snorted.

"I'll spend it on push-up bras." Now I was fifty thousand,

plus interest, richer: Smith's survival bonus. Maybe I'd donate it to Maxine.

At precisely ten the next morning, Duncan Zadinsky knocked. My accompanist liked to breakfast with me after a concert to discuss all the mistakes we had made the previous evening. Sometimes I think he enjoyed the postmortem more than he did the performance. Today, however, music was not uppermost in his mind. "You missed the party of the century," he crowed, seating himself at the trolley a steward had just wheeled in. "I was dancing till dawn."

"Four-fifteen, dear. I heard you come in with a few elephants."

Duncan constructed a meticulous still life of granola and prunes before submerging it in tomato juice. He had read somewhere that this alleviated baldness. "Paula's one hell of a dancer. She's got hips like butter. Feet like feathers."

Brain like Iago. Bobby was just her Moor. "I'm sure you swept her away."

Duncan tucked half a muffin into his mouth. "After our dance, she left. Why settle for second best?"

"Sorry to disappoint you, but she had a staff meeting. Whom did you ravish next?"

"Justine Cortot. A very attractive woman, believe me."

No kidding: White House press secretary. She and Bobby had graduated from the same high school in backwater Kentucky. Both had gone to the same Ivy League law school, but only Justine had won the Rhodes Scholarship. While she was in England, Bobby had married Paula. "I hear she shot Marvel a long time ago. Missed his balls by inches. He was gentleman enough to call it a hunting accident."

"That's absurd! Where'd you hear that?"

Maxine had sent an unexpurgated bio of Bobby Marvel

along with my ticket to the White House. Great bedtime reading, if you were a satyr. "Don't remember."

Done with the prunes, Duncan attacked a mound of beignets. Maybe they cured impotence. "I'm surprised you believe rumors," he chomped. "Of all people."

A dank wind, heavy with ghosts, blew by. "So what did you think of the concert?"

He launched into a note-by-note recap of our horror show: twangy piano, poor lighting, cold audience, mushy acoustics, jet lag, insufficient rehearsal . . . obviously my accompanist was a saint. Never in our years together had we performed under humane conditions. "We've got to work our asses off before New York," Duncan concluded. "We've been out of action for months. Playing live upsets me now."

It upset me, too; I just didn't let anyone know how much. I went to the window. Outside the hotel, a sheik deboarded from a stretch limousine. All that white hurt my eyes. "How about staying in Washington a few days instead of going to New York?"

"Don't tell me you hooked up with that marine at the White House!"

On the pavement, three veiled women followed their leader into the hotel. I wondered if they fought for his attention or jeered at him behind his back. "There are a couple new exhibitions in town."

"I suppose I could do some research at the Library of Congress." Duncan speared a sausage. "Meet Justine for lunch. She'd be delighted if I changed my mind."

"Cortot invited you out?"

"For God's sake! Am I a leper?"

Not completely. Duncan was just a fidgety old maid whose idea of an orgasm was playing Chopin's *Minute Waltz* in fifty-eight seconds. What could Justine possibly want with him? "She's probably tired of senators," I said. "Wants to try her luck with a piano player."

"Aren't you catty this morning! Justine's a lovely girl."

"Girl? She's ten years older than you. And she's a politician. Don't ever forget it."

"I'm forty-one! I'll forget what I like!"

Give up, Frost. I returned to the table. Duncan had left me five prunes. "Great weather. Maybe I'll rent a Harley for the afternoon."

"Eh? I thought you wanted to see some exhibitions."

A knock interrupted further pleasantries. In the hallway stood a porter burdened with deep purple orchids. He smiled, my pulse tottered: just a few hours ago I had seen an identical arrangement in Barnard's apartment. As the fellow sashayed to a sideboard, Duncan snatched the envelope. Intercepting notes on my bouquets was one of his professional duties, right up there with frowning at my apparel and passing judgment on my boyfriends.

"Orchids," he sniffed with the usual disdain. "How decadent. *'A cliff-hanging performance.'*" Tossed the card away. "Who's your admirer this time?"

"No idea."

I spent the afternoon riding through the Virginia hills, inhaling the first delicate scents of autumn, wondering who could have seen me dangling from Barnard's balcony last night. Duncan was half an hour late for our rehearsal at five. He played beautifully, mysteriously, like someone in love. Neither of us mentioned his lunch with Justine.

Chapter Two

The DOORMAN BEAMED as I left the hotel: I was in silk and diamonds again. No violin tonight, though. Just a little of Barnard's blood in my purse. "Cab, Miss Frost?"

"Thank you." Heat rose from the asphalt, pressed down from the clouds, wilting humans in a moist, invisible sandwich. "Ford's Theatre, please," I told the driver.

"I won't be able to drop you outside," he said, pulling onto Pennsylvania Avenue.

"Why not?"

"Bomb threats. We're supposed to avoid the area."

Great. As predicted, traffic stalled five blocks from destination. I joined those abandoning their vehicles and walked the rest of the way to Tenth Street, wondering why Barnard had bought a thousand-buck ticket to an outdated play. Maybe someone else had blown the grand for the opportunity to sit next to her. Blind date? I was suddenly nervous, unprepared to step into her shoes. Totally unprepared to swallow a tampon. However, curious little gambler that I am, I crossed the police line outside Ford's Theatre. Sailed by the metal detector in the foyer as an attendant fished through the pile of platinum I had dropped onto his plate. "Enjoy the show," was all he said.

Ford's Theatre looked much the way it had in April 1865, when Lincoln had taken a bullet in the head. Heavy green curtains framed a modest stage; the audience sat on barely cushioned chairs. Slender beams supported two shallow balconies. Despite the crowd and the lights, my heart skipped upon entering this place: it felt the residual evil lurking here. I walked quickly along the rear wall, checking exits, aisles, faces. Everyone looked rich and terribly important, or attached to such a person. Finally I headed toward second row center: typical Barnard. She had probably planned to arrive three seconds before opening curtain so that no one could miss her entrance.

Three chairs in the second row remained empty. Left of them loomed the immense Vicky Chickering. Seeing me, she broke off speaking with a younger woman at her side. For just a wee moment, disbelief grayed her face. But recovery was swift. "Leslie!" She ooched over a few inches to make room. "I thought you left town last night!"

Had I told her that? "I make exceptions for Schnitzler." I wedged into the three-quarter space she had left me. "So you're a fan of endangered species?"

"As is the First Lady." Vicky's eyes leapt to a more strategic beast behind me. She not only stood up for this one, but pronounced her name in French. "Justine!"

Egad, Duncan's dancing partner. Looking right through me, Justine Cortot began wedging down the row as a man in bow tie and Fu Manchu glasses followed closely behind. Very hard to believe she was twenty years my senior. She looked more thirty than fifty. Cortot had packed her ninety-eight pounds into a white Lycra sheath that stretched to the max at bust and butt. Lipstick matched the stiletto heels and her blondish hair had been poufed into an enormous French twist. Her cubic zirconia jewelry glared in the yellow light. This lady was pedal-to-the-metal competing: she had expected to be seated next to Barnard. What a pathetic contest that would have been. It was still pathetic.

I pretended to read the program so that Justine and Vicky could exchange public intimacies like "Did you get my memo?" and "We're confirmed for next Friday." Justine's acquired Etonian accent grated on my nerves. Twice I caught her date looking down my décolletage. Justine noticed me not. She only had eyes for Vicky, and vice versa; if either of them had come to hear Schnitzler, I'd eat my diamonds.

The hall quieted. I looked toward the loge at stage right, where Lincoln had been assassinated. That space would remain unlit, unoccupied, forever. But—rusty me—I didn't take the fact full circle. Only when a Secret Service agent made a final pass by the first row did I realize that the two empty places in front of me were reserved for the Marvels.

This ticket was hotter than hell!

Justine suddenly acknowledged me. "How is dear Duncan?" she asked, never introducing herself. That would have been insulting—to Justine.

"Fine, thank you."

With a smirk, she buried her face in the program. The Secret Service drifted quietly to the exits, penning us in as the U.S. Marine Band played a few ruffles and flourishes. All stood. Arm in arm, the Marvels entered. Bobby's face was flushed; beneath Paula's rouge I detected fury. They had been brawling again. However, politics being one of the minor performing arts, both bared their gums and waved to the crowd. From a distance, it would look genuine. Just before taking his seat, the president narrowed his gaze from the universal to the specific. Had I not been watching his eyes, I would have missed the shift from anger to shock to utter vacuity as he discovered not Barnard, but me, in her place. We stared for a split second as a few million volts passed between us. Then, smiling as if I had tickled him, Bobby turned his back and sat down.

Ice crept through my guts as the lights dimmed. I had not been expecting such a reckless game, not even from Barnard. What had Marvel's smile meant? Perhaps I had misinterpreted his glance . . . and perhaps the earth was flat. Without intermission, Schnitzler's saucy play came and went. Trapped between giant on the left, pygmy on the right, president's head looming like a cannonball two feet in front of me, I saw nothing onstage. Each time Vicky Chickering resnuggled into her seat, she squeezed me another few centimeters toward Justine, whose stuporously sweet perfume should have been buried in a canister in Nevada. After Schnitzler bit the dust, we were treated to idolatrous speeches about animals. Paula pinned a medal on the oldest actor's lapels. Everyone applauded. Then the Marvels left.

The lights came up. Vicky stood, breathless; she had been clapping herself silly for the last twenty minutes. "What a treat!" she preached, scribbling one last note to herself on the little pad hanging from her neck. We began shuffling toward the aisle. "You were so lucky to get a ticket!"

Fishing? I'd nibble her line. "Someone sent it to my hotel."

"Is that so! And you just came here out of . . . *curiosity?*"

I winked. "Wasn't you, was it?"

She stiffened. "You live dangerously."

Get off the soapbox, sister. I concentrated on Justine's plummy rear end, wanting to get out of that theater, out of Washington, out of America. I wanted to be back in my studio in Berlin, playing Beethoven to my plants, slithering unnoticed into the night. I didn't like Bobby Marvel and now he was part of the job. So was Chickering. So was this gremlin in front of me. God! What had Barnard been doing with them?

Engulfed in bodies, I shuffled up the aisle. Then a tap on my shoulder: I faced an egg-shaped man in a flax suit. His fluorescent tie clashed nicely with the "Save the Ocelots" badge. Slicked-back gray-blond hair, around fifty with the round eyes of either a naïf or a hopeless degenerate. Smelled of heavy money. "Leslie Frost?" he asked with that annoying local familiarity. "What a pleasure. My name is Fausto Kiss. Your recording of the Sibelius concerto is the greatest."

I had never even listened to it: the performance had cost me two lovers. "Thank you."

"So sorry I missed you last night but I was out of town. Never mind. I detest concerts in the East Room." The man confronted Chickering. "How's that three-ring circus at the White House, dear?"

For him, she smiled. "Getting by, Fausto."

Half hummingbird, half blimp, he whirred back to me. "How long will you be in Washington?"

"I'm leaving tomorrow."

"Could you join me for a drink tonight?"

"I'm afraid not."

"Breakfast then?" When I laughed in his face, Kiss tucked a business card into my hand. "Call any time. For any reason. I'm at your service." With lubricious delicacy, his mouth brushed my fingertips. "Do take care of these."

Chickering's indulgence evaporated as Fausto's enormous yellow suit melded into the crowd at the rear of the theater. "Maybe he sent your ticket," she snorted. "Fausto loves to play practical jokes."

I eventually reached the sidewalk. Halos of humidity sanctified the street lamps. Now that the Marvels had taken off, bums and taxis had been allowed back to work the throng on Tenth Street. I wanted to walk far and fast away from there, neutralize the acid burping through my system like a tank of bad gas. I needed a Harley, a cold shower. Too many people had seen me and I, dully relying on providence, had seen nothing in turn. I had made a huge mistake coming here unprepared to play poker with my life—and win. Now, out in the night, my feeble antennae sensed crosshairs on my back. I hunted in my purse, dropped coins onto a beggar's blanket as my eyes flitted over the crowd. Took only a moment to find the shadow across the street. She stood in front of the house where Lincoln had died. A column of dark flesh amid a sea of legs, heads, hands: Maxine.

We drifted to F Street. I waited on the corner as she crossed to my curb and without a sideward glance, continued toward Union Station. I gave her half a block then began to follow her past ever tawdrier storefronts and raunchier women. The Queen was dressed like a tart and her epidermis matched the demographics of the neighborhood: few locals looked twice. Leading her bejeweled, lily white agent through this scorched earth was obviously another of Maxine's little rehab exercises: if I couldn't fend off a couple of drug addicts, the odd gang or two, I obviously wasn't up to Barnard's killers. I saw men approach her, then drop away. They didn't touch me, either; perhaps they sensed the claws and fangs behind my nail polish and lipstick. That didn't prevent them from exercising their right of free speech as I passed by, of course. After a dozen invitations to sit on a face, I would almost have preferred a fight.

My stiletto heels were not designed for inner-city hikes. Well aware of that, the Queen maintained an Olympic pace, finally diving into the Metro station at Judiciary Square. Different world down here, clean, quiet, devoid of pushcarts. Until the train *whoosh*ed in, Maxine and I observed our companions on the platform. Most of them wore neckties and vapid stares, at least until they got a load of Maxine's knickers and my slightly overexposed breasts. I followed her into a car and sat at the opposite end, kneading my feet until she sprang out at Woodley Park.

We stalled at the turnstiles until everyone had gone, then took the steep escalator to Connecticut Avenue. The only person who had boarded with us at Judiciary Square strode uphill, scything the thick air with his briefcase. The Queen cut into a dark street bordered by woods. Finally, when my shoes were ruined, she disappeared into the brush. Hilly, heavy going; I could only pant after her and curse the branches clawing my face. Sweat trickled into my eyes, down my cheeks. My dress was history. She slid through a clever break in a chain-link fence. We hit macadam, signposts: the *zoo?* Maxine veered into a thicket tittering with crickets. A second uphill slog and suddenly I was alone against a wall of rock. Had she flown away? No such luck. With the heel of a dead shoe, I tapped the rock face. When the sound turned hollow, I ran my fingers over the warm stone. A small depression, smaller *ping* as the hinges gave way.

The single halogen bulb snapped on only when the door had shut behind me. I stood in a cell crammed with the tools of my other trade: keyboards, monitors, slots. Inch for inch, this playpen had probably cost as much as a space probe. The Queen was already taking two cans of soda from the minifridge. She hadn't even broken a sweat, but she was more panther than human. "Eleven seconds behind," she said, dropping into the only chair. "You really are out of shape, Smith."

"Let's trade shoes and try again," I retorted, frowning at a stain on my hem. "Nice little hideout."

"Glad you like it. You're the second tenant."

Poor Barnard. "Where are we?"

"Between the wolves and lions." Maxine grinned at a wide run in my stockings. "How was Schnitzler?"

"Couldn't tell you. Bobby Marvel's head blocked my view." Removed my other shoe: looked as if it had been through a lawn mower. "I sat between Vicky Chickering and Justine Cortot."

"His and her White House staffs? That must have been a farce in itself."

"On the way out someone named Fausto Kiss introduced himself."

"Humpty-Dumpty meets Oscar Wilde. Bet he liked you."

"He liked my Sibelius concerto. Invited me over."

"Don't disappoint him. Who sat behind you?"

"No idea." I hadn't looked: bad, bad.

"So you still don't know where Barnard got that ticket."

"Don't laugh," I said, sliding to a small space on the floor. This room was designed for only one occupant. "But I think it came from Bobby Marvel."

The Queen laughed coldly. "That's what I was afraid you'd say." Her slender finger touched a video button. "Watch."

On screen appeared an opulent bathroom, daytime. Surrounded by plants and potpourri, a blue ribbon in her hair, Barnard soaked in a marble tub. She was a staggeringly beautiful woman. Door opened and in tiptoed Boy Marvel wearing only a white towel. When Barnard opened an eye, smiled archly, he dropped the towel and stepped into the suds. Great tight ass, considering how much time he'd been sitting on it over the past few years. Barnard poured champagne, their mouths moved, they laughed. Then Bobby grabbed his bathing partner. The water began to churn. Barnard nearly drowned, giggling all the way. Marvel left the tub. After Barnard flung her champagne at him, the screen went black.

I looked across the table. "Touching."

"It's a copy. I found it here. God knows who's got the original."

"Any messages with it?"

"Barnard never liked sending interim reports."

"Whose bathtub?"

"It ain't at the White House."

"Is the picture real?"

"Nothing in this town is real. But you can be sure Barnard made that tape on purpose. My guess is she was trying to flush someone out of the bushes." Maxine took a long swig of soda. Quite a compliment, really, exposing her throat to me like that. "On July first, we picked up some e-mail from Krikor Tunalian to Louis Bailey."

Tuna I knew: arms merchant. Should have been dead twenty years ago. "Who's Bailey?"

"An ethnobotanist." The Queen couldn't resist translating for me. "Jungle medicine. Witch doctors. Natural hallucinogens. Oxford trained. Now he's a big-shot professor at Richmond. Studies plants, sees if they might contain a cure for cancer or AIDS. Almost won the Nobel Prize two years ago."

"What would Tuna want with him?"

"Nothing too noble. They met at Bailey's home in Virginia. Next day Tuna wired five million dollars to a Swiss account in Bailey's name. When the doc left the country, I put Barnard on the case. She took a crash refresher course in botany then went to Belize. That's where Bailey goes whenever school's out."

"How'd Barnard manage to blend into the woodwork down there? Wearing a monkey suit?"

Maxine looked down at me. "She posed as a researcher

collecting specimens for the International Red Cross. Put on a little bandanna and stumbled into Bailey two weeks after setting up camp in the jungle."

She must have made one hell of an impact. "Let me guess. She became his assistant."

"They worked together for six weeks." Maxine looked bleakly at me. "On September first he disappeared."

Excuse me? No one ever got away from Barnard. "How?"

"I got no field reports. Could have been equipment failure. Jungles have a way of eating communications gear."

"Whatever you say. Bailey disappears. Barnard follows his trail to D.C. but still doesn't fill you in?"

Obviously not. Our group didn't work like that. We were paragons of independent study and the Queen knew better than to interfere with an agent teetering on the brink of extinction. "I suspect she was chagrined at losing her man. It was the first time." And the last. "All I know is that she set herself up at Watergate. Soon she was screwing the president. You know the rest."

"Did she ever find Louis?"

"Couldn't tell you. No one else has seen him. If he's here, he's invisible."

"Where's Tuna?"

"Panama City. He hasn't heard from Louis, either. Probably thinks the doc is still in the jungle."

I opened my purse and laid the tampon on the table. "Bloodwork." The Queen stared a moment before putting Barnard's only remains in her pocket. "Give me a few leads," I said.

"Yvette Tatal is the Mother Teresa of Belize. Specialist in dengue fever. Expert in jungle medicine. Louis has known her for years."

"Anything else?"

"Louis Bailey is the vice president's brother."

Maxine had just dumped a ton of sludge on my dainty white parasol. I needed a long moment to dig out. "Is that why Louis came to Washington?" I asked hopefully. "To see Jojo?"

"No one's seen Louis," she repeated. "Anywhere."

"Are the feds looking for him?"

"What for? No one knows he's missing. He lived alone and was out of contact with the world for months on end. Besides, Jojo's in no position to miss his only brother. Brain's mush. It's just a matter of time."

Hell, life was just a matter of time. Suddenly I didn't want mine to end with a tampon down my throat. "I'm not sure I can handle this."

"Sure you can." Again she drank, exposing that luscious, chocolate neck. "Start with Fausto."

"I've got three concerts in Frankfurt next week."

"Curtis canceled you until mid-October. Tendinitis."

"Son of a bitch!" Winged my shoe across the floor. "What am I supposed to tell Duncan?"

"Say your wrists hurt." As Maxine stood, the small knife in her belt glimmered briefly, softly, as a firefly. "Get going. September is hurricane season."

"In Washington?"

"Belize. Fly through Miami. Your bag's waiting." She tossed me a key, pushed a red dot on the wall. "I want to know who killed Barnard." A latch clicked, the lights went out. I saw a faint spray of stars as the Queen melted into the night.

After Maxine left our little pen, I played with the toys therein. Everything was smaller, faster, smarter, than my setup in Berlin. In six months, of course, the next generation of software would make this one obsolete: meringue pies had a longer shelf life than did the tools of this trade. I entered my passwords, tapped a few keys: up popped a map of Belize, the former British Honduras. Wedged between Mexico and Guatemala, it was a lush green rectangle about the size of Massachusetts, blessedly overlooked by both superpower and guerrilla. Offshore lay the largest barrier reef in the Western Hemisphere; inland, the rain forest attracted scientists and that strange nineties fungus, the ecotourist. Barnard and Jojo Bailey's brother had situated themselves in the western Cayo district, amid mountains and Mayan ruins.

I watched the bathtub video a few times, wondering why she would cherish such a lousy lay, even if it was with the president. Unable to detect anything remarkable about the scene but Bobby Marvel's ass, I fed Barnard's face to my computer. Its database listed just about every troublemaker on the planet, which roughly translated into politicians, millionaires, failed politicians, and failed millionaires. ID, I typed. The computer burped twice before her driver's license flashed on screen. Gorgeous smile: my stomach writhed. POLLY MASON. Bogus address and Social Security number.

> HERBALIST, BOTANIST
> RED CROSS RESEARCHER
> UNMARRIED

That was it? The Queen had shielded her well. I ran Bobby Marvel under the scanner.

> POSSIBLE ID ROBERT CHARLEMAGNE MARVEL
> PRESIDENT, UNITED STATES OF AMERICA

Possible? I rewound tape: sure enough, when the president entered the bathroom, his left ear faced the camera. Mating, his right ear stayed in the suds. When Barnard hit him with champagne, Bobby's hands went up to his eyes—his ears—as he whizzed away from her. Without a right ear on film, the computer couldn't nail him. I zoomed to Marvel's thighs, locating scar tissue about five inches southwest of his balls. That would be the spot where, years ago, Justine Cortot had shot him for marrying Paula. Marvel all right.

Thoughts of succeeding Barnard in the bathtub agitated me so I cut to FAUSTO KISS. On screen appeared a rather dated picture, judging by the puffy face I had seen last night at Ford's Theatre. Time had only burnished the caustic gleam in his eyes. He was born fifty years ago in New York City.

> ROYAL COLLEGE OF MUSIC
> HARVARD UNIVERSITY—BA PHILOSOPHY 1978
> NET WORTH: $470 MILLION
> INTERESTS: ARTS, POLITICS
> UNMARRIED, SEXUAL PREFERENCE UNKNOWN

A philosopher with 470 million bucks? Ludicrous. So was the bit about sexual preference: I had seen Fausto's eyes. Why no degree from the Royal College of Music? I hit PHONE. Fausto picked up after one ring. "This is Leslie Frost," I said. "Sorry to be calling so late."

"Not at all. I'm just sitting down to supper."

Alone? "My plans have changed. I could join you for breakfast tomorrow."

"Excellent! How do you like your eggs?"

"Benedict."

"Will you be bringing your accompanist?"

"I don't think so."

"We pour coffee at six, dear. I'll be waiting for you."

What a pro: conversation not too long, not too short, the perfect blend of deference and contempt. I bet no one in

Washington knew Fausto's political affiliation. He was one of those cunning neutrals who played no sides and all sides, who heard all the confessions and got a kick out of manipulating a legion of tin soldiers because no matter what harm they did to the country, each other, Fausto's 470 million bucks would cover his ass forever. He hadn't run into me at Ford's Theatre by accident.

Finally I took a look at Louis Bailey. Studied internal medicine at Oxford. Disciplined for unethical conduct. Medical officer in Vietnam, where he may have gotten his first taste of jungle medicine. Returned to school for a second degree in botany and never looked back. His list of awards was impressive. At a price, however: divorced, without family except for bro Jojo. Pulled Louis's picture on screen and saw nothing in his thin face but ego and ambition. I wouldn't want him anywhere near my bed. But I wasn't a botanist.

Shut down the machines and slipped out of Maxine's playpen. A wolf howled as I passed its cage. I was not looking forward to sleeping with Bobby Marvel.

Chapter Three

FAUSTO KISS lived in a swank neighborhood near the vice president's mansion. Area residents had built gigantic homes to within a few feet of their property lines, then had crammed the remaining space with tennis courts, pools, sculpture: if their money couldn't buy acreage, it could at least obliterate what little the zoning laws allowed. As my cabdriver ascended the winding street, squinting at house numbers, a silver Mercedes pulled inches behind us. Tailgated for a hundred yards before zooming past: Justine Cortot at the wheel. "Follow that car," I said. We both pulled into a driveway dammed by a gabled mansion.

Justine was just ending a mobile phone chat as I reached her car. She must have been up since four braiding her hair into that intricate twist. Flawless makeup, adorable little glasses. Her white skirt clung deliciously to her hips: power dressing elevated to an art form. I supposed I'd have done the same if I stood only four feet ten. "Good morning," I said. "Long time no see."

She didn't look particularly glad to see me, but this was the third party I had crashed in three days now. Also, my white skirt was tighter than hers. "Playing for your breakfast?" she asked innocently.

"Dancing for yours?" I walked up a few steps and pressed the bell.

The door swung open: hello Fausto, in blue pajamas and white kimono embroidered with strawberries. "Girls!" Kisses. "You know each other?"

"Hardly." Justine had evidently visited this foyer often enough to ignore the Rembrandt above the credenza. "Coffee on yet, Fausto? I have no time to dawdle today."

"Waiting inside, precious. Autograph the guest book then you can run along." He watched Justine's fanny bob between two wide doors. Then he took my arm. "Amusing little copperhead, isn't she?"

"Not really."

"Bobby ruined her, poor thing." Fausto handed me a heavy gold pen. "Please sign my guest book." A dozen names were already inscribed beneath today's date. After I added my own, Fausto ushered me into a sunny parlor, where other guests had already begun to eat as three televisions stuttered quietly in the corners. I recognized many of their faces as they glanced my way. Some of the older ones had passed through Berlin during my father's ambassadorship there. I had sat on their laps, toyed with their buttons . . . now we all played headier games.

"Quite a diner you run here," I said after making the rounds.

Fausto drew back a chair, smiling as a server appeared with my eggs Benedict. "Tell me what brings you, dear."

I swallowed perfect hollandaise. "Boredom."

"Ha! I'll do my best to amuse you."

Enter Aurilla Perle. Today the senator wore a dress with a thick black belt excellent for tanning hides. As her eyes swept the room, she digested its contents with the aloofness of a tarpon swimming openmouthed through a sea of herring. In her wake was the beige assistant, in another prim suit. "Good morning, Fausto." Two air kisses. Aurilla poured herself a cup of coffee from my pot, then extended a cool hand. "Still here?" She didn't wait for the explanation I didn't offer. "Perhaps you'd have time to hear my daughter now." Her hard eyes sought Fausto's. "Wouldn't that be wonderful?"

Host didn't disappoint guest. "Leslie, do hear the girl. She's amazing."

Aurilla opened her appointment book. "Seven tonight?"

"Sure."

She placed a business card next to my orange juice before espying her next item of business, a congressman with a face full of pancakes. As she crossed the room, swinging her round hips, part woman, part wrecking ball, conversation dipped respectfully. Only Justine ignored her.

"Aurilla knows she's going to be vice president," Fausto observed. "If Jojo cooperates, of course. Ah well, no one lives forever. Especially if they get in that woman's way." He leaned over my ear. "Be nice to her, sweetheart."

I watched Aurilla manacle the congressman with a handshake and icy smile. "Don't tell me she's a stage mother on top of everything."

"Who cares? You just received the hottest invitation in Washington. No one goes to Aurilla's place. Not even I, believe it or not."

"Why not?"

"She tries to keep her private life private."

"What's hubby like?"

Fausto momentarily stopped diluting his cream with coffee. "Hubby's dead. He was a senator from New Jersey. Plane crashed in midterm. Aurilla replaced him and has been running the show ever since. Not one misstep in eight years. Marvel thinks she's God and he hasn't even taken her pants off."

"What about the girl?"

"Gretchen? You'll see." Fausto dismembered a third croissant. "Aurilla's the perfect VP for Bobby. With her on the ticket, no way he won't be reelected, despite the bimbo problem."

Problem? Try addiction. About a year ago, Bobby's inability to keep his cock between his own legs had nearly led to his impeachment. He had saved himself, as only an American politician could, with a tearful confession about temptation, forgiveness, and redemption. Since then, in a phenomenal display of fortitude, he had limited himself to one mistress at a time. "Aurilla does have a certain probity," I agreed. "Unlike poor Jojo."

Fausto sighed wistfully, as if Jordan Bailey's demise actually saddened him. "Tell me about yourself."

I discussed my future engagements, neglecting to mention that Curtis had just canceled nine out of ten. Fausto reapologized for having missed my concert at the White House. We touched on Stradivarius, Sibelius, and Schnitzler as he occasionally tiddled a finger at incoming guests. "Were you always a music lover?" I asked.

"Worse. I was a musician. Piano. I thought I was the reincarnation of Franz Liszt." Like me, Fausto had studied with a great teacher, practiced ten hours a day, and performed all over Europe during his childhood.

"Why'd you stop?"

He cackled so harshly that all conversation in his breakfast room withered. For a moment I thought he'd choke. "Couldn't cut it," he finally whispered.

"Lousy business," I said after a moment.

His smile exposed teeth the color of bamboo. "Yes, for those of us who don't sleep with conductors. Mind if I smoke?"

"Just blow it the other way."

Fausto lit a cigarette. "You don't believe in tempting fate?"

"Not with tobacco."

He studied my face for the next half inch of Dunhill. "How does it feel to be a widow?"

Blam went the blood. I returned his even, taunting gaze. "About the same as it feels to be one hundred pounds overweight, I think." While he was trying to laugh, I asked, "Why aren't you married? Can't find anyone who loves you for yourself?"

A few puffs. "No one's had a chance. I haven't been myself."

"Since when? You stopped playing piano?" I patted his hand. "Maybe that's just as well. You would have made a lousy husband. Maybe a lousy pianist, too."

The philosopher blew another cloud at the gods. "May I ask something? Why'd you come to breakfast?"

"I was hungry. Why'd you invite me?"

"I adore women with talent. And secrets. They're so much more challenging than politicians."

For a horrific instant, I was certain that Fausto had seen me hanging off Barnard's balcony, that he knew exactly who I was and why I endured his insulting familiarity. *Calm down, Smith. His tongue is his only weapon.* "Too bad you gave up music." I sighed cheerfully, smiling across the room. "Is it more edifying to feed a pack of wolves?"

"Depends on who's eating my eggs." With great deliberation, he rubbed his cigarette into the ashtray. "You don't like Washington."

"Not my style."

"No? Men here are no different than anywhere else."

"The roulette wheel spins a little too fast here."

"Don't be a hypocrite, darling. Musicians have so much in common with politicians. Always onstage, polishing the image. Always trying to subdue the orchestra, charm the press, always aware that one slip could finish them."

"Nice try, Fausto. I'm just a fiddle player."

"Really? You married a conductor thirty-five years your senior. Now dead, poor chap. Your last lover was the director of the Leipzig trade fair. Also dead. Not to mention that dashing young recording engineer. But I'm sure they all expired in various stages of ecstasy."

I folded my napkin. "Get to the point."

"What point? I envy them all." My host smiled. "You like powerful men."

"I like powerful brains."

"Then we've got a lot in common." Fausto offered me his elbow. "Would you like to see my little concert room?"

Now that he had wrecked my appetite, why not. I accompanied him to a capacious hall decked with tons of brocade, oak parquet, and a Steinway D. "I'd be delighted if you rehearsed here," Fausto said, lifting the piano lid. "It's so much nicer than the East Room. What's your accompanist's name? Zadinsky?"

"Duncan." The score of the Brahms sonata we had just played at the White House rested on the music stand. "Aha, you *have* been practicing."

"Good God, no! I haven't touched that piece in years."

Then what was it doing on the piano? I played a chromatic scale: the tuner had visited within the last twenty-four hours. Fausto had been expecting me. *Don't disappoint him,* Maxine had said. "Maybe I'll bring Duncan over this afternoon."

"Lovely." Fausto glanced lazily out the window, registering comings and goings. "I don't know whether it's you or the planets, but no one's leaving with the person they came with today." We peered outside just as the secretary of defense was ducking into Justine's Mercedes. "Dennis has been trying to screw her for three years," Fausto said.

"Really? I thought he was gay."

"Screw figuratively." Fausto dropped the curtain. "Who told you about Dennis?"

"Minister Klint," I lied.

"Damn Germans. Always know twice as much as they let on." We returned to the foyer, where Fausto stared at my mouth, at the dark mole above my lip, with a lascivious disinterest that made my stomach ache. "As long as you're coming back," he said, fishing in a sideboard drawer, "take that red car outside. My knees can't cope with stick shifts anymore."

He pointed to a Corvette ZR1. Six speeds driving four hundred horsepower, happiest around two miles per minute. A cannonball with steering wheel: my right foot began to get an erection. "That's very kind."

"The thin one is the house key. My home is yours. I promise you will never be bored here." Fausto wrapped my fingers around metal just as Senator Perle strode into the hallway. "Run along now. I'll take care of her." I slipped away as his robe billowed in her direction.

Drove the Corvette to Brandon's Blossoms, a designer hothouse in Foggy Bottom. Inside, the slightly sour odor of carnations triggered memories of my dead mother. I had been a youngster when she died. Acres of these tight, frilly blooms had surrounded her casket; ever since, I had hated them. In the refrigerator, dainty nosegays awaited quivering nostrils. Nearby, a man stood wrapping a huge arrangement in cellophane. "I go all out for funeral sprays, even if they end up at the crematorium," he confided. "How can I help you, sweetheart?"

"Are you the famous Brandon?" Affirmative. "I received a gorgeous bouquet from here the other day. Thank you."

"Thank *you!* So few people show an *iota* of appreciation!"

"Deep purple orchids. I'd like to return the compliment

but I don't know who sent them. Do you remember anything about this?"

He fussed with a big bow before finally peering at the card in my hand. *A cliff-hanging performance.* "I could look it up," Brandon said hesitantly, beginning to cough. "Deliver the flowers today."

"I would prefer to deliver them myself."

"No! No! Never! That would be violating a customer's confidence!"

"Could you give me a few hints, then? My curiosity is killing me." I placed a C note on the counter. "Boy or girl?"

"It—it's—" Brandon threw the money back at me. "Please! I can't tell you! It's a matter of national security!"

"In that case"—I sighed, tucking the bill into his apron—"please tell my admirer not to be so shy next time."

Brandon could only wheeze in fright. I left the shop, holding my breath as I passed the carnations. Whoever sent those orchids had made quite an impression on the florist. A matter of national security? Get serious. More likely the client had threatened to break Brandon's neck if he didn't keep his mouth shut. I plopped into the Corvette and roared through Georgetown. M Street writhed with students, tourists, panhandlers, and, occasionally, exquisite women. Everywhere, guts and butts: two across blocked the entire sidewalk. This was a nation of hogs, and the situation wasn't much better in the street. Confused by the dead ends and one-ways preventing their escape from the main drag, drivers crawled along, braking timidly at each intersection. Why was Georgetown a tourist attraction? M Street was nothing but a strip mall minus the mall. The constant stop-go didn't suit the Corvette. It was edging toward meltdown when I finally noticed that an old gray Chevy had been behind me for too long. Driver wore sunglasses opaque as my own, white baseball cap. Dressed like an aimless slob but he didn't tailgate like one. The shape of his face, his nose, looked familiar, but he was out of context. As I was taking another look, he suddenly grinned and cut away.

Coincidence, Smith. Unconvinced, I took the Corvette for a spin along the canal road into Maryland. The Chevy might be gone but Fausto's shadow remained. I wondered if he always conducted such intimate conversations with strangers or if I were a special case. Either way, aggravating. Although I hadn't told him anything, I was sure he'd learned exactly what he wanted to know, and I had learned . . . nothing.

An hour later, out of gas, I returned to the hotel and made some noise with the Strad. Come what may, I still had a concert in Carnegie Hall on Saturday night. Senator Perle's secretary interrupted once, confirming my seven o'clock appointment with the daughter. After a few hours, I quit. Wrists hurt, intonation splattered. Instead of seeing notes, I saw Barnard bleed as I dug a pin into her neck. Her blood was not red, but the rich purple of orchids. It smelled of grilled pineapple. I couldn't believe she was dead.

The door connecting my room and Duncan's flew open. "What is that god-awful odor?" he cried, flopping onto the bed.

"Herbal tea. Good for the joints. Have some."

"Please! I've just had a *very* nice lunch!" The king of hypochondriacs suddenly realized what I was telling him. "What's the matter with your joints? Tendinitis? It's probably from squeezing the brakes on that fucking motorcycle!"

"I haven't squeezed anything in days. Who sprang for lunch, you or Justine?"

"Nobody sprang for anything. Will you stop prying into my personal affairs?"

So Justine had bought again. I looked pointedly at my accompanist's loud new tie, obviously a gift from his inamorata. Duncan would never buy himself anything red. "How many hours did you practice today?"

"Zero. I know these pieces backward and forward."

"Let's get going, then. I found a new place to rehearse."

"Oh God, not another boyfriend's house! I hope the piano is decent!"

"Should be. He used to play two hundred recitals a year."

That put a dent in Duncan's cheer. He became even more upset at the sight of Fausto's Corvette in the hotel lot. "Where'd you meet this guy?"

"Ford's Theatre. He gave me the car at breakfast today." I let Duncan's imagination run amok as we drove past the zoo. "Name's Fausto. Don't embarrass me now."

I nosed the Corvette into Fausto's driveway. Duncan frowned at the house as he followed me up the walk. "Why do I feel like Hansel and Gretel going to visit the Wicked Witch?" he asked as I rang the doorbell.

Still in pajamas, our host answered. Purple half-frame glasses matched the violet in his eyes. "Welcome back. Had lunch yet?"

Duncan glared at Fausto's embroidered kimono. "It's three o'clock," he announced, striding in. "We've eaten long ago."

"You must be Duncan Zadinsky. I'm Fausto Kiss."

Their palms grazed. Duncan swiveled his head about the foyer, searching exaggeratedly for a long black object with eighty-eight keys. "Would you mind if we got right to work? I'm pressed for time."

Grinning, Fausto led us to the music room. "I'd love to hear your program," he said, "but I'm in the middle of a Scrabble game." He closed the doors quietly.

"Scrabble," Duncan muttered, following me to the piano. "How degenerate! Does he ever get dressed? Or can't he find anything to fit?"

"Calm down, Duncan. He hasn't touched a piano in years."

We rehearsed hard. Fausto was correct: the acoustics here far excelled those in the East Room. Of course Duncan dis-

liked the piano. The place was too warm. His music didn't
stay open. Finally he stopped playing altogether and motioned for me to come to the piano bench. "He's listening at
the keyhole," he whispered.

"So what? We're not exactly cloning sheep in here."

"You know I can't stand eavesdroppers! Make him go
away!"

I opened the faraway doors: no one. "Done so soon?"
Fausto called from the breakfast room.

He really was playing Scrabble. "Just getting a glass of
water," I said, going to the sideboard. "Don't let me disturb
you."

"Not at all." Fausto extended an arm. "Come, I'd like you
to meet an old college friend."

His opponent lifted his head from the game board. When
his green eyes met mine, I felt a mild, delphic shock. "Mr.
Kaar."

Fausto whirled on his old friend. "You sly bastard, Ben."

Bendix took my hand. I was struck by his quiet yet arrogant possession of my flesh. "You're looking a bit happier
today," he said.

"Happier than what?" Fausto asked.

"A few nights ago at the White House," Bendix replied.

"You went to that tacky affair? Why didn't you tell me?"

"You didn't ask." Bendix had not let go of my hand.
"How nice to see you again."

I took a step backward, breaking contact. "We'll be done
in an hour, Fausto."

When I returned to the music room, Duncan was leafing
through the house copy of the Brahms sonatas. "What stupid
fingerings," he huffed, tossing aside the score. "No wonder
no one ever heard of him." After Brahms, he insisted that we
practice Messiaen. Since I hadn't yet told him about our

cancellations, I had no choice but to humor him. But I wanted this rehearsal over now that Bendix was listening.

Finally Duncan glanced at his watch. "My God! Look at the time!" The wife of some cultural attaché had invited him to dinner. "Will you step on it!? I can't keep foreign dignitaries waiting!"

"Give me ten seconds to say good-bye."

The breakfast room was empty. Duncan snatched a note from a silver platter in the hall. " *'I'm in the bath. Feel free to join me.'* Gad! Where do you find these people?"

I unlocked the front door. "Come on."

Rush hour: red lights, redder tempers. Cabs, horses, and prams choked Connecticut Avenue. Duncan was accustomed to Berlin, where jaywalkers at least had the courtesy to step a little faster while they blocked traffic. After a few minutes, realizing that nothing was to be gained but a robust case of laryngitis, he stopped shouting insults out the window and sank into a pout. As we passed the long boundary of the zoo, he suddenly perked up. "You met Fausto at a play?" he asked in an oddly conversational tone.

"Ford's Theatre. Justine didn't tell you she sat next to me?"

Duncan frowned. "Was there a good crowd?"

"Packed. Bobby and Paula were there, too."

He waited three seconds. "How'd you get a ticket?"

My accompanist had about as much finesse as a trash compactor. "Why does Justine want to know?"

"What a stupid question! Will you stop picking on her!"

"Someone sent it to me," I sighed. "I don't know who." Duncan would pass along the fib.

"And you *went?*"

"Why not? I love Schnitzler."

"Maybe it's the same guy who sent the orchids. Could be a stalker."

I zoomed through a yellow light. "Any more questions I can answer for your girlfriend?"

"She asked about your love life," he whimpered finally.

"What'd you tell her?"

"That after Hugo you only had one serious fling. But with two men." Thanks a mil, Duncan. Very elegant. "She wondered if you were seeing anyone in Washington."

"For Christ's sake! I just got here!"

"That's what I said." Duncan was sinking into a funk. "Now that I think about it, every other question was about you. Justine's not interested in me at all."

"Come on. She was just trying to break the ice." Against my better judgment, I extolled her virtues until we arrived back at the hotel. Duncan ran smiling to his room and I spent an hour in the gym converting guilt to sweat. Although women were much more invidious adversaries than men, I knew I could handle Justine Cortot. She was nothing but a feisty amateur with an ability to see one step ahead of her enemies. To survive in this town, however, she'd need to see ten steps ahead—twenty behind—and Justine was a little too smug to pull that off. Sooner or later she'd go down. I didn't want Duncan dragged down with her.

My room reeked of wilting orchids. I threw them out. Last thing I needed tonight was a musical exhibition by Aurilla Perle's daughter. However, since the invitation smelled totally rotten, I was obligated to go. Showered, dressed in narrow pink pants and fuzzy halter. At precisely seven o'clock, parked the Corvette in front of Senator Perle's castle a few miles up the Potomac. Wide balconies, a chandelier in every leaded window: she obviously didn't need a husband for economic survival. A man stopped me at her front stoop. Holster under the arm, audio pickup in left ear: armed guards, and she hadn't even been named vice president yet. "Leslie Frost," I told him. "The violin teacher."

"Leslie Frost," he repeated into the intercom, poising me in front of the camera.

Senator Perle answered. She wore the same dress as that morning, but without the power belt. Her hair was still perfectly glacéed but the twenty-four-hour makeup was nearing the end of its shift. I had not seen her wearing glasses before. She looked her age. "Thank you for being punctual," she said as a second guard ran a metal detector over my bra. "My daughter is waiting."

Aurilla's unnamed assistant, a pastiche of earth tones, emerged from a large first floor office. "Have you met Wallace?" her boss asked.

"Gretchen's so excited that you're here," Wallace assured me, crushing my hand as if it were a stress relief ball. "So am I."

"Hold my calls," Aurilla commanded. I followed the proud mother to a beautifully appointed parlor. It was like the senator's hairdo: not an atom out of place. Looked less like a room than an extension of its owner's will. In the middle of the carpet lay a mound of French fries.

"Gretchen dear," said Aurilla, stepping over them, "this is Miss Frost."

Motionless as a doll, arms resting on the chair as if it were her throne, a girl of maybe eight watched my approach. One was tempted to ruffle the flyaway black hair, pat her adorable cheeks, until one saw the eyes. I understood why Aurilla had thanked me for arriving on time. "Hello," I said.

The girl spat. We both watched a gob of potato cling to my thigh before dropping to the carpet.

"Gretchen!" Aurilla snapped. "Miss Frost is a famous musician! Shake her hand!"

Sliding off the chair, the girl extended her hand. I was about to shake it when she tried to kick me. Bad move, even for an eight-year-old. I caught her foot and flipped her to the floor. Luckily, the French fries cushioned her fall. "Nice to meet you," I said.

Neither of them moved so I tuned the violin lying on top of the sofa and ran a few scales up and down. Aurilla had bought her daughter an expensive instrument. "Get up and play something," I said after a while, handing it to her.

"I don't want to."

Wouldn't a mother have rushed to her humiliated flesh and blood, screamed for the security guard, had me thrown out? Conversely, wouldn't she have reprimanded the girl again? Aurilla merely stood in place with that ghoulish, plastic smile.

"Don't play, then," I shrugged. Tucked the violin under my chin and, strolling about, began a Paganini caprice. Nothing in this room told me anything about Senator Perle except that she had money and a ruined daughter. Eventually I cut short the fireworks. "How long have you been studying?" I asked the girl, yanking loose hairs out of the bow.

"Four years."

"Like it?"

"No."

I resumed playing, waiting for Aurilla to make her move. Why did people in this town always have to involve a third wheel in their petty machinations? I wandered to the window. In the driveway, three black cars had come to a halt. Two men alit from the first and last vehicles. The four of them fanned out, adroitly taking positions along the perimeter of Aurilla's property. The rear door of the middle car opened. Four men in suits clustered a fifth, hustling him to Aurilla's front door. As the bell rang, I smiled at my own stupidity: textbook Secret Service. Aurilla had been waiting all along for Bobby Marvel. Maybe he had come to give her some acting tips for Jojo's funeral. *Fat chance, Smith.* He had come to see me.

"You could get a hundred grand for this," I told Aurilla, setting down the violin. "Why don't you cash in and send Gretchen to the Citadel."

After a soft knock, the door opened. Aurilla's assistant peered in. "Excuse me. The president is here."

"Thank you, Wallace." Aurilla's android smile rose a notch. "Gretchen, play something for Miss Frost. Right now." She left.

I sat on the girl's chair. "Got a checkerboard?"

She finally got up from the cushion of French fries. "I want to play my violin."

I handed it over. "Not too loud, please. I can't stand squeaks."

She didn't make many. As I had suspected, the girl was very gifted: not many chromosomes separated psychopath from prodigy. "Nice," I said when the Mendelssohn had ended. "Who's your teacher?"

"Uncle Bendix." While my mouth was hanging open, Gretchen added, "But he hasn't given me a lesson in a long time."

I sighed. "Play something else."

Mozart. Gretchen's face became wise beyond her years; I recognized the look and pitied those who would someday become her lovers. After she finished, I showed her a few bowings. We were deep in horsehair when a voice interrupted.

"Wonderful." Bobby Marvel, three feet away.

Gretchen immediately reverted to form. "Who asked you?" she snapped, cracking her boot against the president's shin.

Marvel managed a smile as he rubbed his bruise. "Evenin', ma'am."

Aurilla appeared. "What's going on here?"

As Bobby straightened up, a few fries fell into his cuff. "Just tying my shoelace."

"You were not," Gretchen cried. "Buzz off!"

"Gretchen Perle! Mind your manners!"

Ah, if Maxine could see me now. I put down the violin and patted the girl's head. "Keep up the good work, dear." Now for the tricky part. "Good night, sir."

He wouldn't let go of my hand. Worse, his thumb was wandering. "That was such a fantastic concert the other night. I could listen to the whole thing all over again."

When I didn't offer to play the whole thing all over again, Aurilla stepped into the breach. "President Marvel's quite a musician, you know."

Spoons? Washboard? "I brought my cornet with me to the White House," he boasted. "Still play it sometimes with the Marine Band."

They must just love that. My hand was beginning to sweat but Bobby held on through a long-winded paean to his cornet teacher. "One in a million," the president blubbered, eyes bright with tears. "I still think of him every day."

I finally got my hand back. Nearly ran to the Corvette but my getaway was not quite fast enough. As I was buckling my seat belt, a Secret Service agent caught up with me. "The president would like a word with you, ma'am. Just wait a moment."

My usual reply would have been a fifty-foot swath of rubber. However, I was a member of the armed forces, he was my commander in chief, so I walked dutifully to the car waiting in the shadows. No voters here, so Marvel didn't need to act presidential; in fact, he sat in the backseat with his legs curled, the better to massage the welt on his shin. I sat in the corner and tried to appear awed. After Barnard's video, it just wasn't possible. "Hurt?" I asked finally.

"Goddamn brat. Did you like Mr. Schnizzler?"

Took a moment to figure out whom he meant. "Not really. It was a bad translation. Badly acted." Bobby watched as I crossed my legs. "Lousy night."

The president suddenly leaned forward, chin jutting like a pit bull. At last he looked like the guy on fifty-cent postcards. "Someone else was expected in that seat."

As my heart thumped against my halter, warm French perfume blossomed in the dark. *Go! Now!* I leapt over the cliff. "Polly gave me her ticket."

He gasped. "You know Polly?"

"We're old friends." A drop of sweat inched down my side. I smelled like a bitch in heat, and Bobby noticed. "She tells me everything."

"Is that a fact. What does she call me?"

I viciously raked my brain, exhuming only that message on Barnard's answering machine. "Something to do with ice cream, I think." Bobby grunted unpleasantly. *Roll the dice!* "If I were you," I said, slowly recrossing my legs, "I'd forget about her. She has a short attention span."

The buttons on his shirt rose and fell as he teetered on my advice. "I don't think you understand," Bobby seethed at last. "I'm the president."

"What can I tell you? She prefers princes." I reached for the door handle.

He grabbed my sore wrist. I winced: years on the campaign trail had given him a bionic grip. "You tell your friend," Bobby whispered, "I am not amused."

I brushed away his hand. "Tell her yourself."

He couldn't even choke out a good-night. I aimed the Corvette for the Beltway and started to weave in and out of traffic, not that I was in a rush to get anywhere, rather the Corvette wasn't made for going only seventy in a straight line. An exodus of commuters, grandmothers puritanically obeying the speed limits, and yuppies in their budget BMWs made this road more dangerous than the Autobahn. Good: kept my mind off that clod Marvel. When the sun sliced into the horizon, I finally saw that a gray Chevy had drifted across the dotted lines behind me once too often. The driver, still in the baseball cap, never allowed me more than three cars leeway: maybe that was a compliment. I veered right, poked along the shoulder. Chevy copied. I tapped the gas, notched left: soon we were back in the fast lane. Fear riddled my gut as a million phantoms began to thaw and writhe. Where had I made the fatal error that six of Maxine's seven agents had made before me? For miles I purred in the wake of a rusty Caddy, awaiting a slim coincidence of exit ramp and fender gap. I got it at the Merrifield turnoff. Ripped the 'Vette right, screeching across three lanes, barreling around the cloverleaf. Chevy never had a chance.

I drove in a few loops before ditching the car at a twelve-screen cinema in Fairfax. Sat through a loud, bloody movie as my watch crawled forward. When the hero destroyed his nth opponent, I left. Bad place, movies: shallow sex, shallower death, all so sickeningly easy. I cabbed back to Washington. Night had not relieved the heat, but it had decimated the tourists around the Reflecting Pool. I took the Metro to the Zoo. Connecticut Avenue still pulsed with people who either hated air conditioners or didn't own one. Cut into Rock Creek Park and followed the black, burbling water to the bear house. There I slipped into my pocket in the rocks, grateful as the door sealed me in with my machines.

JUSTINE CORTOT, I typed. Her face came up in a second. Native of Kentucky, where mothers groomed daughters to become Miss America or marry tobacco. Same alma mater as Bobby Marvel. Rhodes Scholarship, English major. History would have been more relevant, but Justine wasn't interested in events larger than herself. Twice divorced from minor dignitaries, zero kids. Once she and Bobby put that little shooting incident behind them, Justine had joined his carnival winding from state senator to governor to president. Had she known about Barnard? Hell, Justine had probably procured her! The press secretary saw a hundred supplicants a day, made or destroyed dozens of careers a week . . . yet she had found the time to lunch with Duncan Zadinsky three days running. Unbelievable.

Next, BENDIX KAAR. The computer finally located him under Political Contributors, a subset of white-color criminals. After serving with distinction in Vietnam, Bendix had made his fortune in exotic hardwood. Ten years ago he'd sold his business to play environmental consultant to any PAC that could afford him. He had given Bobby Marvel enough money to be invited regularly to the White House and had been Aurilla's Svengali since her first day in the Senate. Age fifty-three, two grown children, no known wife. Fausto had said they were old college friends: which college? I cruised through the Harvard file: nothing. The Royal College of Music wasn't even in Maxine's database so I switched to e-mail, asking if Bendix Kaar had ever graced their hallowed halls. That answer might take weeks, so I moved on to superwidow AURILLA PERLE.

Born in Chicago, full scholarship to Princeton. She had tied the knot with a family of meat packers who supplied the entire Northeast with pastrami. Hubby appeared fairly masculine in the early photos; then, as Aurilla's smile inflated from shy to imperial, he began to age drastically, as if she were sucking his blood. His death in a plane crash had had no effect on her mouth. Gretchen, three days old, appeared in only one photo; even at that tender age, the child had impressive fists and a face ready to explode. Aurilla's political record, like her smile, was mathematically perfect.

I snuggled the cassette from Barnard's answering machine into the tape recorder. My breathing paused as her sultry voice, now forever silent, filled the headphones. "Sorry, darling. Let me know you called."

"Darling," Fausto mimicked acidly. "We missed you last night. Naughty naughty."

I played the next message several times just to kill my doubts. "The ice-cream man will see you at midnight. Don't be late": Justine Cortot speaking. Should have recognized those overworked *t*'s the moment I heard her voice at Ford's Theatre.

I phoned Berlin. "Good morning."

The Queen would have gone to bed only two hours ago. "What's up."

"Barnard and Marvel were for real." I told her about my little palaver in the president's limousine. "He's most upset at losing her."

Maxine laughed huskily: join the crowd. "How'd you learn that?"

"Aurilla Perle invited me to her house to hear her daughter play the violin. Marvel happened to drop by."

"Her idea or his?"

"Couldn't tell you. Aurilla had already bugged me about her daughter the night I played at the White House. Bobby's been eyeballing me since Ford's Theatre. And it could have been an accident. None of this would have happened if Aurilla hadn't caught me at Fausto's."

"You don't run into the president of the United States by accident," Maxine yawned. "Sorry."

"There were two messages on Barnard's answering machine," I continued. "One was from Fausto telling Barnard she had misbehaved."

"Eh? How did Barnard know Fausto?"

"Didn't she tell you anything?" I snapped. Of course not. Damn. "The last message was from Justine Cortot, arranging a tryst with Marvel."

"Cortot's in on the act? Have we got two pimps here?"

"Maybe she handles scheduling after the first date." I

sighed. "Bendix Kaar happened to be playing Scrabble with Fausto as I rehearsed there this afternoon."

"People do lots of things in the afternoon. How was breakfast, by the way?"

Insulting. "Fausto wants me to practice at his place. He loaned me his Corvette. I'd take it out more but I'm being followed."

"Surprised? You're screwing around with every heavy in town."

Beautiful. "I hope Marvel's discreet. I don't need his wife coming after me with a two-by-four."

"Wouldn't worry about it. Nothing upsets Paula but a dip in her husband's approval rating. Listen, I got a lab report on Barnard's blood. The only compounds we could identify were zonirene and gamma-gafrinol."

"Okay, I give up."

"Phytochemicals found only in the rain forest. Not synthesized, not really known outside of the military."

"Application?"

"Paralytics. Once Barnard took it in the neck, she could only watch that tampon go down her throat." A moment of black static. "Bastards."

"I've got one last concert Saturday night," I said. No big deal. Just Carnegie Hall. "Then I'll go to Belize."

"Barnard left some surveillance gear behind. You might pick it up while you're down there."

"She left it behind?"

"Just get it back," Maxine said wearily. "Everything's on the map in your kit."

My kit was burning a hole in a locker at the Miami airport. I turned off the lights and headed into the woods. Whatever Barnard had left in the jungle, it was more than a camera.

Chapter Four

$\mathscr{I}$ HAD STRIPPED and was about to step into the shower when the phone rang. "Hello, Leslie." Marvel sounded agitated, as if he had been calling for hours. "I'd like to see you."

Shit! "When would be good, sir?"

"Now. A car's on its way." He hung up.

Sixty seconds wet, another sixty yanking on clothes. No time for underwear. I painted the face, blew on a little scent. Just as I hit the revolving doors, a Lexus pulled up to the hotel. Chauffeur nodded, I got in. No president in the backseat. No surprise: he'd be the soul of discretion until his re-election. The car sailed past the White House. "Where are we going?" I asked.

"Out of town." He joined the Beltway herd. "Sit back and relax."

City lights eventually faded, as did traffic. Without a word, we headed deep into Virginia. I had been here on the Harley just the other day, trying to forget about Barnard; now I was rushing into her lover's embrace. I hoped Bobby hadn't invited me out here to take a bubble bath. Maybe he wanted to ask a few more questions about the only woman who had ever dumped him. Ah, Barnard. Why had she lured him into that bathtub? And who had the original video? Were it with a friend, Bobby would probably have seen it by now. Foe? He'd have no idea.

Eventually the Lexus turned onto an unmarked dirt road. Pine branches swished at the doors as darkness engulfed us. Many bumps, one last swerve before a guard with walkie-talkie and submachine gun blocked our path. He checked the driver's ID, asked me to step out for a modest pat-down. That done, he unchained the gate. Bobby's discretion now verged on the paranoid: I liked that.

The president, plus cigar, waited on the porch of a spacious old house. Since our chat in his limousine, he had changed into khakis and sport shirt. I stood next to him a moment inhaling smoke and cologne, running my eyes only once over the hair on his chest. Now that Marvel had put aside the presidential act and reverted to his natural state, stag in heat, he seemed much more dangerous than he had a few hours ago. "Thanks for coming." He peered at my face in the dim light. "Can I get you something?"

Gin and a chastity belt. While he was inside, I looked around the yard for Secret Service agents. Exceptionally well hidden, wherever they were. Maybe in the trees. Over the past three years Marvel had probably asked them to get lost so many times that invisibility was a job requirement now. As the president returned to the porch, he motioned to a swing in the corner. "You were out tonight," he said, serving me.

Zoo. "Rehearsal. I have a concert in New York this weekend."

Bobby smiled insipidly. "Ah. Will you be seeing Polly?"

"You never know."

Chains creaked as the swing moved in tandem with our breathing. "Where did you meet her?" he asked.

"On a beach in France. She was with a Hungarian count." I had been buffing this story for the last hour. "I next met her in Paris. She was with an Italian from one of the sports car families. Our paths have crossed a lot since then. She was always with a different man." I swallowed gin. "If it's any consolation, you're her first American. Where did *you* meet her?"

"At a fund-raiser. She was with Fausto Kiss. A different sort of prince." Bobby chuckled coldly. "What did she tell you about me?"

"Nothing."

"Then how did you know my nickname?"

"Polly said I'd be sitting behind a hunk of ice cream. I had no idea she meant you."

Bobby's irritation increased. "Did she say why she wasn't going to be there?"

"She had a date with a football player." I tried to look embarrassed. "Unlike you, he left his wife at home."

"That was the problem? *Paula?*"

"You wouldn't understand. It's a woman thing."

"But our going to that play was official business!"

Unless he was the best actor in the universe, Bobby had no idea that Barnard was dead. Why was he so upset now? Did he have genuine feelings for her? Or was the concept of anyone leaving him insupportable? "Official for you, maybe."

"Shit." He got himself another beer. I looked into the trees, around the lawn: no witnesses but the stars. Bobby's bodyguards had no idea how easily I could assassinate their charge and slip away into the night. Maybe they did know and were keeping their fingers crossed. The chains wheezed as Bobby returned to the swing. "You don't live in America, do you?"

"I grew up in Berlin. It's home to me."

"Will you be going back soon?"

"After a few more concerts."

He laid a warm, thick hand on my thigh. "That's not much time."

So much for genuine feelings. I put my drink on the floor and looked Bobby full in the face. His mouth was inches from mine and closing in fast when I said, "May I use the bathroom?"

It had to be upstairs because of the skylight. Behind the first door I found the marble tub and potted plants I had seen in Barnard's video. Camera not too cleverly stashed atop the linen cabinet, aimed at the bathtub: Barnard would have noticed it within seconds. Maxine was correct: Barnard had made that video on purpose. If I went to the toilet, I'd pass right in front of the lens: no way Frost would go on record here. Not yet. First I wanted to know who'd be watching. I went across the hall and saw another camera aimed at the gigantic bed.

Bladder unrelieved, I returned to the porch. Bobby was staring at an airplane as the head on his beer opalesced in the moonlight. He had slid another five inches toward my side of the swing. I detoured to the railing, inhaled the damp breeze. "Whose house is this?" I asked the trees.

"A close friend gave me the keys on Inauguration Day. Every president needs a special hideaway." Bobby slipped behind me. I caught my breath as he kissed the nape of my neck. After a moment he drew my hips backward, against his pelvis. Maybe he had stashed a piece of the Manhattan aqueduct in there.

I turned around. "What about Polly?"

Now his lips started in on my collarbone. "She's history."

"Not to me."

Bobby smiled indulgently, as if I were kidding. "I've never made love to a woman who didn't want me." He resumed at my throat. "On the other hand, I never met one who didn't."

I was beginning to understand how he had convinced the voters to put him in the White House. My stomach fluttered as he nibbled with absolute concentration beneath my sternum. Resistance impossible: this man's gift was persuasion. With crowds, on the tube, he was reliable as a diesel; one-on-one, he was overwhelming. As his hand slid beneath my dress, wilted a moment as it encountered no underwear, enlightenment struck. Forget about his mark on history: Bobby Marvel lived to fuck. Being president was just the best means to that end. He truly believed he was conferring some sort of Purple Heart on the women he seduced. What higher honor than to be taken by *the president?* His sincerity was stupidly endearing. But I had known too many finer men.

"You're very nice," I sighed, retreating. "However, not my type."

Momentary disbelief, then that dazzling smile. "No one's made me wait in twenty years." Bobby sniffed his hand languorously, ecstatically, as if inhaling purest cocaine. "Believe me, you're *my* type." He jerked my hand to the ridge in his pants.

"I didn't come here for this," I snorted.

"No? What did you come for?"

"Professional courtesy."

Two fingers dug between my legs. They felt as thick as his penis. "Next time you don't wear panties," Bobby whispered, "you'd better mean it." One quick, rough kiss and he sprang me loose. The driver came to the porch. I got back to Washington after four in the morning. Duncan was not in his room. I couldn't sleep: bodies were apolitical, and mine had wanted Marvel's.

Several hours later I returned Fausto's Corvette to his driveway. Judging by the paucity of cars outside his house, not many people had felt up to breakfast this morning. But that lurid orange sun lurking above the smog would drive any sane human into the hills. Only the truly depraved, like Justine and I, would still want to eat. Her silver Mercedes occupied the space closest to the front door: she had arrived first. Maybe she had slept over.

Fausto greeted me in flowing white pajamas embroidered with watermelons. Weak flesh puffed around his eyes. His complexion matched the smog. No smile: maybe I should have phoned beforehand. "Darling." He squeezed my fingers. "Come in."

I signed the guest book. A dozen visitors looked up as we entered the dining room. I got fewer, but longer, stares than I had yesterday. Justine actually stopped chewing for a few moments to check out my dress. She looked delicious, a little wild, as if she had been up all night. When she actually smiled at me, I knew with whom.

Fausto settled into his chair in the corner. "I had no idea you were such an early riser."

"Jet lag." I told the butler to bring just coffee and bread. "Sorry we missed you after the rehearsal. Duncan is not into coed bathing."

"I forgive him. He's a good pianist. You've been playing together a long time?"

"From the beginning." I stuck a toe in the water. "I try to look out for him."

"Ah, you're worried about Justine? Join the club." Fausto lit a cigarette. "No secrets in this town, my dear. And the two of them are not exactly discreet."

Last I had seen Duncan, he was barreling off to some dowager's dinner party. That had probably ended around midnight: seven long hours ago. "Okay, let me have it."

"The evening started mildly enough. Apparently your accompanist loves to tango. He burned up the floor at the Argentine embassy."

"His mother made him take dancing lessons for ten years." I sighed. "Then what."

"I understand he carried Justine to her car. They cooled off a bit in the fountain in front of the Capitol Building. They hit a disco, then committed a few carnal sins on the steps of the National Cathedral." Fausto waved at Vicky Chickering, who had just entered with a glum attorney general. "Thereafter Duncan may have reconsidered his antipathy to coed bathing. Justine rolled in an hour ago with stars in her eyes. Extraordinary."

Damn! "What does she get out of this?"

"A priceless opportunity to make Bobby jealous. Not to mention stud service." Fausto patted my hand. "There, there. Duncan's a grown boy."

Across the room, the servicee broke into girlish laughter. It was the same frequency as that laugh I had heard over the Watergate fountain the other night. Was I denying the simple, obvious possibility that this woman had fallen in love with Duncan? I was a possessive woman, even when I didn't own the gentleman in question. "I hope he's got enough energy to rehearse this afternoon."

"If he's been screwing Justine, he won't need to sleep for a week." Fausto waved to Aurilla Perle as she cruised to the coffee urn. "The first week, anyway. Incidentally, my friend Bendix is most taken with you. Are you seriously involved with anyone, darling?"

I daubed my lips with a napkin, wondering why this did not feel like an incidental change of subject. "I'm a serious girl."

Fausto extended a hand as Senator Perle and her slave Wallace approached. "Good morning, ladies. You're looking lovely today, Aurilla."

Lovely was stretching it, but the VP-in-waiting had spent the night with a grenade named Gretchen. I now understood why no one was invited to her home. "Thank you for listening to my daughter," Aurilla said to me. "You must come back again. She has two new pieces prepared."

A pall asphyxiated the table. I finally caved. "How's four this afternoon?"

"Perfect. Thank you."

Wallace wrote it down then caught up with her idol across the room. Deep in thought, Fausto watched Aurilla snare a senator. "How is the girl? Last time we met she tried to kick me."

"She's still kicking."

"What a waste of your time. No reason for it." Fausto looked at me slyly. "What does Aurilla think you can do for her?"

"I was hoping you might answer that." No way, of course. "Maybe she's more of a stage mother than you think."

"Darling, Aurilla hasn't given that girl ten minutes since the day she was born." He lit a cigarette. "The little monster has become a major political liability. If Aurilla had half a brain, she'd get her out of the country."

Across the room, Justine broke into that irritating, silvery laughter once too often. I stood to leave. "I'm not about to adopt her. Thanks for breakfast."

Fausto bobbed to his feet. En route to the door, he steered me within slapping distance of Duncan's inamorata. "How is the water in that fountain, Justine? Warm or cold? I've always wondered."

"Warm," she replied.

"How unlike the president to give you the night off," he continued. "And how unlike you to take it. However did Bobby pass the time without you?"

"He watched football." Justine pointedly resumed her conversation with the speechwriter at her side.

"Poor thing," Fausto muttered as we headed for the door.

"Whatever she's swallowed, it's clouded her judgment. I hope she doesn't drag your pianist to too many coke parties."

"You're not serious."

"Afraid I am. Justine's been high on one substance or another for the past thirty years. I was there when she discovered LSD."

And what had Fausto been discovering? The twenty-third Psalm? "You go back a long way."

"We met at one of my recitals in London."

"She's a music lover?" I couldn't picture Justine in the same room with the Waldstein sonata.

"She attended the concert with a friend of mine. It was a night to remember." Naturally Fausto supplied no further details. At the door, he kissed my hand. "I'm so glad you practice here. It's delicious to have music in the house again."

We both smiled, honoring the lie. "Will you be playing Scrabble with Bendix this afternoon?"

"No. He's going with Aurilla to visit Jojo. They've got to rehearse looking sad."

"Fausto! There you are!" Vicky Chickering lumbered down the hall. "Paula wants to thank you for the fantastic ointment. Wherever did you get it?"

"Can't tell you, Chickie. You know it's not FDA approved."

As Chickie brought Fausto up-to-date on the First Lady's arthritis, I thumbed through his guest book. Polly Mason had signed in, loud and clear, the day she died and the six mornings before that. So Bobby had told the truth: Barnard had indeed connected with Fausto, prince of another sort.

Chickering eventually returned to the dining room. "She didn't even say hello to you," Fausto remarked.

"Why should she? I'm a lowly fiddle player." That earned

an amused silence until I hit the ignition. "Let's play together sometime."

"Definitely." Fausto's mouth turned grim as he watched me drive away.

Back at the hotel, I could hear Duncan snoring regularly as a metronome on the other side of the wall. Inspired, I practiced mechanically for a few hours, exercising fingers as the brain grazed over craggier terrain. What had Barnard been doing at Fausto's? Was he aware that she had been bathing with the president? I wondered if Fausto already knew about Marvel and me and how he would amuse himself with that information. What was Bobby after, flesh or information? I didn't think I was worth killing yet, but my perspective was stunningly myopic. As Maxine had said, nothing in this town was real. Everything had happened too fast. And where the hell was Louis Bailey?

Around one, when Duncan began a major flood in his bathtub, I checked my e-mail. Surprise, a reply from the Royal College of Music: Bendix Kaar, composition major, had left school a semester after Fausto. Never graduated. I laughed: a failed composer? Bad news. The worst, in fact.

All this ruptured music made me curious, so I went to the Library of Congress and sifted through old microfilm of the *London Times*. Maybe a critic had gone to Fausto's last concert. I began looking about thirty years ago, when recitals dispelled, rather than induced, depression. Came across a review of my husband Hugo, who had not conducted Mahler properly. What a joke: even now, this critic was still trashing heterosexuals. I hadn't gotten a good word out of him ever. Duncan usually received honorable mention since his sexual persuasion was titillatingly ambiguous.

Fausto had gotten a rave from our friend. The artiste was thoughtful, brilliant, daring . . . unbelievable. I couldn't take the notice at face value, not from that critic, not about Fausto. Cut to the *Observer* for a second opinion.

VIOLIN SINKS. At first I thought it was a review.

> Five partygoers aboard a cruise boat jumped into the Thames in an attempt to rescue a priceless violin which had fallen into the water. Mr Richard Poore, a tugboat captain, apparently saved the lives of Mr Fausto Kiss, his mother Ethel, Mr Louis Bailey, Mr Bendix Kaar, and Miss Justine Cortot by repeatedly tossing a life preserver into the current. "Silly fools," Poore said. "I nearly rammed the London Bridge." The violin was not recovered. Police are investigating the incident, which occurred shortly before dawn.

Louis Bailey? I read the article again: as Fausto had said, a night to remember. Five people overboard? Whose violin? I inched through several more newspapers but saw no further details of the episode. There were two more reviews of the recital, both excellent. Apparently Fausto was best with the hard, fast stuff. I could understand his jumping afterward into a filthy river. But Justine in her perfect makeup? Fausto's *mother?*

Almost four o'clock: time for Gretchen's music lesson. I drove to Aurilla Perle's house. No Secret Service today, thank God. A maid answered the door. She had the despairing look of an unransomed hostage. "I'm Leslie Frost," I said. "Gretchen's expecting me."

This time the little vixen charged from the right. I caught her foot inches from my shin. "Hey! Nice to see you!" I cried, lifting her ankle high in the air, forcing her into a lopsided reverse. "Love your boots."

"Let go! That hurts!" she screamed.

I took her arm, swung her in a wide arc, let her fly into a divan. "Next time you go through the window," I smiled.

For a few seconds the only sound in the foyer was that of the grandfather clock striking four. "I hate you!" Gretchen shrieked, stomping upstairs.

I turned to the terrified maid. "Is Senator Perle home?"

Of course not. She was at the vice president's bedside, pretending she'd rather hear Jojo rave about whales than hear herself taking the oath of office. "Please wait here," the maid said. "I'll bring Gretchen down."

"Don't bother," I replied, mounting the wide stairs. "I'll find her."

Peered into an airy room with paisley curtains, canopied bed, four television sets: Aurilla's mission control. Passed a gym, again with four TVs, then a pair of guest rooms with less media presence but more canopied beds. I would not be able to sleep with all that lace hanging over my head. No sign of the girl so I climbed another round of stairs. "Gretchen?"

Her room looked like FAO Schwarz after a cyclone. Maybe she had used the walls for batting practice. Gretchen sat on yet another canopied bed fit for a czarina. She appeared to be reading a book. "Get out of my room," she said, not looking up.

"Your mother said you wanted to play a few things for me."

"I don't want to play anything. Go away."

Couldn't do that so I waited as Gretchen nonchalantly turned a few pages. Then the phone next to her bed rang. "I'm sure it's for you," she said.

"No one knows I'm here."

"*He* knows."

The phone stopped midring. Gretchen kept turning pages.

After a few moments we heard footsteps on the stairs. "Miss Frost?" the maid called. "For you."

Gretchen suddenly lunged at the phone. "Don't answer," she whispered, clutching it to her chest. "He'll take you away. Like Polly."

I tried to smile. "Who's Polly?"

"My friend."

"She came here to your house?"

"Yes. She was prettier than you."

"Miss Frost?" the maid called anxiously.

"Give me the phone," I told Gretchen. "I'm not going anywhere."

"Yes you will! I know it!"

"I'm counting to three then I'm picking up downstairs. One. Two." Gretchen threw the phone at me and buried her face in the pillows. "Yes?" I snapped into the receiver.

"Aurilla mentioned you'd be with her daughter today," said Bobby Marvel. "How's it going over there?"

"Fine, thanks."

"I enjoyed our talk last night. You're a fascinating woman."

"Could we pick this up some other time? I've got my hands full here."

"Wouldn't you rather have your hands full of me?"

Wasn't this idiot supposed to be running the country? I hung up. "Did you hear that, Gretchen? I'm not going anywhere." Her face peeped from the pillows as I sat at the foot of the bed. "Tell me about Polly."

"She helped with my science homework. I liked her a lot. She played in the backyard with me and Wallace and Herman."

Wallace was the gofer. "Who's Herman?"

"My friend."

I kept smiling. "How do you know Polly's not coming back?"

"Because Mom couldn't find her anymore."

I sat miserably through an hour of Gypsy dances. No visitors and Gretchen refused to talk further about her friends Polly and Herman. When I returned to the hotel, a fresh bouquet of purple orchids waited on the dresser. *See you soon.* Bobby? Louis? My message light was blinking: Justine Cortot commanding me to call the White House at once and Bendix Kaar wondering if I were free that evening. Rather than disappoint either of them, I flew to New York. Too damn muggy down here.

My accompanist blew backstage at Carnegie Hall about four minutes before show time. "Traffic was unbelievable," Duncan cried, heaving his garment bag over the dressing table. He began stripping. "Grab my shirt, would you?"

I stared a moment at his pink string bikini. In ten years I had never seen Duncan in anything but voluminous boxer shorts. Fingernails had recently raked three delicate, parallel lines between his nipples. "Wildcat attack?" I asked, handing over his pants.

"Where the hell are my cuff links?"

A knock: Justine, tousled and radiant, with Duncan's patent-leather shoes. "You left these under the bed," she chided.

"Oh my God! Thanks, doll!"

"And take this for your nerves." She tucked a few pills into his palm.

Duncan had told her about his stage fright? That was one of his deep, dark secrets, buried far back in the closet along with fantasies of becoming the next Horowitz. "Right!" he cried, sweeping into the bathroom. Within seconds the sounds of violent intestinal disruption blurted through the green room.

I tuned my violin and ran over a few scales. "He won't be out for a while," I said, glancing at Justine in the mirror. She was repairing a few minor wrinkles around her mouth. "Why don't you go find your seat."

Instead she inspected my gown. Moss green, clinging to all the best places. Soon two thousand people would be staring at it, mesmerized. That was too much for Justine to stomach. "You shouldn't have ignored my message."

"Sorry." I fixed my lipstick. "I find Bobby Marvel quite unattractive."

"What *you* find *him* is irrelevant." After I laughed, Justine tried the confidante angle. "You've only met once."

"Three times. He didn't get any better."

Her eyes flared: panic? "Let me give you some good advice. Next time the president asks for you, move your ass."

"Let's make a deal. You drop my pianist, I screw your boss."

She mulled that over for three seconds. "You screw Bobby Marvel," Justine decided, heading for the door. "Period."

Duncan, pale and quivering, emerged from the bathroom. "Where's Justine?" he wailed.

"Finding her seat."

"My head's killing me," he moaned, dropping to the couch. Before I could stop him, he ate Justine's pills.

"Do you have any idea what you just swallowed?"

"Beta-blockers. I think they're from Sweden. Justine's an expert on that stuff."

I tugged him to his feet as the stage manager knocked. As always, my accompanist died many deaths 'twixt green room and stage door. He cursed me for dragging him into an arcane profession that gave him nothing but an inferiority complex. "Looks full," I said, peering into the auditorium.

The stage manager motioned expectantly at the two of us. For a second, terror ran wild from head to foot: I wanted to be anywhere on earth but that stage. Then another beast, a larger one, engorged my fright. That was the demon who lived in the shadows of the blood, who pushed me in front of orchestras and off balconies because it knew that life was sweetest when oblivion was just a breath away. I felt my brain lock on to a violin, music: for the next two hours I would be a supercomputer with fingers. "Try not to step on my gown, would you, Duncan," I said, walking onstage.

Applause, warmth. The auditorium looked smaller than I remembered. Duncan managed to locate the piano bench without passing out. I waited as he twirled the knobs a few dozen times, fussed with his music, his handkerchief: poor sod, Carnegie Hall was no place for mere humans. Finally his eyes met mine. I smiled the secret smile that only Duncan saw. He began to play.

We got off to a better start than we had at the White House: here I wasn't distracted by a pair of jesters in the front row and Duncan played with the acuity of the profoundly afraid. After a few minutes, however, we began to drift. Didn't sound bad, but it wasn't what we had rehearsed. Slower, fatter. . . . Brahms over, Duncan bowed dreamily. I walked offstage.

"That was very nice," he said.

"Come here." Held his face under a light: pupils dilated, slight flush. His skin felt cold. "How are you feeling?"

"I told you. Very nice."

"Tired?"

"A little." Yawning, Duncan turned to the stage manager. "Could you turn up the heat?"

"You mean turn down the air-conditioning, sir?"

He frowned. "Whatever makes it cold."

"Get some coffee," I told the man. "Duncan, drink it before I get back."

"You know I never touch caffeine after breakfast!"

Into the auditorium for solo Bach. When I returned backstage, Duncan was puking into a garbage can.

"What are we going to do?" the stage manager whispered.

I lifted Duncan's head. "Feeling better?"

"I think so." He wiped his mouth. "Let's go."

We ended the first half with a sonata that had recently won a Pulitzer Prize. Fortunately, few people in the audience knew the piece and it was the sort of music that sounded incorrect anyway. The composer had just died, so everyone clapped appreciatively afterward. Duncan went straight to the couch in the green room. Justine barged in almost immediately.

"Zadinsky, that was superb," she cried, beelining for the cadaver, pressing his hand to her cheek. Between Brahms and intermission she had turned pinker, faster: chemical assistance. "Worn out, poor thing?"

He smiled weakly. "Just getting my second wind."

"Got any more of those pills?" I asked. "Duncan really enjoyed his first dose."

She ignored me. "Save some energy for me, tiger." After many kisses, she left.

Long, testy silence. Duncan finally opened his eyes. "She was only trying to help." When that got no sympathy, he added, "Justine's had a hard life."

Who the hell hadn't? As I was trying to focus on the second half, someone knocked. Enter Bendix Kaar, confident and sinister in a double-breasted suit. His eyes lingered on my naked shoulders. Maybe he was just counting moles and diamonds. This being our third meeting, he kissed my mouth.

Duncan squinted at him. "You're the guy with the Corvette?"

"No, that's Fausto."

"Ah, how could I forget! He invited us to a three-way bath." After ten years backstage with me, my accompanist was expert at distinguishing musical admirers from sexual predators. He usually got the admirers, I the predators. "We don't like visitors at intermission," he sniffed, as if Justine hadn't exited minutes before.

"I don't like crowds after the encores." Bendix returned his gaze to me. "I've been trying to reach you."

"Get in line," Duncan called. "Take a number."

Bendix touched my arm. "You won't be running away afterward, I hope."

Let him guess. "What is with these people?" Duncan asked after he had left. "Do they think they can just come back here and carry you away?"

"Probably."

"Animals. It's those dresses you wear."

Dresses? Radar. Most men picked it up but only a few had the guts to follow the signal into terra incognita. I had a soft spot for that sort of bravery. "Ready to roll, Duncan?"

Cursing, he staggered up from the couch. The second half went better than it should have, all things considered. Three encores later we were backstage for good. "I wish you'd stop rushing that ending," Duncan complained, gargling with mouthwash. "You're always going for the burn."

His aggravation vanished the moment Justine walked in. "That was so *hot*," she swooned, pronouncing the word as Mick Jagger would.

Duncan extended his arm. "Ready to tango?"

Unfortunately, the lovers' getaway was impeded by a dozen well-wishers, most of them relatives of the dead composer. They had brought champagne. I let Duncan deal with that bomb squad while I did a little time with Mr. Godo, president of Kakadu Records, and four of his major distributors. They adored me: I was one of the company's primary cash cows. Sushi, anyone? Duncan was obviously engaged but Bendix Kaar, hovering conveniently at my elbow, stepped into the breach. We exited to Fifty-sixth Street.

Justine tucked herself into the first limousine at the curb while Duncan, addled with champagne, bade us adieu. Making his final turn, he tripped. We all watched his head hit the sidewalk with a fruity thud.

"Duncan!" I bent over him as Godo & co. fretted in Japanese.

Under normal circumstances, Duncan would have demanded an ambulance and the city's finest neurosurgeon. However, not wishing to appear fatuous to his beloved, he raised himself to a sitting position. "It's nothing," he said, rubbing a welt over his eyebrow.

I helped him up. "Bag the dancing. Go to bed."

"They go to hospital?" Godo asked as the limo pulled away.

"They go dancing." What the hell, it was Duncan's skull, not mine.

Bendix followed me into the second limousine as Godo directed him to a sushi palace on Madison Avenue. "Your accompanist is bewitched," he said, amused at the violin I had placed between us.

I scowled. "Is the feeling mutual?"

"Hard to say what makes Justine tick."

"Do you know her well?"

"We met at Fausto's a few months ago."

Liar. You met on a boat thirty years ago. I watched a hooker sashay down Fifth Avenue. Why did she get truthful answers so much more often than I did? "You and Fausto go way back, though."

"We went to the Royal College of Music together."

Wow, a straight answer. "What did you study?"

"I wrote operas."

"I'd love to take a look."

His voice hardened. "That's not possible. I've burned them."

Didn't matter. Bendix had just revealed the story of his life. Nothing he ever did, no mountain of money, prestige, or power, would ever compensate for the death of those operas. This was a dangerous man. I took his hand. "Pity."

"I have no regrets." Lie number two. "How do you know Fausto?"

"He introduced himself at Ford's Theatre a few nights ago."

Bendix didn't ask how I had gotten my ticket. "He's a fascinating man. Clever as the devil."

"Why'd he stop performing? He must have been pretty good."

"He was more than pretty good. His mother's death devastated him. He just stopped when he was twenty-one."

About the year of my birth. Maybe I was his musical reincarnation. "Fausto was that attached to his mother?"

"Everyone was."

We pulled in front of an Upper East Side restaurant. Our party chewed fish as Godo raved about my concert at the White House and passed around toothy thrill-of-a-lifetime photographs of himself shaking hands with President Marvel. He was ecstatic that Kakadu Records now had a friend in the White House.

Bendix wrote a number on the back of a business card. "The secretary of commerce would be a better friend," he said.

Godo nearly swallowed his gold tooth. "May I ask what is your business, Mr. Kaar?"

"I'm a political consultant."

Godo gasped. "You were at White House! Dancing with Vice President Perle!"

A millisecond pause. "Mrs. Perle is still a senator," Bendix corrected, a hair tight and high.

"Very handsome couple," Godo beamed.

Bendix refilled everyone's glass and ordered another bottle as sly old Godo began plying him with questions about Washington, well aware that had I not been at the table, this conversation would have cost him thirty bucks a minute. In exchange, Godo handed Bendix the priceless opportunity to impress me with the story of his life: lower-middle-class childhood, service in Vietnam, socially responsible lumber business in Third World, gravitation toward Washington . . . give me a break. The only missing item here was the envelope containing Bendix's lecture fee. Not a word about classical music: the orator would not want us associating him with dead, white European males. Or with catastrophic personal failure. Godo listened raptly although he was one of those corporate villains Bendix had spent the last half hour skewering. Maybe Godo knew that beneath all this bluster, Bendix was just another millionaire trying to pass himself off as an altruist. "You good friend with Mrs. Senator," Godo pronounced, awed by Bendix's crowning achievement.

As flattery oozed like acid from a battery, I passed the time imagining which of them would be worse in bed. Finally, when all four of Godo's yes-men looked ready to pass out, I stood up. "Thanks, Godo."

He sprang to his feet. "You go to Berlin?"

"I go to sleep."

Bendix shook hands all around and accompanied me to the limo. "Thanks," he said. "I couldn't have kept that up much longer."

True: no one outdrank Godo. I lobbed Bendix a few more softballs about his apostolic life. Soon I had him where I wanted him, tipsy, torn between lust and propriety, dependent on my signals, which might yet go either way. Outside my hotel I took his hand. "How long have you been giving Aurilla's daughter violin lessons?"

I felt him recoil. Maybe he had been expecting an invitation upstairs. "Four years."

"I thought you were a composer."

"I also studied violin. She's very talented, isn't she?"

"Yes. What does her mother expect me to do?"

Bendix's pulse elevated: lie en route. "Maybe you could get Gretchen into Juilliard. You have connections, don't you?"

Gretchen didn't need me to get into Juilliard. "Why'd you stop teaching her?"

"She became too difficult."

I needed to ask Bendix about that little diving party on the Thames, ask why he had left Aurilla to attend my concert tonight; ask if he kept in touch with Louis Bailey as closely as he did with Fausto . . . but to procure any answers, all that asking would have to occur in bed: information, as yet, not worth the price. "Thanks for coming to the concert," I said, dropping his hand. "Let's play Scrabble sometime."

Bendix pecked both my cheeks. "The Brahms was beautiful. Brought back many memories."

Anguished ones, I hoped. Smiled and went inside.

My accompanist was not in his room and I belatedly realized that Bendix Kaar had not posed one personal question the entire evening. Respect or arrogance? The phone eventually interrupted that weak riddle.

"My wrist is broken," Duncan announced. "Swelled like a

grapefruit as soon as we left you. Justine took me to the hospital. My arm's in a sling for three weeks."

"That's awful!" Actually, too good to be true: now I didn't have to tell Duncan about our canceled concerts. "How's your head?"

"Hurts." He moaned a bit, leading up to the critical question. "Are you going to get another pianist?"

"I don't think so. We'll just bag the tour. What's a hundred thousand bucks between friends."

"My God! You'd do that for me?"

"I might. Curtis might not. I'll give him a call." Dialed my house in Berlin. "Curtis."

Short silence as my manager computed New York time, presumed the worst. "How'd it go?"

"Better than last week."

"How about Duncan."

"OD'd on beta-blockers then broke his wrist." Now for the bad news. "He plans to recuperate in Washington. Assisted by a new sweetheart."

"A woman?"

"Occasionally. I need this like a hole in the head."

"I'll see what I can do." Curtis would arrange master classes in Baltimore, Charleston, put Duncan on a few arts panels . . . remove him from the line of fire. "When are you coming back? Dresden's threatening to replace you with Bing Bing Chin."

Another eight-year-old who played like a CD. Audiences loved it when the kid was only a few inches longer than her violin. "When?"

"October twentieth."

"I'll be there."

We talked shop for a while. My manager was accepting engagements for five years hence, as if I'd still be alive to play them. He wanted to send me the score of a new concerto I'd be performing in Vienna that summer. The composer, who had made a fortune writing musicals, wanted to prove that he still had artistic integrity. "What's the piece like?" I asked.

"A long commercial. But good exposure. Great fee." Curtis wisely changed the subject. "Someone named Aurilla Perle called this morning. Is that the senator?"

Damn! "Siccing her kid on me again?"

"What kid? She wanted to arrange a private concert this Friday night. A program like the one you did at the White House. No question about your fee."

Ergo no question about Curtis having accepted it. "What's the occasion?" I sighed.

"None of your business. She didn't request 'Happy Birthday.' "

"What am I going to do about a pianist?"

"How about Fausto Kiss? He was good once."

"For Christ's sake! Get serious!"

"Should I start asking around?"

"Haven't you done enough damage for one evening?" I slammed down the phone, unwilling to become Aurilla's circus dog, even if she had paid the going rate. Her little party would be a rehash of Bobby Marvel's in the East Room: same guests but better alcohol, same postprandial farce as a passel of Little Caesars feigned appreciation of sounds beyond their comprehension. Why me? Aurilla could have hired a string quartet for the same price.

Do your job, Smith. I made one final call. "Fausto. Am I catching you at a bad time?"

"Never." I heard a match flare, a languid inhalation. "What are you doing up at this hour?"

"I have trouble getting to sleep after a concert."

"Good old Carnegie Hall! I played there once. It was the only time in my life I nailed all the leaps in the Schumann

Fantasy." Fausto pulled on his cigarette. "How was Duncan?"

"Fine. But he broke his wrist afterward."

"How? Servicing Justine with a dildo?"

"Tripped. He's out of action for a while, which is why I'm calling. I have a concert Friday night. Private. Short program. Interested in playing with me?"

Words were replaced by an intense dialogue between Fausto's cigarette and his lungs. "I don't think I'm up to it, darling," he replied after an aeon. "Thanks anyway. I'm profoundly flattered. But I don't think so."

He spoke with regret: a soft no, malleable as clay. "Aurilla Perle's buying," I persisted. "Dinner included. Come on, Fausto." Silence. "You pick the program. I can start rehearsing Wednesday. We'll go all day and night if you want. Nice change of pace from that indolent life you lead."

"But you've never heard me play."

No, but I had read his reviews. "So surprise me. I'll pay you five thousand bucks. God knows you need the money."

"What if I say no?"

"It's you or nobody." I hung up as his cigarette hissed like an angry cat.

Hooked my laptop to the airline schedules. Next flight for Belize left JFK in two hours. Layover in Miami: perfect. I dozed, listening, but Duncan never returned to his room. Down in the lobby, a maid stood polishing fake marble columns as the night clerk admired her gelatinous hips. The place reeked of chemical lemon and musty carpet. I stashed the Strad in the hotel vault. Outside, nothing moved but stray cats and clouds in a gray pink sky: in a few hours Manhattan would fry. I cut through Central Park, checking that no one followed me, then caught a cab to Flushing. The driver, in horn-rims and a fifties crew cut, looked like a pederast about to become a serial killer. "You that model?" he asked, staring at the mole above my lip.

"No." Irritating, this mole. But it was now part of my act, like the Harleys and leather pants. Until last spring, it had been a good hiding place for the poison Maxine required all her girls to keep handy in case of insurmountable difficulties. Great concept; too bad it hadn't worked in practice. After my boo-boo last spring, Maxine had supplied me with another poison, this one guaranteed to work. Trade-off was it wouldn't be painless. But I wouldn't hurt for long.

Traffic to JFK was light and passive. All-night drunks stuck to the right lane, as did beach-bound families of ten, aware that today an overheated radiator could cost them their lives. The cabbie weaved expertly between potholes, mufflers, and huge rinds of rubber on the expressway as he listened to a radio talk show. Callers were uniformly incensed that Bobby Marvel had appointed yet another New Age judge to the federal bench. "Pussy-whipped draft dodger," my driver fumed as a mattress commercial blasted over the air. "Country's goin' down the tubes." He quieted down as the next caller accused the oil companies of murdering Vice President Jordan Bailey. Someone else opined that the environmentalists had eliminated Bailey for brown-nosing commercial loggers. "Somethin' odd there," the cabbie agreed, nonchalantly cutting off a motorcycle. "You don't die of mosquito bites. Not even big mosquitoes."

The next caller trashed the medical profession for allowing one of the century's finest public servants to turn to farina. Someone else countered that the vice president had been brain dead since the inauguration. Debate raged concerning his replacement: the country was ready for a woman; a black; a homosexual; a Jew; a general. Bobby Marvel had to be very careful with this one, as he was running for reelection in November and could not afford to of-fend more than six voting blocs. Aurilla Perle seemed to be the heavy favorite. Then one listener suggested that Marvel demote himself to vice president and give the man's job to his wife Paula, who had been running the show for almost four years anyhow. I left the cab as enraged female callers flocked to the First Lady's defense.

Checked in for my flight as Cosima Wagner, my favorite alias. Plenty of seats: unless you were a hurricane, equatorial zones were not popular destinations in September. I looked ghoulishly pale compared with my fellow passengers, handsome Cubans and Germans, all strung with gold. Throughout the trip the Berliner across the aisle stared at me with that look of vague recognition I both craved and abhorred. Had I been carrying a violin, he would have pegged me. Witnesses everywhere, the down side of fame: thank God classical musicians were third-rank celebrities.

Landed early in Miami. I took a stroll around the terminal, fighting for right of way with the elderly in golf carts and pregnant teenagers in microshorts. Finally located the locker matching the key Maxine had given me long ago at the zoo. Inside was a beat-up carry-on. I went to a phone. "Out of Armani totes, dear?"

Maxine didn't laugh. "What's your time frame?"

"Two days."

"I thought you were off for a month."

"Something came up with Fausto."

"Great." Maybe she said *Shit.* "Take your medicine. Follow the map. Call when you get back."

She knew better than to wish me luck. I brought my bag to a ladies' room. Bolted myself into the handicapped cubicle, inventoried my very light load. Binoculars but no heat scopes, no computers, phones, global positioning equipment. Instead the Queen had packed a variety of drugs in disposable douche packets. Sewing kit was nothing but hypodermic needles. Zero weapons: I didn't know how to interpret that. Jabbed my ass with a megadose of immunoglobulin and amphetamines, the high-octane formula for those jobs involving infectious diseases, many square miles, no time. I wouldn't be needing food or sleep for the next two days. Nevertheless, Maxine had provided me with two thousand bucks and a manicure set designed for locks rather than fingernails. I changed into hiking gear, all Salvation Army reissue. Cosima Wagner would blend into the scenery all right.

Chapter Five

𝓕ROM MIAMI I took my seat in another nearly empty airplane. With the amphetamine high came paranoia. A chubby
brown baby peered through the crack between the seats
ahead of me: maybe a little young to be credible, but a witness nevertheless. Across the aisle, an islander wearing large
gold rings and a straw hat kept checking out my legs. Behind me, a businessman tapped his laptop. Had either of
them followed me on this flight? You never knew until it
was too late. I stared out the window at huge Michelangelo
clouds and tiny boats flecking a turquoise sea.

Maxine had left a map of Belize in my shirt pocket. An
X about forty miles inland, deep in the Maya Mountains:
Louis Bailey's campgrounds. Barnard had abandoned her
equipment at a nearby X: San Ignacio, a hick outpost on
the Macal River. The third X marked Belize City, the former capital, on the Caribbean coast. Louis's doctor friend
Yvette Tatal worked at the hospital there. On paper the trip
looked simple, but I was thinking in terms of paved roads,
potable water. While I was studying a topographical map,
the plane shuddered. Sabotage? I glanced outside. Murky
jungle had displaced the sea. The clouds had turned gray

and fretful, as if evil genies writhed therein. The plane flew between bolts of lightning, over rainbows and sidling olive rivers. Disneyland, I thought . . . until the first beads of sweat trickled down my jaw. The cabin was getting hotter. Baby began to cry as the plane nosed toward the swollen treetops. My pulse jumped: that green was too thick, too *alive*.

The ground crew rolled a staircase up to the aircraft as its internal temperature rose by the second. I said good-bye to the pilot, stepped into incinerating light and heat. After a moment's shock, my skin began to weep in rebellion. Walked quickly to the terminal, only to discover it was the same temperature as the tarmac, minus the breeze. Tried to collect myself for the customs agent as the archaeologists in line chatted with the snorkelers. Easy for them: they all had legit passports. As the queue shuffled forward, I studied the whirring fans, rehearsed my smile. Finally I stood in front of a woman with red lipstick and skin taut and black as an olive.

"How long will you be staying in Belize?" she asked Cosima Wagner.

"Two days."

Sweat poured past my ass, past my knees, as she peered at my immigration card. "You're a journalist?"

"I'm writing an article on jungle medicine."

A pause, then *thunk* went her stamp. "Enjoy your trip."

Sure. I was already down a quart of water. I went outside, where the air was more active but no less crushing. Palm trees rustled beside a fraying strip of macadam. A dilapidated yellow bus, crammed with passengers and poultry, rattled past. Two more bumps and its gearbox would be road kill. I got a cab.

"Vacation?" my driver asked in soft, undulant Creole,

tooting his horn at children on bicycles. Punta rock throbbed from the radio.

"Yes." The car reeked of warm vinyl. Already I yearned for a shower, a Tom Collins.

"You wish a guide?" He passed a business card to the backseat. "I am Pablo."

Minutest pressure on the accelerator produced thick gurgling from the vehicle's underbelly. Heat and dust streamed through the windows as we passed wooden shacks on stilts and construction crews on perpetual coffee break. Once the cab entered Belize City, a shanty town in need of paint, sewerage, and perhaps another hurricane like the one that washed it away thirty years ago, Pablo tooted the horn every few seconds, signaling friends, policemen, other cabdrivers, children, dogs, fruit vendors, and women, none of whom moved an inch out of his way. Those who could honked back.

"You may rent my car," he offered in that delicious singsong. "Very reasonable."

"Sorry, I've already got one."

He smiled, shrugged: no problem. "You are hungry? I know a fine restaurant."

I dropped thirty bucks into the front seat. "Just get me to the car rental. Fast."

Speed was relative in the tropics. Swishing around a few corners, Pablo crossed the narrow bridge at Haulover Creek. To my right, gulf water lapped at dinghies. We cruised past dull Caribes and dusky shops selling only sneakers. No ATMs, no bagels, cell phones, air-conditioning, yet the populace looked perfectly content. Soon the city petered out and we were back to shacks on stilts.

Already three o'clock. I rented a jeep, bought water, and headed west past halfhearted housing projects gouged from the brush. More vehicles stood, cannibalized, in front yards than used the highway. Every mile or so someone waited patiently for the yellow bus that would eventually appear. I passed dozens of tiny settlements whose inhabitants downshifted from slow to motionless in order to eyeball the jeep. Far ahead, the land heaved bluish mountains. I kept driving toward them. Sunlight became intermittent as the road began to rise. Just a few minutes from the Guatemalan border, I reached a steep, unpaved turnoff seamed not with ruts, but with gorges: slip into the gulch between two narrow bands of ground, kiss axle good-bye. I checked my map: fifteen miles on this moonscape, another five on foot, and no lingering sunsets at the equator. I wouldn't get to Louis's camp before dark.

First, I drank. Then I got the lug wrench from the toolbox. Killed the AC, opened the windows. As heat flooded in, my sweat glands mounted a ferocious defense. I shifted into four-wheel drive and left the last pavement I'd be seeing for a while.

The baseball-size rocks weren't a problem until the road suddenly lurched downward, putting the jeep's ass so high in the air that one good bump would pitch it over the hood. I fought to keep all four tires on the highest ridges. No help when the sun disappeared and shadows came alive, blurring width and depth. The wind shifted, red dust blew in. I looked at the speedometer and laughed: five miles an hour. I could have walked faster than this. Finally the jeep reached the bottom of the hill. The road evened out for a few revolutions of the tires before boomeranging upward again.

Beyond the hum of the engine, I heard a cacophony of insects and birds. Spooky, all that noise but nothing in sight. I disliked being the spied upon rather than the spy. Flipped on the headlights and inched skyward, chipping rocks into the wayside ferns. Did cougars pounce into cars if they were hungry enough? Maybe I should roll up the windows. *Get a grip, Smith, you're not even in the jungle yet.* I went as fast as I dared. The jeep began to creak like a cricket. With each bounce, I half expected to see the transmission in the rearview mirror. The sun was dropping faster than I was climbing and the heat never quit. As the light waned, apprehension increased, I began to smell and hear with feral acuity.

My failing intellect fixed on the odometer. All this rutting around may have added a tenth of a mile to the reading. Maxine's map had directed me to a pile of stones at 15.3 miles off the highway: overshoot that and the forest would devour me. I slowed to a crawl. Had that little mess been a pile? Did three stones equal one pile? Each time I hit a bump, my headlights ricocheted into the trees, surprising birds, bats, beetles big as my fist. Light was draining from the earth like blood from a slaughtered bull. The sky was almost black when I saw the tiny stack of stones.

Hid the car behind high ferns and dug in my bag for insect repellent and flashlight, neither of which would protect me from anything here. I was checking out the pile of stones when a tarantula scuttled over my boot. *Jesus Christ!* Humans I could handle: animals were different. *They're more scared of you than you are of them.* Bullshit! I didn't have fangs loaded with venom or jaws that could tear a rabbit in half. I didn't have wings to fly, legs good for forty miles an hour, ears bristling with radar. I didn't have quills, talons, scales, or antennae. I was just open fillet, and this was dinnertime.

Glutinous fronds stroked me as I plunged into the forest. The path was slippery, littered with rocks and small bones. Odors of blossom and rotting entrail saturated the air. The blindness was nowhere near as terrifying as the noise. Each time I heard a nearby grunt or the heavy snap of twigs in the dark, I braced for a dozen teeth in my intestines. The chirring of cicadas hit me in huge, throbbing waves, as if I were amid an army of angry maraca players shaking their gourds inches from my ears. Add hoots, caws, screeches, and heat, always the goddamn heat. Sweat dribbled down the crease of my ass, joining the sweat dribbling down from my navel in a salty, musky confluence that drove bugs wild. Whenever I stopped to drink, they swarmed my ears, fed on my wrists. Maxine's repellent had shot its wad about half an hour ago. I had slogged almost two hours when the flashlight went black.

Had I buried myself alive, the darkness could not have been more total. Raided my pack for matches, violently scratched one aflame. Ten seconds of feeble light convinced me I'd never find wood dry enough to make tinder, let alone a torch. I could either sit here and wait to be eaten or plug ahead. As the match sputtered out, I saw a footprint in the path. A second match proved I wasn't hallucinating. Memorized the impression, sucking all possible hope from it. When the match died, I crawled slowly as a worm toward the next dip in the earth.

All thought melted into a sinkhole of adrenaline. Following less a path than an absence of forest, feeling for the footprints that miraculously recurred at fifteen-inch intervals, I proceeded a fingerling at a time, patting the dirt ahead of me so that snakes and rodents, hearing the vibrations, might flee. The insects stayed, and they ate. Flying things strafed my ears. After bumping into a dead armadillo, I began to go a little mad. *If Barnard could do it, so can you.* Crawled for ages in black, shrieking hell. Then the path tricked me and vanished. Suddenly I saw millions of fireflies. Stars. *Grass?* I crept ahead, muttering as my knees sank into the sod.

A swish preceded blinding light. "Who are you?" a voice demanded.

I could only blink as the brain fast-forwarded ten million

years along the evolutionary chain. I staggered to my feet, brushing compost off my knees with hands that looked like raspberry trifle. "Cosima Wagner. I'm looking for Polly Mason."

The light didn't move. "You came here on foot?"

No, in a Checker cab. When I tried to smile, my lower lip split. "On my knees, actually. Flashlight died."

"You're alone?"

"Yes." I looked at my watch and nearly choked: one in the morning. This field trip was already half a day behind schedule. "Is Polly asleep?"

"Polly's been gone for weeks."

I tried to look shocked. "Where to?"

"I don't know."

I upended my water bottle over my head. By the time the water reached my shoulders, it was hot enough to percolate coffee. I waited as it dribbled down my back, my front, met at the lower fork, wept toward my ankles, fed the grass: still no invitation to stay. "Could I trouble you for some water?" I asked finally.

"What's that in your belt?" he asked. I threw away the lug wrench. "I do not believe you have come looking for Polly."

"I'm not out on a bird watch."

"If you are after Louis, go back where you came from."

The gnats had relocated my ears. "Listen," I said, swatting futilely at nothing but humidity, "I don't give a shit about Louis, whoever that is. I want to know what happened to Polly."

The beam finally left my eyes. "Come with me," he said. We crossed the lawn to a thatched hut. As my host lit a kerosene lamp, I saw a finely hewn brown face that could have graced a Mayan frieze. His feet matched the prints on the trail. Black hair, bright black eyes. The body of Tarzan, maybe twenty-five years too young to interest me. "My name is Ek. I'm the only one left here now."

"Why are you sticking around?"

He looked surprised. "Because Louis will return." Ek offered me a glass of water from a covered pitcher. "Don't worry, we have our own well."

I sank into the only available chair in a hut about the size of my shoe closet in Berlin. Wooden bowls cluttered a rough table. Mortars, pestles, and glass beakers crammed the shelf above a stone sink. An array of machetes hung on the back of the door. If Ek slept here, it was in the hammock suspended from two beams. Why would Bailey abandon a state-of-the-art facility in Virginia for this shack? "Could you tell me what happened to Polly?" I sighed. "From the beginning?"

Ek studied my filthy face. "You do not want to sleep?"

"I took drugs to stay awake."

Rummaging beneath the sink, he found a bottle. "I'll stay awake with you then." He quaffed most of its contents with a shudder. "You are a brave lady."

Brave? I was just a two-bit narcissist who wished to die recognizable. Ek settled into the hammock. "I have known Louis my whole life. Every summer he worked with my father, who was a country doctor. I helped them carry plants back from the mountains. Louis studied them under a microscope while my father made medicines for the villagers. They did this every year until my father died last spring."

"Your village is here?"

"No. This is a secret camp. You are the first person to have found it."

I wouldn't be getting a door prize. A breeze wafted through the cabin, cooling nothing. Every second I waited, my body lost another few drops of precious fluid. "Polly came to study plants," I said. "That's all I know."

Ek brushed a beetle off his shoulder, drank some more. Finally he spoke. "At the beginning of July, Louis came to my village in the middle of the night. He had come to Belize through Guatemala so no one would know he was here. 'Come with me,' he said. 'I need you.' We went into the mountains and built this hut. Day and night we gathered plants. Louis had brought some equipment and a computer that ran on solar batteries. No one bothered us for a long time."

I went to the window and inhaled unseen, voluptuous blooms. "Then what."

"One morning we heard chopping. We went toward the noise and saw a woman." Ek paused. "She was tall with yellow hair."

I wondered how long they had stared at her in awe and delight. Barnard had probably kept chopping, then spritzed water over her neck so that her blouse would cling to her breasts like cellophane over tomatoes. Maybe she'd sit on a log, lasciviously peel a banana. Better yet, she'd break her machete. Swear a little.

"She broke her machete," Ek continued. "After Louis gave her his, she brought us to her place. She lived in a cave near a waterfall. Inside were her herbs and books. She even had pictures on the wall."

I wouldn't have been surprised to hear that Barnard had AC and track lighting. "Bet she and Louis hit it right off."

"They were a good team," Ek agreed. "He was a different man around her."

All men were. "Did she move here or did he move there?"

"A little of each. But it was not what you think. They spent most of the night working."

The ultimate erotic high, on a par with me playing the Brahms concerto with Furtwängler. No melding of flesh could compete with that. "Working on what?"

"Chemical analysis. We spent days searching for special plants. Once Polly brought back a branch with little black leaves. Louis was very excited. But the rain washed away the trails and she couldn't find it again. Louis was angry. He said she remembered perfectly well where she had found it but was keeping it a secret."

"What do you think?"

His calm eyes held mine. "I think Polly was a very clever lady."

And Ek was a very clever assistant. "Researchers are competitive. Not trusting."

Ek shrugged. "One day Louis told me he wanted to go to San Ignacio. He had a favorite café there named Koko's. We went by canoe. Polly wanted to meet Dr. Tatal so I took her to the clinic while Louis went to Koko's."

"Who's Dr. Tatal?"

A nearby bullfrog belched eight times before my host regained his tongue. "Louis's friend. She comes to her clinic in San Ignacio once a week."

"Why'd Polly want to meet her?"

Ek looked surprised. "Because she's famous."

Brrrripa. Brrrripa. "Was the visit a success?"

"No. Dr. Tatal wasn't in." Several drops of sweat fell to Ek's shorts, leaving dark spots near his fly. "Polly and I went back to Koko's. Louis was not there."

"Where'd he go?"

"I have not seen him since that day."

Brrrippa. "What did Polly do?"

Ek looked at me with annoyance, as if I were insulting his intelligence. He was probably right. "She went looking for him. I never saw her from that day, either." His eyes followed a spider, or a fuzzy golf ball with six legs, across the table. "Polly was not really a botanist, was she."

My pulse clunked, forehead wept: misjudging the assistant was such an elementary, costly error. "She went to medical school."

A tiny iguana zipped over the windowsill as Ek took another swig from his bottle. "One night after I had gone to bed, Polly stood by me for a moment, like my mother used to. I pretended to be asleep. She went to the clearing and began walking in circles with something against her ear. I heard her say 'Max' a few times."

"Maybe she was calling her boyfriend."

"We have no phone here."

I sniffed. Something burning: my nerves. "Did you tell Louis?"

"No."

"Why not?"

"I did not wish to trouble him. He was already agitated that his experiments were going so slowly. I kept a close watch on Polly after that. She never called the man Max again." Ek smiled to himself. "I never found a telephone."

My knees creaked as I stood. "Could you take me to her cave? I'm a little pressed for time."

Ek filled our canteens as I sprayed fresh repellent over my insect bites. He lit a torch and, without a word of instruction, handed me a machete. We returned to the shrieking, shuddering forest and began whacking the green stuff. Heavy going, complicated by the shadows streaking from Ek's flare. Hemorrhaging water, I kept as close as possible to the light as we followed a trail of notched trees. Once I heard a snap, a deep grunt, inches away: big, whatever it was. My nervous system ratcheted into hyperspace.

We crossed two mountains. Finally, stumbling down a ravine, I heard water. The forest fell away and Ek stood at the edge of a torrent. His flare reflected white, rabid tiers of froth. He ignored my dismay, or maybe he just didn't understand it. "The bottom is slippery," was all he said. "Can you swim?"

Thunder downstream: even in a barrel, chances of surviving that mother were zero. "No problem."

We stripped to our underwear. "I can take the machete or the flare," Ek said. "Not both."

"Take the machete." I balled our clothing into my backpack.

"You're bringing that?"

"I can't live without my insect repellent."

He finally smiled. Maybe my lies were beginning to humor him. "Aim there." He pointed upstream and slid into the liquid death.

Warm at the fringe but it quickly went cold and malevolent as the bottom dropped away. My backpack was heavy as a Siamese twin. Swam like a banshee but I was drifting toward that distant thunder. Felt bottom for three accelerating seconds then *pow!* over the edge of the first falls into choking, pummeling darkness. I let the whirlpool spin me above and below the surface; third time up, I kicked with all my strength. Broke free of the maelstrom but the current was dragging me downstream again. Something pulled my thigh as I was swept over a second falls: *Wake up, Smith.* Quieter in this pool but that was because the bottom would drop out of it any second now. I thought of Maxine and, strangely, of Fausto: I had wanted to play a concert with him. Steeled for a bone-crushing end then my head hit a log. Comets behind my eyes as I embraced it. The torrent sucked lasciviously at my legs. As the snagged trunk shifted toward the thunder, my optic nerve picked up a thin line of red at the horizon. I'd be going over the falls at dawn, the hour of love: how that would amuse the mischievous gods. One free fall in the mist, maybe in a rainbow, and I'd be out of this wretched jungle forever. I almost surrendered.

Then my brain flashed to a cheerful, tinkling fountain. I floated back to a moon-drenched night, again transfixed by—*God*, what was it—something lithe and wonderful . . . music. Ah. Yes. A woman's low laugh. I had envied her. The log lurched another foot downstream, losing height as well as position. As water rose to my neck, the laugh grew more radiant. I began clawing toward shore, toward *one more time*. Some primordial beast made the final yank and I rolled onto rock.

Lay staring like a dead fish at the slash of red at the horizon. A while later, Ek found me rubbing ointment into the gash in my thigh. "That pack was heavier than I thought," I said, tossing over his clothes.

He took a long time tying his sneakers. "Is there something special in it?"

"I told you. Insect repellent."

"Are you a soldier?"

Buttoned my filthy shirt. "No. I'm just athletic."

"Like Polly?"

"Yes." To prove the point, I stood up. My thigh nearly split in two. "Tell me something, Ek. Did anyone ever see the three of you together?"

"Just the fat man. Fausto."

I had to sit down again. "Fausto was here?"

"You know him?"

"Not well." But well enough to know that he wouldn't endure this green hell unless his life were at stake. "I thought you said no one visited the camp."

"We had lunch in Belize City. To celebrate Louis's birthday."

Louis came out of hiding, Fausto flew two thousand miles, to blow out a few candles? "How sweet," was all I could say.

"Everyone drank a lot of beer. Fausto asked Polly to run

away with him. He said they wouldn't have to spend much time together and she would be rich. I think he was not joking, though he pretended to be. Louis swore that Fausto would live to be one hundred."

What drivel. "When was this?"

"The middle of August."

Think, Smith. Something else had happened around then: a bundle of loose ends caught fire but my brain couldn't penetrate the smoke. "Did Louis see Fausto after that?"

"No."

"Did Polly?"

"I don't know." Ek stood. "We should continue before the sun gets too high."

I followed him up the third mountain. Conversation impossible: not enough oxygen to make myself heard over the warbles, caws, and trills. Any creature lucky enough to have outlasted the night was trumpeting its survival. The noise was kaleidoscopic, literally dizzying . . . how useless my years in cities had made me. With daylight came more heat. My clothes steamed. Ek followed a thin path, frequently slipping on the steep grade. Near the peak, he stopped. "Here we are."

In the rock I saw a hole the diameter of a kettledrum. Barnard had the balls to crawl through *that?* "To keep the snakes out," Ek said, removing a screen from the aperture. He found a flashlight like mine, only in working order, at the threshold of the cave. "Put the screen back after you."

We wriggled into a damp tunnel. The floor ended at a ledge overlooking a cavern about twenty feet high and wide. Three thousand years ago, Joe Mayan's castle. Now it smelled like an apothecary. I saw why as Ek's flashlight played over piles of leaves, roots, dozens of jars . . . rectangular glass. "What's that?"

"Louis's spectrograph. It worked better here."

Of course: the temperature and humidity of a cave were constant compared with that of the open jungle. Barnard had probably hooked up the solar panels for the batteries in a clearing nearby. Ek and I slid down a rope to the cavern floor. I was shown Barnard's bed, her books and clothing; even here, she'd look soignée. Silk panties hung on a string, still trying to dry. "She was here gathering plants a month before we met," Ek said.

I saw no weapons, no communications gear: either Barnard had taken everything with her or Ek was the most accomplished liar in Belize. Next to the spectrograph lay drawings of leaves, bark, twigs, berries, all with their chemical and pharmaceutical properties. Nothing here smelled like grilled pineapple. I found cures for constipation, impotence, insomnia, parasites; douches to induce birth and prevent conception; unguents, powders, infusions . . . this was saintly, painstaking work. If only Barnard had been a saint! "They didn't put any of this into a computer?" I asked.

"It was always breaking down." Ek lifted the spectrograph. "Would you like to see Polly's pictures?"

I stared at the snapshot of Senator Perle in that whopping yellow suit. She stood at a microphone, catechizing with the humorless vehemence that American voters always mistook for leadership. Next picture she was kissing Jojo Bailey's flushed cheek. That poor sod looked either drunk or heavily under the weather, but speeches had never been Jojo's rush; he preferred parades and talk shows. I leafed through a few more photos of puffy dignitaries, then Jojo getting into a cab, arm around a woman's rump. The last picture was of Paula Marvel dancing with schoolgirls in dark pinafores. Her dress, white with a dozen orange bows up the front, would have looked more professional on a clown.

"What's this all about?"

Ek tapped his sputtering flashlight. "The environmental conference."

"It was in Belize?"

"The week after Louis's birthday. Polly wanted to see the famous people up close, especially after the stories Fausto had been telling us about them." Ek pointed to Aurilla's hideous mouth. "He said that this lady was in bed with her plastic surgeon when her husband died." He laid a brown finger on Paula Marvel's billboard-size bows. "He said this lady sprained her wrist punching the president." Paula's bandage attested to that. No need to ask why she had punched Bobby. Ek found the picture of the woman bending into a backseat with Jojo Bailey. "Fausto said he had a video of these people making love on an airplane."

I gushed sweat. "Fausto is full of stories. All bullshit."

"Louis believed him," Ek said defensively. "And he's the man's brother."

I dropped the pictures into my pocket. "Did Louis go to the conference?"

"No. He was too busy."

"Did Fausto?"

"He said he had enough of these people in Washington."

Did a glutton ever have enough spaghetti? I slithered toward the light and heat at the entrance of the cave. Mosquitoes already swarmed the screen. Several sucked my blood as I applied more insect repellent to flesh already smothered beneath a slick of grease and guano. The gash on my thigh was oozing badly at the edges, so I got the sewing kit from my knapsack. Ek emerged from the cave just as I was knotting it all up.

"What are you doing?" He watched in horror as I doused the mess with disinfectant. "That is not the correct medicine! It will hurt!"

"It hurts already." I choked the area in bandages. We were

so far behind schedule that I'd need a time capsule to make my plane. "What's the best way to my car? Without another swim, if possible."

"Over those mountains."

Next time Maxine sent me here, she'd better pack a helicopter. As the sun continued its climb, I wished I had swallowed more of that waterfall. Humidity weighted me like a lead jacket. The birds called it quits and soon even the cicadas dropped to a monotonous shiver. We passed through bogs so thick that I half expected to see tyrannosaurs foraging on the other side. But Ek's machete kept whacking at the green and I kept following his rear end. We stopped only once, to bury our faces in a stream high in the mountains. "Tired?" he asked.

Dizzy: Maxine's uppers were beginning to clash with my sputtering endorphins. My thigh was screaming and I was hungry. In the last twenty-four hours I had probably burned fifty thousand more calories than originally budgeted. "I'm all right."

Ek refilled our canteens. "Why is it so important for you to find Polly?"

Several lies sprang to the tip of my tongue, squirmed, died. "She was like a sister," I said, realizing too late that I had used the past tense. *Stay sharp, Smith.*

Ek had caught the mistake. "Louis would never have hurt her."

I watched an iridescent blue butterfly skitter above the stream. Winged delight, if you were a human; winged death, if you were a leaf. Perspective depended on your rung in the food chain. "Why did he run away?"

"He was afraid that people were looking for him. Once a man tried to follow us back to camp after we went to San Ignacio. But we lost him." After fishing a stone from the stream, Ek sharpened his machete with short, angry strokes. "When he returns, Louis will explain what this is all about."

After two grueling hours, we reached road. Clouds had shrouded the sun but the air remained miasmal. The jeep waited undisturbed in the ferns. "Thanks," I told Ek, tucking five hundred bucks into his pocket. "Go buy yourself lunch."

"Maybe I should come with you."

"Better not." As I pressed the clutch, my bad thigh shrieked. Rainballs pelted the roof. "Am I going to get out of here?"

He touched my forearm. "I think you'd get out of anything, Cosima."

Within minutes the rain turned ruts into lakes. I began to hallucinate that I was no longer on a road but on a huge, writhing eel. Finally I chose a ditch, there to stare at my watch as the storm cleared the mountain, leaving steam and rainbows in its wake. At noon I rolled into San Ignacio, a colorful wreck of a town lacking only posses and Mae West. Dogs, schoolgirls in pinafores, and fossil-like Mayans thronged the main drag. The worst slobs, Caucasian tourists, congregated on the porch of Koko's, a rickety café wedged between souvenir stands. Barnard had ditched her surveillance gear *here?* I drove the filthy jeep past. No point shopping in this town unless you wanted crucifixes or rubber sandals. Thirty seconds later, San Ignacio ended.

I was beginning to feel light as a firefly. My fingers shook as I rummaged through Maxine's diminishing supply of uppers and antibiotics. The needle felt like a grenade in my thigh. Swallowed another quart of water then located Yvette Tatal's clinic, little more than an inferno on a side street. Patients who made it up the rickety stairwell were detained in a room redolent of skin and garlic. Only an occasional blink proved that the bodies occupying the chairs were not stuffed. On the wall hung a photograph of Paula Marvel and an attractive woman on the steps of a run-down clinic. "Is that Dr. Tatal?" I asked a nurse.

She nodded. "Are you waiting for Dr. Llosa?"

"No, Dr. Tatal."

"You'll see Dr. Llosa or no one. You! Come here!" She yanked a boy behind the scuffed mahogany door.

Silence save the jangling of a woman's bracelets as she fanned her cheeks. "Dr. Tatal goes to Xunantunich on Mondays," she said. "To dig. Everyone knows that."

"Xunantunich," I repeated. Sounded like a sneeze but I knew they were the Mayan ruins up the road. "Thank you." Back to the jeep. As the highway shriveled to a ribbon of dirt, it veered ever closer to the river running alongside. The water was green, merry, seductive, only a Frisbee toss wide. I almost drove by the entrance to the ruins. The tip-off was a soda cooler next to two mestizos selling stone carvings. I jammed on the brakes. "Can you take me across?"

They pointed down a slope. At its end floated a raft just a little longer than a horse. A little man beckoned me aboard. As he cranked a greasy shaft, we began to pull toward the opposite shore. Whenever he stopped cranking to wipe his brow or admire a fish, we stopped moving. Nine minutes later, landfall: I put the jeep in gear and tore up a rocky trail ending in parking lot. Had to hike the last, steepest, quarter mile to the ruins. Leg loved that. The sun leeched all water from my vital organs. Light burned down from the sky, up from the limestone. All my senses fried: *Keep together, Smith.*

Passed souvenir shop, tool shed, outhouses. No one was charging admission and only bees ate at the picnic tables. One last ridge and I stood in a plaza dominated by three gigantic mounds. Where their grassy skins had been scraped away, ancient stones lay exposed to the sun: autopsy in progress. A couple stood atop the largest of the monuments. Fifteen stories below, I could hear them conversing in Dutch. The man was pointing to a trough halfway down the face, explaining that if his companion were still a virgin, that's where Mayan priests would be tossing her. I circled the mound, searching for Tatal on the scaffolding. Not there so I climbed the tiny stairs winding up toward the top. No guardrails, no warning signs: one slip and I'd be eating rocks far below. *Nice and easy, Smith.* When I finally reached top, the Dutch were doggy screwing on a ceremonial slab. They wouldn't have noticed a spaceship touch down behind them.

Through my binoculars I saw Tatal tapping stones on the third mound. I watched her brush away the dust she had made, peer at the limestone, tap some more. In an afternoon, she might clear off a few square inches. Epidemiologist, archaeologist . . . she'd have trouble finding an interesting man: no wonder Louis Bailey topped her heap. I wanted to ask where they met, get a reading on the state of their union. If anyone, she would know where he was now. Should I take the direct or oblique approach? Direct always worked better with women of intelligence, but cancel all bets if she were in love with the guy. As I plotted, the Dutch giggled and left. Finally Tatal headed toward the outhouse.

Nearly swooned when I saw the tiny stairs I'd have to descend. Below, a handful of tourists were nothing but pinheads drinking beer in the shade. I hesitated, dreading my first step, wishing I were a rat, a roach, anything but a hobbled biped. Every few seconds the wind took another heavy puff at me. My thigh oozed molten glass. *Go! Now!* Forever later, earth. Tatal had still not returned to her little dig. I loitered by her toolbox but began feeling cold inside so I took her spade with me to the outhouse, a two-holer with, ludicrously, powder room. Vinyl roofing tinged my skin green.

Abominable stench. I couldn't circumvent a cloud of happy mosquitoes. Tatal's feet, in awkward rag-doll position, rested behind a flimsy door.

"Tatal?" I whispered. No answer. "Tatal?" Inched open the door. The poor doctor, pants at her ankles, stared at nothing. Her pubic hair moved and I saw, coiled in her lap, a fer-de-lance.

My life expectancy shrank to five seconds. Terror trickled up my back as the viper raised its triangular head. *No sudden movement.* With infinite care, atom by atom, I faded from the cubicle. Sweat wept down my jaw more quickly than my legs moved my body. I had reversed only halfway out of range when I heard a laugh, a thud: the Dutch.

As she burst into the powder room, the fer-de-lance struck with horrifying speed. My optic nerve traced the motion of the viper's head, my brain ran a billion calculations, mounted an instantaneous defense: instead of hitting my wrist, the snake slammed into Tatal's spade. Tiny *ping* as fang met iron. I hacked off its head while Gouda Ball sailed into the next cubicle. As she pissed over rocks, I saw the mesh box on the ledge above my head. No birdcage, that.

The corpse and I were finally alone again. Tatal had nothing in her pockets, poor thing. I arranged her with spade and two pieces of fer-de-lance in a tableau of mutual assured destruction, then strolled behind the outhouse. A head moved too quickly in the bushes so I went after it. Thorns, rocks, fronds, tore at my pants and face. Took a while to realize I was chasing someone on a mountain bike. Its wheels were still spinning when I caught up with it at the riverbank. The water had widened to a good hundred yards here; on the opposite shore, women stood knee deep in laundry. I stared dully at the green current. Finally, far downstream, a head surfaced, a figure waded toward the woods. White male. He turned around. For a horrifying moment, our eyes met.

Sank to the mud. Didn't dare stick a hand in the water: typhoid and diphtheria there. My hands looked as if they had been kneading barbed wire. The gnats found my eyes. I began to cry because the jungle never quit for one fucking second. It was a seething, insatiable maw that came at you with snakes, bugs, water, plants, heat, microbes, light, dark, belching death with such polymorphic virtuosity that you finally let it eat you. *Hang on, Smith. You're almost out of here.* Oh? Where was Aladdin and his flying carpet? I sat watching centipedes twiddle the mud. I spun the wheel of the mountain bike, counting clicks as it decelerated to a standstill. But I didn't get up.

Two boys, tired of watching their mother scrape rags against a washboard, swam over. I impassively watched their brown, bright faces bob above the water. "Is that your bicycle?" one of them asked.

Humanity: riddles: something sparked inside my head. "Get me to the ferry and you can have it." The boys returned with a farmer's barge and rowed me to the ferry landing. I dragged myself back to the ruins. Still no action at the outhouse: poor Tatal and the fer-de-lance would rot before anyone discovered them. That was the up side of the Third World.

Another day was quickly fading so I drove straight to Koko's. The bar was jammed with riffraff cheering a three-month-old NBA playoff. Elsewhere, chubby mestizos stuffed their cheeks with tortillas. Two waitresses brought margaritas to a table of backpackers. Men in jungle fatigues laughed it up beneath a flag of Belize. I sat in the corner with a fan. My elbows stuck to the grimy vinyl tablecloth, my pants to the chair. By the time I ordered a bowl of chilemole, all twenty tables were full.

Placed end to end, the bric-a-brac on the walls, the dingleballs hanging from the chipped ceiling, the booze and stemware in the bar, and the keepsakes for sale by the cash register would circle the globe. Instead of paying for their meals, generations of customers had perhaps left a small memento—value not to exceed fifty cents—behind. Overhead fans made every ounce of trash flutter spasmodically. Bravo, Barnard: there was no better place to hide a camera, no less likely place to stumble upon one, than here.

The waitress brought watery black soup spiffed up with the rib cage of a fowl. I studied the room as I ate. Two corners wouldn't work for surveillance: plastic flowers blocking view. Television blared in the third corner: I was probably sitting beneath Barnard's equipment. An excellent vantage point . . . if the gear functioned, of course. Heat and humidity had fried everything else she had brought to Belize. I checked the wall behind me: posters, menus, crowded flypaper, dolls. On the top shelf, plates and Christmas ornaments. When I saw a plastic angel playing the violin, I stopped looking.

I was chomping on a rubber egg when a white male in fatigues came to the table. Crew cut, hoop earring, muscles, beer: if he couldn't join a fight, he'd instigate one. "Name's James. My mate and I have a little bet," he said, taking the chair opposite me. "I hope you don't mind settling it for us."

East London accent: were the Brits still here? They had run a jungle training camp up the road when Belize was still British Honduras. "No problem."

"My friend Simon thinks you're a violinist named Leslie Frost."

I laughed. "Never heard of her."

"I'm very glad to hear that. You just won me a hundred dollars." James waved to the waitress. "What's your drink?"

"Château Margaux, 1990. I didn't notice it on the wine list."

He ordered beer. "Visiting? I can show you places tourists never see."

"I've seen enough, thanks."

"Here alone?"

"Why don't you go back to your mates like a good boy."

Maybe I was too grimy to fuss over: he didn't press the point. "This country isn't as safe as you think, luv. If you get into a jam, call me." He dropped a card on the table.

I glanced at his job description, forced a yawn. "Soldier of fortune?"

"That's right. Used to be a lot more action down here. We're all thinking of returning to Africa now."

"Even your friend Simon?"

"Yo. He's bored silly." James looked toward a tall, lethally athletic man across the room. "Owe me a hundred bucks, you ugly bastard," he called.

The fellow barely smiled, but he had had an exhausting afternoon with a fer-de-lance and a high-speed retreat through the jungle. Hadn't even bothered to change into a dry shirt before joining his buddies. Twenty feet away, I could read that twisted, burning lust to kill in his eyes: why the hell did these people always listen to classical music? "Tell him my name's Cosima."

Who walked into Koko's but the fornicating Dutch. I watched them hit the bar, call for margaritas: either they had no inkling I was here or they were pros and I was dead. "Friends?" James interrupted.

"No." I shook his hand. "Happy hunting."

The ugly one's eyes followed me as I headed for the door. How shocking that Simon had recognized me, covered with mud, thousands of miles from a concert stage. But a soldier of fortune would have a gimlet eye and few idols. Would he follow me out? Would James? How about the Dutch? *Easy, Smith. Just leave.* Without a gun, without even a knife, I had little choice.

Already dark outside. I was teeming sweat again: maybe the gash in my thigh was going septic. Ek stood in a corner of the porch. I continued down a steep alley to the Macal River. Huge moon, distant thunder: this was a night to wade into the water and just float away. I took Ek a bit downstream before wheeling on him. "What the hell are you doing here?"

He held out a tiny jar. "I brought ointment for your leg."

"Oh Christ! My leg is fine!"

A branch snapped behind us. Ek and I slid into the water. It was warm, gentle . . . rife with vermin. Couldn't worry about that now. I took a deep breath and gave myself to the current. The instant I came up for air, I saw a streak. *Pish:* inches from my head, an arrow sliced into the water. Knapsack and I didn't sink quite fast enough before the second arrow grazed my left shoulder. *Damn!* That was *just* the spot I rested my violin! Drifted with the fish until my lungs nearly burst. This time I put just my nose above water. Another *pish* a few inches from my head. I cursed the bright moon. Where was Ek? The river made a sharp bend, nudging me toward shore. No snakes, please: I grabbed an overhanging vine. Rolled behind a fat, slimy tree and ripped off my backpack. Willed my fingers to work in the seething, chittering moonlight. As I filled my last hypodermic I could hear someone pounding through the brush.

Rolled over and played dead. The footsteps stopped abruptly a few feet from my head. Either my assailant didn't know how to proceed or he was loading his quiver for one final shot. Where would I get it next? In the liver? The eye?

"Don't do that," Ek cried.

I plunged steel into the nearest leg. It jerked away, snapping off my needle. Several steps, a grunt, staggering, then a body fell to the ground. Eleven seconds: Maxine had actually met spec this time.

I lit a match. Ek and I stared at the twisted face, the huge eyes. The corpse's hand clutched a long machete. Beheading: why hadn't I thought of that. "He's dead," I said. "Recognize him?"

"Yes. He was the man who tried to follow us back to camp." Ek's voice wobbled. "Why was he shooting at you?"

"Because I saw him kill Dr. Tatal this afternoon." I plucked half a needle from the still leg. "I'm sorry. You weren't meant to be involved in this. Not at all."

"He killed Dr. Tatal?" Ek wailed.

"I found her at Xunantunich with a fer-de-lance in her lap. He dropped the snake on her from an overhead cage in the toilet. Go see for yourself. She's probably still there."

Ek's eyes went white and blind as the moon. "Why'd he do that?"

"Don't know." I chuckled stupidly: Simon would have left me in two pieces. "Did this man ever see Polly with Louis?"

"Yes. At Koko's café the day he tried to follow us back to camp." Ek shuddered. "You killed him!"

"*I* killed *him?* See that machete? He was about to cut my head off. Yours would have been next." Ek didn't move. "Look, I didn't start this."

"Did Polly?"

"No, Louis did. Whatever he's working on, it's trouble."

Besides the machete and the arrows, Simon had been carrying a stiletto and a bit of smooth cord. Nothing in his pockets but a few rumpled bills and a passport. A few feet away, I found the heat scopes. "Take a look," I said, handing them to Ek. A gasp as he found some beast munching on the opposite bank. "What was Louis working on?"

Ek finally let the scopes fall to the mud. "He was trying to make a medicine."

"For what?"

"I don't know."

"Did he succeed?"

"I don't think so."

"Did Polly know?" Shrug. The boy was traumatized. "Go back to camp, Ek. Forget you saw this."

Without reply, he cut into the forest. I drooped to the riverbank. Soon the nearby trees shivered with insects. The frogs resumed their monotony. Strange: now that I had killed a predator, my fear of the jungle suddenly receded. I had passed a primeval initiation and entered the kingdom of the wild. Even the heat didn't seem as crushing anymore. Took a few minutes to realize that only one animal in Belize now threatened my life, and I had just let him walk away.

The bugs had already found Simon. I memorized his passport number, rolled the body into the current: by morning there wouldn't be much soft stuff left. As he floated away, I began to feel afraid again. Hacked my way back to San Ignacio. The town was dark, Koko's empty. A bobby pin got me in. Now that all the fans were off, the place was hot and stinky, thick with the exhaust of the evening's meals. I cut to the corner with the plastic angel on a shelf. Barnard had hidden her camera beneath its skirts, bored her lens cleverly in the wings. I stuffed it in my knapsack and ran to the street.

Drove east, toward the coast, scattering rodents and necrophages. Almost ran over a Mennonite couple and their horse-drawn cart. As the sun cracked the horizon, women in brilliant skirts and men in their grandfathers' suits appeared, looking for the bus that might unload them in Belize City. I whizzed past a development bursting with rich, industrious, monolingual immigrants from Hong Kong. Good luck in Central America, guys. Twenty bucks got me a room with running water. I hit the shower. Scrubbed my blue thigh, pried a leech from my navel. The gash from Simon's arrow could have been a streak of red ink on my shoulder. I had accumulated bites and scratches everywhere, as if I had been scourged by a horde of Lilliputians. Somehow I had managed to get a sunburn. Everything was beginning to hurt: Maxine's booster was winding down and I had no more needles.

Bedlam at the airport. A plague of divers infested the terminal. They all looked tan, fit, mindlessly American: three out of four would have difficulty naming the day of the week. Overhead fans circulated vaguely distasteful biological aromas as ecotourists tried to get triple air miles and Lebanese families checked in with fifty pieces of near dead luggage. Children shrieked, PA system blared. I saw with dismay that no major coffee chain had set up a dispensary here.

The customs agent collected my departure fee. "You have nothing to declare?"

Two bodies, but I was leaving them behind. "No."

One last trek across a searing tarmac and I thudded into my seat. Neither Ek nor the Dutch had followed me aboard. The cabin was cold as a crypt. Something tore inside my chest as the airplane lost contact with the runway. A sharp pain, like that of leaving a lover. Perhaps I was nothing but an animal at heart. I had felt so acutely alive in the sweltering, green bosom of the earth, where death was close as the next cloudburst and creatures hunted without pity or conscience because their law was absolutely clear: Eat or be eaten. Now I had to return to scheming, dirty people? Totally unprepared for that. With a shudder, I drifted into knotted, colorful dreams.

Chapter Six

I HAD BEEN ASLEEP for twenty-four hours when the phone rang. "Don't you have a rehearsal tonight with Fausto?" Maxine asked.

My head felt more distant than Pluto. I was drenched in sweat, but no longer in the forest: something wrong here. "What day is this?"

"Wednesday. You're in New York. How'd it go?"

I arranged aching bones into a sitting position and tried to convert events of the last three days into words. After a silence, all I could say was, "Not sure."

"Did you find Tatal?"

I saw a long, brown fer-de-lance. "She was dead."

"Did you get Barnard's gear?"

I smelled grime and fried banana. "Yes."

"Did you see Louis's camp?"

I felt a crushing darkness, heard waterfalls and the noise of a trillion cicadas. And I felt Ek. "Yes." This room was so cold. What happened to all the bugs? Who was this woman who had interrupted my dreams? I wanted to go back to sleep.

"Smith!" Maxine called. "You're expected in Washington tonight."

I drew back the covers, stared at the swollen gash and the itty bites covering my legs. All this stigmata didn't jibe with the ironed sheets. "I'm tired."

"Eat. Go to the gym."

More exercise? No way. "There was a casualty."

"Witnesses?"

"One." God, my head hurt. "He'll keep his mouth shut."

For the moment, Maxine let that delusion slide. "You've got a rehearsal with Fausto Kiss," she repeated. "He's playing piano. You're violin."

The very word flooded my system with strange chemicals. My fingers tingled. A little door in my brain, behind which Europe hid, cracked open. I inspected my swollen fingertips: just enough callus there to depress an E string. Beneath several fingernails lodged slivers of black earth. Mud . . . heat . . . I felt a rush of longing, a violent confusion. But the violin won. It had been there longer and I was in another jungle now, one thick with phones, lights, people: survival here required a different set of synapses. "Fausto," I repeated. More images, more confusion.

"Can you get back to me tonight?" Maxine asked.

Ah, that little cave in the zoo: one place in America where I might feel at home. "Depends on the rehearsal."

Maxine hung up.

In a trance, disoriented by the absence of shrieking birds and insects, I flew back to Washington. Its heat and humidity were pale cousins of conditions in Belize. White, not green, predominated here: all that sparkling stone grated on my eyes. Thousands of people, heavily overdressed, rushed everywhere. I made airport to hotel without breaking a sweat: machines, not Mother Nature, ruled this cosmos. In my room, messages from Justine Cortot, Fausto, Bendix,

Curtis. I didn't answer any of them because I wasn't prepared for people yet. Duncan was a cross between the Energizer Bunny and a kangaroo, so I let him in.

"Where the *hell* have you been?" he demanded. "I've been calling for days!"

"I told you I was taking some time off. How's your wrist?"

"Still broken." Duncan tossed a newspaper onto the couch. "Did you read that review?"

Of course not. "Good or bad?"

" 'Leslie Frost appeared in Carnegie Hall last night, assisted by the unflappable Duncan Zadinsky,' " he read.

"That's a decent start. Where does it go from there?"

"Nowhere! I didn't get another word! Unflappable! What does he think I am, a shingle?"

After two days in the jungle, black ink on grotty paper had zero connection to reality. Nevertheless, I read the review. It was mostly about the composer who had just died: critics had nothing more to say about Brahms or Bach, who had been demoted from demigods to wallpaper. "Could have been worse."

"Justine called the critic up and chewed his ass out."

"Excellent. You won't get called unflappable again."

Duncan passed on to his next open wound. "I understand I've been replaced by Fausto Kiss."

"For one hour. Hope you're not too upset."

"Of course I'm upset!" he screeched. "Why didn't you just say no?"

"The hostess was paying the going rate. You know Curtis."

Duncan couldn't argue with commerce. "Is Fausto any good?"

"No idea. We're rehearsing for the first time tonight." I

tried to look resigned. "He hasn't touched a piano in thirty years. I bet his fingers are about as swift as cigars."

The phone rang: concierge sending up a fresh bouquet of orchids. "Again?" Duncan cried, fishing out the card. " 'Welcome back.' Who is this? A stalker?"

"Give them to Justine."

"She likes roses." Duncan peered at my face. "What happened to your eyebrow?"

"I walked into a door. Have you been keeping yourself out of trouble?"

"I've been working like a dog! Master class at Peabody tomorrow. NEA panel all next week. People know I'm here."

True to his word, my manager was keeping Duncan off the target range. "How's your girlfriend?"

"Fine. She's arranged a private tour of the White House for us."

"I just saw it last week. So did you."

"This is the off-limits stuff! The kitchen and bedrooms!"

"Bobby Marvel's boudoir doesn't interest me. Thank your Aunt Justine just the same."

Glancing at his watch, Duncan headed out. "She's had enough of this place, you know. She's thinking about coming to Berlin."

Power was a drug, politicians were hopeless addicts. Justine was as likely to kick the habit as I was of throwing my Strad into the Potomac. "Isn't this the pinnacle of her career?"

"She hates Bobby Marvel."

"What was she high on when she told you that?"

The door slammed. My accompanist wouldn't speak to me for days. On the other hand, our verbal exchange had been a nice little reintroduction to civilized conversation. I picked up the phone. "Still on for tonight, Fausto?"

"I've been practicing my weenie off."

"I can hear your metronome. What's the program?"

"Let me surprise you. Sixty minutes, you said?"

"That's what Aurilla ordered."

"Perfect. See you at seven."

This did not sound like the Fausto of yore. I ate a huge lunch then began to practice. Fingers were stiff and the gash on my shoulder wasn't happy with a hunk of wood pressing on it, but the moment sounds began, another demon seized my brain, squeezing jungle out, artistry in. In a few hours I was half back to warp speed, ready for whatever Fausto might throw at me.

As I was dressing, Justine called. "You've been away." When I didn't explain, she continued, "You're expected at the White House tomorrow at three."

"Sorry, I've got a rehearsal. And I never screw married men in their own beds. It's unethical. By the way, I hear you're coming to Berlin. Duncan's beside himself."

"He told you that?"

"He tells me everything. Would you have any more of those pills you gave him backstage at Carnegie Hall? I might need a few for Fausto. God knows if he can get it up for Aurilla's concert."

"Fausto can fend for himself." Justine hung up.

The phone immediately rang again. "You've been away," said Bendix, inflection half amity, half accusation. Somewhere in the back of my brain a branch snapped, a carnivore growled.

"I've been visiting friends."

"I enjoyed our dinner the other night. And congratulations on your review. I'd like to drop something off for you at the hotel. Will you be in?"

"In and out. Just leave it at the desk. I'll get it eventually."

On to my next beast: I drove through clots of traffic to

Fausto's. He came to the door in bow tie and linen pants. There was an effervescence about him I had not seen. When he kissed me, I smelled talcum and stage fright. "Hi darling. I'm nervous as a bride."

"Relax, you've got the gig."

We went to his music room. Scores were piled on top of the piano, as if Fausto had been sifting through every piece in his library. He had been fortifying himself with a mound of steak tartare. My stomach curled: I had seen enough ground meat lately. Fausto watched me unpack my violin, perhaps wondering where I had gotten the scratches on my face. "I've been practicing day and night," he said. "People think I've gone mad. Would you like something to eat? Drink?"

"No thanks." This room was too damn cold. Too clean. Utterly artificial. *Get in gear, Smith.* I tuned to his A. "What have you got for me?"

"One of my favorite pieces." Fausto handed over a worn score.

Triptyche by Camille Saint-Saëns? Off to a sick start. Someone had marked bowings on every inch of the music. We played the first piece through. Fausto was with me all the way, like a perfect dance partner. Against my will, I could feel myself leaning into him. "You've only been practicing since Sunday?" I asked.

"Dear, I know this piece like the back of my hand." He wiped his brow. "And playing the piano is like sex. You never really forget how."

Next, *Vision Congolaise,* Saint-Saëns' evocation of Africa. Absolute *merde.* The third piece in the triptych was one of those perpetual motion affairs where I played fifty notes to one on the piano. "Odd," I said afterward.

"French! Saint-Saëns was a genius."

I checked my watch. "That took thirteen minutes."

Fausto rooted around his pile of music. "Next I thought we might do this." More decadence, this time by Jenö Hubay, a Wagner wannabe. Piano and violin oozed enough chromaticism to generate a second fin de siècle. Fausto relished his part as he would a Sacher torte. He was one hell of a pianist: deep inside, beneath the rubble, part of me trembled. "Well?" he asked afterward.

"It's harder than it sounds."

"Sorry, darling. Maybe you'll like this better."

Now he hit me with Wieniawski's fantasy on motifs from Gounod's *Faust*, the musical equivalent of peanut brittle. "Your signature piece?" I asked a little testily, pulling several broken hairs from my bow. "This is supposed to be after-dinner entertainment, not the Tchaikovsky Competition."

"Oh come on! We may as well have a little fun!"

I'd be inside all week practicing this dreck. Maybe that's what Fausto intended. I looked at my watch. "Eighteen more minutes."

"The grand finale," he announced, spinning a handwritten score across the piano. "You are going to love this."

I could hardly decipher the title. "Sonata by . . . Bendix Kaar? Are you out of your mind?"

"Trust me, darling. I know what I'm doing."

"Is Bendix going to be at this dinner?"

"Who cares?"

"He might, for one. You don't want to humiliate the man."

"What? We're paying him the ultimate compliment! At least try it before passing judgment."

"I can hardly read the notes."

"Just muddle through. Believe me, this time my part's harder than yours."

Inside the score was an old program of Fausto's. Pushed that aside, frowning in anticipation of the next hour. The piece opened with a siege of tone clusters. Then came an itchy scherzo. Bendix's penchant for disharmony reached an excruciating climax in the slow movement, which he had subtitled *Elegy*. After a ten-ton fugue, the sonata petered out on the G string. I now knew more about Bendix than I ever wanted to know. "You want the program to end with this?" I asked my accompanist.

"Absolutely. We need a serious piece."

Saint-Saëns, Hubay, Wieniawski, Kaar: the molasses and roughage here would give the most ardent music lover indigestion. "When did Bendix write this?"

"Ages ago. I commissioned it for my mother's birthday."

"Birthday? It sounds like something you'd commission for a funeral."

Fausto's face went fiery red. He calmed himself with a hill of raw meat. "You promised I could choose the program."

"All right, all right, we'll play it. It's got some good spots." Like the spaces between movements. We drank lemonade in utter silence. Fausto was very far away. "You sound great," I said finally, patting his hand.

"Are you surprised?"

"No." I squinted at the name on a score. "Who's Ethel Kiss?"

"My mother. She was gifted. Not like you, of course. You sight-read these pieces better than she played them after practicing for years."

"This program must bring back a lot of memories."

"You're worth it." Fausto returned to the piano. "Care to review anything?"

"No thanks." Fausto had chosen a recital impossible to screw up: he could skip a page, I could drop my violin, and not seriously undermine the artistic impact. No one would be listening anyway. Well, maybe one person. "You'd better warn Bendix."

"Why? I paid him plenty of money to compose this piece. He accepted it."

"I don't think he's the type who likes surprises. He told me he tore up all his operas."

"Come now! That would be like burning his child at the stake!" Fausto poured himself a few inches of champagne. "Why are you so concerned about Bendix's feelings? It's me he'll be angry with."

"What the hell, he's your friend."

I could hear the thoughts galloping through Fausto's head as he walked me to the Corvette. Suddenly he put a hand on my arm. "I've got two tickets to a fund-raiser tomorrow. Can you come?"

"Whose funds are you raising?"

"Bobby Marvel's."

Forget it, I almost said. *Look after Fausto.* "We won't stay long," I sighed.

"Only as long as you're amused."

I hit the ignition. "I have a high amusement threshold."

"Wear your flimsiest dress," Fausto called as I drove away. *What had he been doing in the jungle?*

I cut through the woods near the zoo with laughable ease. A smattering of bush, a few stones: no jungle this. Middling heat, tepid smells and it never got dark. City lights had denatured night into a weak, stalled dawn. I missed the cicadas; without them, nature here lacked a pulse. Didn't lack noise, though: cars, far-off radios . . . mechanical beasts, harmless. Still, I had to be careful. Armed guards knew the zoo better than I and midnight was not a legit visiting hour. A cougar roared as I crept by its cage. Two nights ago that sound would have traumatized me. Now I just kept walking: in Washington, only humans threatened my survival.

Paused outside Maxine's hollow in the rock. Where was

Ek tonight? Louis? Who had dared welcome me back with orchids? Only half-sure I was alone, I pressed a tiny button in the stone face. Door clicked ever so slowly open. I sent Maxine a report about Louis's camp and Barnard's cave, about waterfalls and Ek. I told her about dead Tatal, visiting Fausto, about Koko's café and Jojo's conference . . . and Simon.

When the phone rang, my pulse constricted. "You killed a man?" Maxine asked incredulously. "And let your witness go?"

"The witness saved my life. If Ek hadn't distracted him, I would have gotten my head chopped off."

"Since when do you practice charity? You should have taken care of him."

What did Maxine know? The closest she had ever gotten to a jungle was the Tiergarten. "Ek won't say a word until he sees Louis."

"Don't count on it." I heard keys tapping: Maxine raking over my report. "So the camp left you clueless. The boy was probably hiding something. He says Fausto visited for Louis's birthday? That's unbelievable. Did you rehearse with him tonight?"

"Yes. He invited me to a fund-raiser for Marvel tomorrow."

The Queen stuck to her original theme. "Why would Barnard leave behind the pictures she took at that environmental conference?"

"Maybe the conference was just an alibi to get to Belize City. To a real phone. Obviously the mobile unit didn't work in the jungle."

"She didn't call me from Belize City." Maxine swallowed something, maybe spit. In Berlin it was too late for booze, too early for coffee. "Do you think Ek ratted to Louis about Barnard's phone call?"

"He told me he didn't. Said Louis was jittery enough already."

"Take everything that kid says with a grain of salt, okay? I wonder why someone would want to kill Yvette Tatal. She was like a saint in Belize. And why that particular day?"

"Everyone knew she went digging on Mondays."

Maxine clicked to the top of my report. "Let's go over this again. Louis seems to have been looking for some sort of magillah plant. For whom or what, we don't know. Fausto visits for a birthday lunch. A week later, the environmental conference goes down. Every Washington heavy but Bobby Marvel makes an appearance. Week or so later, Louis hits Koko's café while the boy goes with Barnard to Tatal's. Louis disappears. Barnard goes after him and winds up dead. You try to see Tatal, she's dead. You chase Tatal's killer, he gets away." Maxine's travelogue halted in disgust.

"He was on a bike. I didn't have a chance."

"You go to Koko's, where you are recognized by the killer, a mercenary named Simon. Ek turns up with a bottle of liniment. Do you realize how *preposterous* that is?"

"Keep going, Maxine. Don't lose the thread of the story." She was leaving so much out: darkness, heat, terror . . . the real stuff.

"The merc knows you've trailed him through the jungle. He tries to clean up after himself by going after you with a few arrows. You counter with lethal injection. After Ek distracts him, of course. So the poison worked this time?"

"Like a champ," I sighed.

"Did you happen to notice if Simon was shooting any arrows at Ek? Sorry, you were too busy ducking. So Ek claims Simon once tried to follow them back to camp. Good thing they lost him. I suspect Louis would have ended up like Tatal. Any idea who may have hired Simon?"

None whatever. Maxine's clicking finally ceased: a deceptive silence, like that of the eye of a hurricane. "After Simon floats away, you retrieve Barnard's camera and call it a night. Quite a trip!" That was Maxine's way of saying *Thanks for risking your neck.* "Did anyone miss you back in Washington?"

Someone fond of orchids. "Duncan. Justine and Bendix. Maybe Fausto."

"How's Marvel?"

"Out of sight, out of mind."

She sighed. "We don't know shit here."

"Maybe we've got video," I said after a silence. Barnard's camera was a fine replica of a cheap aim-and-shoot. She had programmed the computer inside to recognize Louis's face. If he walked into Koko's, film would roll until he left. No audio unless she had managed to replace one strategic button on each of Louis's shirts, but I doubted that had been a problem: Barnard was hell on men's clothing, particularly buttons and zippers. I nestled the camera into a notch in the wall. Tiny whirs. Soon a digital clock appeared in a corner of the screen in front of me.

July 20, 1310 hours. Barnard must have just hooked up with Louis. The two of them waded through a clutter of chairs and backpacks to a table at the far wall. Barnard had dressed in baggy shirt and shorts. Unfortunately she couldn't tone down her height, face, or legs, so her arrival was noted by everyone in the café. Louis Bailey looked as desiccated on film as he had appeared in my computer file. Barnard's height, without her curves. He walked as if shards of glass lodged inches from his vital organs. Neither hands nor eyes made contact with the beautiful derriere ahead of him. Had Barnard finally met a man impervious to her charms? Maybe that's what had derailed her.

The button microphone worked perfectly. "Tortillas are excellent here," Louis said. Thin tenor voice. They ordered.

As soon as the waitress left, Louis plunged into a molecular analysis of malaria, not divagating from the topic even as he and Barnard left twenty minutes later. He referred to Dr. Tatal once, praising her work during the last epidemic in Belize. On the way out, Barnard rolled her eyes at the camera.

Next transmission August 10, again around lunch. This time the picture was acceptable but audio dicey: those button mikes had been corroding in the jungle for several weeks. Although Louis looked even more disheveled, he still monopolized conversation: fallout from a Mach 5 brain. Today's subject was biological immortality and the advances scientists had made in keeping animals alive far beyond their natural terms. Barnard wasn't even trying to keep up with Louis anymore. As he spoke, her eyes roamed the room, picking off men: she probably hadn't had one in a month. Her eyes kept returning to a corner of the café, lingering, toying. Finally even Louis caught on.

"You're not listening to me," he said.

"Yes I am. Ichneumonid wasps."

Mollified, Louis resumed where he had left off. Barnard wasn't through with her corner, however. Eventually Ek came to the table. "I have our provisions," he announced. "We can go now."

"Pit stop." Barnard exited. The camera picked her up at the back exit, a man at her heels.

Ek took her empty seat. Louis called the waitress. After a few shots of tequila, he looked impatiently toward the doorway through which Barnard had disappeared. When she finally returned, her hair looked mussed. As Ek relinquished her seat, he studied the far wall. I hit PAUSE as Barnard's man returned to the dining room, face to the lens.

Simon.

Ek's face betrayed nothing. Barnard suddenly became quite lively. Pulled Louis's ear a couple of times, poured herself a slug of tequila. She didn't look again in Simon's direction. Maybe he was gone. After a few minutes, she left with Louis and Ek.

"Nice little quickie," Maxine commented.

"That's Simon. Think she just picked him up?"

"She obviously wasn't getting any action from Louis."

"But hitting a stranger in a tortilla joint?"

"She's done it before."

"Maybe she wanted him on film." His passport number was in my report so Maxine looked him up. Simon Kingsley was born in Liverpool. Joined the Merchant Marine and brawled his way from sea to shining sea. Navy wouldn't take him after he KO'd a captain so he joined the Foreign Legion, abetting fifteen years of tribal warfare in Africa. When that became redundant, he moved to Central America. Close body work his specialty.

"Nice guy to screw in a back alley," Maxine commented.

"The boy noticed. He didn't appear very surprised."

"You don't think so?" I rewound tape. "Look. He's in shock. Barely moving." *Polly was not really a botanist, was she.* I forwarded to the next transmission. September 1, lunchtime. Louis sat alone at Koko's. No audio: those buttons had been in the jungle too long. He looked cadaverous, drained by the heat. Barking at a waitress, he flopped into a chair with an *International Herald-Tribune.* Turned the page and nearly dropped his tequila. Brought the paper inches from his eyes and read slowly, aghast. His mouth was still open when Krikor Tunalian, patron saint of aspiring Nobelists, tapped him on the shoulder.

Louis coughed violently, pounded his chest. The microphones twitched on. "Hello, Louis," the arms dealer said, seating himself across the table. Delicate man with thick, drooping brows and a dangling earring, maybe a crucifix. The

Indian motifs on his shirt could not conceal crescents of sweat at the armpits. "I'm so glad you remembered our meeting."

"What have you done to my brother?" Louis croaked.

Tuna looked amused. "You have a brother?" he asked with exaggerated dismay.

"Don't joke with me! I know how you people operate!"

"You've been working too hard. I'm glad to see that." Tuna laid a thick envelope on the table. "Here's some spending money. I understand you have a beautiful assistant. Spoil her a little."

Oh Christ! Did everyone on the planet know Barnard was down here?

Louis was stunned. "What makes you think I have an assistant?"

"My friends eat at Koko's, too. By the way, I'm delighted that you worked on my poison rather than visit that environmental conference. You will finish on time for me, won't you?"

"I'm going as fast as I can." Louis shakily poured himself a long tequila. "My brother's got hemorrhagic dengue. I just read it in the paper. I don't believe it. Something's wrong."

"He looked fine at the conference. A little drunk, but it could have been the heat."

Louis stood up. "I've got to see Tatal. She'll tell me what's going on here."

"Don't get sidetracked," Tuna warned. "You're working for me now."

"Go to hell! I work for myself!"

Not after accepting five million bucks in a Swiss account, he didn't. "Good-bye, Louis," Tuna smiled benignly. "You'll see me again soon. With results, I hope."

After Tuna left, Louis emptied the bottle of tequila as he reread the article in the *Trib*. The camera followed him to the phone in the rear of the café. He made one quick call before hurrying out the back door, never to be seen again.

"Zoom to his mouth," Maxine said. "See if we get anything."

Rewind, focus, patch to video decryption program. One syllable at a time, an electronic voice blurted through the speakers. "FAU-STO WE'VE GOT TROU-BLE I'M COM-ING UP."

The screen went black. "September first was a Monday," Maxine said after a grand pause. "Tatal must have been out digging. Could Louis have hitchhiked to the site?"

"Easily."

"She probably helped him out of the country. Of course, the boy would have known Tatal wouldn't be in her office. He took Barnard there on purpose so Louis could meet Tuna alone. Smart little sucker." That's what I loved about Maxine: she always looked for the best in people. "Too bad everyone's dead," she continued. "Now we're left with Fausto and your Tarzan. And Louis, if we can find him."

"Don't forget Tuna."

A guttural laugh. "He flew from Panama City to Washington last night. Maybe he's looking for a refund."

"Apparently Louis is making a poison for him. Any idea whom he'd like to hit?"

"No. And I don't particularly care." Maxine sighed in disgust. "Louis didn't have much trouble choosing between the Hippocratic oath and five million bucks."

That reminded me of something. "His file says he was disciplined for unethical conduct at Oxford. Could you look into it?"

We dabbled with a half dozen scenarios, all flawed. Finally Maxine told me to glue myself to Fausto, our only lead. Maybe I'd get a little closer to solution than Barnard had before the curtain dropped.

Chapter Seven

I WAS DRIFTING asleep when the gouge in my thigh began to throb, as if a demon percussionist were beating *The Rite of Spring*—in my bone marrow. Soon all my other bruises were pulsating in sympathetic vibration, churning up a sweat. I switched on the light, half expecting to see blood on the sheets, but the wound was clean, my stitches intact. I was already up to the eyeballs in antibiotics; painkillers would lull me into a dangerous doldrum. So I lay back and tried to displace the pain with music. That little exercise only brought me around to Fausto. Why had he gone to Belize? Suddenly I heard water and smelled earth baking in the sun. I felt Ek's steady eyes watching me from the mouth of a cave: *adios,* slumber. A man would have come in handy but bah, I was alone. Creaked over to the window. Clear night, about over. I'd take a ride.

Before hitting the ignition, I searched every inch of the Corvette. No bugs: how insulting. Pulled onto the Beltway, scanning the rearview mirror as I weaved past cars containing one passenger and one cup of coffee. Only the insane would commute to work at four in the morning, but Washingtonians believed they were a superior race rather than a mutant breed of rat in a toilet with a four-year flush. Traffic pressed forward at a grim seventy-five miles per hour as I veered into Virginia. The roads were so smooth, cars so fast . . . nature so docile. A human could almost feel in control here. When light and heat dissolved the dawn, I just cranked up the air-conditioning.

Left the highway near Richmond. Louis Bailey lived in a woodsy neighborhood that must have seemed futuristic about when the Beatles did. Now all that plate glass and globe lighting looked merely inefficient. Bailey had the tallest crabgrass on the block. Careful: his neighbors might be keeping an eye on the property, hoping that one blessed day a FOR SALE sign would appear out front. At the moment, they all seemed to be asleep. I parked the Corvette blocks away, cut through several backyards, entered through Bailey's back door. No alarm system, but nothing looked worth taking. Scientific papers covered the sofas, beds, counters, floors. Reams of Internet detritus—all about the latest Nobel Prize winners—gathered dust in the bathtub. Looked as if Louis had left in a rush: phones on, beer in fridge. I combed the house for artifacts but the great doctor had left none behind. Maybe he didn't live here at all. Maybe he slept at the university and just used this place for storage. Outside the kitchen, sparrows twittered at an empty feeder. A car passed, then silence returned.

Tiny click as I went from kitchen to book-lined den. Two videotapes lay on a new VCR. The first was a puffy campaign documentary about Bobby Marvel's life, the second a dub of the interview wherein a tearful president swore off adultery forever as Paula beamed at him adoringly. Behind the desk hung an autographed photo from Bobby Marvel— "To my great friend Louis"—as well as a framed baloney letter thanking him for his generous contribution to the party. A copy of the letter lay on the desk, with Bobby's signature traced in red pen.

I crawled under the desk to check for valuables in the wastebasket and noticed red near the wall socket. Panties, French, expensive. Slid my hand in the narrow space between desk and wall, pulled out a matching bra. Barnard's size, her favorite push-up style. Put it to my nose and smelled Miss Dior, the only perfume she wore. I went to the wide plush sofa, found two long blond hairs: Barnard had definitely been here naked. *With whom?*

Another click as I left the den: bad coincidence so this time I stopped. Backed up a step: click. I dropped to the floor. Embedded in the door frame, about knee height, was a metallic eye no larger than an iguana's. Fresh sawdust beneath it. Passed my finger in front of the infrared beam, tripping the sensor a fourth time.

The bookcase sputtered. Behind me, Bailey's refrigerator coughed as the bullet tore a hole in its side. Had I been standing, my lungs would have been blown all over the kitchen cabinets. Nauseating thought so I rolled to the bookshelf, where specks of paper still floated in the delicate sunlight. Found the gun, a Smith & Wesson .38, in a wrecked dictionary.

Would have preferred a bar but I settled for a diner near the highway, swallowing a dry bagel and Lestoil-tinged coffee as I tried to figure out who would be smug enough, or desperate enough, to plant that little booby trap.

"More coffee?"

No, more brains. I drove to Richmond, where Louis Bailey taught when he wasn't defoliating Belize. His lab stood at the edge of a beautiful campus where the boys looked masculine and the girls feminine. The scene was a little unbelievable, like colonial Williamsburg. I brought a smoothie and a steno pad to the patio outside the lab. Sipped, smiled, waited: soon the great-great-grandson of a Confederate joined me. He introduced himself with first, middle, last name, and *ma'am*: ah, nothing like southern manners to wilt a lady's honor. Furman was a graduate teaching assistant. Once again I became Cosima Wagner, researching an article on dengue fever for a leading women's magazine. It was a chic disease now that the vice president had it. My editor had told me to get a few quotes from Dr. Bailey, world authority on the topic. Bailey hadn't returned any of my calls so I thought I'd catch him in person.

"That might not be possible," Furman said, tearing his gaze from my open blouse. "He's on sabbatical."

"But I've got to finish this article tonight!"

"Maybe I could help."

"That's so sweet! Thank you!" I opened my pad. "Can you catch dengue by . . . ah . . . making love?"

"No, ma'am. It's not a sexually transmitted disease."

"Our readers are going to be *very* happy to hear that. How do you catch it, then?"

"Generally, you're bitten by an infected *Aedes aegypti* mosquito, which breeds in standing water in urban areas. That would most commonly be slums where rainwater collects in basins and tires."

When the hell had Jojo been near slums, basins, and tires? "Is it a big mosquito?"

"No, it's small, green, and quick. The female is the carrier." Furman cast his first line. "As usual."

I obliviously wrote that down. "Could you describe the disease in simple terms? For girls who will be drying their nails while they're reading this article?"

"Shortly after they're bitten, victims will develop a rash, fever, headache, and horrible pain in their joints. That's why the disease is sometimes called breakbone fever." Furman tried again. "The victims will definitely not feel like making love."

"Then they die?"

"Hardly ever. There are four strains of dengue. But even the most virulent form, hemorrhagic fever, kills only about ten percent of its victims. And that death rate has a lot to do with genetic predisposition."

"So it's not fatal like AIDS? My editor's not going to like that." Frowning, I flipped a page. "What do you mean, genetic predisposition?"

"Unlike victims of measles or chicken pox, who develop antibodies that prevent them from getting the disease again, people who suffer dengue once are *more* likely to get it worse the second time around."

"Why?"

"It's a little complicated. It has to do with overstimulated immune systems."

I scribbled away. "What's hemorrhagic dengue?"

Furman deliberated a moment as I rearranged my ponytail. "Your heart pumps blood through the arteries. Those are the main highways in the circulation system. The highways get smaller and smaller until, in the capillaries, they're only wide enough for one blood cell to pass through. When you've got hemorrhagic fever, the dengue virus bores holes through the capillary walls so that the platelets leak out."

"So you have a billion microscopic hemorrhages?"

"Exactly. Your capillaries become sieves. Tiny red spots appear all over the skin as the subdermal bleeding continues. Eventually the virus overwhelms the circulation system. You'll drown in your own blood."

"How horrible! There are no vaccines?"

"Not yet. But we're working on it."

Good luck, honey. "Was Louis Bailey involved with the vaccine?"

"No, ma'am. He never came anywhere near that lab."

I chewed the tip of my fountain pen, as if it were a tiny, tasty penis. "My editor's never going to buy this dengue business. It's just so . . . African! Do you know where I could get in touch with Dr. Bailey? Maybe he's working on something more cool now."

"You won't find him," Furman said. "And you're not the only one looking."

I tried to shrug. "He doesn't have an assistant?"

"No, ma'am! Bailey works completely alone."

"Why's he so paranoid?"

"Researchers get that way, especially if they're on to something." Furman leaned over my ear. Maybe he was just getting a better angle on my blouse. "Last semester, just before he went on sabbatical, I saw him muttering to himself. You'll never guess what was in his hair. A fat orange caterpillar. At first I thought it was a Cheez Doodle. Then it moved. I nearly passed out."

"Come on, Furman, I can't write about this." Perturbed, I brushed a few crumbs into the grass. "Is anyone around here working on something my readers care about? Like waterproof mascara?"

"I'm researching the mating habits of catfish," he said.

I looked at my watch: get inside *now*, Smith. "That's more promising. Could you show me just a little bit?"

Behind the security desk sat a corpulent guard with fingernails as intricately painted as Fabergé eggs. She munched a doughnut hole as I signed in. Furman kindly showed me Louis Bailey's locked office on the second floor. A dozen memos were taped to the professor's door, as if the university weren't certain whether he was really gone or just working antisocial hours. Little traffic, zero surveillance here.

Bailey's lock would resist me for about ten seconds. I oohed/aahed at Furman's catfish then excused myself to begin writing my new article. He walked me to the door with exhortations to call any time.

I hugged him. His neck smelled of soap and youth. "Thanks so much."

Circled the building before returning to the front desk. The guard was studying the box on her lap as if it contained doubloons rather than doughnut holes. "I must have left my car keys upstairs," I told her. "Should I sign in again?"

"Just change your Out time."

Across campus, a clock chimed eight as I entered Bailey's office. Weak, fuscous light seeped through drawn blinds. More drivel about the Nobel Prize and some blank grant applications crowded his desktop. Forgotten cardigans drooped from every chair. As I was studying one of his honorary doctorates, I stepped on something about the size of a bullet. Held it up to the light and gasped: I had just crushed one of Louis's button microphones. He had been here. I hit redial on the phone.

Eleven digits, two rings. "You've reached the Federal Bureau of Investigation," answered a machine. "If you know your party's extension, you may enter it at any time."

I unscrewed the mouthpiece. There lay a tiny mike and a transmitter. Wonderful!

"Find your keys?" asked the guard downstairs, tossing her empty milk carton into the trash.

"Right where I left them."

As I was editing my sign-out time, another guard appeared behind the desk. "Leave me any doughnuts, Cheryl?"

Her chair squeaked as she abandoned it. "Not this time. You're late."

We left the building together. Within two steps Cheryl had freed shirt from belt. Now it fluttered like a tablecloth in the breeze. "You have the graveyard shift?" I asked. "I did that once in a restaurant. Only lasted two months."

"You get used to it after a while."

"I guess this building goes twenty-four hours a day."

"Yeah, those scientists never know when to quit. They're all crazy. Ask them how to fly to the moon, no problem. Ask what they had for breakfast, forget it."

"I know what you mean. I had an appointment with Dr. Bailey."

"Bailey? He's the worst."

"I came all the way from Atlanta and he's been gone for months."

"Give me a break," Cheryl said, peeling a Mars bar. "He was here about three weeks ago."

"You saw him?"

"Sure. Four in the morning, middle of a thunderstorm. He looked like the Unabomber. Scared my pants off. Hey, have a good one."

She cut into a parking lot. I wandered to a phone inside the gym. "Maxine? Trivia question. Did Jojo ever have dengue?"

"Hold on." Heavy clicking. "Never. Why?"

"The chance of getting hemorrhagic fever first time out is practically zero." I smiled at a guy wearing sweat pants, no jock. Pecs smooth as pears and a soft mound between his legs. "I'm at Louis's lab. He's been here. His phone's bugged. Any reason why he'd be calling the FBI at four in the morning?"

"Give me a date."

"About three weeks ago, during a thunderstorm. Security guard saw him. I was at his house this morning." I told Maxine about the lingerie. "Looks like Barnard finally got her man." That earned a derisive laugh so I skipped to the videos of Bobby Marvel and the gun.

"I hope you left everything there."

"I left the videos."

Silence, then a sigh. "Whatever."

A jogger puffed up to the phone. His tiny, erect nipples made my tongue ache. "Check out the thunderstorm, would you?" I hung up.

"Mornin'," said the boy. His sweat smelled like apple juice. That body would stay hot and hard all day. I saw myself slung over his shoulder, carried off to a sunny room with white sheets. Ah, for just a few hours with this sweet, unsullied creature . . . but that would be vampirism, wouldn't it. Handed him the phone and drove back to Washington, where I spent the afternoon practicing Bendix Kaar's thorny sonata. When that turned rancid, I stared at the old recital program that Fausto's mother, once upon a time, had tucked into the violin part. Her boy had played Beethoven, Liszt, and Scriabin . . . then jumped into the Thames.

Wished I could have been there.

I arrived at his house promptly at five. Fausto eyed my outfit with wry dismay. "Who died, darling?"

"What's the problem? We're going to a fund-raiser, not a nightclub."

"I don't see much skin," he lamented.

No kidding. Too many bug bites and scratches. "I'm a modest girl."

"Aha." We began a long, rather unnecessary rehearsal. The only piece that still needed work was Bendix's sonata. Fausto's part sounded better than mine, but he had probably given it more thought. "Get yourself a drink. I'll be right back."

I went to Fausto's kitchen, opened a few cupboards. Found the phone box in the utility closet: his wires were red and white. Glass in hand, I returned to the music room. My host appeared minutes later in a green linen suit. He drew what looked like a handful of marbles from his pocket. "Just so we don't disappear into the woodwork. Turn around." He draped a rope of black pearls around my neck. "That should help."

Help what? "They're stunning."

"They were my mother's. So was this. Don't move." He combed my hair with three lascivious fingers before snapping a diamond barrette into place. His body was close, warm, enormous as the sun: for a depraved instant, I wanted him. "I love dressing women. Go freshen your lipstick and we'll leave."

The air was thick and hot, sick with rain. M Street was clogged with cars, students, and beggars with just enough appendages to simultaneously smoke and hold a tin cup. Fausto drove. I found myself staring at his round hands, wondering if he liked to undress women as well as dress them. Ah lust, fallout from that errant .38 this morning at Louis's. Fausto's silence only aggravated my curiosity. "Why are we going to this fund-raiser?" I asked finally.

His round eyes flickered absently to my face; his thoughts had been elsewhere. "I promised the hostess."

"Really? I think you're just looking for trouble."

Fausto cornered smoothly onto Pennsylvania Avenue. "I never look for trouble, dear. Diversion, maybe. Trouble, never."

"Isn't trouble more gratifying?"

"Trouble is far too easy. Diversion takes finesse. It's like the difference between playing Chopsticks and *Clair de lune*."

"I see. Do it right and no one ever knows what hit them."

Fausto's cool eyes met mine. "You seem to know a lot about diversion."

"Not really. I'm more familiar with delusion. This town's got plenty of it."

"That's what makes the diversion so much fun."

"Cut the word games, Fausto. I think you're just a gambler who likes to play with everyone else's chips."

His plump hand patted mine as we pulled in front of a suburban mansion. Its owner was famous for parties and ex-husbands. "The chips are all mine." He braked under the portico. "You say the word, we leave."

First a little touchie-feelie with the metal detectors at the front door, then air kisses from the indebted hostess, an elf in a blue jersey gown. All that cling looked slightly obscene on a bulimic seventy-year-old. "Fausto! I'm so glad to see you!"

"Wouldn't let you down, Judith. Not for ten grand a plate. This is Leslie Frost."

Fausto hadn't mentioned violins, therefore Judith didn't either. As her eyes breezed over my half million bucks of jewelry, a sixth sense told her that whatever wealth I had, little of it would end up in Bobby Marvel's coffers. "Hello."

My date sniffed a white rose from a gigantic arrangement. "When do you expect the guest of honor?"

"He's on his way."

"My God! We'd better find the oysters before he does!" Fausto took me to the rear salon, where a hundred guests clustered buffet and bar. The men looked corporate, the women excited: Marvel the Magnificent was about to touch them. Another calcium-deficient septuagenarian approached. "You're the violinist, aren't you? We saw you in Paris. You wore a divine St. Laurent."

"Really! What did I play?"

Her eyes bulged, as if I had just asked her age. "I love classical music."

She loved being seen at events with exclusionary ticket

prices. Fausto downed two glasses of champagne as she castigated the government for abandoning the arts. America was becoming a nation of barbarians.

"Correct," he agreed, spearing a strip of smoked salmon and dangling it high above his mouth before swallowing it whole. "There's no self-control in this country anymore." Four olives went down the hatch. He sidled his leviathan stomach inches from the woman's plate of hors d'oeuvres. "Thank God Bobby's in charge."

She hesitated: even his most adamant supporters knew Marvel was one of the lamest presidents in memory. "Think of the alternative."

"I do! Every day!" Fausto delicately harvested three chicken livers from a passing platter. Suddenly he stopped chewing. "Look what the wind blew in!" We left the woman floundering with a mouthful of tapenade. "If only money bred class," Fausto sighed, waving to friends. "Or even wit. Hello, Justine. That dress is absolutely volcanic."

Duncan's beloved, attired in a spin of red feathers and red spandex, glared back. "Thank you."

"How's your wrist, Duncan?"

"Mending," he scowled.

Justine wrested her eyes from my necklace. "Shouldn't you two be home practicing for your little concert?"

"You know how it is. Every so often you've got to give the digits a rest." Fausto swallowed his last chicken liver. "I hope Bobby's oiled his tongue tonight. Judith's packed the place with horny women. Yourself excepted, of course."

"Oh for God's sake!" Duncan interrupted. "I need a drink! Come on, babe!"

We watched them huff away. "Isn't he on his high horse," Fausto said. We circled the room, garnering many sidelong glances: were we or weren't we, and if so, how? Fausto seemed to be enjoying our degenerative game of Beauty and the Beast. I played along, clinging to his arm, curiously shielded by his girth and wealth. Nothing got to me without first passing him: tonight, I was grateful for that. But there was not much call to even open my mouth here. Fausto's jewels did all the talking for me. That was the up side of consorting with the rich.

After a while we retired to the backyard, where the air was dense with camellias and imminent rain. A harpist swished Ravel in the corner of a tent as white-jacketed waiters fussed over silverware. "You've got to see Judith's orchids," Fausto said, leading me past a dozen round tables. "They're the only reason for coming here."

At the edge of the lawn stood a conservatory about the size of the Jefferson Memorial. Through the huge panels of glass, beneath yellow lights, I saw a riot of green: into a jungle again, damn him. At once I began to tremble and sweat. "Do you garden?" Fausto asked, turning a brass doorknob.

"No."

"You should." He closed his eyes as air gravid with perfumes enveloped us. "Ah. Smell that chlorophyll. Beautiful."

Heart lumbered against rib: last time I had been in a place like this, death had stalked half a pace behind. I followed Fausto along the narrow flagstone path, shuddering as palm fronds swished my sleeve. Where was the cacophony of insects, the screech of unseen birds, the sweet smell of decay? This jungle, like everything else in Washington, was a fake. Fausto greeted many plants by their Latin names, bending over them to sniff and fondle. Finally we got to the orchids. Judith grew dozens of varieties, from waxy, prom-date white to droopy pink to the frilly purple I had received in a bouquet three times now. Again, Fausto knew each by name and again, as I watched his fingertips caress their voluptuous, hooded splendor, I wanted him. Strange. "Mother adored orchids. The house was always full of them," he said. "But I prefer roses. Hyacinths."

"Why?"

"Fragrance. Something to keep me company in the dark."

Voices down the path. Fausto let a heavy blossom slip from his hand. First a suit, then our hostess, resplendent in jersey, cut through the fronds. Next, Bobby and Paula Marvel and another Secret Service agent. For a moment we all stared disbelievingly at each other, like the expeditions of Stanley and Livingstone.

"Judith! We were just admiring your treasures." Fausto kissed Paula's hand. "You're looking lovely tonight, madam. As always."

The First Lady was wearing another of those dresses with large bows that matched her pink shoes. Tonight her hairdresser had gotten stuck somewhere between Jackie O and Gidget. Paula's little kewpie mouth barely moved as she accepted Fausto's kiss. In these confines, the two of them hogged more space than a pair of Steinways in an elevator. "I understand you're performing tomorrow night, Fausto," she said.

"My God! Are there no secrets in this town?"

"Not when you spill half of them." Paula smiled thinly. "Thank you for sending that ointment."

"Chickie already thanked me profusely. Just let me know when you need a fresh supply."

Paula drilled me with purest blue eyes before asking Fausto, "Where is your friend Miss Mason? I'm still waiting for that tea she promised."

I looked slowly at Bobby, whose face remained lively as concrete. "You'll get your tea, I'm sure," Fausto responded after the tiniest of eternities. "The girl is probably off harvesting it herself."

"She rather led me to believe I'd be getting it right away. Nothing else seems to be helping my arthritis."

"Do you know that pain can be stress related? And you have so much of that, poor thing."

As if Fausto were her personal physician, Paula engaged him in an intense discussion about degenerative diseases. Each time she made a point, one of her pink bows shook. I tried to maintain a rigid, cocktail party smile while Bobby did a good imitation of a dugout canoe. The Secret Service men kept glancing into the trees, on the lookout for killer apes. Meanwhile, poor Judith was about to explode. On one hand, this fatuous conversation fascinated her; on the other hand, she hadn't dragged the Big Bananoids into her greenhouse to discuss cortisone with Fausto. She was savvy enough to realize that Paula's little sidebar had nothing to do with tea or arthritis but that the longer it continued, the more her stock would slide.

Fortunately Bobby came to the rescue. "What are those flowers over there, Judy?" he suddenly pointed, glowering at Paula. "Tiger lilies?"

Taking the cue, Fausto ducked into a handkerchief as Judith basked in her minute of glory with the ruler of the land. No matter that his wife had contemptuously meandered up the path. Just as well, in fact: no woman, not even a seventy-year-old, would want Paula around when Bobby was revving up the bedroom eyes. Soon Justine, minus Duncan, rushed up the path. Her booze breath blended nicely with the smell of peat. Addressing her old flame, her enunciation reverted from duchess of Windsor back to hillbilly of Kentucky. "For Christ's sake, look at the time! Everyone's expecting you inside, Mr. President."

"Aw Justie! It's much more fun out here!"

Chortling under his breath, Fausto took my hand. We started for the door. Suddenly, whimsically, inches from

Bobby's orchids, he stopped. "Do you remember Leslie Frost, Mr. President? She played in the East Room last week."

"Of course. How do you do." I curtseyed with the eyelashes, he barely twitched. Great performance: not even Fausto would guess Bobby had already had four joints inside of me. Marvel turned toward his wife, a hot pink mirage in the far-off fronds. "Paula! Time to go!"

Fausto stepped deferentially into the dirt, allowing the First Lady enough room to pass. "Remember my tea," she admonished before her blue eyes settled on Judith. "It is hotter than goddamn hell in here."

The hostess actually apologized. Paula didn't hear a word. "That's some dress," she told Justine. "You look like a little rooster."

Justine, sixty pounds lighter than her accuser, merely smiled. "Thank you."

"My wife's had a rough day," Bobby explained to no one in particular.

"Just shut up, would you?" his wife snapped. "Let's get out of here. I need air."

Fausto and I remained in place until the door slammed. "Hail democracy," he said.

I swatted peat moss from my shoes. "Do they all get like that once they're elected?"

"You're putting the cart before the horse, sweet. If they weren't like that in the first place, they wouldn't go into politics."

"Even the women?"

"Especially the women. I see Paula and Justine are still fighting over Bobby." He drenched his handkerchief under a spigot. "Marvel barely noticed you."

"Why should he? I'm not raising a fortune for his war chest. What was all that business about tea?"

"A few weeks ago I brought a woman named Mason to a fund-raiser. She and Paula hit it off like firecrackers and matches. They got into a powwow about herbal remedies. Mason was considered an authority in the field. If you noticed, the First Lady loves to discuss her maladies. She thinks it makes her husband feel guilty."

Dream on. "So why didn't she get her tea?"

He looked long and hard at me before answering. "Because Mason left."

Unless my antennae were fried or Fausto was the greatest liar in history, he did not know that Barnard was dead. If only I could be as sure of Paula Marvel! "Mason left?" I repeated. "And stiffed the First Lady?"

"Some people play games."

"With Paula? Not too swift."

"She didn't give you the time of day either, I noticed." Fausto daubed his forehead with a handkerchief. "Guilt by association."

Association with whom? "What would we have talked about, fifty ways to tie a bow?"

"Paula's a sharp cookie. Don't underestimate her." As soon as we left the greenhouse, Fausto lit a cigarette. "Sorry. I know you disapprove."

I watched his lips grip the tiny cylinder. *Down, Smith.* "Why'd Bobby marry Paula?"

"Simple. He wanted to be president. She's got the brains and the venom he lacks. Not to mention pedigree. Her family's been lawyering in Washington for nearly a century. Paula's intimately familiar with the workings of government."

"Why'd she marry Bobby then?"

"Same reason, sweet. She wanted to be president too. And Bobby's a lovable marionette." Fausto gazed moodily across the lawn, where guests were beginning to drift under the tent. Finally, when the first apathetic drops of rain let go of the clouds, he asked, "Are you up for speeches and dinner?"

"Only if you are."

As we drove away from Judith's party, the rain began in earnest. Fausto's melancholy filled the car. "Sorry," he said finally. "I just realized I'd rather be practicing the piano than yapping with the president. I must be losing it."

I watched hundreds of tiny drops, persistent as hope, reappear on the windshield immediately after the wiper blade had passed. "Are you sorry you stopped playing?"

"That would be like missing an amputated arm. You just accept the loss and try to get by as best you can." He braked, or maybe ran out of gas, at a red light. "And now the arm has miraculously reattached itself. Makes me think about the last thirty years."

The car behind us honked. Fausto rolled forward. "I had forgotten about the ecstasy of shutting myself away with a piece. About time standing still as you become nothing but will and sound, about the odd dislocation as you try to function in reality while music is always playing in the back of your mind. You know what I'm talking about. What's going through your head now?"

Besides lust? "The last movement of the Brahms sonata. What's going through yours?"

"Saint-Saëns. Thank God we're equally disadvantaged." He took my hand. "I stopped because I knew I couldn't have a career. Halfway never cut it with me. But I didn't realize until this week how dreadfully I've missed the music. I don't know whether to thank you or curse the day we met."

I kissed his fingers. "Are you up for tomorrow night, Fausto?"

"Of course. I'm an exhibitionist at heart."

In his driveway, I unclasped his mother's jewelry. The

pearls felt warm as a handful of quail eggs. As always, the cold, immortal gleam of diamonds took my breath away: returning them pained me. "Go practice," I whispered.

A cassette from Bendix Kaar awaited me at the hotel desk: Fausto Kiss performing his piano sonata. *I had completely forgotten about this,* his note lied. *But since you asked* . . . Clever man, Bendix: of all his tapes, he knew I'd be most likely to listen to this one. But not now. I tossed it on the bed and changed into black leather.

The storm pounded Washington until midnight. I waited it out at the cinema in Fairfax, this time with a romantic comedy about two divorced parents. Nobody laughed much except at the sex scenes. Afterward I visited the zoo, checked the serial number of the Smith & Wesson I had lifted from Louis's bookshelf. He had bought it six years ago in Florida. I phoned Berlin.

"No surprise," Maxine yawned. "But I hope you don't think he planted it."

"Why not? He's paranoid. He knows people are after him."

"So he rigs a gun to blow away the first person who comes to his house? Come on. Someone's playing games with you. And it's not Louis. I doubt he's been home since July." As she yawned again, I thought of the bouquet of orchids and the card welcoming me back to Washington. "I traced his call to the FBI. Listen." She patched me in.

"This is Rhoby Hall," said a female. "For your protection, our conversation is being recorded. With whom am I speaking?"

"I can't tell you over the phone," rasped Louis. "Just connect me with someone in charge. I have confidential information concerning national security."

Rhoby Hall was unimpressed by her fiftieth crackpot of

the day. "We suggest you come in during office hours tomorrow. We'd be happy to speak with you personally."

"You don't understand! People are trying to kill me! I know their secrets!"

"Could you be a little more specific, sir?"

"Goddamn it! How much more specific do you need?" Behind Louis, booming thunder. "Let me spell it out for you. Someone's just assassinated Jordan Bailey."

"Vice President Bailey? I believe he was still alive as of the six o'clock news."

"Meet me out front when your shift is over. I'll explain everything."

Less patiently she replied, "I'm sorry. You'll have to speak with my superior before we determine a course of action."

"I risk my neck and you won't leave your desk?" Louis was beside himself. In the background, campus clocks chimed four. "What was your name again?"

"Rhoby Hall. What's yours?"

"Not over the phone! I'm coming over right now! My *life* is in your hands!" Louis hung up.

"She tossed him in the wacko bin," Maxine said after a few seconds. "He does sound completely lunatic."

"Did she meet him?"

"Don't know. But she's still working at the FBI."

I pulled Rhoby Hall on screen. Big-shouldered brunette with a jaw that could crush spark plugs. Blasé college, blasé degree. Looked familiar.

"She's Vicky Chickering's significant other," Maxine said. Right. I had seen her at Ford's Theatre. "Maybe you could take Chickering to lunch. Get to know her a little better." When that suggestion bombed, Maxine asked, "Does she go to Fausto's for breakfast?"

Who the hell didn't? "If I see her next time, I'll chat her up. But she's never brought Rhoby along."

That was now my problem. "How was the fund-raiser?"

"We ran into the Marvels in the hostess's greenhouse. Paula grilled Fausto about some tea that Barnard had promised her. Evidently the two of them had met at a previous fund-raiser." I tried to keep my voice neutral. "Barnard was Fausto's date."

The Queen didn't care about that. "Why'd Paula bring it up? Do you think she really wanted the tea? Or was she fishing?" Maxine blew on something, maybe cocoa, maybe a custom-made bomb. "Think she knows what happened to Barnard and was getting a rise out of taunting the poor fat boy?" Another couple puffs. "Subtext is god. I hope you were watching."

I was watching all right. My date's lips. "We didn't stay. Fausto got bored."

"I thought he lived for that stuff."

"Lately he prefers to practice piano."

The Queen only chuckled. "Did you ask him what he was doing in Belize with Louis? Or don't you know him well enough yet?"

"I can't push this, Maxine. He's too clever."

"You're right on that one. Did I tell you that Louis called Fausto before dialing the FBI? Call only lasted fifteen seconds. Plenty of time to arrange a rendezvous."

More pain in my gut: Fausto knew everything. "Did you get anything on Louis's problem at Oxford?"

"Oh yes. The lad was caught helping himself to a few items at the school morgue. Said he needed them for his experiments. He was studying chemical imbalances in the nervous system. His professor got him off the hook by swearing that Louis was the most brilliant research assistant alive. A few months later, the kid went to 'Nam. No problem with organ donations there, I bet." She took several long swallows of something before asking, "Have you seen Bendix Kaar lately?"

"No. But he's keeping an eye on me. Just sent over a cassette of his music. What's Tuna up to?"

"He spent the day at the National Gallery of Art. Funny how all these boys have suddenly become aesthetes. Why don't you go see if Fausto's practicing now."

That taunt couldn't be ignored. I left the zoo and walked ten minutes to Fausto's steep, quiet street. The night was soupy and dark, perfect for peeping. Most of his neighbors had either gone to sleep or left town for the weekend. I smiled to see lights ablaze in his music room. Good boy . . . sort of. Walked back up his hill, stopping at the ninth telephone pole. Its upper third was shrouded in willow leaves. Held my breath, then jumped. Thigh disliked all that friction but I had to get to the iron hooks, out of headlight range, fast. Soon I was embowered with the black box at the top. Snapped on my flashlight, went down the neat pairs of terminal screws, searching for the red and white wire that ran from here to Fausto's cupboard. Connected two of my own wires to his. Fausto was now sharing his line with a transmitter about the size of a deck of cards. I started down the pole but whoa: car: froze as a Mercedes scuttled past. The driver wore red feathers. She had a passenger.

Dropped the last ten feet to spongy earth. Justine's car was parked in Fausto's driveway. The clouds growled as I raced across his lawn toward the high windows of the music room. Visibility poor through the organza but I saw his hands on the keyboard. Splotches of Saint-Saëns seeped outside. Justine shared the sofa with a man whose head lay in her lap. Duncan? Couldn't tell: too many feathers. The two of them listened to the whole damn triptych. Incredible: Saint-Saëns usually made my accompanist break out in boils. Now he was sitting through just the *piano part* of a duo?

Fausto finished his half-assed recital, to dull applause. Justine stood and so did the gentleman. My pulse dipped when I saw Bobby Marvel.

Last spring the president had been reprimanded for sneaking out of the White House without his Secret Service contingent. Needed space, he had whined. No one had wanted to ask with whom, and Bobby had promised not to do it again. But that was months ago; in Washington, fruit flies lived longer than oaths. I watched the escapee totter to the sideboard, pour himself a drink. Bobby eventually seated himself next to Fausto at the keyboard. One lit a cigarette, the other a cigar, then they began to play the Schubert *Fantasy*. Justine turned pages.

Their musicale so hypnotized me that I didn't hear the van until it was in the driveway. I hit the deck a second before its headlights splashed the wall behind me. What now, the Supreme Court coming to sing *Liebeslieder*? A kid with two pizza boxes entered the pool of light on Fausto's stoop. Half of me accepted him at face value. The other half calculated how many seconds the delivery boy would need to strangle Fausto, put a few holes in Bobby, and drive away.

Fausto answered the door. I held my breath as he let the kid in. No immediate gunshots, but that meant nothing. I crawled to a break in the curtains. Inside, Justine remained at Bobby's side, staring at the music. He appeared to be studying the score as well. They seemed frozen, on edge. Then I saw the hem of Justine's red skirt rise. Bobby's fingers were trilling between her legs and, judging from the arch of her back, precipitating turbulence.

Twenty feet away, Fausto's front door opened. "Thanks," the pizza boy called, returning to the van. Fausto watched it drive away, then lit a cigarette. While he putzed with the flowerpots on his stoop, I found another breach in the drapery just in time to see Bobby heave Justine facedown over the piano and begin ramming her, using the same short, brutish strokes I had seen in the bathtub video. He held her ankles wide apart, as if maneuvering a wheelbarrow full of feathers over rough terrain.

When Bobby's knee crashed into the keyboard, Fausto looked up from his begonias and smiled. Damn, coming my way: I rolled into the shrubbery as his slow steps crossed the patio. Fausto took my post at the window, observing the action between drags on his cigarette. Copulation seemed to excite him about as much as dead fish. He chuckled once before going back inside.

Another crunch in the driveway as a black Lincoln inched next to Justine's Mercedes. Three men, heavily armed, herded a fourth to the door. I probably should have been a little more surprised to see Krikor Tunalian, who didn't even have to knock before Fausto answered. "Come in, come in," he announced grandly. "The president is waiting." Since Tuna had left two bodyguards at the door, I stayed in the bushes. Not for long, though: pizza party broke up in fifteen minutes. Tuna's contingent left first, Justine/Bobby shortly thereafter. Fausto practiced like a madman for another hour before packing it in.

What the hell had just happened? Clueless, I returned to the hotel. About to step into the bathtub when the phone rang. "You've been out."

"What can I do for you, Mr. President?"

"You looked gorgeous in that greenhouse tonight. Sorry I couldn't talk. Paula has eyes like a cougar and fangs to match. She was all on edge, too. Hasn't been herself lately. I ignored you for your own good. Don't take it too hard."

"No problem," I yawned. "Sounds like Polly stood your

wife up, too. Does the First Lady have any idea you two were sleeping together?"

Bobby stuck to the original subject. "You left before dinner. Those two empty seats were like a slap in my face the whole night long."

"What's the problem? Fausto paid the going rate, didn't he?"

"You missed a terrific speech."

Yawn. "Fausto wanted to practice. We've got a concert tomorrow."

"You left *me* in order to *practice?*"

Ah, trick question. "No, Fausto practiced. I went for a drive."

Perturbed silence. "I'm all wound up, baby. Come see me."

"Haven't you had enough excitement for one evening?" I asked sarcastically.

"Just gettin' my second wind."

I stuck a toe in the water. "I'm flattered that you called, Mr. President. But nothing interferes with my bath."

"Bitch! This is the loneliest job in the world," he whined.

"I'm sure it is. Enjoy."

I wasn't about to become the fluff in Bobby's second wind. Sank into the tub, disturbed by twists in current events. Marvel evades Secret Service, an accomplishment in itself, to meet Tuna. He's assisted by the perfidious Justine, whose affair with Duncan does not prevent her from spreading her legs for an old flame. Worst, I kept seeing Fausto's contented smile as he looked up from the begonias. All was proceeding as he had planned. I didn't have one clue in hell what was going on.

I was caught in a torrent, rushing toward a waterfall. Trees and houses shot over the edge, hitting the rocks with a *boom! Boom!* Shuddered awake. Rain pelted the window. Sudden bright lightning, a thunderclap: storm over Washington. Fringe of a hurricane, claimed the weather channel. Duncan barged in as I was watching the news. The blue sling for his cast matched his bow tie. "Justine and I are going to Cleveland," he announced. "She's going to meet my parents."

I waved him quiet. We listened to an update on Jojo Bailey, now sharing his room with wife, mother, and spiritualist. The action cut to Bobby Marvel emerging from the hospital looking puffy and sad, as if he had been up all night administering last rites.

"This is a tragedy for the American people. I ask everyone to join me in prayer."

"Prayer for what?" Duncan asked.

"Swift confirmation of Aurilla Perle."

Duncan scowled: I had reminded him of this evening's house concert. "I danced with her at the White House. She had about as much rhythm as a fire hydrant. Why have you play at her damn party? You don't fit in at all."

"Maybe it's you she wanted."

"Pfuiii! I have no further interest in dancing with that woman! Or her guests!" Duncan helped himself to a brioche from my breakfast trolley. "By the way, you were right about Justine shooting Marvel years ago. She'd really like to know how you found out."

"I think it was on the Net. Did she tell you why she clipped him?"

Duncan munched enigmatically. "He deserved it."

"Something strange about those two, Duncan. Would you hire someone who shot you to be your press secretary? Would you go to work for someone you shot? Maybe they're more attached than you think."

"For Pete's sake, they've known each other forever! It's a family affair!"

"So's incest." I turned off the television when Aurilla's powdered face took over the screen. "When's that cast coming off?"

"About a week."

I wanted both of us out of here by then. "It'll feel good to start playing again."

Duncan merely peeled a banana with one working hand and his teeth. After he left, I practiced. When the rain stopped around noon, I took a long run around the Tidal Basin. This was an annoying town, deep as a Monopoly board. I pounded past the White House, irritated that the president was meeting arms dealers while his press secretary was setting up an innocent pianist for the mother of all falls. I was irritated that a monomaniacal scientist could vanish and that a philosopher *manqué* could control everyone—especially me—like puppets. God only knew what he had in store tonight at Aurilla's.

The clouds reared and rumbled as I jogged by Watergate. Glanced up at the ninth-floor balcony, wondering how many months in advance Barnard had paid her rent. Sorry, friend. Some avenger I turned out to be. Suddenly, convulsively, I missed her. While she lived, I was not entirely alone. Now I was last of my kind, unlikely victor of an undeclared war, survival of which had brought desolation rather than glory. I had not foreseen that.

The sky spat warmly at me as I returned to the hotel. On the table was a fresh bouquet of orchids. *Play well tonight.* That put me over the edge so I called Curtis. "Cancel the concert. Tell Aurilla anything you want. I'm not going."

Agent sinking but this was an open line. My manager had to play his part. "What's the problem?"

I began with the most blatant. "Fausto."

"He can't cut it? You've been rehearsing for days."

"He can cut it. I just don't want him there."

"Sorry, that's not reason enough to cancel. Try another."

"I'm not ready," I whimpered. "Fausto picked a ridiculous program."

"You've got five hours. Plenty of time to get your act together. I thought you said no one was going to be listening anyway."

"That's another reason."

"Poor thing," he said without a shred of sympathy. "Tell you what. I'll call Aurilla, you call Fausto. I'm sure he'll understand." Fifteen seconds of silence. "Feeling better?"

I heard the teakettle whistling. Curtis was in the kitchen, probably wearing his plaid apron. Maybe he had a batch of oatmeal cookies in the oven. I violently wished I were home, milk glass in hand, watching his perfect round rump. "Can you come to Washington?" I whimpered.

"Sorry, I'm tied up with your accountants. How's Duncan?"

"Screwing merrily toward Big Bang."

"It'll do him good. Hold on." I heard the oven hinges squeak. "Derschl called this morning. He wants Beethoven the last week of October. I told him no problem."

"What are you baking?"

"Kirschtorte. Just play the concert, Les. People are counting on you."

Ah, Curtis: the mere sound of his voice soothed my wretched life. I couldn't disappoint him, even if I went down in the process. Practiced a little more, trying not to think about Fausto. Not possible so, yielding to temptation, I listened to the cassette Bendix had sent over. His sonata was awful but Fausto's performance was brilliant. Once again, I lusted to get close to the brain behind those sounds: no aphrodisiac like talent. Perhaps I was not completely alone after all. Picked up the phone. "Ready to roll, Fausto?"

"I'm a little nervous, sweet. You're the only person I'd ever admit that to."

"What are you wearing?"

"A tux, naturally."

"Black?"

"Is there any other color?"

"Just checking. Wouldn't want to clash. Are you interested in trying Aurilla's piano?"

"Hell no. It is what it is."

Duncan would have demanded a three-hour dress rehearsal, with tuner present. Then again, Fausto and I were playing charades, not a real concert. "Dinner's at eight. I presume we make noise around ten."

"We forgot about encores. Why don't you come over at six and run through a few."

I spent the rest of the afternoon watching bulletins about Jojo Bailey, who was fading fast. What a crass time for his successor to be throwing a dinner party.

Where the hell was Louis?

Chapter Eight

*D*ESPITE HIS GIRTH, Fausto looked excellent in a tux. Five thumbtack-size diamonds glistened between tie and cummerbund. He had combed his hair straight back, revealing a stark widow's peak. I smelled cologne and excitement. "Eh, you dog."

His round eyes traversed my pink satin gown, upswept hair. "The hell with Aurilla. Let's take my plane to Paris and dance till dawn."

"You dance?"

"Every civilized man does. Oh well. Another time." He swished through the doors to his music room. "Business before pleasure."

As I laid my violin case on the sofa, the downdraft lifted a red feather into the air. It settled near a pillow as I tuned the Strad. Fausto hadn't bothered to straighten the embroidered throw on top of his piano, which now looked like an unmade bed: I found that mildly insulting. "What treasures have you got for me this time?"

"*Flight of the Bumble Bee.* The perfect encore." Cute, but so were most pieces about insects. I played it so fast that he had difficulty keeping up. "Obviously one of your favorites," he breezed afterward. "If they keep clapping, we'll do this."

A Joplin rag immortalized by *The Sting*. Clever piece, but I wasn't in a ragtime mood. "Is all this bug and sting shit one of your inside jokes? Isn't that in rather poor taste, considering Jojo's condition?"

Fausto looked up from the keyboard. "You're taking this seriously?"

"Perhaps you've forgotten. This is how I earn my living."

He burst out laughing. "Oh, you're just a poor widow trying to make ends meet? That's why you're doing this?"

Careful: after all these rehearsals, he knew me too well. "Aurilla called, my manager booked it. Period."

Fausto smiled sourly. "Did your manager tell you to hire me?"

"No, that was spur of the moment. I thought that up all by myself. I wanted to know if you played as well as you talked."

"And?"

I stared at his eyes, his rosy mouth. *Backstroke, Smith.* "We haven't gone onstage yet."

Without a word, he tucked his music into a briefcase and went upstairs. I heard numerous footsteps, then the toilet flush twice: for someone who wasn't taking this concert seriously, my accompanist was exhibiting classic symptoms of stage fright. When he finally came down, he brought more of his mother's jewelry, this time a square brooch paved with sapphires. "Wear this for me, would you? It was her good-luck charm."

Fausto's cold fingers brushed my throat as he pinned it on. I had to admire his choice of weapons: gems and music. "Do you think I need luck?"

"No." He was so quiet en route to Aurilla's that I almost asked if he had taken any tranquilizers. But I kept my mouth shut, just in case he was thinking about his piano part: Duncan always did his most earnest practicing half a mile before show time. Besides, sympathy was useless now.

He looked over. "Sorry I was a little testy before. Thanks for asking me to play with you. You took a huge risk."

I was still taking it. "So did you."

"No matter what happens, I want you to know that you gave me a very happy week." He kissed my hand. "I'll never forget that."

As his skin touched mine I heard soft, ecstatic laughter from a faraway place. I almost asked him to pull over and kiss me again, on the mouth, but that was a dangerous thing to do to your accompanist before a debut performance. So I merely smiled.

We left the Corvette with a valet outside Aurilla's mansion. Since my last visit, her gardeners had planted asters along the front walk. Brass doorknobs gleamed in the fading light. The place looked more like a movie set than ever. "I wonder what she did with Gretchen," I said.

Fausto rang the doorbell. "Let's hope she's upstairs in a straitjacket."

A maid led us to the concert room, a cream and brocade extravaganza about the size of Fausto's but with more chairs. I placed the Saint-Saëns on an ornate music stand. "Sure you don't want to run through anything?"

"Absolutely not. Bad luck."

"Where's the green room?" I asked the maid. "Where musicians hang out beforehand. A room with a toilet." She didn't know what I was talking about: obviously Aurilla didn't sponsor many musicales. I gave her my violin. "Put that upstairs. Keep the door locked."

Fausto handed the maid a stack of lavishly printed programs, instructing her to place one on each chair. We were shown to the backyard, where two dozen guests were tank-ing up at a canopied bar. No manicured fund-raising crowd, this. Aurilla's crew was scruffier and deadlier, the Gamblers Anonymous who had helped her arrive and were prepared to sacrifice everything for a few asterisks in the best-seller that would hit the bookstores in a few years. Aurilla, in a gold-white-black pants suit, looked every ounce the queen bee. Drone Bendix stood at her side, collecting handshakes and collusion. The two of them looked triumphant as newly-weds. Fausto leaned over my ear. "I don't play *Pomp and Circumstance*. Neither do you."

We paid our respects. "Fausto! I'm finally able to reciprocate for all your breakfasts." Aurilla gushing was like an iceberg melting. "We're so looking forward to the program."

She wouldn't be hearing one note. "How's Gretchen?" I asked.

A nanosecond of dead air: who the hell was *that?* "Very well." Aurilla excused herself to speak with some real guests.

Bendix kissed my hand. "I haven't seen that brooch in a while, Fausto."

"Over thirty years since Ethel wore it. Just think."

Whatever the memory, it wasn't pleasant. Bendix turned to me. "What's on the program tonight, Leslie?"

"This and that. Easy listening." Gad, I needed a drink.

"Nervous, Fausto?"

"Hell no. I'm looking forward to it."

Bendix eyed his old friend. "You won't be dancing on top of the piano, will you?" he asked, only half joking.

"Not yet," Fausto replied.

Very few words later, Bendix excused himself. "He smells something," I said.

"Good! He should!"

Whatever their game, I was obviously not included. "I hope you're having fun," I snapped. "I'm not."

"Hold on, sweet. The evening's young." Fausto dredged a shrimp through cocktail sauce. It was almost in his mouth when he spied someone across the patio. "My God! What's she doing here?"

A zaftig redhead, highball in hand, backed away from the bar and into an elderly man, spilling his drink. Something about her looked familiar. "Who's that?"

"Jojo Bailey's girlfriend." Fausto watched her mop tomato juice off the man's tie. "Myrna Block. Maybe she's trawling for a new job."

Ah: that rear end. I had seen it before, in one of the photos Barnard had taken at the environmental conference in Belize. "How long have they been an item?"

"Years. She's one of Jojo's staff. He doesn't go anywhere without her."

"What about his wife?"

"She's a psychiatrist. Can't afford to leave her patients alone too long or they might get better." Lifting a cigarette from an antique gold case, Fausto explained that the old man was New Jersey senator Phil Pixley. Although Pixley had served seven terms with absolutely no distinction, he had been Aurilla's first ally in the Senate, so she owed him a few favors before dropping him. Pixley had just gotten himself reelected for the eighth time by eloping, after sixty years of bachelorhood, with a Latina beauty queen on Halloween night. The Hispanics all voted for him and it was too late for the gays to withdraw their support without looking petty. "Typical Washington marriages. Damn, I could use a drink."

"You're abstaining on my account? I'm flattered."

Fausto exhaled at the stars. "I don't want to let you down. Hello, Wallace. Nice party you've thrown together here."

Aurilla's aide-de-camp smiled. One hundred degrees outside and she was still wearing a poplin suit and stockings. Technically I suppose she was still at the office. "We're so glad you could come." After shaking my hand, she looked anxiously across the yard at her mistress. "Excuse me."

"That's Aurilla's rottweiler," Fausto informed me.

"She looks like a hamster."

"Precisely. Oh God, look what just sailed in."

Vicky Chickering and partner Rhoby Hall. Chickering had dressed for the occasion in one of her flashier tents and plenty of Indian jewelry. She lingered on the porch, wrapping up a cell phone call, while Rhoby fetched drinks. "Bestowing Paula's blessing?" I asked Fausto as they headed toward the hostess.

"Of course. Aurilla's toast without the First Lady behind her. Look out, here they come." Fausto flicked his cigarette into the hedges. "Hello, ladies. How's that traffic jam at the White House, Chickie?"

"Moving right along."

Rhoby took my hand. She was a healthy brunette maybe half Chickie's age and weight. Like her consort, she wore no makeup; unlike her consort, she didn't need any. Her skintight black pants suit revealed muscle rather than curve. I guessed she ran sixty miles a week and hadn't menstruated since Christmas. "I'm Rhoby Hall. I'm really looking forward to the program tonight. I used to play the cello."

"You still play," Chickering corrected. "Very well, too."

"In that case, we'll read a few trios someday," Fausto said. "I've got all the music."

"Oh no! I couldn't! I'm not that good!"

"Yes you are," Chickering corrected again. "Stop apologizing. They'll play with you."

"Victoria, please. I can handle this myself." Rhoby's smile returned when she looked at me. "What's on the program? Aurilla's kept everything so hush-hush."

"Saint-Saëns, Wieniawski, Hubay, and a surprise."

"Uh-oh," Chickering clucked, pausing in whatever she

was scribbling in the little notepad around her neck. "Your idea, Fausto?"

He only smiled. "Bendix's."

Rhoby forced her eyes away from either Fausto's brooch or my cleavage. "Have you two played together before?"

"No. Tonight's our debut."

"Gad! Are you nervous?"

"Terrified."

She couldn't tell whether or not Fausto was joking. "Well, I think it's wonderful Aurilla invited you to play," Rhoby continued. "To tell the truth, I wouldn't have come otherwise."

Chickering's frown now involved her entire face. "Is that a fact? I wish you had told me earlier."

"Victoria, stop it. You're such a wet blanket."

Chickering's glare could have sparked a forest fire. "Excuse us," she commanded, steering Rhoby toward the hedges.

I watched them commence a peppery dialogue. "Rhoby must be the only person in Washington not terrified of the old girl."

"That's why the old girl needs her. Poor Chickering. One blessed day she's going to pay for that weakness." He lifted a snail from a passing platter. "Everyone does sooner or later. Desire is the ticket to destruction."

I looked calmly at his round eyes. "What do you desire?"

"The most impossible prize of all, darling. Time." He chuckled. "You?"

I looked over the lawn full of dedicated, desirous people, all closing in on that pot of gold at the end of the rainbow. Too many of them had the suicidally exultant look of skiers zipping downhill ten feet ahead of an avalanche. "I don't want anything."

"You do realize that wanting nothing is the greatest desire

of all. Fortunately I don't believe you." His fingertips brushed my cheek. "And you're blushing."

His darts were landing a little too close so I went inside to check on my violin. The frazzled maid sent me upstairs with a key ring and instructions to open the first door on my left. I obeyed, only to interrupt Chickering deep in discussion with Wallace. They were probably hashing out seating plans at Aurilla's swearing-in. Chickering broke off in midsentence, glaring as I said, "Excuse me. The maid told me first door on my left. I'm just checking my violin."

"It's across the hall," Wallace said pleasantly. "Can you find it?"

Duh, I think so. "Sorry."

My Strad lay unharmed on a chaise longue. Someone familiar with backstages had provided water, fruit, and extra toilet paper. Didn't see Gretchen under the bed with a blow torch so I returned downstairs. Fausto was chatting nebulously with strangers. I huddled at his side like a chick with mother hen. Soon the dinner bell drew everyone to a pale peach room where round tables floated like gigantic lily pads beneath a chandeliered sky. Nine pieces of silverware and three goblets outfitted each Limoges plate. Bouquets and candlesticks vied for the remaining open space. Beneath portraits of illustrious Perles, Aurilla's butlers awaited her signal to empty the kitchen.

"Impressed?" I asked my accompanist.

"Worth the trip."

We were busted to musicians' ghetto in the darkest corner along with the other least consequential guests, namely Myrna Block, Senator and Mrs. Pixley, and a Mr. Tanqueray Tougaw, all of whom seemed quite drunk already. Poor Myrna could not blather three sentences without crying, but her social status was about to go six feet under with Jojo. Pixley sported quite a tomato splotch on his tie. His twentyish bride Pila was insulted to be seated next to Tougaw, a black man wearing twice as much gold as she. Twice Pila told a butler that there must be some mistake, then settled into a loud pout with her martini. Tougaw I couldn't place. Maybe he was a cricket player.

After introductions and a toast, Tougaw got things off to a rocky start by asking Myrna how Jojo was feeling. "Horrible," she wept, not at all indignant that a complete stranger knew about her liaison with the vice president. "He's unrecognizable."

"Now now," consoled Pixley, donating his handkerchief. "Nothing you can do about these tropical diseases. Everybody down there catches 'em."

"One day he was fine," Myrna sobbed. Her curls and breasts shook when she blew her nose. "Just a little headache from the heat. A few aspirin and it went away. He made a terrific speech. Next day he was still fine except for another headache. But he had made every meeting on the agenda. Next day he was sick as a dog. I don't understand."

"You catch de dengue from de mosquito," Tougaw said in a lovely tropical drawl. I lost my breath, momentarily flung into a writhing jungle.

"Everyone knows how you catch it," Myrna snapped. "Why did one have to bite Jojo?"

"He mus' have de sweetes' skin." Smiling at his brilliant deduction, Tougaw lifted his glass. "To a fine gen'leman. May his suffrin' soon be ovah."

Pixley shook his head as Myrna fled the table. "She's a nice girl but none too bright. Headaches from the heat, my foot. Bailey was sloshed from the beginning to end of that conference. He could have been bitten by a tiger and not felt it."

Tougaw looked up from his chestnut soup. "You were dere?"

"Of course." Pixley puffed like an adder. "I'm the number one environmentalist on the Hill."

"You're the oldest one, at any rate." Pila Pixley drained her glass as if it contained Kool-Aid.

"Jojo got his green conscience from me," her husband continued after a generous little laugh. "I knew his daddy from the minute he came to Washington. Now there was an outstanding public servant. One of the best secretaries of state we ever had."

That explained Jojo's refuge in the bottle and perhaps Louis's refuge in the jungle. Two tables away, Rhoby Hall beamed at me. "So politics runs in the family?" I asked.

"Absolutely. Old Bailey intended to be president himself. Ironic that Jojo, who's a mere shadow of his father, would get within a heartbeat. Ah well. It's all a crap shoot."

"How amazing that Jojo alone got dengue," I said. "Considering all the people who went to the conference with him."

"Madame is missing of information," Tougaw broke in. "Dere be two more suffrin' as we speak. But we do not read of dem in American newspapahs. Dey be Belizean school-girls who performed one afternoon."

Right: Barnard had taken a picture of Paula Marvel and the obligatory dancing locals. "They were so cute," Pixley cried. "Why didn't I hear of this before?"

"They don't vote," his wife sniffed. "Will they die, too?"

"Dey are younger," Tougaw said diplomatically. "Stronger."

Pixley whipped out his gold pen. "What are their names? We'll send flowers."

"Babette and Iris Auclair." Tougaw paused as a waiter removed his soup. "Dey stay at Dr. Tatal's dengue ward in Belize City. Sain' Elizabet'. It is de place to go for dese sicknesses."

Obviously news of Tatal's death had not yet made it to Washington. My heart skittered into my throat as Fausto said, "Are you a friend of hers, Mr. Tougaw?"

"Oh yes. I see her at de conference. She introduce me to vera important people."

"Aha." No more questions. Maybe Fausto was too beset by preperformance demons to continue.

Myrna blubbered back to the table. "I'm sorry. I have to pull myself together."

"That's the spirit," Pixley bellowed, positioning his empty glass beneath a butler's upended wine bottle. "Life goes on. You have too many good years ahead of you to let something like this bog you down."

Aurilla Perle, who had been slowly working over the room, now blessed us with her attention. "How's everything here?"

"Couldn't be better." Pixley kissed her hand. The gesture looked less like gallantry than a plea for mercy. "Fantastic meal you've cooked up, Senator."

The soon to be ex-senator wisely skipped over Pila. "How are the musicians?"

"Fine," Fausto replied for both of us. "Thank you."

"Tanqueray?"

"Dis is de bes' evening of my life."

"I'm so glad to hear that. And how are you, Myrna?"

"I'll be all right."

One big fucking country club. Worse, I was just one of the golf balls. As Aurilla transferred her unsmile to the next section of minions, I realized that someday she would be president. Ghastly thought, not because the woman wasn't bright, persuasive, or connected. Maybe she even had principles. But I had seen that same bloodless glint in a mercenary's eye in a run-down Belizean café. I had seen it in the obsidian gaze of the fer-de-lance that killed Yvette Tatal. It wasn't a human look. Bobby Marvel didn't have it, but his wife did. Bendix, too. Fausto was capable of it. I conjured a weak variant of that look each time I walked onstage, but I was just a musician, my foe imperfection. The look got more evil as the stakes got less noble. Those eyes in the Oval Office? Look out, America.

Aurilla's departure left a reverent hole in conversation, which Myrna filled by asking Pixley for highlights of his career. The senator was delighted to furnish a Homeric history that took us through a rack of venison, a fussy composed salad, fiery sorbet, and many more glasses of wine. He finished with the recent funeral of one of his colleagues in the Congressional Cemetery, where Pixley hoped to repose someday himself. The place was a mess, though. Scandalously neglected, a national disgrace, an insult to the patriots buried there.

Finally Pila Pixley, who had been playing footsie with Tougaw ever since her husband's riveting account of JFK's assassination, couldn't take any more. "Will you stop!" she cried. "Who's going to visit you in a cemetery?"

Pixley switched to a soppy paean to Aurilla Perle, spewing encomia as if the candlesticks were bugged. Maybe, deep down, he knew as well as the rest of us that once she was sworn in, all the doors he had opened for her would be slammed in his face.

"A vera intrestin' story," Tougaw said as a waiter removed his panne cotta and fresh currants. "But did you not meet otha fine women in Washington? Marilyn Monroe?"

"She was a sweet girl with a nice voice." Becoming melancholy now, Pixley took a long drink. "And I'll never forget Ethel Kiss. She was magnificent."

"I just told you to cut out the dead stuff," Pila snorted.

Fausto's entire bulk became still as earth. Beneath the table, I touched his thigh.

"Who was dis?" Tougaw persisted.

"Fausto's mother. She was lovely. Talented. A princess. She made us all laugh. The whole town came to a standstill when—when we lost her. It hasn't been the same since." Pixley looked across the table. "I still miss her, Fausto."

"Don't we all."

Silence as the waiters brought coffee and chocolates: after this repast, Aurilla would have better served her guests with a three-mile hike, not a concert. "Tell us about Jackie O," Pila said.

"She's dead," Pixley snapped.

Fausto licked the vestiges of cream from an antique spoon. "Heard from Louis lately, Myrna?"

"No. Nothing. He's somewhere in the jungle. Probably Belize, but no one knows for sure. We won't hear from him until it's too late."

"Madman," Pixley said. "What's he doing there?"

"The usual. Boiling plants."

"Who is Louis?" Tougaw asked.

"Jojo's brother. He's a scientist."

"Does he know Jojo's sick?" Fausto's voice rose a tiny notch. I noticed, but I had been listening for it.

"I doubt it. We don't know where he is and we're not about to send a search party into the rain forest. Last time we did that, they were gone for two months. I don't hold out much hope that he'll make the funeral." Myrna edged close to sobs again. "When was the last time you heard from him, Fausto?"

"June sometime."

Tougaw was impressed. "De jungle is a dangerous place. He goes alone?"

"Sometimes he takes an assistant," Myrna said. "A Mayan boy. I forget his name."

Fausto didn't offer it. "Louis will turn up. He always does."

"Now there's a man who should've gone into politics," Pixley boomed. "He had all the right stuff. Twice the brains of his brother. Sorry, Myrna."

"Jojo has more personality," she retorted, conceding the brains.

"Old Bailey thought Louis was going to carry on the family tradition. Then I remember the boy went abroad. England, I think. Something disgraceful happened. His father nearly died of shame. Know anything about that, Myrna?"

"That was before my time."

Pixley's glass clanked his plate as he replaced it, empty again, on the table. "That's the game. One little slip and you're out, sometimes before you've even started. Something always comes back to bite you in the ass. At times I wonder how I've managed to survive all these years."

By farting with the wind, of course. Everyone knew that, including Pixley. "Soon you can retire," Tougaw said brightly. "Move to Florida."

Pixley glared at him. "I hate Florida. Nothing but swamps and mosquitoes."

Far away, Aurilla tinkled Reed & Barton against Waterford. Fausto folded his napkin, looked over at me. "Excuse us. Musicians are not required to stay for speeches."

I followed him to the foyer. "Wasn't that a fascinating dinner?" he asked. "No one paid the slightest attention to you but Rhoby Hall, and the poor girl was two tables away."

The maid took us to the bedroom directly above the speeches. My violin was untouched. "What a fairy tale," Fausto said, flopping onto the bed. The canopy didn't collapse but its ruffles flounced like startled geese.

I sat next to him. "How do you feel?"

"I'm still dying for a drink."

"You didn't eat much."

"I will later."

"Nervous?"

"Just excited. I'm so looking forwa—" Bolting upright, Fausto peered at my face in horror, as if it had sprouted mushrooms.

"What's the matter?"

He outstretched his arms and slowly wiggled his fingers, staring at them as he had at my face. His complexion went from pink to gray. "Lock the door, Leslie." As I obeyed, he unhooked his cummerbund, removed his pants: surprisingly shapely legs in yellow silk shorts. "Please do as I say. In a moment I'm going to be sick. Don't be scared. Don't call for help. It will go away." Fausto slid his arms into the pants, crossed them in front. "Tie me in back. I don't want to be smashing any of Aurilla's treasures. You can gag me with the cummerbund if you like. Don't worry about my tongue. I won't swallow it." I knotted him up. Seconds after he lay on the bed, Fausto's blue eyes slid out of sight, into his skull. His body went rigid then snapped into convulsions, as if he were on the receiving end of a thirty-thousand-volt prod. Aurilla's antique bed began to hop. As I was pushing the night tables out of range, Fausto broke into tormented snarls. When they turned fortissimo, I gagged him. A pillow over the face would have been more effective, but I didn't dare: those tremors were already taxing his body to the point of collapse. Twice Fausto almost fell out of bed. Took all my strength to keep him from hitting the floor: that would put a dent in palaver below. Already Aurilla's guests would be misinterpreting the commotion above their heads.

After a few horrible minutes, the tremors stilled. Fausto's body stank, as if he had been half-fried. Red patches spattered his skin. When his eyeballs regained their proper axis, they were bloodshot. "What happened?" he whispered.

"You fainted," I said, untying him. "Stage fright."

He ran a heavy hand over my disheveled hair. "I don't think so." He shut his eyes. "Damn, I'm going to vomit."

I got one of Aurilla's frilly wastebaskets under his mouth just in time. Up came deer, truffles, sorbet: the stench almost brought my dinner up as well. "Sorry," Fausto rasped, dropping his head back to the embroidered pillow sham. "It's almost over."

As I was getting rid of his puke, he slumped against the bathroom door. His shirt was unbuttoned. Without pants, he looked helpless as a little boy. A gigantic little boy. "Just throw me in the shower, would you, sweet."

"Are you mad? Go lie down!"

"Please, I've been through this before. Just get the clothes off. My fingers are still numb."

Modesty did not exist backstage ten minutes to show time. I stripped him naked and flipped on the shower. As he stepped in, I saw hideous swirls of scar tissue running from shoulder to thigh: third-degree burns. Once, under the spray, he shuddered. I thought he would go into convulsions again. But he held on. "Okay," he said.

I turned off the water, handed him a towel. He dried off what he could reach, namely, a penis hiding beneath a convexity of flesh. I dried the rest. "Those are bad burns."

"Penance."

I got his clothes back on and plopped him in the chaise longue. Fausto slept while I repaired my face and hair. Downstairs, shuffling and laughter as Aurilla's guests migrated to her next party room. I finally had to wake him. "Are you up for this? Tell the truth."

He managed a wilted smile. "You've got the hard part."

"What if you have a relapse out there?"

"I'll fight it." He half sat up. "I didn't intend for you to see me like that."

"I've seen Duncan worse," I lied. "Look, let's cut out a few pieces. Aurilla's not going to sit there with a stopwatch. It's so damn late already."

The maid knocked. "Hello? *Scusi?* Downstairs now?"

"Coming," I called. Tuned the violin, feeling cold inside: the old demons were back. I would have given ten years of my life to be home in Berlin, eating kirschtorte. But I smiled at Fausto. "Let's go, champ."

He pulled himself together the moment we went public: a born performer, as he had said. We shuffled downstairs. In the concert room, spotlights brightened the piano and, over the fireplace, a recent portrait of the hostess; elsewhere, illumination was mercifully dim. Aurilla stood under the glare introducing the entertainment as if we were her running mates. Despite the hour, not one of her guests had dared leave: they knew this party was the first skirmish in a four-year war of attrition. Fortunately the heat, darkness, and general intoxication would carry them off to La-La Land minutes after the hostess took her seat in the front row.

"Psst! Miss Frost!" Daughter Gretchen, flanked by two maids, sat just inside the door. Someone had dressed her in a pinafore and gigantic hairband, perhaps in the hope that, looking like Alice in Wonderland, she would behave as such. She was holding a small stuffed animal. "Mom said I could listen."

A suit interrupted. "This will just take a second," he apologized, stroking Fausto and me with a metal detector. My brooch made it nervous but the Kiss trinkets had that effect on everything.

"Marvel's inside," I told Fausto as he straightened his mother's sapphires.

"Who cares?" Applause: I wanted to evaporate here, condense anywhere else. Fausto patted my rear. "Go earn your living, widow."

We walked to the front, where Aurilla stood applauding our entrance. Two air kisses, then she nestled between Bendix and Bobby Marvel, whose wife had stayed home tonight. Chickering filled in at the president's side. Next to her, Rhoby Hall clapped furiously.

Fausto gave me a soft A. I tuned, caught in that terrifying chasm between contact and chaos. Was he going to make it? Then I heard a perfect introduction to the Saint-Saëns. He did what we had talked about in rehearsal, only more so: Fausto was one of those magical accompanists with whom it would be impossible to play badly. He forced me to listen to him because he reinvented as we went along, daring me to respond to the tiniest change of accent, a fleck of rubato: performers didn't try this without monumental reserves of confidence. The last time I had felt such electricity was years ago, in Vienna, with my future husband Hugo conducting. There had been a thousand concerts since then, all decent enough to leave me satisfied, my audience impressed, my agent paid. But once every aeon, maybe three or four times a career if you were lucky, the gods gave you a break and brought you into their fold. In between, just to keep you going, they sprinkled the divine dust on you for a phrase here, a movement there, but never from first note to last. The only musicians who reached ecstasy regularly were the composers, the creators, but they didn't have to contend with real time and human frailty. Performers got hit with memory slips, stage fright, cold halls, elephantine orchestras . . . the odds were against them from the first note. Somehow, tonight, Fausto was doing the impossible. I wasn't that surprised: he had genius. But I never thought he'd share it with me.

We rolled with Saint-Saëns, Hubay, Wieniawski. Five feet away, but in another world, Aurilla counted notches in the ceiling, exactly as Paula Marvel had at the White House.

This time Bobby stayed awake, studying the sway of my hips as if I were a belly dancer. Bendix listened to our musical oddities because he had to. Chickering scribbled repeatedly in the pad around her neck, earning black looks from Rhoby. Aurilla's shadow Wallace sat straight as a ramrod, blinking occasionally. The rest of the audience either dozed off or tried to look beatific as they fought to keep digestive gases under control. Aliens, all of them.

"Now for that little surprise you see on your program," Fausto announced from the keyboard. "In appreciation of Bendix Kaar, who is highly responsible for having brought us together tonight, we would like to perform a sonata he wrote over thirty years ago. The slow movement is an elegy. We'd like to dedicate it to Vice President Bailey, who is in all our thoughts tonight."

Bendix's mouth dropped open. Aurilla frowned: surprises in this town were generally fatal. Marvel was all smiles. "I didn't know you composed, Ben," he called over the applause.

Having been led to believe they would be hearing something melodious, the audience was unprepared for grating tone clusters. Their wrinkled noses and sidelong glances reminded me of children smelling boiled turnips. No one dared walk out, of course. Fausto and I continued to perform expertly. But the piece didn't fly. Never would. It was first cousin to fingernails scraping blackboard.

Bobby and Aurilla never relinquished their utterly delighted smiles. Bendix looked ready to burst into flames, but this sonata was his proud, perfect child, blossom of his blood: each note clawed at his soul. He was overwhelmed to hear it again but furious that Fausto had reduced him to postprandial bonbon. Ah, poor composer, forever misprized! Which was the greater torment, oblivion or botched resurrection?

By the time Fausto and I got to the elegy, the audience, with the exception of the front row, had slipped back into its torpor. Even Fausto got bored for a few measures. Then several rows back, down by the shoes, I thought I saw a ball of black dart across the aisle. Long tail. Rat? Too round. Monkey? Unbelievable, not here. Then I remembered the lump in Gretchen's lap.

I kept playing, bracing for a shriek that never came. Perhaps the animal had curled up harmlessly in someone's pocketbook. Once, at a summer festival, a skunk had wandered in, traversed the open-air theater, and left; Gretchen's pet could do the same. Then I noticed a ripple across the fifth row. Furball on the move. I concentrated on a nasty set of trills. When I finished, Aurilla's eyebrows had risen a good inch. A split second later, I heard why.

The monkey had jumped into the piano, burying Bendix's elegy in an avalanche of twangs. "Bloody hell!" Fausto snapped, looking inside the lid. The ensuing scream would have knocked King Kong off the Empire State Building. A Secret Service agent, leaping from a side chair, threw Bobby to the carpet. Another slammed the lid of the piano. Vicky Chickering fainted.

A second shriek, piercing as a train whistle, froze the room. "Herman! He killed Herman!" The wails gradually receded as Gretchen was carted upstairs.

From the sound of things, Herman was not only alive but multiplying. I stepped over Marvel to get to Fausto. Flushed, wheezing: last thing we needed here was a reprise of his performance in the bedroom. "Are you all right?"

"What was that filthy beast?"

"Gretchen's pet monkey."

"Oh God! That's too funny!"

Bendix didn't think so. He flung up the piano lid, grabbed the terrified animal by the neck, and stormed out. Aurilla kneeled over Bobby as her dismayed audience whispered nervously, wondering how to react. Chickering, regaining consciousness, slid like a giant amoeba back into her seat in the first row. Finally the president was helped to his feet, having suffered only a minor rug burn on the tip of his nose.

"Now that's what I call a rip-roaring performance," he announced with a twenty-tooth smile. Everyone laughed and clapped. "Thank you both!" I got a hug and sloppy kiss. Fausto was embraced like a brother. "And thank you, Aurilla, for a thrilling evening! Never a dull moment, eh!"

Her smile returned about three seconds into her standing ovation. When that finally died down, the gracious hostess thanked her musicians, as if our concert had come to a natural end, then her chef, then Bobby Marvel, her eloquence thickening as she ascended the social ladder. Guests surrounded her for a farewell blessing as the butlers returned with more coffee, brandy, and chocolates.

Chickering shuffled to the piano bench, leaning heavily on Rhoby Hall. "You're a man of many talents, Fausto."

He remained seated. "I was inspired. Feeling better now?"

"Much. Did Bendix really write that sonata? I had no idea he had a musical background."

"Ask him about it sometime. Did you like the piece?"

Chickering took cover in the mother of all insults. "It's interesting."

Rhoby pumped my hand. "You gave me the shivers!"

"Let's play together sometime," I said.

Myrna, eyes red and rough as bricks, hugged Fausto. "At least someone in this rat hole thinks of Jojo. What a gorgeous piece. I was beside myself! Until that dreadful animal got loose."

"Really, Myrna," Chickering scoffed. "We should send it a dozen roses."

Rhoby was mortified. "You don't know a thing about modern music, Victoria. All you can play is Mozart. Stop wolfing down those chocolates, would you? Geez!"

Fausto squeezed my hand: time to blow this joint. "Stay here," I said. "I'll get our things." Leaving him with the ladies, I worked my way down the clogged aisles. A few people interrupted their impromptu policy meetings to nod at me. Tougaw, brandy in hand, stood at the door.

"You are so fine," he said. "But how 'bout naughty Herman. He goes back to Belize."

I went upstairs to the guest room, where a faint odor of vomit still mingled with potpourri. Sight of the rumpled bed stopped me cold: last time I had seen such distressed sheets, Barnard's body had sprawled thereupon. Sorry, friend: I was no closer to finding her murderer than I had been that first night in Washington. I had even let her corpse get away from me. Suddenly I felt a rush of guilt for being here, dressed in satin and sapphires, making music while Barnard rotted in a secret grave.

The heavy door clicked shut. Bendix: for a moment I thought he'd strangle me. "I hope you two amused yourselves."

"Not really. Your piece was harder than hell." I picked up Fausto's music bag. "I get about ten manuscripts a week from composers all over the world. In a year maybe three of them make the cut. I accepted yours sight unseen."

"Why tonight? Why here?"

"Why not? You wrote the piece. You don't own it."

"That bastard did it to humiliate me."

"I would have thought he paid you the ultimate compliment."

"That's not the way Fausto works." Bendix boiled quietly, dangerously, like a cauldron of lead. "He'll pay for this."

"Oh stop it. If you hadn't noticed, this was his first recital in thirty years. You can't blame him for going with pieces he's done before."

"He hasn't done this piece before. You just played the world premiere."

What was I missing here? "But his mother's writing is all over the score."

"She died before the first performance. Fausto didn't tell you? I suppose you don't know each other as well as I thought." The composer's fury intensified as he looked at the disheveled bed. "All that noise and no communication. How do you two screw, by the way? Sideways?"

I tucked my violin case under an arm. "Thank that monkey for me, would you?"

"Get out." Bendix dropped to the bed, lost his face in the pillow. "Just get out."

Guilt rolled over me: I had just stomped on a failed artist. That was on a par with mugging grandmothers and tearing the wings off butterflies. "I liked the trills in the elegy," I said from the door.

Bendix didn't acknowledge the compliment. I carted my things downstairs, afraid that he might trample me from behind, like a gored bull. Fortunately Fausto had maneuvered himself to the crowded foyer, where he was rubbing date books with Rhoby Hall between slugs of champagne. He looked not only sharp, but energetic: incredible, after what his body had just been through. "Up for Brahms trios tomorrow night?" he called over the din.

Hadn't he wrecked enough evenings with music? "Should you be drinking that?"

He had also cadged a large sandwich from the butler. "Hard work up there, darling. Have a bite."

Pileup at the front door: Marvel leaving. As he was shaking Aurilla's hand for their hundredth good-bye, he glanced over and up, found me on the staircase. For just a second, his jaw stilled, eyes flared: I felt like a dinghy caught in a light-house beam. Bobby had flashed me the same look at Ford's Theatre last week. This time Aurilla caught it. Across the room, I saw her face change: she had learned something. The information would be tucked away, retrieved when most useful. Bobby didn't know it yet, but he had just lost a pawn.

Chickering wrapped an acquisitive arm around her lover. "Time to go, Rhoby. You've got to get to work."

"Forget it! I'm calling in sick! Tonight I'm practicing Brahms!"

"You go to work at this hour?" I asked innocently.

"Graveyard shift at the FBI," she replied. "You can call me there after midnight."

As Fausto burst into laughter, Chickering realized too late that she should have left Rhoby home. "What is so funny?" she demanded.

"Nothing that concerns you!" Fausto chomped his sand-wich. "Please tell Mrs. Marvel we missed her tonight. You were so kind to come in her stead. And to bring along your delightful partner."

Rhoby nearly curtseyed. "Can you check your date book and call me ASAP?" she asked me.

"No problem. I just dial the FBI and ask for you?"

"Right."

Chickering lugged her away. "What are you up to, Fausto?" I asked.

"Nothing! I thought you liked chamber music!"

"You're doing this to torment Chickering."

"And you're not?" He washed down the sandwich with the rest of his champagne. "Let's go. I'm beat."

Senator Pixley dammed traffic at the front door as he bab-bled with Aurilla about forming a committee to restore the

Congressional Cemetery to its erstwhile grandeur. "Scandalous," he kept repeating. "Weeds up to your knees!"

"I'll look into it," she finally snapped. "Good night." Her composure returned after she had processed the dozen myrmidons ahead of us. "Leaving so soon, Fausto?"

"Breakfast at six," he replied with a loud smooch. "You know how it is. Where's Bendix? The least he could do is thank us for playing his piece."

"He's inside with his guests, I'm sure."

Still no apology for the monkey. On the one hand, that burned my ass. On the other hand, we had been spared the brutal fugue at the end of Bendix's sonata. "Give our love to Gretchen," I said, shaking her mother's hand. "We're so glad she could make it."

Aurilla turned to the next in line.

By the time we reached Fausto's Corvette, his second wind had blown away. Plopping like wet concrete onto the passenger seat, he said nothing until we were back on the freeway. "God, what a night."

I took his hand. "You're a great pianist."

"Thanks for indulging me, sweet. I owe you." He closed his eyes. "Next time I promise we'll play real music."

I zipped past a BMW that was going only twenty miles over the limit. "I saw Bendix afterward. He was a little agitated."

"He'll calm down. Bet you a thousand bucks he kills the monkey, though."

"Can you tell me something? Why did you play his piece?"

"Someone occasionally needs to remind Bendix that he has feet of clay. That's what friends are for, after all."

"You reminded him all right. He intends to pay you back."

"He can't do that, sweet. He doesn't know what I want."

More inverse riddles: I had had enough of them tonight. "I don't understand. Aren't old friends the only ones you can trust in this town? Look at the Marvels. They've paved the White House with people they went to high school with."

"Old friends are a double-edged sword. They know all your youthful follies."

"So you know a few of Bendix's deep, dark secrets. If you haven't spilled them already, why would you now? And if they're so bad, why hasn't he shut you up by now?" Dumb questions: secrets were blue-chip stocks. Only a fool would cash them in before maximum appreciation. "Some friendship you've got."

"Ah, Leslie, let us play our little games. It's how we keep each other going."

I ran a red light. "How'd Bendix hook up with Aurilla?"

"They met on some island about ten years ago. She was on vacation and he was on a business trip. After Aurilla's hubby kicked the bucket, they got down to serious business. Took a gamble on Bobby and it paid off. They're right where they want to be now. It was a matter of luck as much as perseverance."

"What does Bendix want out of this?"

"The taste of victory, love. He'll never get it writing music." Fausto rubbed his puffy eyes. "It's probably my mother's fault. She filled him with glorious tales of Washington when she came to visit me at school. No surprise that the White House became Bendix's alternative Everest."

"Does he want to be president?"

"No, no. Much better to be an éminence grise like me."

I left the Beltway. "Aurilla sure knows how to repay you for all those breakfasts. I never sat at such a table of losers. Myrna's pathetic. Pixley's a psycho. All that raving about cemeteries was bizarre."

"He's been in the Senate over forty years. What do you expect?"

"Who was that fellow Tougaw?"

"Aurilla's designated eavesdropper. She had one at every table."

"Nobody said anything important."

"No? You weren't listening very hard, then."

Silence as Fausto dozed and I tried to figure out what important bits of gossip I had missed. Unenlightened, I crawled the car down his quiet street, past willows, high gates . . . phone taps. Killed the engine but he didn't move. For a terrible moment, I thought he was dead. Touched his lips, felt his slow breath. Still with me, thank God. Without him I wouldn't last a day in this jungle. "Fausto," I whispered.

He slowly turned his head. "Home?"

"Can you make it inside?"

"I think so." He took a few deep breaths. "Just walk me to the door, if you would."

I walked him to his bedroom, a gigantic space above his concert hall. A beautiful Pisarro hung over the fireplace. Elsewhere, Turner and another Rembrandt: Fausto kept his best paintings private. Exhausted, he stood at the foot of his bed as I began undressing him for the second time that evening. I put his diamond tacks on a dresser laden with pictures and sterling hairbrushes. While he was in the bathroom, I took a closer look at the photographs. Fausto had been a very handsome boy: tall, slim, Lisztian. He resembled his mother, whom Senator Pixley had described perfectly. I could understand why Washington had stumbled without her. Fausto and Ethel posed in front of Swiss alps, London bridges, Carnegie Hall, the White House, looking proud and mischievous, either on the verge of a great joke or the tail of a great concert.

The bathroom door creaked open. Fausto stared a moment, as if he had forgotten bringing me here. "You remind me of her, all dressed up like that."

I laid Ethel's brooch next to her pictures. "I see why you miss her. Who's that?"

"Lydia Varnas. My piano teacher. She used to travel with us."

The gorgeous boy, now a bloated ruin, shuffled under the covers. What had gone wrong? Other sons had survived—nay, overcome—the deaths of their mothers. Fausto had had more than enough cause to pick up the pieces and continue. But what did I know? Everyone had a breaking point. The unlucky ones reached theirs too soon, before a thousand middling disappointments could fuse into a protective shield around the heart. I went to his bed. "Are you going to be all right?"

He knew I wasn't referring to the hours between now and his next breakfast party. "Do me a favor," he whispered. "Stay here tonight."

I turned my back. "Unzip me."

Fausto's hand crept down my bared spine, slowing as it came to a three-inch scar, souvenir of a wayward Austrian bullet. "What's this?"

"Penance. Maybe my sins weren't as great as yours." Ha. I was just a little more adept at postponing retribution. I let my pink gown slide to the floor. He saw the crude stitches on my thigh. "Biking accident," I explained.

"Please don't shower," he said, lifting the sheets.

I shut out the light. "You like stinky women?"

"I like the smell of you. It's even more intense after a concert." Moving with the unrushed, luscious sensuality of large people, he sniffed my sternum, throat, chin, stopping an inch from my lips. "Does it feel strange to be here?"

"No."

He kissed my lips. A warm tide of lust overtook me but I dared not lead this dance: perhaps Fausto didn't know the steps. "Will it feel strange in the morning?" he continued.

"I hope not."

He kissed me again. A finger played with my hair, a nipple. Then, to my dismay, he rolled back to his own pillow. "If you're gone when I wake up, I'll understand." He caressed my shoulder in the dark. "Just do it quietly. It would kill me to hear you go."

I brought my mouth inches from his. "What happened to you tonight?"

"A few wires got crossed. It's happened before. Nothing to worry about."

"You take medication for it?"

"Not now. I haven't had a spell in years."

"What brings it on?"

"Causes unknown."

"But you can tell when it's about to happen."

"Everything becomes outlined in brilliant turquoise. Then I have about a minute."

I remembered him staring in horror at his hands. "Last time this happened, you got those burns, didn't you."

He didn't answer for a while. "I was smoking in bed when the blitz came."

"You'll call your doctor in the morning?"

"Promise."

I returned to my pillow. For a while we both stared at the ceiling. "Why do you think Aurilla invited me to play tonight?" I asked.

"I was just asking myself the same question."

"Do you think she knew I would bring you along?"

"No. She doesn't have that much imagination."

Pauses between question and answer were becoming ever longer. Fausto drifted off while I stared at the ceiling, again reconstructing dinner: who had said what that I should have caught? From the slobbering Myrna, nothing but lachrymose details of Jojo's heroics at the environmental conference. Aspirin hadn't helped and no one was even looking for brother Louis. From Tougaw, zip except that a couple of Belizean schoolgirls had also fallen sick with dengue. Pixley was a tapestry of senile bathos, obsessed with burial at the Congressional Cemetery and his own flimsy shadow over American history. He had mentioned Louis's uh-oh at Oxford. That was all.

Hour by hour, lust dissipated into pale, unslaked fatigue. Fausto had chosen sleep over me: insult or blessing? Outside, a few birds began to twitter. The hour of love and here I lay, not daring to wake a man up. I silently gathered my things and left in disgrace, praying he would open his eyes and miss me.

Chapter Nine

*A*S THE FINAL insult of a humiliating daybreak, the gray
Chevy followed me away from Fausto's. Driver made no at-
tempt to be discreet but this morning I was too weary to respond. He cut away as I pulled up to the hotel: sorry, pal.
We'd play tag when I felt like punching again. I crawled into
bed then called Rhoby Hall, whose shift at the FBI was
about over. "I checked my calendar. Tonight's good for me.
What time were you and Fausto thinking of rehearsing?"

"Six o'clock?" she asked back.

"Fine."

"The B Major Trio, right? I don't want to be practicing
the wrong one!"

Whatever it was, I'd be sight-reading it. "Could you let
him know?"

"Sure! God! I'm so excited!"

Take an aspirin and call me after ten thousand concerts. I
didn't really give a damn about Rhoby and her phone skills
at the FBI. I wanted to see Fausto again: chamber music furnished the perfect excuse for doing so. He'd be eating breakfast now—if he had awakened at all. Had he remembered
anything of last night? Fits? Kisses? Fingers in my hair?

Would he be ashamed that I had undressed him twice and he hadn't risen to the occasion once? Probably not: how infuriating.

Duncan pounded on the door. "I know you're in there! Open up!"

"Good morning, dear." No problem with the seersucker suit and white bucks. But the white hat made him look like a reject from a barbershop quartet. "Coming or going?"

"Going. I have important NEA business today."

"How'd Justine like Cleveland?"

"We didn't go. Something came up." He strode to the phone and ordered breakfast. "Get my coffee here in five minutes or start looking for a new job."

"That's a nice line," I said as he helped himself to a Coke from my minibar. "Where'd you learn it?"

He frowned at my smooth bed. "You didn't sleep here last night."

"Did you?"

"Yes." Duncan burped loudly. "I hear the concert was a howling success. Except for the very end. What do you call a monkey? An act of God? Serves you right."

"The only person who suffered was Bendix Kaar."

"Serves him right, too. He bought the monkey."

Jesus, Duncan was quicker than CNN at getting the poop these days. "For someone who refused to go, you sure know a lot about the concert."

"A man's got to be informed. Especially when some schmuck's trying to elbow him out of a job." Back at the minibar, Duncan twisted open a tiny bottle of rum.

I watched him pour it into his Coke. "Learn that from your girlfriend, too?"

"You'd be surprised at what I've learned. So! Do you still think Fausto's got fingers like cigars?"

"He's not bad," I lied. "For someone who hasn't practiced in thirty years."

"Only 'not bad'? Why'd you sleep with him, then?"

"Who says I slept with him?"

"You went to his house afterward. You only left an hour ago."

I sat on the bed. "Okay, Duncan. Why is Justine spying on me?"

"You're absolutely *paranoid!*" he screeched, guzzling the last of his drink. "She couldn't care less about you! Someone calls *her!* She doesn't ask for the fucking information!"

"Who calls her?"

"How should I know? Some guy. He paged her at six o'clock this morning."

"And she called back?" I picked up the phone. "Get me the number. Now." He still balked. "If you ever want to walk on a stage with me again."

That did it. "This is Mr. Zadinsky, room 507. Yes, I know I'm calling from 508, don't be a wise-ass! I made a phone call an hour or so ago. . . . What? No, from 507! I need to know the number. Just get it!" He scratched furiously on a hotel pad. "Where's my breakfast? What kind of room service do you run in this clip joint?" He slammed down the phone and threw the paper at me. "There. I hope you're happy."

I blinked: Justine had called Louis Bailey's home in Virginia. Careless woman! "She talked with a man at this number?"

"She answered a page from that number! What are you going to do about it? Go there and beat him up?"

Not if he had booby-trapped the joint like he did last time. I rubbed my forehead: what was Justine doing in this demolition derby? "Do me a favor. Don't tell her you gave me this."

"Sorry, can't do that! We have a pact! No secrets! Forever!"

"Your choice. You blab, you look for a new job." Duncan would be looking for one anyway if he had started swilling rum and Coke for breakfast. "So when's Justine finally going to meet your parents?"

"Next weekend. For sure."

Room service knocked a minute later, but Duncan was gone. I sent the prunes and tomato juice to 507 and took that shower I had been persuaded to forgo last night. Whatever scent Fausto had admired had been displaced by a ranker odor: fear. *Face it, Smith.* I had been a sitting duck the moment I took Barnard's place at Ford's Theatre.

The phone rang. "I missed you this morning. Terribly."

I forgave him. "Couldn't wear my gown to breakfast, could I?"

"You could have eaten upstairs with me."

Ah, what a fool I was. "How are you feeling?"

"Fine. Very fine. Rhoby called. So we're taking a whack at Brahms, are we?"

"Do you think she can play?"

"Does it matter?"

Spoken like a true philosopher. "Did you call your doctor?"

"It's a little before office hours."

"Who's at breakfast?"

"The usual brigands. No one we saw last night, though. Aurilla kept everyone up too late."

"Is Justine there?"

"Just walked in. Looks like she slept on a bus. Why doesn't she ever bring her boyfriend over? Don't musicians live on free meals?"

I almost told him about Justine's phone call. *Leave Dun-*

can out of it. "He's impossible at breakfast. Besides, he thinks you're trying to steal his job."

Short silence. "Duncan's got nothing to worry about."

Ouch. Served me right. As usual, I was confusing business with . . . life. After a few sentences I terminated the conversation. Seconds later the phone rang again. It wasn't Fausto.

"Hello, Miss Frost? This is Gretchen. I'm sorry about wrecking your concert."

I was sorry I had picked up the phone. "We'll survive."

"You looked so pretty in that pink dress."

"Thanks. How'd you sneak your monkey past the guard?"

"He thought Herman was a doll. Everything was okay until you started to play that scratchy piece. Then Herman wanted to leave."

Sharp little guy. He should go into music criticism. "Did you apologize to Uncle Bendix yet?"

"No! He threw Herman out the window!" Gretchen began to cry. "He's lost."

"Put a few bananas on the deck. I'm sure he'll come back."

"No he won't! I hate Uncle Bendix!"

"You can always get another monkey."

"Herman was my special present!"

"Give it a day or two. If he doesn't show up, we'll go to the animal shelter and find something else. An alligator maybe."

She stopped crying. "Someday I'm going to kill Uncle Bendix."

"I'm sure you don't mean that."

Like her mother, Gretchen didn't believe in retraction. Instead she sniffled off to stash bananas around her backyard: God help Bendix if the animal didn't return. I wondered if he'd be calling Fausto today, maybe dropping by for Scrabble and a duel. Some friendship! Whatever they had on each other, it was deep. No time like the present to check it out.

Walked across the Mall, looking for tails. Nothing out there today but tourists and lower staff *fress*ing out of paper bags. A few trees had already begun to shed into the Reflecting Pool and during lulls in traffic, I could hear the feeble chirp of crickets. Insects were so anemic here. I suddenly missed autumn in Berlin . . . yet I wanted to linger in Washington. Too soon to tell whether Fausto was a sign of recovery or another tango with suicide. I ran up the Capitol steps. No one huffing in my wake, but that only eliminated the amateurs. Whoever knew about me was slicker than that. So I threaded around the Senate offices before cutting to the Library of Congress.

Back to the microfilm. I searched for hours but didn't find a word in any London paper about a scandal involving Louis or Jojo Bailey. I did find a stomach-wrenching review of Bendix's opera. Even taking into account a limey critic's anti-American prejudice, this was a trashing for the ages. I could understand why Bendix had burned his pencils afterward, poor sod. I would have hired a hit man.

On to more cheerful topics: didn't take long to find Ethel Kiss's obituary, but she had gotten nearly as many column inches as had the Tet offensive. Ethel came from a distinguished line of robber barons, specialty railroads. Granddaddy, tired of dealing with middlemen, finally bought himself a Senate seat around the turn of the century. Ethel's mother had died fairly young; Ethel's father spent the rest of his life hunting game until a charging rhino put an end to his safaris. After finishing school in Europe, Ethel had a string of spectacular liaisons on either side of the Atlantic. She scandalized her sixth and final fiancé, an English marquess, by eloping with an American pilot she had met in a London bar. He went off to war but ran out of luck over Dresden. Six months later, Fausto appeared.

Almost at once, mother and son began a reign of terror among hoteliers on every continent. They were famous for traveling with a pet tiger and a piano teacher named Lydia Varnas, for their midnight concerts in presidential suites, and literally tons of luggage. Suddenly it all stopped. Fausto immured himself in a conservatory and Ethel retired to Washington. One spring afternoon, she slipped off a parapet of the National Cathedral. No witnesses but the organist, who thought she was reaching for a bird.

I cut to the society column. Ethel's death stunned Washington. Several distinguished men (including Senator Phil Pixley) claimed to have been engaged to her, on the grounds that they had asked and Ethel had not given them a definite no. Even the president made a special trip to her coffin the night before the funeral. Mourners, including Ethel's jilted English fiancé, overflowed the National Cathedral. After her burial in the family plot at the Congressional Cemetery, Fausto had everyone back to his house for a party that lasted seven days.

Switched off the screen. Thirty-plus years later, gone to seed, Fausto was still officiating at his mother's wake. Why would a woman like that lean over a parapet, tempt fate so? A few months earlier, Ethel had jumped off a boat in London. Dress rehearsal?

I cabbed to the Congressional Cemetery, where Ethel moldered in the plot begun by her grandfather, the senator. A row of squat, identical monuments lined the main strip. Celebrity alley: John C. Calhoun, Preston S. Brooks, Henry Clay . . . once upon a time, this must have been the most prestigious resting place in town. Now the cemetery was bordered by tenements and a huge jail. Vandals had wrecked the front gate and overturned dozens of headstones. Everywhere I saw dead, ivy-strangled trees, overflowing garbage pails, weeds high as my knee: that sot Pixley hadn't been exaggerating. This place was a disgrace.

"You want to visit J. Edgar Hoover's grave?" my driver asked. "John Philip Sousa? Tip O'Neill? Private Matlovich?"

"How about Ethel Kiss."

"Can't help you with that one. There's a directory in the chapel." He stopped outside a simple structure in the center of the graveyard. Thick weeds brushed its stucco walls. Windows boarded, doors secured with corroded chains: the last service here may have been during the influenza epidemic of 1918. "Good luck."

Bouncing over potholes, the cab left. I circled the chapel, looking for a way in. Best bet was to unpry the boards and NO TRESPASSING sign that had recently been nailed over a bulkhead door. I'd need a crowbar, though. And I didn't really want to poke around a desecrated church. Even at midday this cemetery spooked me. So green, bright, still, yet I sensed corruption wafting from the graves of the illustrious dead, as if they wanted to come back, win a few more elections . . . escape hell for a while.

Thunk: down the hill, a thin black man patted earth with his shovel. I walked over, waited for him to pack in a headstone he had just righted. "Excuse me, are you the caretaker?"

He wiped his brow with an old handkerchief. Age anywhere between fifty and one hundred. He could have been a ghost. "No, I just try to keep the place up a little. Live across the street."

"It sure needs work."

"Oh yes." He offered me hot water from his dented canteen. "You lookin' for something?"

Careful, Smith. "My guidebook gave this place two stars.

Is the chapel open? The cabdriver said I could find a map of all the famous people buried here."

"You won't find no map in that chapel. Vagrants were living there. Wrecked the place. A few weeks ago they finally chased them out and closed it up. Won't open again until they find some fix-up money. Your best bet is to walk along the rows and read the headstones. All kinds of folks here. Lots of history."

Just ragweed now. "Okay. Thanks."

In death as in life, the heavies congregated on the hill. Slaves and Indians lay in the gulch by the jail. I hurried past the public vault, with its crooked iron doors agape. Didn't take long to locate Ethel Kiss just a stone's throw from another outstanding American, John Philip Sousa. Their beautifully tended graves were roses in a wilderness: I guessed the marines and Fausto came out here once a week with fertilizer and hedge shears. Granddaddy Senator's black granite stele rose like a gigantic railroad nail, dwarfing lesser memorials in the vicinity. His name was etched in six-inch letters, challenging the reader not to recognize it. His daughter, Ida, Ethel's mother, got four-inch letters on the north face, but she hadn't lived as long. Ethel lay beneath a gorgeous pink granite headstone. "Her son Fausto," I read with a shudder. Just a date and a dash: a death in progress.

Morbid curiosity drew me to their numbers. Granddad hung around a long time but his wife had died at forty-six. Ethel's mother Ida had died at forty-nine. Ethel had died at forty-seven. I looked over the last half-entry in the plot. Tremor inside as something dark and heavy winged by: next month Fausto would be fifty-one. Way beyond the Kiss shelf life.

"Find what you wanted, miss?" asked the gardener.

No. Never. "I think so."

Back to the Library of Congress, this time to find Ida's

obituary. A snap since I knew the day and date. Ida had died at home following a short illness. Due to the heat, burial had been immediate. I went back a few more decades to check out the demise of Ida's mother. Big headlines and a long article listing the nabobs who had attended the funeral. She had also died at home following a short illness. Immediate burial. Bah.

The afternoon was shot and I was tired, empty, dusty with death. Returned to the hotel and plummeted asleep. Then the phone rang.

"You've been avoiding me," fumed Bobby Marvel.

"I've been busy." Looked at my watch: five-thirty. If I didn't get out of here in one minute, I'd be late for a Brahms rehearsal. "How's your nose?"

"Damn rug burn stings. I want to see you. Tonight."

Men always got so territorial after a concert. I suppose it was a compliment. "Send a car to Fausto's around ten," I sighed. Bobby was my best link to Barnard and it was time for a few more questions. "I can drive around with you for an hour. Or come in if you want. You two can play a few duets."

"Me? Play duets with Fausto? That's not what I would call fun."

He'd seemed to enjoy it well enough the other night. "We'll order pizza."

"I hate pizza," Bobby growled. "You're spending too much time with that repulsive weasel. I'd be careful if I were you. He's a dangerous man."

"And you're a safe one?"

"Absolutely. But I can be extremely jealous."

"Look, I've got to run. See you at ten."

"Wear that fuzzy pink top for me, will you?"

I was beginning to understand Paula Marvel's forty extra pounds, her wardrobe of virginal bows, and her arthritis.

Small price to pay for running the country, and she could always divorce Bobby when they were busted back to Kentucky. Still, a bad marriage was like secondhand smoke: sooner or later it would kill you. Paula had been inhaling for thirty years. I threw on the fuzzy pink halter and dashed to Fausto's.

Pulled the Corvette behind a Hummer in his driveway. If Rhoby's taste in cars was any indication of her musical talent, this was going to be a long evening indeed. I let myself in and stood at the door of the music room. Unaware of my arrival, Rhoby and Fausto were futzing with chairs and stands. He wore a light blue smoking jacket and black pants: ducal in comparison with Rhoby's grunge. As always, smoked fish and effervescent liquids waited on a sideboard. Fausto looked over and half smiled. "Ah, there you are."

"Miserable traffic. Sorry."

He watched my approach but didn't kiss me hello. Rhoby did, however. Now that she was with arty types instead of politicians, she wore a nose ring and a few tiny barbells in her eyebrow. "I could have given you a ride," she said. "Nothing gets in Hummer's way."

"I'll bet." Aware of both their eyes on my fluffy pink halter, I tossed my violin case on Fausto's divan. Bad choice, this outfit. Should have worn a chador.

"It's so great to be here!" Rhoby shivered in delight. "I've been practicing all day!"

"Our pleasure, believe me," Fausto replied. "We're always looking for new diversions, aren't we, sweet?"

"Right." Wrong. Disaster in that cool voice: did Fausto know I had been spying on him all afternoon? "How long have you been playing the cello, Rhoby?"

"Fifteen years. I sort of dropped it since coming to Washington. It doesn't fit into the lifestyle, if you know what I mean."

Fausto gave a pensive A and watched me tune. His look lacked the conspiratorial warmth I would have preferred after bedtime events of last night. Ah well, at least he had straightened the rug on top of his piano. "We're here to enjoy ourselves," he said without a scintilla of smile. "Set for Brahms?"

He began the trio with magisterial poise, as if he had been playing it for years: no question who was going to rule this soundscape. Phenomenal tone. But Fausto had the advantage of plush fingers, pudgy arms, deep center of gravity . . . stuff a cigar in his mouth and he'd even look like old Johannes. It melted my brain all over again. *Mind the gap, Smith!*

Fausto handed his phrase to Rhoby, who came in with the mellifluence of a strangled loon. Once she got over her nerves, she just played louder. She could count like a son of a bitch, though. Out loud. "Excellent," Fausto called after the first movement. "You've got a marvelous ear."

"Thanks!" She retuned, for reasons unknown. "What tempo would you like in the scherzo? You've got all those nasty repeated notes."

"Anything you can handle, dear. I'll do my best to keep up."

Rhoby took a running leap at the opening. After her fourth miss, she said, "I guess that's a little too fast."

"Just a hair slower, then. We can always ramp up later."

Brahms took another beating. Few human inventions inflicted worse aural pain than a badly played cello, whose woofs and shrieks originated somewhere in the Ninth Circle of hell. Even Fausto needed a break after the second movement. "Whew! Can I get you something to drink?"

"Just a little juice, please."

He mercifully brought me champagne. I was gratified to see him swallow a belt of bubbly before the adagio. What was he trying to accomplish here? Without Rhoby, the two of us could have been reading violin and piano sonatas in perfect bliss. "Have you played this trio before, Rhoby?" I asked.

"Oh yes. With Chickie."

"My God!" Fausto exclaimed. "Is she a pianist?"

"I wouldn't go that far. She only studied for a few years." I glared at him. "Ready when you are."

He began with eight quiet chords. Then violin and cello had to play with each other for three bars. Here, at least, Rhoby had the courtesy to cringe a little, muttering "Oops" and "Sorr-eee!" as she trashed our duet. Soon I just closed my eyes and pretended she was Yo-Yo Ma after a lobotomy. Fausto got her next, in an extended section for cello and piano: excruciating. An orchestra could absorb a deadbeat string player or two, a trio never. But I humored him: music wasn't uppermost on Fausto's agenda tonight.

We plowed to the end. "Wow!" Wet and exhilarated, Rhoby laid down her cello. Since neither of her colleagues had stopped to make corrections, she may have presumed that we had liked her performance. "You guys are great! Let's do it again!"

Fausto hit the food trolley. "Have a bite first," he called. "Brain food. Les? What can I get you?"

Earplugs and hatchet. I got another glass of champagne. "We should form a trio," Rhoby said, making herself a sandwich. "There's potential here."

It probably wasn't Rhoby's fault that her self-esteem swelled in inverse proportion to her talent. She had gone directly from Sesame Street to Capitol Hill. "One problem," I said. "I live in Berlin."

"You're going back? I thought you'd be here for a while."

Why would she think that? "Not the case."

"How long will you be staying, then? We could play a

benefit before you leave." The studs in Rhoby's eyebrow quavered as her jaw mashed the sandwich. "Chickering could pack the place."

"No time. I'm going back in a few days."

Touché: Fausto momentarily ceased chewing pâté. We all ambled back to the piano. "Tell you what," he said, closing the Brahms. "Let's read a little Haydn."

Rhoby's trepidation dissolved as she discovered that the cello part was identical to the piano left hand. All she had to do was imitate Fausto, who had had the foresight to bring the champagne bucket over to the keyboard. By the end of the third trio, he and I were fairly ripped: a good way not only to play Haydn, but to listen to him. We ended our reading session with Mozart. Rhoby thought her part was easy because she didn't have many notes.

Fausto had become more remote with every page. Finally he stood. "That was fun, ladies. Let's get some dinner. I know a great French restaurant."

"Can't." I looked at my watch. "Someone's picking me up in half an hour."

For the first time that evening, he looked me directly in the eye. I flushed redder than Justine's feathers. "In that case, I've got some bouillabaisse kicking around the fridge. Rhoby, have a drink. You earned it."

She followed him to the Scotch bottle. "Not too much. I still have to work, you know."

"I would think a little nip would help you through the night. All those nut cases calling in their conspiracy theories." Fausto poured Rhoby a hefty highball and led us into his kitchen. "How does a cellist of your caliber end up at the night desk at the FBI?" he called, half disappearing into his Sub-Zero.

"I auditioned for orchestras for five years. They all discriminated against me because of my sexual preference."

That was a joke, considering that nine out of ten conductors were gay, not to mention ninety-nine out of one hundred artistic administrators, music critics, record company executives, and concert agents. Fausto clucked sympathetically. "Tough going out there."

"Then I met Chickering at my National Symphony audition."

"My God! She plays the violin, too?"

"No, she was in the lobby of the Kennedy Center with Mrs. Marvel. It was love at first sight." Rhoby sighed at me. "For Chickie anyhow."

I smiled back. "How long have you been together?"

"Two years. To preserve my sanity, I got this FBI gig. Now the only time we see each other is after dinner. If Paula doesn't need baby-sitting, of course. She thinks Chickie's her slave. And Chickie sure loves her keys to the White House." Rhoby finished her Scotch. "This town sucks."

Fausto brought over three bowls of bouillabaisse and a rare white wine. "Did she recover from her faint last night?"

"Oh yeah. She was her old self by the time I got her back to Annapolis. I guess she doesn't like monkeys."

Rhoby spilled the story of her life to the only people in Washington to have asked her for it since she moved here. Fausto was an expert interrogator, smooth and cool as his bouillabaisse. Rhoby made conversation the same way she played chamber music: oblivious of all other parts but her own. When Fausto rounded her yet again to her job at the FBI, I understood why he had invited her over. "So you man the phones, eh? Who would call between midnight and eight?"

"You'd be surprised. People who are scared. Paranoid. People who have important information to pass on. This is great soup, Fausto."

"Thanks. What do you do? Meet them?"

"Screen them. Sort the nuts from the legit callers. You get pretty good at smoking people out after a while."

Sure, Rhoby. "Sounds more interesting than playing in an orchestra."

"I wouldn't know," the victim replied. "But there are psychos out there."

Fausto refilled her glass. "Vicky was worried about a call you got the other day. Some madman insisting on seeing you after your shift. Now that sounds dangerous."

"She told you that? Stupid bitch! That stuff is all confidential!"

"*Please* don't tell her I mentioned it!" If Fausto was fishing, he had just caught a whale. "Didn't you call her that morning?"

"She likes to know when I leave work."

"She was eating here when the pager went off. Poor thing was nervous for you."

"She's worse than a fucking mother-in-law."

I stopped slurping soup. "So did you meet the guy?"

"No way. I called the cops. They carted him away. Along with two other guys he was fighting with. I saw it happen right outside my window."

"Three of them?" Fausto smiled insouciantly at me. "Good thing you played it safe. Don't you wonder what your lunatic caller had to say? What if he saw a real Martian landing? The Loch Ness monster in the Potomac? Now we'll never know."

"Not my problem," Rhoby replied, swabbing her empty bowl with baguette.

It was nearly ten. "Don't get up," I said, bringing my china to the sink. "I'll wait outside. Nice playing with you, Rhoby."

She wrapped me in a ferocious hug. "Can I look you up if I'm in Berlin?"

"Sure." I caught Fausto's eyes on my ass. "Take it easy."

He accompanied me out to the thick, hot night. No moon and the crickets were getting louder. I flashed back to Ek, suddenly missing the clean life-and-death struggle of the jungle. I'd rather fight that waterfall again than deal with the perverted bestiary here. "Hope you enjoyed yourself," I told Fausto. "Whatever game you're playing."

"It's no game," he replied as a long, dark car rolled down the driveway. "Who's that?"

"Who do you think."

Lightning over the treetops. "Bobby Marvel."

Fausto had merely to move one inch, brush me anywhere with any part of his body, say one word, blink an eye, clear his throat, and I would send the car away. But he remained absolutely still as three vehicles halted beside Rhoby's Hummer. "You're right," I said.

He grunted quietly. "Leaving your violin behind?"

"I'll come back for it."

His warm, heavy fingers closed around my wrist. "Tonight?"

Great confusion, greater lust: I had to get inside that mouth again. "I don't know."

He watched me get frisked but he didn't watch me leave. Great drops of rain pelted his stoop as I ducked into the armored limo, where Bobby was relaxing with a beer. Tie gone, shirt unbuttoned: he looked whipped. "Hey, sugar. Was that your chaperon out there with you?"

I flopped into the opposite seat. "You're getting a little bold, aren't you?"

"Paula's in Seattle tonight with Chickering. Fausto knows when to keep his mouth shut." Bobby handed me a glass. "You drink gin, if I recall. What did you tell him?"

"That we were going for a ride."

Bobby looked moodily out the window. "Come sit next to me. I won't bite."

Maybe not, with a driver and a Secret Service agent on the other side of the partition. I slid across the abyss. "Coming from a fund-raiser?"

"No, I was at the hospital with Bailey. Poor bastard is nothing but a big blood blister. How he can still breathe is beyond me." Bobby inhaled his beer. "I wish he'd die. Put himself out of his misery."

"How much longer do you think he'll hang on?"

"No one knows. His doctors are astonished." Bobby fell silent as great sheets of rain drummed the roof. "He was my friend. We go back a long way. Matter of fact, your boy Fausto introduced us."

Tread lightly, Smith. "Really? Where?"

"It's a long story."

"I've got an hour. Where are we going?"

"Just for a drive," Bobby sighed, abnormally flat. "As you wished."

Poor schmuck. They all wanted to lead the world, inspire fear and awe in millions, and at the end of the day, when that charade collapsed of its own weight, they always came crying to mama. I tossed back the gin, patted my lap. "Put your head down. I'm listening."

He didn't need a second invitation. Bobby kissed my navel. "Why aren't you afraid of me?"

"You don't play the violin." The downpour outside slowed the limo to parade pace as I stroked his hair. "So how'd you meet Jojo?"

"It was a long time ago. We were still in college." Bobby closed his eyes, taking a few moments to arrange events with optimal spin. "You don't know this, but I used to date Justine Cartot. She was a very hot lady then. I guess she still is." Couldn't argue with him: just two nights ago Bobby had been boffing her on top of Fausto's piano. "She had been studying in England on a Rhodes Scholarship. I came over for her graduation."

"That was kind of you."

"Actually, the purpose of my trip was to tell her I'd be marrying Paula."

"If Justine was such a hot number, why were you marrying Paula?" I pulled his hair. "Never mind. So Justine was expecting to become Frau Marvel?"

"Welllll . . . . we had been going out since we were twelve. . . . She may have been counting on it. So I took her out for dinner and broke the news. Then you know what?" Bobby chuckled. "She shot me."

"Jesus! In the restaurant?"

"No, no. In a field."

"Aha. One last roll in the hay, then you told her. Weasel."

"It was wrong, I know it. I should have written a letter." Bobby smiled up at me like a kid who had just caught a touchdown. "Aren't you going to ask where I got shot?"

"Where you deserved it, I'm sure. And I'm not interested in seeing your scar. Didn't the neighbors hear something and call the police?"

"It was late. She only fired once."

"Where'd Justine get hold of a gun? It's a little tougher to carry one in England than it is over here."

"You know, I never had the heart to ask. But I suspect Fausto. He has a talent for giving ladies their heart's desire."

I frowned. "What does this have to do with you meeting Jojo?"

"Okay, okay, I'm shot and bleeding badly. Realizing what she'd just done with her slightly illegal weapon, Justine called her doctor friend. His name was Louis Bailey. He was studying medicine at Oxford. In ten minutes he arrived with

Fausto." Bobby's face nuzzled my thigh. "Who was a little slimmer back then."

"What was Fausto doing in Oxford? I thought he studied in London."

"Maybe he had a concert. In any case, they brought me back to Louis's flat. The two of them slapped me on the kitchen table and went to work. Bloody mess. Justine missed my femoral artery by half an inch. Afterward, Fausto drove me back to London. I stayed in his place until I could walk again."

"Some nurse he must have been."

"Nurse, hell. The next day Louis dropped by with his little brother Jojo, who got baby-sitting detail. Louis and Fausto took off."

"Where to?"

"They didn't say and I didn't ask. Fausto flew me home in his private plane and managed to convince Paula that he had accidentally shot me while we were fox hunting. It wasn't a complete untruth."

Bobby owed him big time. Justine had a major IOU floating in the ether as well. "I guess you and Jojo got to know each other pretty well during your convalescence."

"Better believe it. Fausto's apartment was bigger than Buckingham Palace. Women broke down the doors to get in. He must have had two hundred birds in his address book and they all showed up the next week."

Outside, rain. Inside, thunder as I imagined the young, slim Fausto and an army of eager women . . . bah. Maybe they had made him happy for a few moments. "Who knows about this little escapade?"

Bobby counted on his fingers. "Just the four of us. And you."

Keep counting, honey: Maxine knew about it. So did

Duncan. The ship wasn't as tight as Bobby thought. "So why are you telling me?"

"Because you asked. I suspect you won't tell." His smile disappeared. "And Jojo's about dead. It's one of those nights."

Bobby's head vacated my lap as he got another beer. "I guess you've forgiven Justine," I said.

"She's forgiven me is more like it." Bobby burped softly as he lay down again. "We're one big happy family. That includes your sweetie pie Fausto."

"Does it include Louis Bailey?"

"I haven't seen him in years." Bobby shuddered, or maybe he was just trying to mash his nose a little deeper into my belly button. "Funny you mention it. I had a nightmare last night. I was back on Louis's operating table. What was horrible wasn't the blood or the pain but the look in his eyes as he bent over me. I think he likes to dissect living things."

"What was Justine doing with him?"

"They went to concerts together. Louis was fanatic about music. He'd drive all night to see an opera. At the time, Justine was trying to swallow as much European culture as her cracker stomach could tolerate." Suddenly Bobby laughed. "Know what Louis was talking about all the while he was operating on me? Bendix Kaar's opera!"

I needed another gin. "How'd Bendix get into this?"

"Doesn't Fausto tell you anything, sugar? They went to school together."

"Oh. Right. What was Louis saying about the opera?"

"He was trying to get Fausto to burn it. Fausto said he couldn't do that, Bendix had been working on it for five years."

Too bad no one had taken the doctor's advice. "Did you ever ask Bendix about it?"

"Hell no. Music like that is an embarrassment for life, like

herpes. Everyone makes a few youthful mistakes." Bobby
smiled winsomely at me. "I just can't figure out why Fausto
had you play that awful thing last night. Aurilla was mortified. I had nightmares afterward. Bendix was ready to kill.
Fortunately no one was listening."

"What can I tell you? Fausto picked the program. I as-
sumed it was some sort of inside joke. All in the family."

"Hmmm." Bobby closed his eyes. We rode in silence for a
mile. "How well do you know Fausto?"

"I met him a week ago."

"Is he screwing you?"

"None of your business."

"You spend a lot of time over there."

"He's a great pianist."

A half dozen deep breaths, all of my mons veneris. "Did
Fausto ever tell you about our little chat in his airplane?
No?" Bobby smiled dreamily. "We were flying back to the
States after Justine shot me. Drinking champagne. I was all
excited because I was about to marry Paula and enter my
first election, for state senator. Suddenly Fausto dropped
something into my glass. It was the bullet he and Louis had
fished out of me. 'Just a reminder that you sold your soul,'
he said. 'What are you going to buy with the proceeds, now
that you've ditched Justine for Paula?'

"I told him I was going to be president. He looked me up
and down, smiling in that twisted way of his. 'Why would
you want that?'

"I said I wanted to be the most powerful man on earth.

" 'Powerful?' Fausto laughed. 'You'll be nothing more
than a rat in a cage. The lowliest animal could take everything away from you like *that*.' " Bobby snapped his fingers.
"I threw the bullet back at him. 'Let's see you try,' I said.
'When I'm president and you're nothing but a piano player.'

"Fausto said it was a deal. I never forgot that conversation because with every election I became a bigger rat in a smaller cage while Fausto just spread his wings over Washington. On inauguration night he came up to me and dropped something in my pocket. 'Remember I'm just a lowly animal,' he said with a wink. It was the bullet, of course."

"What's he going to do?"

"How would I know? But he's had thirty years to think it over. God knows I've got skeletons in my closet and I'll bet Fausto knows every damn one of them. I don't think he'd hurt me, but I'm a poor trusting country boy."

"Maybe he's just trying to keep you humble. Like he did with Bendix by playing that awful sonata."

"Oh, now Fausto's our conscience? That's a good one. Do me a favor, would you, sugar? Don't tell him what I just told you. Let him think I was just huffin' and puffin' here like an animal. I don't want you to get hurt."

Bobby dozed off. Two men asleep on me in two nights: I must be losing it. I let him be as our caravan rolled through the mist. We were making a big circle, heading back to Washington, duration of trip one hour precisely. Why had Bobby told me this adolescent tale? As Maxine had said, in this town subtext was god, and no one got to be president without mastering the art. Maybe, like Fausto, Bobby was toying with me, dangling the bait, waiting for me to snap at it. . . . The oddest thing about his behavior tonight was its reticence. Not one pass in fifty miles. But how would I react coming from the deathbed of an old friend? Wouldn't my thoughts dwell on how we had met? How we'd soon part? Wouldn't I want my head in the lap of a neutral stranger?

Lulled by the rain and my soft belly, the leader of the free world lapsed into gentle snores. Poor guy should have become a car salesman, not a president. He just didn't know what it was all about. In forty years he still wouldn't know, because at heart Bobby Marvel was a people person, not a leader. He lacked a cold, hard core and the fangs to bite popularity in the face. Joke was, he'd get reelected for those very reasons. Ah, America. Maybe this lump in my lap was the best it could produce.

We rolled along the watery highway. My thoughts became diffuse and runny as the windows of my glass cage. I wondered why Fausto had been so distant tonight. I wondered if Barnard had driven around in circles like this with Bobby Marvel and how she had handled him. I wondered why I hadn't found Louis yet and why Bendix's opera kept bobbing like a cadaver to the surface of an oily pond. And those purple orchids . . .

A sudden cataract sprayed the side of the limousine. Looked out the window just in time to see the Chevy float insolently past.

Maybe, through his ears, Bobby sensed my elevated pulse. He awoke with an erection and absolutely no memory of the previous fifty minutes in our mobile confessional. "Must have dropped off," he said, drawing my hand to the storm in his pants. "Feel that, sugar. It's all for you."

Next he'd be swearing he'd had a vasectomy. "Tell me something," I said. "Does Paula know about this kind of stuff? Or doesn't she ask anymore?"

"Paula's needs and mine are very different."

"That wasn't the question. Does she know?"

Bobby tried another tack. "I try to protect her feelings."

"That's big of you." I squeezed tumescence. "Did she know about you and Polly?"

"God no! Blondes make her crazy!"

"Did Justine know?"

"Of course. She arranges everything for me."

"How does Justine feel about your ongoing harem? Sometimes you're not too bright, Bobby."

He sat up. "I take good care of Justine. Always have. She knows where she stands with me."

I fiddled a little with his belt buckle. "How many times did you see Polly?"

"See her?" Bobby thought about it. "Six."

"I said see, not screw."

"Six is the answer to both your questions. She wasn't quite the puritan you are." Bobby nosed under my pink halter and kissed my stomach. "Not that I'm complaining."

Six. They must have gone at it every night. "Where did you two get together?"

"We met once at the White House. Four times at the country place. Once right here. She was fantastic." Bobby rushed me to the cushions. "All this talk is making me horny." He rolled on top of me. "I want you, sugar."

And I wanted one more piece of information, for which I was willing to get a little saliva on my nipples. I held Bobby's ass, which felt surprisingly mushy, considering what I had seen in Barnard's bathtub video. He weighed a ton. "Who owns the country place?"

"Aurilla," came the muffled answer.

Aurilla? Damn.

Bobby's mouth left my breasts and headed south. Failing to master the zipper in my pants, he took care of his own. "Get these off," he whispered, digging under my waistband.

I locked my knees around his neck and flipped both of us to the floor. Luckily the president ended up on bottom. While he was staring at the ceiling like a stunned fish, I bit his earlobe. "I never fuck in backseats." Rolled to my banquette and tucked the boobs back into the halter. "Put that poker back in your pants. Your hour is up."

He put a few fingers to his ear. "You bit me," he cried when they came back bloody.

I rapped on the partition. Nothing happened. I picked up

the intercom phone. "Pull over, please. I'll be getting out here. Thank you."

Bobby was still flat on his back as I unlatched the door. "Meet me in the country house," I said. "Next time, try to stay awake."

Slammed the door and blew a kiss, as if my companion rode upright in the backseat like a gentleman. As the caravan pulled away, I started walking. Seconds later, Chevy reappeared. License unreadable, of course. Driver the same white male, alone. Sign at the first intersection put me at Sixteenth and Florida, not too far from the zoo.

For effect I looked a few times over my shoulder before ducking into a long woods that led to the lions and tigers. City lights reflected off the clouds, mitigating the darkness: if my tail lost me here, I had nothing to worry about. Stayed close to Rock Creek for half a mile, listening for the occasional snaps and thumps in my wake. He was stalking all right. When we were deep in the woods, I bolted into the bushes. Let's see how well you kept up now, pal.

Wilder terrain, heavier night. Rock Creek Park was no jungle; it was no golf course, either. My tail was not only keeping up, but getting closer. I went faster, fueled by the first little licks of panic. Forests were my specialty. In my entire career no one had bested me on this turf but Ek, who was more animal than human . . . and Simon, who had cheated by wearing heat scopes. If the man behind me were wearing those, he was probably carrying a gun as well. Damn, I should have screwed Bobby and called it a night.

Craggy rocks ahead: closing in on the zoo. I scrambled up twenty feet and waited behind a sharp, very opaque boulder. Heard footfall, calculated distance to target, dove. Big bastard but I bowled him over. The fool wore a ski mask. We wrestled over a patch of soggy earth. No amateur but he was rusty, a millisecond dull, like an outfielder on opening day.

He saw my nail file just before the tip of it disappeared beneath his collarbone. Not too deep: I didn't want to kill the guy. Just deface him a little.

Realizing I was about to yank off his mask, he clicked into overdrive. I got tossed to the rocks hard. Lost my wind, balance, nail file. Spun into a tree, saw comets behind my eyes: instantly I was on the receiving end of this fracas. As I dropped to my knees, head spinning, he reached into his jacket. I expected gun, knife, oblivion: instead he tossed something at my feet and ran off. I finally reached over: an orchid.

With a soft *whoosh*, rain returned to the forest. Hauled myself to the top of the rocks and waited. Nothing. He was gone. Odd fight. Nonfight. Why the mask? God, my shoulder hurt. So did my tattered thigh. I was deeply tired, perhaps defeated, no longer invisible, no longer free. Why had he walked away without naming his price? What had he gained by revealing his existence? In my line of work, that was an incredible blunder. I could have led him to bigger fish, richer blackmail . . . evidently not what he wanted. What did he want, then?

I dragged over to the zoo, to my pocket in the rocks. Stared at that crushed flower for a long time. It was my death warrant. Why should I be surprised? No one expected to last long in this profession. That was why most of us had joined in the first place: death by old age was proof of cowardice. Strange that the older I got, the more I saw of the sun, the more I played Bach and loved men, the more an early death seemed . . . proof of cowardice. The real heroines tried to live, to keep playing one last card against a dealer who always won in the end. Like that unseen woman laughing by the fountain the other night. I had desperately wanted to laugh like that again. The odds against it had just skyrocketed.

Switched on my computer. If nothing else, I knew I was getting closer to Louis Bailey. Tonight Rhoby had said that rather than meet her deranged caller, she had notified the police. Outside her FBI window she had seen three men hauled into a paddy wagon: her caller and two assailants. The date, according to Maxine and thunderstorms, would have been September 5. I tapped into the D.C. police rap sheets. Bingo: at 0822 hours, Figgis Cole, Mohammed Jones, and Donelle Boozer had been booked for aggravated assault, willful destruction of a federal building, and resisting arrest. No one had posted bail but everyone had pleaded not guilty. The judge busted them to the district jail to await their case. I cut to the prison files. Three arrivals duly noted, but within the hour Jones and Boozer had become violently ill and had to be removed to the hospital down the street.

I accessed hospital records for September 5. The ER had admitted two black males, both in cardiac arrest, at 0935 that morning. This being an unusual coincidence for a pair of twenty-somethings, the warden had thought they were faking and had delayed calling an ambulance until it was nearly too late. Once the paramedics got their hearts pumping again, the victims had developed fever, mumps-size thyroids, and acute diarrhea. Doctors eventually blamed a tic carried by bats and ferrets, although neither victim had been near such animals. They had just been discharged from the hospital two days ago. Having coughed up bail, they were allowed home until their trials. Mohammed Jones may have bolted to Detroit, his listed address. Presumedly Donelle Boozer went to nurse his ragged rump in an apartment on Florida Avenue.

I cut back to Figgis Cole at the district jail. The fool had flashed a Guatemalan passport but hadn't demanded to speak with the Guatemalan ambassador about his incarceration. He hadn't asked for a lawyer or a translator. He hadn't gotten sick.

Welcome to Washington, Dr. Bailey.

I moved to another keyboard, this one connected to transmitters, receivers, Fausto's phone tap. I was calm enough until I heard his voice. Then a virulent case of stage fright kicked in: didn't know what I was about to hear. The next few minutes could kill me.

For a man about town, Fausto spent remarkably little time on the phone. I caught him speaking with tailor, banker, landscaper. Then Justine Cortot called.

"He's becoming impossible," she said, voice cold and edgy. "I can't control him much longer."

"Your usual method isn't working?" Fausto replied with equal warmth.

"Do something fast. He's losing it." She hung up.

Who was losing it? Duncan? Justine had made the call yesterday, late afternoon, just before I'd showed up to take Fausto to our concert. Maybe it hadn't been nerves at all. His next call was to me at the hotel, around six in the morning. "I missed you," he said. My stomach rolled all over again. "Terribly."

"Couldn't wear my gown to breakfast, could I?" I had replied. Ball breaker! I replayed our conversation about Rhoby, breakfast guests . . . and Justine, who had just walked in. Fausto asked why she never brought Duncan with her to breakfast. "He thinks you're trying to steal his job," I had told him.

"Duncan's got nothing to worry about."

I had hung up in a huff. Stupid, but that's what happened when you became too fond of your major suspects. After speaking with me, Fausto had made a few more inconsequential calls. Around lunchtime he'd dialed a number in Belize.

"Koko's," a woman answered.

"Eh, Florita. Is Simon there?"

"I look." Short pause. "No. We have not seen Simon in a long time."

"Did he leave a message for me?"

"No. He just stopped coming here. His friends worry."

"Put one of his friends on, would you?"

Please, oh God please, not James. "James here," said a familiar voice. "That you, Fausto?"

"Lost track of Simon, eh?"

"He disappeared. I think he's shacked up with a bird. That's the only explanation."

"How so?"

I nearly threw up as James said, "Last week some hot babe walks in at dinnertime. Simon takes one look and bets me a hundred bucks that her name is Leslie something or other and she plays the violin. I go to her table, chat her up. Not exactly a friendly sort, if you know what I mean. Anyhow, Simon's wrong. Her name's—shit, I can't remember. It's not Leslie, though."

"What did she look like?"

"Long dark hair. Green eyes. Little mole above her lip. Great body. Looked like she needed a bath and a good fucking."

Long silence. Maybe Fausto was throwing up. "Did you see Simon leave with her?"

"No, but he followed her out. Couldn't take his eyes off her ass. You know how he gets once that happens."

Another silence capped with a dreary sigh. "If he turns up, have him call, will you."

"Sure. Everything okay up there?"

"Fine."

End of conversation. End of my life: of all people on the planet, Fausto was the last one I would want to know about my trip to Belize. I cringed, remembering how he had stared at the stitches on my thigh last night. What had I told him? Biking accident? He hadn't pressed the point then, but he sure as hell must be reconsidering now. I should have known the moment I walked into that trio charade that something was off. Fausto hadn't said two words to me. Why should he? I had betrayed him. But then he had asked Rhoby questions that would lead me directly to Louis in jail. Why hand over that priceless information? Why the hell was everyone giving it away tonight?

I sat very still, trying to digest the frozen watermelon in my gut. Nothing moved. Finally, with a mammoth shiver, I reconnected to the phone tap. After calling Belize, Fausto had dialed a number in Panama. "This is Fausto Kiss. Is Krikor in?"

Tuna eventually came on the line. "Everything's on schedule," Fausto reported. "I'll keep you fully informed."

"Thank you, my friend."

No further calls of significance. Fausto had probably spent the afternoon practicing Brahms, concocting retribution. He knew my secret. So did my masked assailant. *Last stop, Smith. All out.* I called the Queen. "I found Louis. He's in jail under the alias Figgis Cole."

"Doing what?"

"Chilling out until his hearing." I got Maxine up to speed on the amazing detective work required to locate him, neglecting to mention that Fausto had fed me clues like pablum.

"If Louis was willing to go to the FBI about a purported assassination of his brother, why is he hiding under an alias, in jail of all places?"

"Before he even left Belize, he was spooked that someone was after him. Used a Guatemalan passport to enter the country. He didn't go to jail on purpose. That someone attacked him in broad daylight in front of the FBI building would confirm his fears that he was a target. I say he's lying low, trying to figure out his next move."

"Who would want to kill him?"

"Tuna?"

"Try again. Tuna wants him alive so he can get his poison."

Shit. "Louis is afraid of Fausto."

"He called Fausto first, before dialing the FBI."

"Maybe he's afraid of Barnard. Must not know she's dead."

"That's ridiculous. Who were the two men he went to jail with? Accomplices?"

"I'll know in an hour." I tried to keep the pout out of my voice. Difficult to do when Maxine belted me from endgame back to square one.

"How's Marvel?" she asked brightly after a pause.

"I haven't taken a bath with him yet, if that's what you mean."

"How's Duncan?"

"Oblivious of anything beyond Justine's tush."

"I hear Fausto's a pretty good pianist."

The Queen knew musicians were my downfall. I might as well give her something to worry about. "I've tapped his phone. He's been trying to reach Simon in Belize."

"Why would Fausto be contacting a mercenary?"

No answer yet. "The good news is, no one knows Simon's dead. The longer he rots in the jungle, the less chance there will be anything left to find." Bad news was, Fausto knew I had been to Koko's. No need to rile the Queen with that.

"Speaking of rot," Maxine said, "Jojo Bailey won't last the week. I want you to wrap things up before Aurilla gets herself sworn in. You've been in Washington too long."

"I've had concerts."

"One concert. It's over."

"Bobby likes me."

"Are you so naive to think that the *president of the United States* would take the risks he has just to see *you?*"

"You weren't in the back of a limo with this oaf's head in your lap."

"Know what, Smith? I think you're having so much fun in the water that you don't see the sharks coming at you from twenty directions."

I saw them all right. Trouble was, I'd have to wait for one of them to take a leg off before making my next move.

"What's happening with Aurilla Perle?" Maxine continued.

"She hasn't spoken to me since her party."

"She invited you for a reason. It wasn't a musical one. Ever find out who's sending you flowers?"

Sure! I just went five rounds with him! "No."

"What's Chickering up to?"

"She's threatening to sit on me if I go near her wife again."

"She sat next to you at Ford's Theatre."

"So did Justine. The ticket came from Bobby. They're all one happy family."

"How's Paula?"

"Nursing her arthritis."

A short guffaw. I braced myself. Maxine always saved her best questions for last. "What's with Fausto? Skip the part about what a good pianist he is."

But that was ninety percent of the puzzle. Where to begin, what to omit? I had to be extremely careful here: Maxine's forte, besides puncturing my theories, was connecting the dots and hanging me with the line. "Two nights ago, after the fund-raiser, he played a private recital for Marvel and

Justine. Strange thing was, there was no Secret Service around."

"Ain't easy for a president to slip out of the White House."

"He's done it before. Nearly cost him his job. But he did it again."

"Gee, that sounds a little cagey for the innocent sex maniac you've been seeing."

"I didn't say he was totally stupid." Damn, where was I. "When Fausto left the room, Marvel took the opportunity to fuck Justine."

"I thought he was besotted with you. And I thought Justine was servicing Duncan."

"Maybe it's just a habit."

"Nothing you're saying makes sense. But continue."

"Who comes down the driveway but Tuna. He meets with Bobby for about ten minutes then splits."

"Why would Marvel secretly meet an arms dealer? Was Fausto in on the meeting?"

"No, he was outside while they talked. I think he only set it up."

Maxine sighed profanities. "Too bad you couldn't tap more than Fausto's phone. Would have been nice to hear what went on between Marvel and Tuna."

"Give me a break. Fausto's with me every second I'm in his house. I was lucky to get away with a phone tap." One Pandora's box at a time, for Christ's sake! "Could you look up a Richard Poore and Lydia Varnas for me? He's a tugboat captain. She's a piano teacher. Both in London. If they're alive, they're old."

"What does this have to do with Louis?"

"It has to do with Fausto."

Momentary quiet. "Just remember that your primary mission is to identify Barnard's killer and get out of there. You're spending too much time with Fausto."

I sighed in frustration. "Everything seems to revolve around him."

"Absolutely not. Everything revolves around Bobby Marvel."

"I'm telling you, he's not that smart!"

"Exactly what Barnard said," she replied. "Look who's still walking. Watch your ass at the jail."

Talking with Maxine was more exhausting than playing chess with Deep Blue. She had the advantage of distance and dispassion while I was the grunt in the trenches. At least she hadn't told me what to do. She never did: the Seven Sisters always got to step on their own grenades. Nearly one in the morning but now I had a little errand to run. A futile one, perhaps, but better than standing like Bambi in front of on-coming headlights. I took a cab about three miles east on Florida Avenue.

"Sure you got the right number, lady?" the driver asked. "I ain't goin' wait for you in that neighborhood. And you ain't goin' find a cab back neither."

"Tell you what," I said, dropping a hundred bucks into the front seat. "How about selling me that crowbar I know you're sitting on."

He pocketed the bill. "It's a bowie knife."

"I'm not choosy."

With each block, Florida Avenue lost glass and gained graffiti. Must have been a nice place to live during the Civil War. Pretty coned dormers, high windows, inset door-ways . . . now a cockroach would think twice about moving in. The liquor stores were armed fortresses. We passed cars without tires, buildings without roofs, squares of neon hawking tarot, lotteries, tattoos . . . this was a jungle within a jungle. Different animals but same Darwinian struggle, and without a gun I could not consider myself among the fittest here. Only two slim points in my favor: the rain and my lethal curiosity.

No idiot, the cabbie didn't directly unhand his bowie knife. Instead he opened his door, left the knife on the street, and U-turned back to civilization. I tucked the bowie in my belt and looked around. Nothing moved but the stormclouds and a twitching police flasher two blocks away. Donelle Boozer didn't live far from the hospital where he had just spent a wonderful three weeks shitting his brains out. I rang the doorbell of a brick tenement: no buzzing inside. As I waited, heavy raindrops spattered the jalousies. Someone was trying to eke one last tomato out of the vine in the milk box. Lightning whitewashed the street for several seconds before a loud, close *boom*.

I took a few steps back, saw an open window above the porch. Climbed up to a small, hot room where a black man, naked, slept alone. A dozen bottles of medicine cluttered the night table. He hadn't yet removed the bandage over his IV drip. I took the largest bottle to the window and read the label. Take two teaspoons every three hours to relieve diarrhea: Boozer all right.

He slept on his stomach. Nice ass. Didn't look dangerous, but his eyes were shut. According to his rap sheet, Donelle was a fifth-rate hustler who had never graduated beyond un-armed robbery and friendly pimping. Couldn't be too dangerous if he slept with the windows open. With a few of his polyester ties, I secured one wrist and two ankles to the bed frame. "Donelle. Hey." When he lifted his head, I straddled him, twisting his free arm back. "Don't even try to get up. You're tied to the bed."

A couple of tugs convinced him that this succubus was real. He didn't seem to mind. "You're wasting your time, woman," he said calmly. "I got no cash at all. I been in the hospital with a very nasty disease."

"I know." Outside, intense lightning. Thunder shook the house. "I have a few questions about that."

"Look, if you're here about that guy, I'm sorry. He was one motherfuckin' tornado. I'll give you a refund soon's I get back on my feet." Donelle struggled to look at me. "You a cop?"

"Worse." I shoved his face back into the pillow. "I'm the sanitation crew. Clean up everyone's mess. And you messed up." I laid the bowie knife on the sheet a few inches from his nose. "Start from the top and stick to the facts."

"Can I go to the bathroom first? You got my insides all riled up jumpin' on me like that."

"You can crap all you want after I leave. How'd you get this gig?"

"Someone phones me four o'clock in the friggin' morning askin' if I'm lookin' for quick easy work. Two grand cash was waitin' in my milk box downstairs. All I do is haul myself down to the FBI in half an hour. If a thin honky shows up, I shove him into my car and drive to the cemetery down the block."

"The Congressional Cemetery?"

"Whatever's down by the jail. I said I couldn't do it without help since I never saw this guy and what if he's a strong sucker? So I get my cousin Mohammed to come along."

"How'd you get this job?"

"I got a little network, you know what I mean."

"Sure. So you and Mo get to the FBI building and see this guy."

"Yeah, a tall honky, thin as a coke straw. Little round glasses like those revolutionary dudes. Stank real bad. Me and Mohammed mosey up nice and slow like, one on each side. But he's expectin' us and starts swingin' and spittin'.

We can't get a good grip on him. 'Fore you know it, he's jumpin' in the bushes and throwin' dirt. Then a police car comes by. Shittin' bad luck."

Outside, a long flash followed by gigantic ripping sounds and cascades of rain. "So you all go to the police station. Then what."

"Me and Mo tell the cops we just walkin' by mindin' our own business and this guy starts hammerin' us. That don't cut no mustard since the cops know me. So we get brung to jail. Me and Mohammed bein' very good, very polite, 'cause we know we done nothin'. Then all of a sudden I get these motha pains in my chest. I think I am goin' die. I was chokin' for air. Then Mohammed gets it too. We rollin' on the floor and goin' out fast when the ambulance finally come. Me and my cousin spend three weeks in a hospital with a stomachache and the runs to die. I still hurtin' bad all ova."

I dismounted but kept Donelle's arm in a twist. "What was supposed to happen once you brought this guy to the cemetery?"

"Why you askin' me? I jes' do my job and clear out."

No use asking if he knew who had hired him. "Any idea why you got sick?"

"Sure! This guy, he done it. He bite me here, on the hand. And he bite Mohammed on the arm."

"Try again. He's not a dog with rabies."

"He somethin' odd, you believe me. Hot like hell and he wears rubber gloves. And he smells so bad, like a dead skunk. Not a people smell at all."

"What happened to the rubber gloves?"

"Cops made him take them off when they fingerprint him. Throw them away."

Adios, evidence. A little ecotoxin on latex, touch an open

wound: bingo. Louis wasn't going down without a fight. "Did he talk?"

"Only two words, loud and clear. *Not guilty.* The lawmen laugh him out of the room. That's one wanker there. Me and Mohammed be settlin' when we see him in court."

"When's that?"

"Three days."

"Did you tell your doctor what you told me?"

"He jus' laughed. Stuck-up shithead from India."

To my left, a tiny splat: the roof leaked. "One last question. Where's the money?"

"You not askin' for it back, I hope. This was supposa be a nice easy job. No one mentioned this guy bein' a poisonous snake. In fac, I should ask for another grand in medicine expense. My insides not feelin' good."

I could hear them gurgling all too ominously. "You don't really deserve this," I said, tucking a wad of bills in Donelle's butt. "But at least you tried. Count to ten real slow and keep your head in the pillow. You peek at me and you get a bowie knife in place of those nice clean Ben Franklins. Understand?"

"I read you, sista."

"I never made this visit."

"You got it."

"And you don't repeat this snake man crap. Start counting. Slow and out loud."

I was back on the street before Donelle hit double digits. Overhead raged a violent thunderstorm. I was glad to walk undisturbed under tons of water and a zillion volts of electricity. Reminded me, soothingly, of the jungle, of Ek in his grass hut, waiting, caretaking . . . He had chosen his master and stuck with him. Rare boy. A few miserable cabs surfaced after a mile or so, but I had left all my spare cash in Donelle's rear end. Popped back to the zoo. Maxine had located Poore and Varnas, alive, in London. Breakfast time over there so I called and made appointments with both of them. Checked Fausto's phone tap: inactive, thank God. Got back to the hotel around four o'clock, as Sunday commuters were zipping along Pennsylvania Avenue toward their places of worship. Message light blinking. The first was from Rhoby Hall.

"Leslie, I can't thank you enough for playing with me. That was one of the greatest nights of my life. I'm crazy about you. Let's please get together again."

The second was from Vicky Chickering. "Here's some advice you should take very seriously. Stay away from Rhoby."

Third was from Bendix. "I'd like to see you at your earliest convenience."

Once again, a little overhot in this town. Louis could wait a day. I slept, then left.

Chapter Ten

THE CONCORDE was halfway across the Atlantic when I realized that over the last few days Fausto had phoned just about everyone but his doctor. Maybe he was waiting for another seizure to confirm that his old malady had returned; meanwhile he'd pretend his only health problems were a nicotine craving and a slight midriff bulge. He hadn't called me, either. That hurt, even if I had left him stranded with Rhoby to take a spin with Marvel.

Slept until the slate gray ocean gave way to land. In a few minutes I'd be in London. Europe. Civilization, or what was left of it. Home. Already I felt more human. That was the up side of Washington: it might obsess you absolutely while you were there, but once you left, it vanished like Oz. As I deboarded, a fellow passenger smiled at me. Perhaps somewhere he had seen me onstage in a pretty dress making pretty sounds. Ah, if only I had stopped there.

Called Curtis from Heathrow. "How'd it go?" he asked.

"Aurilla's party? A barrel of laughs." I told him about our concertus interruptus. "Hope she didn't ask for a rebate."

"Not yet. How'd Fausto make out?"

"He's a great pianist. If he ever decides to resume where he left off, you should put him on the roster."

Curtis didn't affirm. We both knew that no matter how great a pianist Fausto might be, his nationality, size, and sexual persuasion presented insurmountable marketing obstacles. "I booked you for the twenty-third," he said. "Beethoven with Derschl."

Couldn't say I'd be there. I rented a car and drove smack into a monumental traffic jam on the M4. Nothing I could do about it but roll down the windows and inhale cow manure. It was a crystalline evening, on the cool side without a whiff of humidity: even the weather was more civilized over here. The scent of grass gave way to curry and exhaust as I entered a maze of increasingly narrower streets. After the grandiose parade routes of Washington, London was like spaghetti. Delivery trucks, cyclists, and one-way alleys dented my timetable even further.

I found Captain Poore in a Fulham pub, as we had arranged. He was short and thick with an impressive thatch of white hair. His pension evidently covered necessities like beer and smokes but didn't cover luxuries like nail clippers and weekly trips to the Laundromat. Nevertheless, he was a cheerful, Father Christmas sort. If he had children, I bet they visited him often. "Captain Poore? I'm Cosima Wagner."

He ordered shepherd's pie and a revolting side of canned peas and mayonnaise. I repeated some old fibs about my journalistic career, listened to tales of tugboat life, then got right to the point because each time a few more people walked into the pub, the proprietor cranked up the music three decibels. "I'm writing an article on river rescues and was referred to you by the people at Charing Cross Pier."

"Is that so! I've made a few rescues in my day."

"I know this is a stretch, but do you remember an incident

about thirty years ago involving five people jumping off a cruise boat?"

"I remember most clearly. You're speaking about Mrs. Kiss."

Way to go, Ethel. "Could you tell me about it?"

"It was a warm evening in June," Poore began. "With a full moon. I was returning to Fulham from the Greenwich Pier. As you would expect, there were a lot of pleasure boats on the water. People were out walking on the bridges and the riverbanks until four or five in the morning. No one wanted to go back inside. I sailed under Waterloo, Westminster, Lambeth, Vauxhall, Chelsea Bridge." The captain paused over each name, conjuring different silhouettes of light and history. "I was just about under the Albert Bridge when I passed a party cruiser. We were so close, I could see the cream on everyone's ale. It was a jolly crowd. They all waved at me. Then I saw a riveting lady on the handrail. She wore an enormous hat covered with flowers. She was surrounded by four young men and a girl. I couldn't take my eyes off her, and it was a good thing I didn't because just a few moments later, she jumped into the water, hat and all. Astonishing."

"You didn't see a violin case fall overboard first?"

Poore's fork abandoned a brownish lump in his shepherd's pie. "Violin case? No, I certainly did not. What makes you think that?"

"An article in the *Observer* mentioned a violin overboard."

"Rubbish. Anyway, within seconds the entire group jumped in after her. I never saw anything like it. Four strong gents and that tiny girl right into the current. I had a devil of a time pulling them all in. Fortunately, they could all swim well except for the woman in the hat. One of the lads got to her in the water and managed to grab the life preserver I had tossed out. She almost didn't make it."

"Did she need artificial respiration?"

"Water wasn't the problem." Reluctant to continue, Poore started playing with his mashed potatoes.

I put my pencil in the ashtray. "What was the problem?"

"The boy asked me not to mention anything."

The boy had probably backed up his request with a bundle of pound notes. "The lady in white died a few months after the boat ride," I said.

"Oh, the poor thing! I wondered what would become of her!" Poore blew his nose. "Well, I suppose there's no harm in telling you. After I pulled the two of them in, she lay still as an anchor on the deck. Suddenly she started shivering in a most violent manner. Her son bent over her, crying until it passed. Meanwhile, mind you, I was flinging every last life preserver into the water. It was bedlam. I nearly rammed the bridge."

"Did anyone else see the woman in fits?"

"No. They had passed by the time I pulled the next lad in. I wrapped them all in blankets and brought out a bottle of whiskey. The boys were all laughing and drinking as if they jumped into the Thames seven nights a week. Ah, reckless youth."

"What about the girl?"

"I took her aside and tried to tell her what a dangerous thing she had just done and maybe she should not be with this group. She laughed and said not to worry, in a week she'd be returning to America to marry her childhood sweetheart."

Wrong horse, Justine. "That's nice."

"Soon the young man's mother sat up and introduced herself as Ethel Kiss, as if nothing had happened. She said that her son had just performed a magnificent piano recital over at the Wigmore Hall and they had been out celebrating. She thanked me most profusely and apologized for all the trouble. I let them off at Cadogan Pier. The next day, a courier came to my boat with an envelope from Ethel and her boy. Inside was five thousand pounds." Poore finished his peas. "So if you were wondering why an old bloke like me would be remembering an evening so long ago, there is your reason."

"That's quite a story," was all I could say.

Captain Poore dabbed his mouth with a napkin. He seemed suddenly exhausted. "I'm so sorry to hear about Ethel. I had always hoped to see her again one day. How is her boy? Still playing the piano?"

Yes, I almost said, then remembered that I was here writing rescue stories. "I could look him up," I said.

"No, no point. It was the mother I took a shine to. A police reporter came by the next morning. I was a bit of a hero for a day." With an effort, he pushed back his chair. "Thank you very much for coming to see me."

I had ruined his evening. Said good-bye and drove to the Royal College of Music, a flat concrete temple of art in Kensington. Grungy students hung out on the stairway, smoking and looking disdainfully at people with less talent but nicer shoes. Eventually a girl with four nose rings and a violin case recognized me. "Are you Leslie Frost?" she asked, dropping a candy wrapper onto the sidewalk.

Her hair looked green, her lipstick black. Maybe it was the street lamps. "Right."

"Playing in town?"

"Just passing through." I looked inside the school entrance. "I was wondering if the library's open."

"Till midnight. Come on, I'll walk you in." I followed her sarong and army boots to the man standing guard over the next generation of unemployed musicians. "Just sign there," she pointed. "It's okay, Harold."

We walked past cracked walls, dirty glass, dozens of posters for student recitals, mental health workshops, parades for justice, zero posters for night courses in business school. Younger students gawked at me. Older ones looked away as I passed. I felt uncomfortable as a freak here, for good reason: I was exactly that. Hey guys, what can I tell you. Natural selection plus I happened to be riding the right merry-go-round when the brass ring whipped by.

"There you go," said the girl.

The female behind the librarian's desk looked like a singer. False eyelashes, built like a rain barrel, she was very busy trying to stamp a stack of checkout slips and hum an aria from *The Magic Flute* at the same time. "Excuse me," I finally interrupted. "I'm looking for old programs of concerts at the school. Do you have an archive section?"

"Sure. Over by the magazines."

I found Fausto's recital programs, all big and brash, all planned brilliantly as a royal banquet. I began to understand why, denied pure music, he would turn to conducting in Washington: politics was the loudest, most treacherous symphony of all. Still, what an enormous waste of talent, of peace. I needed to know the reason for it.

London was a great walking town but no time for that now. I drove toward Hampstead through miles of dark, empty streets barely wider than my bumper. Took a while to reach my next appointment because I made a few wrong turns and there was no such thing as going round the block and ending up where you had started here. *Stay awake, Smith.* Madame Varnas, Fausto's former piano teacher, lived above a baby boutique on Haverstock Hill. If her seven decades behind a metronome had perhaps not produced a first-rank concert pianist, they had secured Madame lodgings in a tony neighborhood. Its shops offered exquisite shoes, belts, gold, cakes, cheese . . . even the vegetarian restaurants had linen and candles. Foot traffic seemed to be ninety percent au pair girls. Just before seven I rang her doorbell.

Lydia Varnas answered the door in a houndstooth suit festooned with old, heavy jewelry that had probably come from lovers sixty-odd years ago, when she could still toss off the Tchaikovsky concerto and ten orgasms a night. With stacked heels she only reached my nipples and I had eaten suckling pigs with bigger butts than hers. However, her blue eyes could stop a gorgon. I wasn't expecting that: Varnas had looked much softer in the snapshots on Fausto's dresser. Those had been happier days. "Hello," I said. "I'm Leslie Frost. Thank you for seeing me on such short notice."

Accepting my bouquet of roses, Varnas led me inside an apartment crammed with the memorabilia of a lifetime in pedagogy. The autographed pictures alone would render a student's fingers numb with fright. Toss in death masks, plaster casts of hands, honorary doctorates, three pianos, a horrifying collection of sharpened pencils, and the line between castration and music lessons became razor thin. She filled in the spaces with cacti and violets. I didn't see a trace of Fausto anywhere.

Varnas seated herself on a small sofa. "What can I do for you, Miss Frost?" Voice sharp as her eyes. "Don't tell me you're interested in piano lessons."

Not with you, honey. "I just played a concert with Fausto Kiss. I understand he was your pupil at one time. I'd like you to tell me as much as you can about him."

One eyebrow arched ever so slowly upward, as if I had just run a saber between her ribs. "Why would you like to know?"

"He's a stunning pianist. I need to understand why he stopped playing."

She breathed with difficulty: I had ruined another octogenarian's evening. Finally, "He became sick."

"With what? The same thing his mother had?"

No answer as Varnas eyed me suspiciously. "He's playing again?"

"Just one concert."

"How'd he do?"

"Splendidly." After the fit had passed.

"You must have enormous powers of persuasion. I congratulate you." Varnas's bony hand stroked her white fox collar as she sized me up, trying to decide whether to humiliate me with silence or blast a lot of pus from old blisters. The blisters won: audiences were scarce at her age. "As you know, I was a very famous pianist at one time. I played in every major concert hall, with every major orchestra, in the world."

Obviously not very well, otherwise she'd still be doing it. I nodded reverently. "Yes, I know."

"At the height of my career, Ethel Kiss brought me to Washington to hear her son Fausto, who was then seven years old. He was a phenomenally gifted child. Ethel proposed that we travel together so that the boy could continue his studies without interruption." Varnas paused melodramatically. "Naturally, I accepted, honoring my debt to the Muse. For the next ten years the Kisses and I went all over the world. We had quite a time. Quite a time." Varnas's reverie curdled into a frown. "Until Ethel became sick. Since we could no longer travel, I insisted that Fausto stay with me in London. It was high time for him to be on his own, away from his mother. She was a free spirit and the boy needed to become more serious. So he enrolled at the Royal College. Ethel returned to Washington. She made frequent visits, of course. But her health deteriorated over the next three years. She would have lucid days and terrifyingly bad days. It agitated the boy tremendously but he continued to perform. London took notice of him."

"I read a wonderful review of a Wigmore Hall recital."

"Yes, that was quite an evening. I was the proudest teacher on earth." Varnas squinted at me through half-closed eyes. "Are you aware of what happened afterward?"

"Was that the time everyone jumped off the boat?"

"Ethel just leapt right over the railing into the water. It was incredible. Had I been able to swim, I would have tried to rescue her as well." A crocodile sigh: perhaps Varnas had been a little in love with her pupil, who was hopelessly in love with his mother. "Her decline after that was swift. She died three months later. Fausto was in Washington for a month. When he returned to London, he was a shadow of himself. But I convinced him that he must go on. Music was his salvation! He shut himself away and practiced like a fiend."

Silence. I waited for the inevitable. "He was at the Purcell Room, in the middle of an electrifying performance of *Petrouschka*," Varnas continued. "When suddenly he just stopped, stared at his fingers, and staggered offstage. I found him lying on the floor having a—a nervous fit. Just like his mother's. It was horrifying."

"Did anyone besides you see him like that?"

"Only his doctor friend Louis Bailey, who had been treating Ethel. Fausto suddenly awoke, perfectly lucid, and went back to finish the concert." Varnas sighed for the last time. "But nothing I could say could get him in front of an audience again. Fausto was petrified of losing his bearings in public. He knew he had his mother's illness. He went home without finishing school. Twenty-one years old and totally ruined!" A resigned shrug. "He'll die early. Every Kiss does.

I wish his mother had told me that before I sacrificed my career for his."

Quit bawling, Varnas: Ethel's golden handshake had probably bought this apartment. "Are you still in touch with him?"

"No, of course not. He disappointed me profoundly."

Debts to the Muse obviously didn't cover compassion. "Were you acquainted with Fausto's friends?"

"Of course. His apartment was an open house."

"How did he meet Louis Bailey?"

"The young doctor? He heard Fausto on the BBC and introduced himself at a concert a few months after we settled in London. They became inseparable. Louis experimented with everything under the sun in an effort to cure Ethel. When she died, he took it personally. I think she was his first medical defeat."

"How about Bobby Marvel?"

Varnas waved a frail hand through the air. "Nothing but a freeloader. I'm shocked he's gotten as far as he has."

"Jojo Bailey?"

"A harmless fool. He was terrified of only two things. His father and an empty Scotch bottle."

"Bendix Kaar?"

Prolonged silence. When Varnas next spoke, her voice lost half its ballast. "Bendix was a classmate of Fausto's at the Royal College. A repellent creature who fancied himself a composer. He clung to Fausto's coattails, perhaps hoping a little talent might brush off. He was always backstage after a concert telling others what could have been improved."

"Fausto played his sonata, though. I have a tape."

"He performed it out of sheer pity. Deep down, Bendix knew he was inferior material. He resented his smarter friends and was a very bad influence on them. So cynical. I was always afraid of him." Varnas's voice almost disappeared. "I still am."

"Why?"

After a moment she pointed to a photograph on the far wall. "Do you recognize that man?" Not really. He looked like a bullfrog with glasses. "That is Morris Morton."

The name sounded familiar. I smiled vapidly. "A pianist?"

"He studied with me for ten years. He was far too intellectual for public performance. He became a great music critic instead."

I waited. Nothing. "That's nice."

"Obviously you do not know that he was murdered in a most brutal manner. It happened two days after he wrote a scarifying review of Bendix Kaar's opera."

Now I remembered the name. Hey, write a killer review, expect a response. For the first and only time, my sympathy lay with Bendix. "That's quite an allegation, Madame Varnas."

"It's the truth! Poor Morton's body was found in Golders Hill Park with the eyes poked out and various pieces missing. Since he was homosexual and Golders Hill is a well-known meeting place, the police called it a sex crime. Never solved."

"Wouldn't Bendix have been a prime suspect?"

"Bendix was as clever as he was evil. He had a perfect alibi." Varnas managed to shudder. "I believe Fausto and Louis had something to do with it. But those were dark times. Ethel had died and poor Fausto had just had his first attack. He was absolutely distraught."

Dark and sick but true: my gut felt it. "Did you know Justine Cortot?"

"Little Justine? When I first met her, I think she was Louis's girlfriend. They were both studying at Oxford. I think she slept with everyone, including that repulsive Bendix, before she finally went home. The girl was always a little too free with drugs and men." Varnas checked the clasp on a massive brooch. "How do you know Fausto's friends?"

"They're in Washington. I've met them all." Well, almost all.

"They were a wild group. So brilliant and arrogant! Inseparable until Fausto got sick. Then it all burst apart." Overcome with history, Varnas said no more.

I stood to leave. "Thank you for seeing me. Fausto never told me about his past. Or about his friends." I was beginning to understand why.

"Even when he was little more than a boy, he was complicated. You won't get to the bottom of him for years." Madame walked me to her door. "I've never told anyone what I just told you. I hope you will respect my confidence."

"Promise."

"Will you play with him again?"

"I hope so."

"Such a loss. He could have had the world in his hands."

What could I say? Fausto had lived up to expectations, albeit in a different way. Walking back to my car, I tried to imagine the dynamic of a group including four such colossal egotists as Fausto, Bendix, Louis, and Justine. If Louis and Fausto cared enough about Justine to pull a bullet out of her lover, why should they mind going a few steps in the opposite direction for Bendix? Laws were mere suggestions, unnatural and imperfect. Thirty years later, the attitude held: nothing had changed for these people but geography.

I called Maxine. "I'm in London for a few hours. Need details on a Golders Hill murder in the early sixties. Morris Morton was the victim."

"The music critic. Sensational case. What does this have to do with Bailey?"

"I think he did it." That shut her up. "Know anyone who can fill me in?"

"Osman Furshpan in Brighton would know. Used to be a police photographer until he started selling his material to the tabloids. He'll have pictures and stories but they won't come cheap."

"I've got five hundred pounds."

"That should do. Hold on." She clicked off the line. "Osman's ready to roll. Tell him Zazu sent you."

I set out for Brighton, a seedy resort town on the south coast. I had played a concert in some kinky pavilion here several years ago but couldn't remember what or with whom. The local attraction was flesh, and a lot of it was still cruising the sidewalks as I pulled onto the main drag a little after midnight. This seaside park attracted a strange subset of females, either overweight or distastefully scrawny, sporting huge manes of dyed hair, tight skirts, and platform shoes. In their wake slobbered a legion of shifty-eyed men who looked as if they had told their friends they were vacationing in Scotland.

Knocked on a bombproof door near a video arcade. A middle-aged baldie with ponytail answered the door. Eyes mean as a terrier's. Perhaps, with a name like Osman, his destiny was foreordained. "Hello, big boy." I was a good five inches taller than he. "Zazu sent me."

Ozzy led me upstairs to a tastefully furnished flat. He poured me a gin then made the mistake of putting a hand on my thigh. In the ensuing scuffle his switchblade gouged a two-foot slit in his leather sofa. "You bitch!" he cried. "That sofa cost me two thousand quid!"

"I want pictures of Morris Morton," I said, dropping onto a wooden chair. "Don't give me a hard time or you'll end up looking like him." I dropped three bills on the table. "We'll start with that."

Osman disappeared into a back room. I wondered what he did by day. Probably wrote poetry. He returned with a large envelope. "There," he said, whipping it across the coffee table.

Morris Morton had paid for his nasty reviews one hundred times over. The pictures of his remains looked cubist. All ten fingers cut off. Castrated. Eyeless head just about severed. Railway nails in his ears. Gutted, sort of.

Osman sidled next to me. "I took those shots. Thrilling, aren't they?"

Only to a musician. I peered at the crushed grass. "Where's his cock?"

"Nicely tucked in on the other side. I've got pictures of that, too."

"What about his guts? Liver, kidneys?"

"Gone. Maybe they got eaten."

One person couldn't have done this much damage. Two minimum, three likely. With four the odds of one wimp with pangs of conscience became too high. I threw the other two bills on the table. "That's all I've got. Tell me about the case. You were still on active duty at the time, I presume."

"Right. We got the call around noon. A dogwalker discovered the body. It had been there at least twelve hours."

"Isn't Golders Hill full of people?"

"They're all busy with other things, if you know what I mean."

"What had Morton been doing that evening?"

"He went to a concert then went to the paper to write the review. The operator remembered a call coming in. Morton left in a rush. A cab took him to Golders Hill."

"Man or woman calling?"

"Man, of course. Morton went directly to a hard-core section of the park. He preferred the rough trade. He was alive when the appendages came off, when the eardrums were punctured, the eyes gouged out."

Hey, write murderous reviews, expect justice. "And throughout all this he didn't make any noise?"

"If he did, it must have sounded like sex."

"There were no hairs, body fluids, razor blades, needles, hatchets, bloody clothes, mad dogs, found at the scene?"

"Nothing. Mind you, a rainstorm swept through London just before dawn and washed most of the evidence away. Footprints and the like. The killers may have listened to the weather report before starting." Furshpan thoughtfully pulled his goatee. "But they were smart to begin with. They wore surgical gloves. And they used professional instruments for the organ removal. That was carefully done. Odd bit is, they used kitchen utensils for the various amputations and disfigurings. Bloody crude work. As if they wanted Morton to suffer."

"So there were two killers?"

"At the very minimum. One to harvest the organs, the other to mutilate him. That never got into the papers, of course. We didn't want a panic on our hands."

"Any suspects?"

"An Indian doctor who was in the body parts business. But that was a cold trail. We interviewed every gay surgeon in London. We hauled in every pothead peddling hallucinogens. We placed decoys in Golders Hill. Nothing."

Of course nothing: these weren't ordinary butchers. "Wouldn't a music critic have a fair number of enemies?"

"Yes. We spoke with hordes of musicians. Very few of them were sorry that Morris was gone. We were rather suspicious of a young fellow at the Royal College of Music who had been the target of a particularly bad review. But he had a solid alibi."

"So who do you think did it?"

"Could have been anyone. Morton lived by himself. He liked violent sex with strangers. He wrote reviews that made people very resentful. He abused waiters. From all accounts, he was a shit. And he could have been in the wrong place at the wrong time." Furshpan sighed. "Wish I knew where the eyeballs ended up, though. I still have bad dreams about them."

Looked at my watch. "Keep the pictures. Don't walk me out."

"Give my love to Zazu," he called.

I drove like a maniac to London. Just managed to chuck the rental car and buy a ticket before the Concorde took off. As it pierced the clouds, I ached for Fausto.

Chapter Eleven

Took almost as long to get from New York to Washington as it had taken the Concorde to bring me back to America. I got to my hotel around one in the afternoon and wasn't surprised to find another bouquet of orchids waiting. *Love from your fan in the ski mask,* said the card. What a clown. Checked my messages. No word from Fausto, damn him. Rhoby wanted to meet ASAP. Gretchen wanted to go alligator shopping since her monkey had still not returned. Bendix wanted to take me to lunch. I called him back. "Am I forgiven?"

"I behaved abominably the other night," he said. "It wasn't your fault."

Perhaps Fausto's eyeballs were lying on the bottom of the Reflecting Pool. "Let's have tea."

Next door, Duncan was relaxing with the soaps. I knocked on his door. "Would you mind turning that down? I'm trying to think."

The latch opened a few inches, revealing a face covered with green mud. "Where have you been? Sleeping with that fat slob again?"

I muted the television. "I thought you were on an NEA panel this week."

"We ran out of money. My God, look at the time! I must get into the bath. Justine and I have a fund-raiser this afternoon." Duncan twirled the spigots in the tub. "You look lousy," he called over the thunder. "Why don't you try some of this mask? It's especially for tired skin."

"No thanks. How's your lady friend these days?"

"Overworked but blissfully happy."

"With you?"

"That's right. I'm the first person to make her laugh in thirty years."

Laughter? Bliss? Why had Justine told Fausto that Duncan was becoming uncontrollable? More to the point, what was she supposed to be controlling? Didn't make sense. "How's your wrist?"

"Much better. Justine's finally coming to Cleveland to meet my folks. We've been arguing endlessly about dates."

"I thought you never had fights."

"They're scheduling conflicts, not fights! Something always comes up." Duncan frowned. "Mom had to put her apple pie back in the freezer three times now."

"Don't tell me Justine puts her work ahead of you. That's outrageous."

"I finally put my foot down. It's this weekend or never."

"That's one way to find out where you really stand," I said, rolling off the bed. "I hope you're prepared to eat crow instead of apple pie."

"You're the one who's going to be eating crow," he shouted after me. "Fausto Kiss serves it to all his friends."

Duncan's comments pushed me over a rickety edge so I called Fausto and let the phone ring fifty-one times before giving up. Bastard! Maybe he and Louis were waiting for me at the jail. I cabbed to that surreal Hilton overlooking the

Congressional Cemetery. Guests here arrived in police cars instead of limos. They didn't bring much luggage and they weren't particularly happy to be signing in, nor was the staff any happier to be registering them. I joined a queue leading to a rotund woman in a bulletproof booth. "I'd like to visit Figgis Cole."

"Coal?" She tapped her keyboard. "Like the stuff you burn in the backyard?"

"No, like Nat King." I still had to spell it for her.

"No Figs Cole here."

"He came in almost a month ago. September fifth."

More typing, more staring at screen. "Removed."

Goddamn it! "What does that mean? He went home?"

"Out September sixth, nine fifty-eight A.M. That's all I can tell you."

Louis hadn't even been here for one day? "Look," I said. "I've got to speak with him. Where'd he go?"

"That's classified information."

I reeled outside to a concrete bench and tried to remember the itineraries of criminals in the U.S. justice system. First they were caught committing a crime. Next they were taken to the police station, there to await arraignment by a judge who either set bail or let them go until the trial. Louis hadn't made bail. He could have tapped any number of friends for the cash, but no: looked as if he wanted to stay behind bars, invisible, for a while. If no one knew Louis was in jail, then who had removed him?

A Department of Corrections van jerked to a stop in front of my bench. Two guards hopped out, unlocked the rear doors, and hustled a sullen passenger into her new lodgings. Before the driver pulled away, I knocked on his window. Good-looking kid, quick eyes, rich mouth, the type who could always use another gold necklace or a little spare cash on weekends. But maybe not. A lot of these sharpies belonged to the Nation of Islam now. "I wonder if you could help me," I smiled. "Do you transport most of the prisoners around here?"

"Me and my buddies, yeah." He looked me over. "My name's Jason. What's a nice lady like you doing in a place like this?"

Jason got one hundred bucks in his lap. "An inmate named Figgis Cole left here at ten in the morning on September sixth. I need to know where he went. Do you think you could have a word with your dispatcher?"

"I don't think that would be a problem."

I wrote down the information. "How soon can you find out?"

"My shift ends at two. I'll try then." He read the name. "Figs? Is this your man?"

He was. I tucked another hundred behind Jason's ear. "Don't make me wait too long."

A promenade in the Congressional Cemetery was slightly less depressing than an hour's wait outside the jail, so I walked a few blocks to the entry gates on E Street. One car was parked in the shade; by yon crabgrass, a few tourists gawked at J. Edgar Hoover's grave. Since my last visit the weeds around the chapel had grown another few inches. The garbage cans erupted with trash. When the breeze shifted, I smelled urine and rotting meat.

Over to the Kiss plot. On Ethel's grave lay a dozen white roses, very fresh, left within the hour. The grass had been trimmed, the gravestones washed. Several plots away, two marines were sprucing up John Philip Sousa's current address. "Was someone just here?" I asked. "A big fellow?"

"He left about fifteen minutes ago," one of them replied.

Fausto had clipped the grass very short, as if he wouldn't be returning for a while. My eyes kept returning to the numbers on the various headstones: yep, I had added right last time. Forty-eight was the average Kiss life span: not a lot of years in which to accumulate wisdom, but they all had probably started early. Who would take care of the plot after Fausto? Too bad he had never come to grips with marriage or reproduction. Both were tough calls for a philosopher.

On my way out, I saw the old gardener still trying to restore dignity to the bottom of the hill. "How's it going?"

He stopped wrestling with either a root or a petrified anaconda. "I'm kind of surprised to see you back. One visit is all most people can take."

Necrophilia was my hobby. "Lots of interesting stuff here."

He returned to the root, I to the jail, where my new friend Jason waited for me. He had changed into a white polo shirt and two little gold earrings. "I was getting worried," he said.

Sat beside him on the scorching hot concrete. "Any luck with your dispatcher?"

"A snap." He read from a little rip of paper with block lettering. "September six, we picked up a single prisoner from here at 10:02 A.M. and moved him to Lorton." That was a penitentiary ten miles southwest. Facilities for all ranges of miscreant plus a youth center for ten-year-olds who set their grandmothers on fire. "He was delivered to the maximum security area."

Just great. "Thanks, Jason."

"Eh—we could take a ride down to Lorton right now. I know the way."

"I don't think my boyfriend would like that."

"You got a boyfriend? Shee-it. What's his name?"

Dropped another hundred into Jason's lap. "Benjamin Franklin." Jumped into a cab that had just discharged someone's unlucky mother at the entrance. "Take me to the Mall," I said, blowing a kiss as we rolled away.

Risky calling Berlin from downtown, but I found a phone

at the end of the Reflecting Pool. Tourists had bagged it for the day, and bureaucrats were beginning to stray into the sweltering outdoors, walking as if they had diaper rash. "Did Osman deliver?" Maxine asked.

"Perfectly. I'm back in Washington. Bailey was removed from the D.C. jail to Lorton less than a day after his arrival. What's the drill here."

No use crying over spilled milk so the Queen said, "One, the warden either thinks Bailey is a danger to the other inmates, or he thinks Bailey's in danger himself and sends him to a more secure facility. Two, the warden receives an order from Justice or Corrections or some heavy to move the prisoner. I'd say the latter since Bailey was trying to lie low. I don't think he'd cause much trouble."

"How soon can you find out?"

"Half an hour."

While Maxine was fishing, I walked to the Lincoln Memorial. Inside, teachers were trying to explain to the young what Honest Abe had done to earn such a big statue. I called her back from a different phone. "Figgis Cole was transferred to Lorton due to overcrowded conditions in D.C.," she said.

"Transferring one prisoner to maximum security at Lorton relieved the crowding? Give me a break. Someone got to the warden."

"He must have left a paper trail." Signatures and seals proving he had just been following orders, he didn't know anything, it wasn't his fault, please guys don't take my pension away. "He just hired a new assistant named Betty-Lou Beasley. Divorced with two kids. She's ten grand into her credit cards." Maxine gave me address, car license, description.

"This is a long shot, Maxine."

"You getting into the warden's office is an even longer one."

I returned to jail. In the parking lot I found Betty-Lou's dented red Honda, its back seat a sty of Tupperware, Wendy's bags, cheap toys. On the dashboard lay three parking tickets: things were looking up. Around five o'clock a white woman, thirtyish and going downhill fast, headed toward the car. Her hair was dyed the color of a trombone. Blondes had more fun? Not this one. "Betty-Lou Beasley?" I asked.

"Speak to my lawyer." She jumped into her car then noticed the green bills tucked behind the windshield wipers. Down rolled her window. "What do you want?"

"Two minutes of your time. I'm not from any lawyer. I have nothing to do with your divorce or your credit cards." I peeled the bills free. "I need your help."

She stared at the possibility of nice birthday parties, new school clothes. "You're not going to kill me or anything, are you? I have two girls."

"I don't kill people." Not on purpose.

"Okay. Get in." Betty-Lou drove straight into a traffic jam on Independence Avenue. "I suppose you're not going to tell me your name."

I gave her the money. "I work for a government agency. We're interested in a prisoner who was transferred from D.C. to Lorton on September sixth. All we need to know is who ordered the move. Your boss the warden certainly has the papers. We just want a copy. He won't get into any trouble."

"Is this like a turf war between the CIA and the FBI?"

"The information is worth two thousand dollars to us. No one's going to get hurt. Your boss was just following orders."

"What about me? Can I get into trouble?"

"Not if you're careful. Two thousand dollars is a lot of money. Tax-free. Three thousand if you get me the information by tomorrow morning."

"I've never done anything like this before," Betty-Lou whined, almost rear-ending the car ahead of us. "I have to think about it."

"Think about it all you want. Just don't think out loud. That could be dangerous." In a few seconds Betty-Lou realized that once she had let me into her car, she was in quicksand up to her three chins. "Drop me behind that bus. I'll call you tomorrow." Patted her arm. "Trust me."

My head felt as if I had just stuck it down the barrel of a circus cannon. I just had to keep reminding myself of Betty-Lou's credit problem and hope she had watched enough television to persuade herself that a mother's first responsibility was to keep her daughters in designer jeans. Screw national security. Back at the hotel, I called Fausto again: still no answer. Duncan was correct: I had been dropped like a hot potato.

That put me in a ruthless mood for Happy Hour with Bendix. I met him in a Dupont Circle bistro impressive less for its food than its absurd prices. The only people stupid enough to pay them appeared to be lobbyists and Asian tourists. "Hot out there," I said, slithering into my seat.

Bendix looked fresh as a scoop of sherbet. "Thanks for seeing me. I was afraid you might have gone back to Berlin."

"I'm having too much fun here." Flagged a waiter and ordered alcohol in slush. "But all good things come to an end. I listened to your cassette. It's brilliant. Why'd you stop? You could have been on your ninth symphony by now."

Bendix was speechless. He had probably planned to round the conversation to this intimate topic after five long cocktails. "You liked it?"

"Loved it. So cleverly written for the piano. Such original thematic development. Fausto turned in a great performance, but the piece stands on its own." I stared him deep in the id. "How'd you get into composing?"

I finally got the hidden history of Bendix Kaar. One day misfit teenager, thinking he's about to hear a Beatles album, drops the needle on his mother's beloved recording of *Romeo & Juliet*. The skies open and he resolves to become the next Tchaikovsky. Learns violin well enough to earn scholarship to B+ conservatory. Transfers to the Royal College because he hates the humiliation of playing in an orchestra and no one in America wants to perform his music. Lo and behold, he has as much difficulty getting a hearing in London as he did in Cincinnati. Life becomes hell.

I swallowed half my drink. "Didn't you tell me you wrote an opera? That got performed, didn't it?"

The composer downshifted from fifth to neutral. "Yes. But not without help. Fausto paid for the whole thing."

"Nothing wrong with a patron, is there? How'd it go?"

Neutral to reverse. "I was booed."

"So what? So was Stravinsky."

"Stravinsky must have had a stronger stomach. I didn't leave my bed for two weeks." Bendix blacked out on the review and his catharsis on Golders Hill. "I decided to abandon music."

"That must have been incredibly painful."

"Amputation beats gangrene. I charted my ship on another course and never looked back—until I heard you and Fausto play my sonata the other night. God, it was good! Stunning, really. I haven't been able to sleep since."

A Japanese woman approached the table. "May I have autograph, Miss Frost?"

I scribbled on her menu. "Composers don't succeed until

they're dead. I think you took the right course. Look at all the good you've done the world."

"The world?" he croaked. "What about me?"

Ah, if only Fausto could see this. "You can always go back to composing."

"But will I have anything to say?" Bendix took a long pull at his vodka tonic. "I may have exhausted all my creative juices in Washington. I'm not a kid bursting with ideas and idealism anymore."

Next he'd want his head in my lap. I was suddenly tired of playing confessor to men who felt lonely at the top. Barnard was dead and one of these miserable wretches had killed her. "Why don't you try writing an hour a day? If Fausto could throw together a recital in a week, you could toss off a two-part invention."

"I've got a lot more on my plate than Fausto." Bendix ordered another round. "He's become quite a good friend of yours, I notice."

"He's an unusual man." How smoothly Bendix had usurped the reins of conversation. Instead of cantering with him, I asked, "How's Jojo Bailey? He's quite a friend of yours, I notice."

"One of my oldest. Goes back to my London days. What's happened to him is horrible beyond words. I wouldn't wish a death like that on my worst enemy."

"Does he recognize you?"

"He's in a coma. Aurilla and I can barely bring ourselves to visit him. I can't stand the sight of blood." Unless it was issuing from a music critic's eye sockets, of course. "Jojo was doing so much good work."

"I don't think the two of you will have to visit him much longer."

Bendix looked sharply at me. "Who told you that? Fausto?"

"Everyone knows he's fading fast. And everyone says Aurilla's a shoo-in to replace him."

"It ain't over until the fat lady sings. Who knows what tricks Bobby and Paula might have up their sleeves."

I patted his arm. "You're just feeling a little stage fright."

Bendix finished his drink. "Maybe. Aurilla and I have worked years to get where we are. Her career started rather unexpectedly, do you know? Her husband died in a plane crash. She finished his term and never looked back."

"Fate."

"You make your own fate. He was a nothing. Aurilla was better off without him." A strange glow, somewhere between an alcohol buzz and a demented ecstasy, suffused Bendix's face. "She'd be a fantastic president." He caught himself. "Vice president. Does Fausto think she's going to make it?"

"We haven't talked about it."

"Right! You two just concentrate on music!" Bendix tried not to snarl. "What does Bobby say about her?"

Cool it, Smith. No secrets in this town. "We haven't really discussed Aurilla. Bobby's been preoccupied with Jojo. He's pretty upset at losing him."

"He should be. Jojo was his favorite drinking partner." A strange remark about the statesman whose impending departure had so pained Bendix just a moment ago. "Does either of those two ever mention Jojo's brother Louis?"

"Louis the doctor? I thought he was lost in the jungle. That's what Myrna said at your dinner the other night."

"What did Fausto have to say about that?"

"He said he hadn't heard from Louis in months."

Crunch went the ice cube between Bendix's teeth. When he smiled, I recoiled: his eyes looked exactly like Aurilla's. "I suppose you find Fausto fascinating," he said.

"Fausto's got a brain."

"A devious one," Bendix retorted. "He likes nothing better than putting his old friends in their places. It's his way of compensating for his own failure."

Gee, Fausto had said more or less the same thing about Bendix. Bobby had said more or less the same thing about Fausto. My stomach turned: had Barnard been caught in nothing more than a monstrous case of sibling rivalry? "I think I can handle him."

"If I were you, I'd go with Bobby. You won't get quite as hurt."

That soulless smile was beginning to unnerve me. Finished my drink. "How's Gretchen?"

"Making life intolerable for her mother, as usual."

"She seems to dislike you."

"Of course she does. I made her practice violin two hours a day. Thought it would straighten her out." Total backfire. "She's going to school in Switzerland next week."

"Is she excited?"

"She doesn't know it yet." Bendix floated a fifty-dollar bill to the table. "May I drop you at the hotel?"

I opted to walk. Outside, the heat devoured us. "Give my best to Aurilla."

"I'll be seeing her in New York tonight."

"Nice of her to let Bobby and me use her summer house."

Bendix barely missed a step. "He needs an escape from that virago of a wife."

I kissed the composer's mouth, which was about as responsive as a nose. "Send me your first invention?"

"If I write it." He squeezed my hand a little too hard. "Thanks for your support."

Thanks for the advice to the lovelorn. I ate dinner alone, haunted by the gleam in Bendix's eye as he talked about Aurilla's glorious future. The evening news was all about defunct Jojo. I thought about driving to Lorton and dropping in

on Louis. Instead I called Gretchen, a younger prisoner.
"How'd you like to go out for a little ice cream?"

"I can't. It's a school night."

"Why don't I bring some over then?"

"That would be okay. I like chocolate-chip mint."

Aurilla's mansion loomed dark and empty now that her
party had ended. Between curb and doorbell, I passed five
bananas in pink saucers. "I'm Gretchen's friend," I smiled at
the woman who opened the door. Each time I came here, a
different maid answered, looking more frazzled than her
predecessor. "Brought some ice cream."

A volleyball struck the maid in the back. "Get out of the
way!" my playmate shouted.

"We'll be in the kitchen," I told the woman, grabbing
Gretchen by the wrist. "That wasn't very nice."

"Ow! You're hurting me!"

Pulled her through the empty banquet hall to the kitchen.
Not quite as impressive as Fausto's galley, but Aurilla enter-
tained less. I stuffed Gretchen in a chair and got two spoons
from a drawer. "How's school?"

"I hate it."

"That's the spirit." Dug into the ice cream. "Guess Herman hasn't come back, eh?"

"He's a bad monkey. I want an alligator now."

"Where'd you get him anyway?"

"In that country Uncle Bendix took me to. Belize."

"You were in Belize?" I tried to choke down the cold
stuff. "That's pretty exciting. Better than Disneyland, I bet."

"No it wasn't. The air-conditioning didn't work."

"Were you on vacation?"

"No! Mom was at a conference. Uncle Bendix made me
play the violin there. I didn't want to. He promised me a
monkey, so I did."

"What did you play?"

"A Bach suite."

Bendix and Aurilla haul Gretchen the Untouchable to Belize to perform Bach during an environmental conference? Something wacko here. "Who'd you play for?"

"People in a hospital. It was too hot and I couldn't stay in tune. I thought Uncle Bendix would hit me. But he clapped afterward. Then he said I could go home." She licked her spoon. "I flew back in a private plane with Uncle Fausto. It was lots of fun. Herman came with me in a little box."

I nearly gagged. "So you went to a hot country, played a concert, and left? That sounds like something I would do."

"It wasn't much fun."

No kidding. "I'm sure the audience loved it."

"They weren't even listening! They were all in bed sleeping. They looked horrible. I brought some nice toys and they didn't even want them."

"I'm sure your mother was very proud of you."

"She didn't come to the concert," Gretchen scoffed. "Only Uncle Bendix. And Dr. Tatal. She gave me a doll."

We concentrated on the ice cream for a while. "So have you been practicing?" I asked.

For once, Gretchen looked sheepish. "I broke my violin. I was angry that Uncle Bendix took Herman away."

One hundred grand in splinters: that had probably earned her banishment to Switzerland. "Can you get it fixed?"

"Mom says no more violin. When can we go shopping for alligators?"

"Why don't you get a dog instead? They're a lot more fun to play with."

"I want the alligator to eat Uncle Bendix."

This was the second time Gretchen had mentioned killing him. Maybe she was the reincarnation of the murdered music critic. "Why do you hate him?"

"Because he doesn't like me. He just likes Mom."

The maid anxiously peeped in. "How's everything?"

Fubar. I put my spoon in the sink. "Back to your homework, Gretchen. I'll come by soon."

I wandered around Georgetown until nightfall. Then I crawled into my little hole in the zoo and, just to torment myself, hooked into the airline files. Yep, Gretchen and Bendix had flown to Belize on August 15. No record of her return, but that was because she had come back in Uncle Fausto's plane. I took a deep breath and cut to Fausto's phone tap. Again, not many calls, but the ones that did get through wrapped my gut in knots. The first was from James in Belize. "Eh Fausto, I've got a bit of bad news."

"What's that," Fausto answered dully, as if he already knew.

"They found Simon in the Macal. Not much left of him, poor bugger. No signs of violence on the bits still intact. Maybe he hit his head on a rock and drowned."

"Ah. Yes."

"Did you need him for anything? I'd be happy to step in."

"Possibly." Signal flat, weak, emanating from another planet. "I'll let you know."

The next call was from Vicky Chickering. "I hear your little pickup trio was a roaring success. Is Rhoby over there now, by chance?"

"No."

"I can't seem to find her. I called Frost's hotel but she's not in, either. You don't suppose they're out somewhere, do you?"

"Vicky darling, I'm not the vice squad."

"Tell me something. What do you think Leslie Frost is doing here?"

A pause. Then, tonelessly, "Enjoying the scenery. Why?"

"I know you're fond of her, but something's not on the

level with that bitch. I've thought so since the night I saw her at Ford's Theatre. She said someone just sent her a ticket. And she *used it!* That's not normal, is it?"

"I'm afraid she's that type of girl."

"Well, where does she go all day? She's never in her hotel."

"How would you know?"

"I have my sources. Where is she now?"

Fortunately, Fausto didn't suggest that I was in London with his old piano teacher. "She's going back to Berlin in a day or two. Then your worries will be over."

"It won't be soon enough. You wouldn't happen to know where Bobby was last night, would you?"

"No. Why?"

"Something happened to his ear. He said he caught it on his comb. Looks to me like someone bit him. Paula's furious."

"Vicky, get a grip. No one could bite the president without the Secret Service going ballistic. Maybe Paula did it herself."

"She and I were in Seattle. You're no help at all, Fausto."

"You're asking for answers outside my area of expertise, dear." My imagination, or had a little spark returned to his voice? "Did Paula get her tea yet?"

"You ask me every time and every time the answer's no," Chickering sighed. "Maybe you should stop asking for a while."

"Poor Paula. How she must suffer."

"If you see Rhoby, tell her I'm looking for her, would you?"

"Of course. Bye-bye, dear."

Good old Fausto: he had given Chickie pebbles for pearls. A call came from Duncan, about eight this morning. "Okay, where is she?" he demanded. "This is Duncan Zadinsky."

"At the White House, my boy. I believe that's where she still works."

"Not Justine, you fool! I'm looking for Leslie!"

"I haven't seen her in days."

"What? You sleep with her then don't even know where she goes?"

"Now that's an interesting bit of information, Duncan. Where'd you get it?"

"Off Justine's pager! It's no secret! The whole town knows! Look, I need to speak with Leslie this second."

"Try the president's hot line," Fausto snapped, and hung up. He immediately dialed Justine. "I understand your pager's been getting a workout. You haven't been keeping your charge under very good control, my dear."

"I've got a full-time job," she snapped. "He's a loose cannon. I told you he was getting out of hand."

"In that case, we're going to move things up a day."

Short silence. "That's going to be a major pain in the ass."

"Take care of it." Fausto hung up and called Tuna. "Get your people ready to go tomorrow."

"You can count on me, my friend."

I felt sick. Walked to Connecticut Avenue. Another hot, dense night, gagging with rain: all the sidewalk cafés were retracting their tables. I cut over to Fausto's street. Since my last stroll here, a few trees had yellowed. Didn't jibe with the eighty-plus temperature. Another autumn already? Each year it filled me with ever more desperate premonitions. I hurried past the dying leaves: since last October I had unwittingly learned a few more words of their secret language.

Red Corvette in Fausto's driveway, exactly where I had left it before my date with Bobby. Downstairs, lights in his music room. I crept to the window. Fausto was playing Chopin's Fourth Ballade. I felt a stab of envy: pianists were so lucky. They got to do it all: melody, harmony, rhythm. No interpretive arguments, no backstage seizures from accompanists. No problems with intonation, no welts on their necks. And a glorious repertoire. From the shadows of lust, envy, and longing, I watched him play. His hands moved so gracefully and familiarly over the keys. Drove me mad. Why didn't I just leave a dying man to his labyrinth? Fausto would never need me. I almost went home. Then the wind stirred and I smelled the foreboding breath of autumn. Suddenly it didn't matter what games he and I were playing: they'd soon be over.

Flat yellow leaves scurried over my feet as I let myself in. Stood outside the music room as the ballade rushed to a dark, tumultuous end. I knocked. My pulse ran wild as I heard footsteps. The door opened. Fausto's round eyes flared but his mouth didn't move. I was acutely aware that I had interrupted him and that he knew I had killed Simon. Hell, he probably knew I had been hanging off Barnard's balcony. I wanted to put my arms around him, tell him I was harmless, get invited back upstairs. "Sorry to drop by like this. I saw lights and thought it would be a good time to pick up my violin."

The little pink mouth altered: perhaps my lies had amused him. "Come in." Fausto's Hawaiian shirt fluttered as he went to the bar. "What can I get for you?"

Gin and an erection. He looked awful. "Have you seen your doctor?" I asked.

"Tomorrow."

"You haven't had another spell?"

"All quiet. Cheers." We clanked glasses. "Where have you been?"

Jails, cemeteries, England. "Waiting for you to call."

"Your pianist is looking for you. He sounds distraught."

"Maybe Justine's about to punt him." I walked to the piano. "Did Rhoby invite you to some sort of luncheon?"

"Me? I'm the wrong gender."

Not a word about Chickering. I diddled with his music. "What are you working on?"

"This and that. Old friends. Everything comes back so quickly. Hard to believe I've been away from it for so long." Fausto tugged a tiny twig from my blouse. "Rolling in the grass, dear?"

I watched his slow fingers snap it in half. "I rode with Bobby for exactly one hour. We did nothing but talk."

"Really now!" Fausto lit a cigarette. "Talk about what?"

"The weather. Jojo." *Go, Smith.* "You and Louis Bailey digging a bullet from his crotch."

Fausto went absolutely still. "He told you *that?*"

"He knows I won't repeat it."

Through hot white clouds, Fausto's eyes burned a hole in me. Maybe he was trying to decide if I had killed Simon for business or pleasure. "Entertaining story, isn't it."

"I liked the part about you leaving him in your apartment for a week." Finished my drink. "Where'd you and Louis run off to? Bayreuth?"

"Oxford. Louis was experimenting with endocrine extracts. I was his guinea pig."

"You volunteered for that kind of stuff?"

"It was the sixties. I was curious and idealistic."

Forget idealism: Fausto had been either collecting or disbursing chits. Huge ones. "Did he discover anything?"

He puffed away. "We're still working on it."

"What does that mean? You're still eating spleens in the name of science? Maybe all that shit is what's giving you the convulsions."

He only stared at my thighs. "I've been thinking about you," he said finally. "Would you play something with me?"

Hadn't been expecting that. "What did you have in mind?"

"Whatever pleases you."

"I've had two drinks."

"I've had four."

He was bigger. However, chamber music being an exalted form of foreplay, I chose the Brahms G Major Sonata. It reflected the willows outside. Before tuning my violin, I poured myself another drink. "When was the last time you played this? Thirty years ago?"

"Something like that." He watched me tighten the horsehair on my bow, straighten the music stand. Even after I was ready, he kept looking. Finally he cleared his throat and played the first serene chords. I smiled: Duncan would have required a two-minute chat about tempo and three pages to settle into a compromise. Fausto just read my mind. I envied the ivory beneath his fingers. Twined my notes around his and rolled with him through a shaded vale that opens only to people making music. As usual with Fausto, in music as in life, he knew my part intimately. I felt enclosed and protected. I had met so few, so pitifully few, men who could rise to that minimal challenge. They were the only ones worth going to the precipice for.

Long, languorous piano introduction to the second movement: if Fausto were trying to woo me, he was succeeding. We slid into a gentle trance beyond time, perhaps beyond passion. I needed another belt of gin before facing the last movement: like much of Brahms, it was about death. Strange that playing those pieces made me want to live forever. The music ended but my pulse just got thicker.

"Thank you," Fausto said finally.

I packed my violin. He followed me to the foyer. I had one hand on the doorknob when his fingers closed around my wrist. *Thunk* went my case on his antique sideboard as he backed me against the door. Fausto's warm tongue took over mine. His hands swept over my neck, down my back and between my legs, as if we had already rehearsed this a thousand times and I had shown him where all the secret places were. Oh God, there was no beast purer than a man finally consummating his lust. Fausto was humid and rhythmic as the ocean: thought I'd fry when his mouth found my nipples. No way we were going to make it upstairs. "Do it here," I said, unzipping my pants. Didn't care how. I just wanted something of his inside of me.

Fausto kneeled as if he were about to propose. He peeled off my pants: years out of the loop and he did a better job than Bobby Marvel, who practiced daily. It had been a while since I had been near water and I knew I smelled like an animal. Welcome to the she-jungle, Fausto. He swung my leg over his shoulder and put his tongue into the core of me. Immediate enslavement: tongue was twin of cunt. Better suited to the terrain, capable of infinitely greater delicacy: when his soft flesh met mine, pushed just an inch inside where all the thunder lay, there could be no escape. That Fausto should be able to poise my entire existence on the tip of his tongue was both horrifying and inevitable. When I felt myself slipping away, I wrapped my legs around his neck so that he wore a necklace made of woman: drown in that, sir. He only made low sounds of pleasure, perhaps triumph.

Afterward I lay like a puddle on the floor. When he finally leaned down to kiss me, I smelled myself. The fragrance was like Man, but more complex. I tried to reach his penis. "Don't bother, darling. Not now, anyhow."

"Later?"

"I hope so." Deep kisses. "You have a gorgeous body." Job requirement. "Your mind's not bad, either. It's just that what I see is not what I get." His tongue wet my throat, his breath dried it. "Drives me mad."

Each of us became lost in our own contradictions and codes of silence. Eventually he slid my pants back on. "Hungry? I've got a few odds and ends in the fridge."

We went to the kitchen. Leg of lamb, smoked duck, three terrines: some leftovers. I sliced bread as he brought a thick yellow soup to the table. "Mulligatawny. Careful, it's hot."

No kidding. I was searching in the refrigerator for yogurt when, behind me, a knife dropped to the floor. Fausto was staring at his hands.

"Upstairs," he said. Didn't have to explain what was about to happen this time. I slung his arm around my shoulder. We staggered out of the kitchen. "I'm not going to make it."

"Yes you are cmon cmon one foot ahead of the other." If he lost it halfway up the stairs, I couldn't hold him. "Fight it. We're almost there."

He was only running on half a cylinder by the time we made the landing. His body was locking up as I loaded him onto the bed, rolled him toward the center, loosened his shirt. A moment of total quiet before convulsions shook him head to foot. They were worse this time and he made awful noises as he chewed up the tongue that had given me such pleasure just a few moments ago. In seconds the Fausto I knew became nothing more than an obscene mass of meat with defective circuitry. As it moaned and gurgled, I felt the same terror that had gripped me in the jungle: how easily nature stripped us of our cherished inklings of godhood. A momentary chemical imbalance and *pouf!* Gone.

Much more shuddering and he'd snap his neck. I could only watch as the spasms slowly petered out and Fausto lay still as a corpse on his embroidered sheets. I leaned over his heart, got a thump rather than a pulse. His breath again smelled as if his internal organs had been left out in the sun. Brought a wastebasket from the bathroom since the first thing Fausto had done upon waking last time was throw up. I petted his arm, waiting for intelligence to return to that waxen face, for speech to return to that mangled tongue. I whispered in his ear. He wasn't bouncing back as quickly as he had last time.

Take a look around, Smith. This could be your only chance.

"Fausto," I repeated.

Barnard's dead. I slipped out to the hallway. The first two doors led to bedrooms that probably hadn't been used since his mother's wake. Third door was locked. Fausto didn't give the slightest indication that he felt me taking the key from his back pocket. I entered his study, which looked like my little nook at the zoo: computers, printers, tape decks . . . Fausto had probably spent a lot of time here before remembering how to play the piano. No incriminating papers, not even a phone bill. I didn't have time to poke into his computer. Almost missed the one-inch fax still in the machine. No headings to help me out with time or origin. It looked more like an error than a message.

SEE YOU AT DULLES TOMORROW NIGHT. ALL CLEAR. JAMES

James the mercenary? Why was he coming to town? Damn, the Queen was right. Witnesses were like little weights: wrap enough of them around your ankles and soon you'd drown. What was *all clear?*

Fausto lay on his bed exactly as I had left him. I returned his key. Still no color in his cheeks, no movement behind the eyelids. Wherever he was, it didn't seem pleasant. It just seemed like . . . death. I took his hand. "Fausto," I pleaded.

He shivered so I kept whispering. After a while he opened his eyes. Stared at the ceiling before facing his witness. "I must have had another spell."

"Just a little one," I lied. "How do you feel?"

Only strong enough to smile. "What time is it?"

"About one."

"Just a little spell, eh? I don't even remember getting up here."

"It wasn't your most graceful trip to the boudoir. How's your stomach?"

Ten seconds later, empty. The pâté didn't look much different coming up than it had going down. "Sorry, darling," Fausto wheezed, falling back to the pillow.

I cleaned his face with a damp washcloth. "What brings these things on?"

"No one knows. They go away for years then come back. Always a little worse." He closed his eyes. "Ah, that feels nice. You're a wonderful nurse. I sense a great maternal instinct. Think about children someday, would you?"

"Cart before horse."

He drifted off. "Don't tell me you would require a husband first."

"I was thinking more on the order of committed baby-sitter. I'm on the road a lot."

"Don't leave the child home. Take a nanny along. Take a few tutors. That's what my mother did. We had a wonderful life."

"Your mother was a special case."

Long silence. Again I thought he had slipped back into his coma. Got rid of the puke and refreshed the washcloth under cold water. As I was daubing his forehead, Fausto half opened his eyes. "Did you enjoy your first marriage?"

"You mean my only marriage? It only lasted a few months."

"Time isn't everything. Answer the question."

"Yes, I enjoyed it. Hugo was the perfect fusion of lover and father."

"Not friend?"

"We didn't know each other long enough."

"Do you miss him?"

I only found out last spring that he hadn't married me for love. Since then, I had stopped thinking of myself as a widow. "Not anymore."

"I'm glad to hear that." With an effort, Fausto rolled over. "Would you marry me?"

He had to be kidding. One, mixing business with pleasure was always fatal. Two, if Fausto hadn't killed Barnard, he probably knew who did. Three, he lived in Washington. Four, I had never seen him with an erection. Five, I didn't know what he had in store tomorrow night. Six, Maxine worked only with bachelors. Seven, he was sick. Eight, without him I would be condemned to my solitary mountaintop, perhaps forever. "When?"

"Right now."

"Aren't you forgetting a few details? Blood test? Marriage certificate?"

"All in the drawer there." Fausto watched as I studied the neatly typed forms. "I hope you're not offended. I have friends at City Hall. Drop in to a clinic with a few drops of blood tomorrow and send the results to the person on that envelope. Then we're all set."

He had listed the hotel as my local address. Some of the boxes, like my age, he had kindly left blank. "You cheeky boy."

"Please. I am a man of exquisite forethought." Maybe he was just an outstanding philosopher. "Tap six on the speed dial, would you?"

"Whom am I calling?"

"The judge. He's a light sleeper." Fausto listened as I held the phone to his ear. "Peter? Would you mind dropping by? Thanks." He let me hang up. "You've got about ten minutes to think it over, sweet." Kissed my hand. "Do something wild. Say yes."

I went to the kitchen and cleaned up the remains of supper. In the bottom of the fridge was a bottle of excellent champagne that Fausto had probably put aside the same time he had fixed the marriage certificate. Three times I tried to think it over. Three times common sense was pushed aside, first by a heady bliss; next by an equally strong peace; and finally, by that soft laughter that made only a few appearances in a lifetime. I had a chance to go over the waterfall again: no greater thrill than that. At the end of the day, what was there to think about? Time was running out and I wouldn't find another Fausto.

I was putting a few glasses on a tray when the doorbell rang. On the stoop stood a handsome man and two twentyish girls. He wore a fresh Italian suit: maybe Fausto had caught him on the way to work. The girls seemed the type that got up only at three in the afternoon and spent their lives demanding more allowance. "I'm Peter Finstein. Judge Finstein. You must be Leslie," he said, shaking my hand as if he married people five nights a week. "These are my daughters Brittany and Carolina."

More witnesses. "Come in. Fausto's upstairs."

Gaga over the interior decoration, the girls were obviously expecting a leading man on the order of Rochester or Carrington. They could barely mask their dismay as Daddy introduced them to the lifeless mound awaiting us on the bed. Looks weren't everything, ladies: we'd talk again in ten years, after a few hundred prettier schmucks had bled you dry. "How are you feeling, Fausto?" the judge asked, wiggling his friend's toes.

"Never better. I've just got a bad back. Excuse me if I don't get up."

"No problem." Finstein appeared relieved to find his

client coherent: in the eyes of the law, weddings were only one step removed from last wills and testaments. With a doting smile, he sent his daughters into the hall for a few moments. "Are you two sure you want to go ahead with this?" he asked sternly when the three of us were alone. The question was not addressed to me, but Finstein probably didn't realize how much money I had of my own.

"Ask the lady, not me," Fausto replied.

I smiled at the judge. "I let you in, didn't I?"

Finstein reached into his briefcase. "Right. Well. I took the liberty of bringing over a brief prenuptial agreement."

The papers in his hand had more fine print than the nuclear test ban treaty. Fausto didn't even look over. "You may now take the liberty of tearing it in half."

Finstein cleared his throat and put the papers back in his satchel. "Is either of you presently married?" No reply. "I take it that's a no. Obviously you're both above the age of consent. No problem with the blood tests?" Silence. "No one under duress? You're both sound of mind and body?"

"Cut the shit, Peter," Fausto interrupted. "It's late."

The justice bowed to the inexorable. "Girls! Would you come here, please?"

Brittany and Carolina tumbled in. This time they paid more attention to the bride. "Would you like me to hold the rings?" one of them asked.

"We forgot them," I replied, moving closer to Fausto's Hawaiian shirt. "Just the no-frills version, Peter."

He arranged a daughter on either side and opened a red velvet booklet. The three Finsteins looked as if they were the ones getting married, not us. "Do you take this woman to be your lawful wedded wife?" he asked Fausto.

Fausto squeezed my hand. "Now and forever."

"Do you take this man to be your lawful wedded husband?" he asked me.

"I do." Three letters, two fabled words: how simply began the most complex treaty of all.

"I now pronounce you husband and wife."

I kissed my second spouse. "Don't bore me now."

"That's it, Dad?" one of the girls finally asked. No flowers, no gown, aisle, music, maid of honor, cake, presents, photographers, dancing, rings? What a joke!

"That's it, honey." Finstein got a gold pen from his coat. "Just sign on this line. You and your sister are the witnesses. That's a very important job."

As Fausto added his name to the document, I opened the champagne. "May I ask a favor? We'd like to keep this secret for a while."

"You mean you just eloped?" the daughter with more mascara asked.

"You heard Mrs. Kiss, girls. Not a word leaves this room until we get the okay." Finstein knew his fee depended on it. "When might that be?"

"Maybe never," I said.

"What? Fausto! This is a major social event!"

"That doesn't mean anyone has to know about it," my husband replied.

I escorted the wedding party out and shut off the lights. When I returned upstairs, Fausto was sitting at the foot of the bed pressing a handkerchief to his torn tongue. "Come here," he said, patting the mattress. Looked exhausted. Before speaking, he studied my face, as if to find a few answers to many unasked questions. Finally he said, "I suppose I'll spend the rest of my life wondering why you said yes."

"I might do the same wondering why you asked."

"That's easy. I have an overwhelming desire to protect you."

"Against what?"

"Evil spirits. Bad men. Indigestion. Despair." Fausto

kissed my hand. "Any champagne left in that bottle?" He watched me divide the last of it. "May all nights be as unpredictable—and as happy—as this one." We drank. "Are you sure you don't want a little ring? Just to remind you whose property you are now? I've got one in that drawer over there."

An inconspicuous little nothing, I was sure. "I think I can remember."

Fausto put down his glass. "May I ask a favor? Go back to your hotel and get a good night's sleep. I don't want to start off on the wrong foot."

I was stunned. "What wrong foot?"

"I'm going to take some medicine that will make me appear dead for quite a while. You've seen enough of that for one evening, I think."

Don't leave him alone, Smith. I kissed his hand. Tonight, and only tonight, I'd be a submissive wife. "I'll call when I get back to the hotel."

"I won't swallow anything until I hear from you." He winced. "God, I think I'm happy."

"Some philosopher you are."

Dead leaves rushed at my ankles as I walked to the Corvette. I was understanding their language better by the hour.

Chapter Twelve

$\mathcal{D}$UNCAN POUNDED on the door as I was on the phone. "Open up!" he shouted. "I know you're in there!"

"It's Duncan," I told the bridegroom. "Any plans for tomorrow?"

"None until I wake up, sweet. It might be late afternoon. Just go about your usual business. Drop by a clinic if you have time. I'll call as soon as I come to."

"I suppose I should put off returning to Berlin."

"Open up!" Duncan shouted again.

"See you tomorrow," I told Fausto. "Maybe this is all a dream."

"Good night, love. Thanks for jumping off the cliff with me."

I opened the door. Duncan smelled like a distillery. His face was a blast of angry reds. "I've been waiting for *hours*," he screeched, marching in. "I almost went to Fausto's to get you."

"Good thing you didn't," I replied, locking my minibar. "What's the problem?"

"Justine's not coming to Cleveland with me this weekend.

I bought nonrefundable tickets. It's the last straw! I've had it!"

"Did something come up?"

"She wouldn't tell me! After we swore *never* to keep any secrets!" Duncan threw himself across the bed. "There's someone else! I know it! It's the guy on the pager! Oh God, I'm a fool!"

"What was the official excuse?"

"She and Marvel have a sudden dinner meeting with the French ambassador."

"Sounds legit to me."

"I called the French embassy. The ambassador's in Morocco." Duncan punched the pillow with his good fist. "Bitch! I'm going back to Berlin!"

"Good idea. This town is not your speed."

"You think it's your speed?" He wobbled to his feet. "Are you really screwing Bobby Marvel?"

"Get serious, Duncan. You know I can't stand cornet players. I wish Justine would check the facts before feeding you her drugged-out fantasies."

He picked up the phone, dialed, listened. "She's still not home! I've been calling all night!"

"Forget her and get some sleep, would you?"

"You think I can just go to sleep after all I've been through?"

I pointed to the other bed. "You can always stay here. That should give your friend something to think about."

He paused. "No, too risky." At the door he turned. "Are you all right?"

"Sure. Why?"

"You haven't stopped smiling since I came in."

I didn't sleep much after he left: that low laughter kept me awake for long, glimmering stretches. When the alarm buzzed at seven, I wasn't at all tired. After a second, I realized why: last night I had won a round. Wanted to call my co-conspirator, but he was asleep. So I drove to his house with a basket of roses.

No one there but the usual breakfast scoundrels. I crept upstairs. Fausto lay flat on his back exactly as I had left him. On the night table stood an empty glass with brownish residue. Smelled vile. Fausto's heart was barely moving. He looked gray as a pigeon. Hands clay. That frightened me so I opened the night table drawer. Fausto owned a beautiful Colt .45—loaded. Inside a small velvet case was a ring with a diamond bigger than my thumbnail. Garish, camp . . . pure Kiss. I put it on and felt better. Left the roses on his pillow.

Justine saw me coming down the stairs. She didn't look her usual hyper-made-up self. For the first time, I noticed the fifty-year hollows beneath her eyes. Even her butt couldn't iron out all the wrinkles in her skintight linen skirt. High on something, as usual. Beneath the smile, I smelled fear: whatever Fausto wanted, she was having difficulty delivering. "Is the old boy sleeping it off?" she asked pleasantly.

"No, we had breakfast in bed. Duncan tells me you're dining French tonight. He just can't figure out how the ambassador's getting back from Morocco in time."

Took her a moment to figure out what I was really saying, but Justine wasn't in the first tier of Washington jackals. She was more like a groundhog. "He's been spying on me!"

"He thinks you're seeing someone. Keeps talking about a pager."

Her Etonian accent vanished. "Christ Almighty! He told you that?"

"Why not? He's beside himself. Thinking of breaking off your engagement."

"What engagement?" Justine laughed hysterically. "He's out of his mind!"

"That's what I keep telling him."

The sunlight caught my ring. Justine nearly fell down the stairs. "Fausto's mother used to wear that," she cried, as if I had stolen it.

"You don't say. Now that's interesting." As I was flashing sunbeams over the hallway, Chickering opened the door. Seeing me, she froze. Her thick shoes desecrated the spot where Fausto had taken me last night. "Chick! Good to see you," I called fearlessly. My husband would protect me. "Is that luscious roommate of yours still practicing cello?"

She tried the blowfish offense. "Perhaps you didn't understand my last message."

"Hey, don't blame me if you can't choose between wife and career. Why don't you stay home in Annapolis? Play a few duets with Rhoby instead of slumming it with Paula every night."

I left her sputtering with Justine. Drove the Corvette to the Beltway, wondering what had become of my friend in the Chevy. Today I could challenge him to a pretty wild drag race. From a rest stop I called Betty-Lou Beasley, the jailbird. "Did you get a copy of the warden's orders?"

"Yes, yes! I just want this over with!"

"Good. Listen. During your lunch hour, walk to the cemetery next to the jail. Go to the chapel in the middle and take a right. Walk a little bit up to John Philip Sousa's grave."

"John Flip Sousa?"

Oh Christ! Didn't these people know anything? "The bandleader. *Stars and Stripes Forever.* You'll see a stone bench at his grave. I'll leave an envelope on top. Your instructions and money will be inside. You'd better be alone because we'll be watching through telescopic lenses. Good luck."

Actually, I'd be the one needing luck. Daffy Duck was more reliable than a water balloon like Beasley. But today I felt invincible, kissed by the gods. Bought myself a new dress and my husband a ring. Got a blood test. A little before noon I entered the Congressional Cemetery. As usual, it was empty. I didn't even see the old gentleman straightening headstones at the bottom of the hill. Dropped an empty Coke can and an envelope containing three thousand bucks on Sousa's bench. Then I climbed a dogwood a little way down the path.

Ten minutes later, wearing a fluorescent jogging suit visible from Mars, Beasley came puffing up the dirt road. As she passed the dogwood, I saw that she was also carrying Mace and a small baseball bat. She jogged to Sousa's grave, tore open the envelope, and read the very simple instructions. *Leave your paper in the Coke can. Go quickly.*

First Betty-Lou's zipper got snagged on her T-shirt. Then she got all tangled up in her Walkman wire. She dropped the Mace at about the same time a black Lexus rolled into the cemetery. I almost jumped out of the tree as the car slowed at the chapel then took a gentle right toward Sousa's grave. Beasley ripped open her jogging suit and stuffed her contraband into the Coke can just as the vehicle halted at her side. A smoked window rolled down. "Hot day for jogging."

What the hell was Vicky Chickering doing here?

"Oh yes," Beasley nearly screamed. "It's my lunch hour." She stomped on the Coke can in her haste to leave. "Have a nice one!"

Betty-Lou ran away, forsaking Mace and baseball bat. Chickering put the Lexus into reverse and crawled back to the chapel. There, she got out and circled the ruin once, very slowly, as if searching for pennies in the grass. But she kept looking back at Sousa's grave. Maybe she scented me up in the tree. I cringed as she walked back to the bandleader's plot. As her madras tent fluttered in the wind, Chickering inspected the detritus that Beasley had left behind. I hardly breathed: one glance at the dogwood during the wrong gust and I was finished. Fortunately her eyesight, like her imagination, remained earthbound. Chickering was about to leave when the wind scraped the Coke can across Sousa's headstone. It sounded like a rock slide. *Leave it there, Chickie!* I prayed to evaporate as she picked up the litter and walked toward the overflowing bin beneath my tree.

Not six feet away, she shook the can of Mace. Kept that for herself but the bat got heaved. Chickering was about to toss the Coke can when she noticed the paper inside. I went cold as she hunted it with an inquisitive finger. Thank God the aluminum bit back. "Shit!" she snapped. Trashed the can and returned to the chapel.

A black man on a bicycle rode into the cemetery. At first I thought it was the volunteer custodian. When I saw the gold chains, I recognized Tanqueray Tougaw. He and Chickering talked briefly before Tougaw gave her a few items for her purse. Then, with a laugh, he rode away. Lexus followed.

I jumped to the grass. Too damn popular, this cemetery. Retrieved Coke and returned to the Corvette, humbled by my own stupidity: at Aurilla's dinner, Fausto had hinted that Tougaw was something other than he seemed. I had let the remark pass. Sloppy work. I zipped the top off the can and removed a soggy paper. Transfer orders all right. For reasons of national security, Figgis Cole was to be moved to Lorton immediately. Signed by Ralphine Preston, Deputy Attorney General, Justice Department. The seal looked authentic. The D.C. warden would have no cause, and probably no time, to question the order. It was just one of a thousand turds lost in the daily bilge.

Called Maxine from the nearby hospital. "Beasley got the transfer papers." I recited them. "That covers the warden's ass. I think something's going down tonight."

"So you'll keep an eye on Marvel?" the Queen asked.

"No, I thought I'd stick with Fausto."

"Marvel's your boy," she insisted.

"Check up on a Tanqueray Tougaw for me, would you?" I tried to spell his name. "I think he's Belizean. He keeps coming back like mildew after a flood." I held up my left hand. At Fausto's house the diamonds had looked like liquid fire. Under the fluorescent lights here they looked like something I had bought in a joke shop. "Remember James the mercenary? He's coming to Washington tonight."

"Coming? What makes you think he's not already there?"

Good point. Why hadn't I thought of that. "I saw a fax from him at Fausto's. It said that everything was all clear for Dulles tonight."

"Okay, be sharp," the Queen sighed. "I'll check incoming flights from Belize. Follow your head. Not that other thing."

My feelings of invincibility began to fade as I drove to Fausto's. They cinderized completely when I saw that his bed was empty. Maybe he had finally gone to the doctor. That little bubble burst when I returned to the hotel and found zero phone messages but another enormous bouquet of orchids. *See you soon.* Damn! The phone rang.

"Hey there."

Shit, Maxine was always right. "Hi."

"What's the matter, sugar?"

"Nothing." I swallowed thickly. "What's on your mind?"

"Meet me at the summer house," Bobby said. "I have things to say to you."

"I'm listening."

"In person. I'll send a driver at eight."

"I'll drive myself. I have things to say to you, too."

"Now that's more like it."

"I can't stay long."

Bobby chuckled. "I was only expecting an hour. I know that's my allowance."

Three hours later, still no call from my husband. I inched

through rush-hour traffic back to his place. Fausto had left an envelope on the bed.

> My sweet, something urgent has come up. I don't know when I'll see you next. Thanks for wearing the ring. It was my mother's. Your adoring F

Miraculous invention, the nervous system: mere seconds after I read the note, my hands began to shake and my stomach charred. Dark blood hammered my forehead: stage fright was never like this. I fell onto the bed, my body so flooded with toxins that I half expected to go into convulsions. I had been outfoxed but how how *how?* What had Fausto gained by marrying me? And where the hell had he gone? Should have listened to Maxine: follow the head, never the heart, not even for one evening. I had been seduced by ten fingers and a tongue. Ancillary villains Brahms, dead leaves, soul-withering solitude . . . bah, I was such easy prey for a clever man.

I lay there like a kicked dog. When the headache only got worse, I went down to the music room: once, a few lifetimes ago, I had been happy here. Now it was time to get my violin and clear out. But it had disappeared along with my husband. I went to the piano. Brahms no longer rested on the music stand. Instead I saw a Schubert duet, the same one that Fausto had been playing one night with Bobby Marvel, before Tuna dropped in. I thought my head would crack open and a thousand reptiles, each a writhing newborn suspicion, spill out. *Get a grip, Smith.* Presidents didn't disappear in the middle of the day to play duets . . . did they? Bah, what did I know. Maybe Bobby had called me from here, with Fausto coaching.

I rushed to the zoo. Called Maxine from the parking lot, a

mess of strollers, vans, and sloppy families. "Find anything?" I asked. "I'm in a rush."

"Ralphine Preston leads a quiet life. The day she signed that transfer order, she got ten thousand bucks wired to her account. Guess where the money came from."

"Fausto?" I croaked.

"Tuna. She's in his pocket. Why would he transfer Louis to Lorton? It's in the middle of the country."

No fucking clue. "What about Tougaw?"

"Nothing comes up on him. I think he's a nobody."

"What about the mercenary?"

"Fits the profile of James Bassinet. RAF pilot with a drinking problem. He became a jungle training instructor in the seventies. Definitely past his prime. Does odd jobs now."

"How odd?"

"Nothing you couldn't handle. He's not listed in any passenger manifest to Dulles. Has Bobby Marvel tried to contact you?"

"I'm seeing him tonight."

"Don't take any baths, for God's sake."

My brain was in tatters. Returned to the hotel. Put on my new dress and started early for my tryst with Paula Marvel's husband, who had a lot of explaining to do. Traffic was brutal way into Virginia, slowed even further by rain squalls. I didn't bother checking the rearview mirror: this time I didn't care whether I led a caravan to Aurilla's summer cottage. Rolled up to the first security check fifteen minutes ahead of schedule. "Leslie Frost," I told the guard. "Marvel's expecting me."

I got frisked. Thick drops of rain, tired of life in the clouds, hit the hood of my car and lay where they fell. I saw Bobby on the porch swing, reading what looked like a term paper. He watched me cross the wide lawn. "Let's go inside," he said. "It's starting to rain."

"Bad day?" I asked hopefully.

"It's getting better." He poured me a drink. "You don't know how you cheer me up."

"Where's Paula?"

"At some ladies' dinner." He noticed my ring. "Now that's a new bauble."

I swallowed a belt of gin. "I married Fausto last night."

"Jesus Christ! You didn't!"

"I did. He didn't tell you this afternoon?"

Bobby slowly blinked. "Was he supposed to?"

"You weren't at his house playing duets?"

Bobby laughed badly. "Would you like to hear about my afternoon? I had lunch with a bunch of shits who contributed fifty grand each to the party and think they own my balls now. Then I had an interview with a shit from the *Post* who's been writing nothing but shit about me for four years. Then I had a meeting with a bunch of shits from the House who are going to screw me on the welfare reform bill. Then I had a fight with my shit of a wife. Then I had a meeting with my shit of a press secretary, who's been less than worthless ever since she started screwing that shit pianist of yours. Then I had a shitty drive out here and have been reading shitty reports about corruption in the Justice Department. Now I hear you married the mother of all shits."

"So you weren't at his house?" I repeated.

"What did I just tell you?" Bobby exploded. He stalked out to the porch and flung his beer bottle into the pines. "Fuck!"

A Secret Service agent stepped into the clearing. "Everything all right, sir?" he called.

"Just dandy!" Bobby reeled back into the house and fell onto a cushion in a window nook. "Why'd you do it?"

"I love Fausto's brains."

"I hope so, sugar. You ain't gonna be getting much of his cock."

"How would you know?"

"Polly told me." His laugh sounded like a groan. "Have you slept with him yet?"

Trick question. "We did get married last night."

Bobby lay inert for a second or two before pulling me inches from his mouth. "Then what are you doing here with me?" he whispered.

There were overt and covert ways to take a woman. I had married the covert and already received my first little lashing. Maybe I had made a mistake. *Careful, Smith.* "I thought you should be the first to know."

"Thanks so much." He kissed me ferociously. I almost washed over to the other side, and Bobby knew it. "Thought I was losing my touch for a minute there."

"You'll never lose your touch." I straddled him and began moving my hands under his shirt. "Last time you saw Polly was here, wasn't it."

"Not her again! Forget that bitch!"

"Where'd you do it? Here in the window? Upstairs after you took a bath?"

"I hate baths. Haven't taken one since I was in diapers."

My hands stopped. "You were never with Polly and a bottle of champagne in that big tub upstairs?"

"She may have misinformed you, sugar. We had a nice time in this exact spot. And I hate champagne."

A shudder in the back of my brain before a great cold splash, like ice shearing off a glacier into the frigid sea. I smiled foolishly. "You hate baths?"

"I just said so."

"And you don't play the piano?"

He stroked my butt. "Your husband plays the piano. I play the cornet. Don't be mixing us up already."

Then who the hell was playing piano with Fausto this afternoon? My foolish smile wouldn't go away. "When was the last time you slept with Justine?"

"Justine? Don't tell me you're jealous of her, too." Bobby's mood was improving by the second. "About two months ago. We were marooned in Toledo."

Oh Christ! Should have known the minute I touched Bobby's squishy ass that he wasn't the guy in Barnard's bathtub! I was stupider than a snail: we had a double here, a good one. But Fausto could afford the best. Then *whop* everything connected and I got twenty thousand volts of insight right between the eyes: whatever the double was here for, he was doing it *right now,* while I deflected the real Bobby. Ah, bravo Fausto.

"Forget Justine," Marvel whispered, kissing my neck. "She's history."

Thoughts buzzed back to Louis Bailey's empty house, to the picture of Bobby above the desk, the videos, autographs, his signature traced in red pen . . . oh dear. Signature. Forgery. The double was going to sign something. What the hell did Bobby sign? Laws. Proclamations for National Pickle Week. Bills. Treaties. None of the above could be forged without dozens of witnesses. *Think, Smith.* What else did presidents sign? Memos? Letters of appointment? Big deal. Didn't need a double for that. Fausto wanted not only the signature but a reasonable facsimile of Bobby Marvel scribbling it. *Think harder, Smith!* I started lobbing anything I had into the cold pot. Tuna: was he in on this? Only deep enough to be double-crossed. Fausto had already duped him into thinking he had met the real president. My spouse was playing a dangerous game. Didn't want to think about that now so I passed on to Bendix. Forget Bendix. He saw the real Marvel too often to be taken in by a fake. Ditto Aurilla and Chickering. How about Louis? Why would Louis need a fake Marvel? To visit him in jail? That was absurd. Presidents didn't go into jails. They put people in jail and got them out of jail. Stays of execution. Pardons.

Bingo.

"Something the matter, baby? I mean it. Justine means nothing to me."

I pulled back. "I have to go."

"Now? Don't tell me you're worried about cheating on Fausto. I did speak with him a few hours ago. Everything's all right."

Grand pause. "What do you mean?"

"He told me to take good care of you tonight."

"Son of a bitch!" I slapped Bobby in the face since he was the same gender. While he was rubbing his cheek, I left the cushion. "Why didn't you tell me that first thing?"

"It was a little tough once I found out you married the guy. Damn, that smarts." He smiled: maybe slapping turned him on. "I tried to warn you about Fausto, sugar. What kind of husband would give his wife away the day after he was married?" Again that boyish smile. "I think I know."

"You don't know shit."

He caught up with me at the door. "Don't run away. I'll give you a wedding present you won't forget."

I gave him a knee he wouldn't forget and ran outside. The Corvette didn't like aquaplaning through puddles at ninety miles an hour but I didn't like being the last maggot to turn fly so we screamed to Lorton in twenty minutes. Parking lot quiet as a morgue: visiting hours long over. I pulled up to the main gate. A guard with a gun looked down from the watchtower as another came to the chicken wire. "You can't park there."

I pushed a little green linen through the mesh. "There's

three hundred bucks. One quick question and I'll leave. Any special visitors tonight?" I got that not-telling-you stare tantamount to a yes so I added two hundred to the kitty and waited. "I'm running out of time."

I was taking the cash back when the guard said, "Warden came out to see some friends."

I stuffed two more bills in the diamond. "How many cars?"

"Three."

Excellent: impostor arrives with two security vehicles, just as Marvel would. Doesn't go in, warden comes out. Dark night, dim lights: who wouldn't believe that was Marvel in the backseat signing a secret executive order releasing Figgis Cole? Last thing the warden would ask for would be ID. Fifteen minutes later, Louis Bailey walks. Fausto was probably waiting for him out here with a bottle of champagne. Then what? *See you at Dulles tomorrow night. All clear.*

All clear all right. Maxine hadn't been able to find James on the inbound passenger lists because he hadn't been a passenger at all. He had been a pilot. I stuffed another hundred into the fence. "When did the meeting break up?"

"About ten."

Fausto had a forty-minute head start on me. I was thirty miles from Dulles. *No way you're going to catch him, Smith.* True, if one discounted a wife's fury. "Thanks."

Traffic was thick but rolling at a placid seventy. I did forty better than that. Screeched into a parking slot at General Aviation, sprinted to the hangar. No private planes pulling onto the runway: either I had beaten Fausto here or he was already at fifty thousand feet. I ran to the kid at the gas pump.

"Did a private jet just leave?"

"Piper pulled onto the runway about fifteen minutes ago."

"Was one of the passengers a fat man?"

"A blimp."

"How many people were with him?"

"One passenger and the pilot."

"Could you describe them?"

"The pilot had an English accent. The passenger was tall and thin."

Sounded like James and Louis: so they had left Bobby's double behind. "Anyone mention where they were going?"

"No."

"You filled the tank, right? What kind of range would that give them?"

"Three thousand miles easy."

I looked down the runway as a 747 thundered toward us and gracefully lifted off, taillights slowly disappearing in the rain. Every ounce of cargo on that flight was accounted for. Its path through the night would be monitored by dozens of controllers and their computers. Somewhere a crowd of people would eventually gather, waiting for it to land. Why put up with that crap? Nice thing about private planes was you didn't have to tell anyone where you were going or who was aboard. You just turned the keys in the ignition, called the control tower, got in line, and flew away.

The gas man heard the far-off tenor whine before I did. "Look there," he said, pointing down the runway. "It was behind the 747."

A pretty little jet stood at the head of the line. It would get clearance in another thirty seconds, when the turbulence from the 747 had dissipated. I thought about making a mad dash for it, clinging to its rear wheels like they did in the movies. Instead I just stood with my heart pounding as it glided past, smooth as a bullet with wings, and joined the clouds. So much for honeymoons.

Slopped back to the Corvette and listened to the rain. Excellent job, Fausto. You got your man . . . and your woman, too. Rolled the Corvette out of the lot. Could have gone to the zoo, reported to Maxine. Instead I drove to Fausto's, to return this hideous ring, find my violin . . . and leave.

His lights were on. I cut the engine, coasted to a halt at the front door. Ever so faint melody tinged the air. I slithered through a sea of dead leaves to the windows of the music room. Fake Bobby sat at the piano mauling a Chopin mazurka. I circled the house: kitchen lights off, upstairs dark. Let myself in, crept upstairs. The Colt, still loaded, lay in Fausto's night table drawer.

I slowly opened the door to the music room. The mazurka didn't stop as a cheerful voice called, "Ah, there you are. Come in, I've been expecting you."

Couldn't believe what I was seeing. This man, down to the eyelash, was Bobby Marvel except for the voice and the dead, cold eyes of a trained killer. He fumbled calmly through the Chopin, unfazed by the .45 trained on his chest. When the mazurka was finished, he lit a cigar. "Put that down, would you? If I wanted to kill you, you'd have been dead halfway down the driveway."

I didn't move. He still had plenty of time to kill me on the way out. "Start talking," I said. Instead he kept puffing so I shot the cigar out of his mouth. My husband could repair the hole in his wall when he returned from his plane ride. "Thank you for not smoking. Sit on that couch." Great ass. That was definitely the one I had seen in Barnard's video. For a long moment we studied each other. "That warden at Lorton must have pissed in his pants when the president came to visit." Impostor didn't say a word so I continued, "Bet you could sign Marvel's name in your sleep by now."

"Clever girl," was all he said.

Not clever enough. "Make you a deal. You tell me your

story, I'll tell you mine." I took over the piano bench. "Start with your name."

"Cecil Ruske. Soldier of fortune. Why'd you kill Polly?"

"Bad start, Cecil. I found her dead. Fausto didn't do it, did he?"

"No. He thought you did."

"Wrong again. Polly was an old friend."

"You were hanging off the balcony the night she disappeared. I was watching from the street."

What the hell, I'd go first. "She followed a man from Belize to Washington. Looked all over but couldn't find him. Two weeks later she bought it. Her body's missing. I've been trying to find out who did it and why. I keep coming back to Fausto. Your turn."

"So you didn't kill her?" he asked incredulously.

"Cut the shit," I snapped. "I found her dead. Her body disappeared while I was dangling nine floors above the pavement. Where'd you get your face?"

"Mexico, about a year ago. Fausto paid for the operation and told me he'd be using me someday. Kept me on retainer until the call came a few weeks ago." Cecil admired his features in a silver plate. "They didn't have to change much."

"You're a perfect clone except for the ass. Marvel's got more mush."

"That's what Polly said, too. You ladies work for the same boss?"

"Irrelevant. What were you supposed to do for Fausto?" I sniffed the Colt barrel. "Don't irritate me. I've had a hard night."

"He brought me to Washington. Stuck me in this house in the burbs with tapes of Marvel and told me to perfect his voice and signature. Said I was going to help him have a laugh with an old friend. That's all he told me. I wasn't about to ask him any questions. But pretty soon I was climb-

ing the walls. Fortunately, Polly dropped in one afternoon."
He chuckled. "Nearly broke my neck."

That was her preferred foreplay. "Of course you never
told Fausto the two of you had met." Correct. "So you en-
tertained each other for a week to relieve the tedium. Then
someone else moved first. Exit Polly. What were you
doing, spying on her the night you saw me hanging off the
balcony? A little jealous, maybe? Wondering if she were
really serious about Bobby Marvel?"

He flushed. "I didn't make the same mistake with you."

"But you followed me. Sorry, tried to follow me. I suppose the orchids were your juvenile idea of a joke."

"I was bored stiff, luv. My only sport was visiting the
florist and following you. There was a car in the garage and
I kept my breakouts to a minimum."

"Fausto didn't order you to follow me?"

"God no! After I told him about you hanging off the balcony, he forbade me to leave the house. But I couldn't tolerate being cooped up for so long. You became my secret
project. A hired man's got to keep himself in trim."

"So you finally got your first role playing president for
Tuna. Poor guy really thought he was meeting Marvel, didn't
he."

"That was a spur-of-the-moment joke," Cecil replied. "As
well as dress rehearsal. Fausto knew I was going mad waiting for the main event."

"What did you tell Tuna?"

"Said I'd try to cut him a couple of deals with the Pentagon. Pure hot air but he bought it. I did well that night."

"Didn't do too badly with Justine, either."

He flushed. "You're a friggin' cat, that's what you are."

If only I had nine lives. "What does that floozy have to do
with all this?"

"She manages Marvel. Gives me tips on his personal habits. Liaises with Fausto."

Repays old debts. "Does she have any idea how far she's sticking her neck out?"

"She'd stick her neck out from here to China if it wrecked Marvel. But that's her problem."

"Why is she screwing my pianist?"

Cecil looked surprised. "I don't know a thing about that."

"Fine. So after you snow Tuna, Fausto puts you on the shelf for another week. You behave except for a few more attempts to follow me. Fausto finally calls tonight to say the show's on the road. Who told the warden at Lorton you were coming?"

"Justine. She rode out with me. Brought him to the car. Made sure I did what I was supposed to do."

"And you came through with flying colors. Why didn't you leave tonight with Fausto?"

"I didn't feel like going back to Mexico just yet." Cecil smiled pleasantly at me. "Thought I'd kill you first. An eye for an eye."

I blew a bullet hole in my husband's priceless red divan. Never liked the color much. "You would have gotten the wrong eye. If you had just stuck around Watergate that first night instead of following me back to the hotel, you would have saved us both a lot of trouble." I laid the Colt on the piano. "You almost killed me at Louis's house."

"I like to see what I'm up against." He took the gun. "You're good."

Sometimes. "I'm surprised Fausto left you behind."

"He doesn't know it yet. He was not what you'd call with it when they loaded him on the plane."

"Listen," I said, sitting next to Cecil, Bobby, whoever the hell he was. "I have to know who killed Polly."

"I wouldn't mind knowing myself. Who was she looking for? She never told me."

"The guy you just sprang from Lorton."

"Shit! Figgis Cole? Who's he?"

"A friend of Fausto's. Can you lie low for a few days?"

Cecil frowned. "I'm getting a serious case of cabin fever, babe."

"Fifty grand." I'd blow Barnard's slush fund to find her killer. "And you jump off the Washington Monument if I tell you to."

"You got a deal."

I stood up. "Who knows about you?"

"Justine and Fausto. That's it."

"Let's hope so." Told Cecil it was time to get invisible and turned off the lights. We were halfway up Fausto's driveway when I noticed headlights coming a tad too slowly down the street. "Duck."

Rhoby's Hummer nearly squeezed me into the curb. As she leaned out the window, her tank top revealed half a boob and lush tufts of armpit hair. The studs in her eyebrows gleamed like fireflies. "Hi Les! I had a feeling you might be rehearsing with Fausto."

"Aren't you working tonight?"

"I'm on my way in. Did you get my message about lunch?"

"I've been really tied up lately."

An awkward silence then, "Chickie hasn't been leaning on you, has she? That stupid bitch! I'll cut her in half!"

"She's pretty big," I said. "I'll call you, Rhoby."

"I've been practicing!" she called after me.

I hooked left on Connecticut Avenue. "You can get up now."

"Who was that?" Cecil asked, unfolding from the floor.

"Another friend of Fausto's." I passed Walter Reed Hospital, where Jojo Bailey had lain in state for almost two weeks now. "Where'd he find you?"

"Through a friend in Belize. Simon. Does all the contracting."

He was contracting with the worms now. I dumped Cecil with a wad of cash at a flophouse in Silver Spring. He'd relax with the porno flicks until I caught up with him in a day or two. *Loose cannon, Smith.* Absolutely right. But he was all the ammo I had. Returned to the hotel, tried to sleep but kept hearing footsteps in the dark so I packed a few things and joined the first wave of commuters on the Beltway. Time to jump jungles again.

Chapter Thirteen

CALLED THE QUEEN from Miami just to let her know that Louis had escaped yet again and I was going after him. "Where's the double?" was her only question.

"Waiting for me in Silver Spring." I tried not to take the ensuing oaths personally. "We're not kidding anyone, Maxine. He saw me hanging from Barnard's balcony. Cecil knew she wasn't just a bimbo named Polly. He doesn't care what my business is. He just wants to know who killed her. Even a mercenary has a sense of vengeance." Plus I was paying him fifty grand.

"What makes you think he's not going to squeal on you?"

"We made a deal."

Maxine sighed. I was so far blown I might as well have tattooed Special Agent Smith on my forehead. Ah well, perhaps I'd step on a fer-de-lance and end her troubles. She could start all over again with seven wilier women. "Where's Fausto, by the way?"

"With Louis."

"It *is* Louis you're after."

"I'll take care of him first."

She didn't ask what loose ends I'd be wrapping up second. The Queen had replenished my insomnia kit in Miami so I gave myself a booster shot before going to the gate. Every television in the terminal was squawking about Jojo Bailey. Poor Bobby, speaking from the hospital, looked as if he had been swabbing his eyes with ammonia.

The plane to Belize was even emptier than last time, but we were flying right into hurricane season. I sat behind a bunch of student archaeologists who had paid two thousand bucks each to excavate someone else's site. Two fiftyish women with long red nails and hair like cotton candy, obviously misinformed about the chances of picking up a second husband in the jungle, struggled past with buffalo-size carry-ons. The two of them filled the cabin with aromas of perfume, sunscreen, mouthwash, talcum, and hairspray, determined against all odds to smell clean during this expedition. A pair of Creoles with teeth like kernels of corn straggled on last. We flew over dark blotches on the Gulf of Mexico, then tree-choked earth: soon all that green would swallow me again. Bumpy landing, inside and out.

Fausto's Piper was parked at the end of the runway at Belize City. I felt nothing: it was just a machine. Harmless. The old headache roared back the instant I stepped onto the tarmac. Already my brain was screaming for water. My clothing wilted halfway to the terminal and the breeze only thickened a film of sweat. Cosima Wagner, back for more puff journalism, sailed past a dull customs official. I rented a jeep. Bought water and machete and once again headed west, passing the same car wrecks under rotting porches, the same laundry on sagging lines, even the same people slouching in the same armchairs. Only the road kill had been rearranged.

After a quick downpour, a plague of frogs flopped onto the highway. I tried not to flatten too many of them but I feared slowing down, letting daylight slip away from me, because with it went my sight and most of my nerve. I buzzed past the bus from hell and, one by one, *les misérables* waiting for it. No traffic whatever at Belmopan, the capital in the middle of nowhere. Rattled across the bridge at San Ignacio. With each mile, mechanical sounds were increasingly displaced by the noises of birds, insects, water, until finally only the purr of the jeep reminded me that I had come from the twentieth century. I made the mountains by dusk.

A few thousand tons of water had pummeled the side road since my last visit: whatever time I had gained on the highway, I lost in the ruts. Muck slurped my tires, shimmied the axle this way and that. Bats zipped inches from the windshield as the sun crashed behind the mountains. *Keep rolling, Smith.* I parked in the ferns. The moment my feet touched moss, the cicadas shrieked. Their noise was ugly, menacing, everywhere: already I was outnumbered a billion to one, and that was only the insects. Would have turned back but Fausto was on the other end of this path, chortling at his cleverness.

Brandishing my machete, I stomped into the jungle. This time around, my fangs grew much more quickly. The heavy smells, the gnats, the sweat, were not unfamiliar and I had a working flashlight now. Would have preferred a rifle and wings but hey, fire and rocks had done the job for the Neanderthals. The terror would never recede, though, not in this darkness. The ratio of appetite to food was just too overwhelming.

Hours later the jungle ended and I hit tall grass. The black sky shivered with stars. Leaves dipped in the slow wind. Anywhere else, props for a romantic evening; here, weapons for the hunt. I played my flashlight over Ek's shack but no one came to greet me. Nothing inside but dead beetles. Even his hammock was gone. I sat on the stoop, watching heat lightning buffet the hills: only one place left to go. First I drank a liter of water. Every seam on my body had turned slimy and fragrant. Dirt had settled in all cavities and I itched from head to toe. Didn't know if I could make this next hike without Ek. If I got lost between here and those hills, no one would ever find me. Was that such a dreadful thing? This time around I didn't think so.

Took my last look at open sky and dipped back into the jungle. Perhaps someone was expecting me after all: Barnard's notches in the tree trunks had recently been refreshed. I thought of Ek as I followed the trail. Was he glad that Louis had come back? Would he be glad to see me again? Then the cicadas went fortissimo, I came too close to a growl in the brush, and subjective thought ceased. I began to hallucinate that Ek's flare was just beyond the next vine. I thought I heard his voice. *Stay with it, Smith. You're almost here.* The hell I was. Sooner or later those notches would lead me to a river.

Crossed two mountains, dreading what lay in my path. Gradually I heard thunder that sounded heavier than the whole planet. The floor of the forest began to slide downward. I skidded to water's edge and nearly cried when I saw the thick green torrent. God, I'd never make it across! *He's on the other side.* Hiked upstream, looking for stones, logjams, maybe a ferry. Night was losing its grip when I finally discerned a rope connecting two trees on opposite sides of the surging water. Gave it a vicious shake, warning the snakes. Put my boots in the knapsack, tested the knot, waded in. Warm as a bath: typhoid pudding but I could worry about that after I got to the other side.

Lost my footing almost immediately. River turned cold and the rope sagged as the current sucked me toward the falls. I went underwater. *Kick up, slide left.* Did that a half dozen times, inhaling more water than oxygen each time I surfaced. Slimy amphibians brushed my legs. When the current warmed again, I knew I was close to land. Swallowed another quart of sewage before the rope broke the waves. I pulled myself ashore. Refreshing little swim. I had lost the machete. Rope burns scored my forearms, boots weighed a ton. I hiked back to where I thought the path might continue. The sun barely peeped above the horizon but the temperature had already begun to rise. Finally I saw a notch.

Every bird in the jungle awoke with a *wee-wee-wee-wee* or *wakKK-wakKK*. Legions of cicadas shivered in retaliation. Eerie gray green light perfused the forest as I struggled uphill, toward the limestone caves. Sweat ran past my eyes, down my legs: my clothes would rot before they dried. What if Fausto wasn't there? *Don't think. Just move.*

Outside Barnard's cave I saw a tent, a dead fire. Peered through the mesh: there lay my husband, in almost the exact position I had left him in Washington. I sat on the low stool next to his cot. His skin was a mélange of unhealthy pastels. I didn't like the noises he was making. Sniffed the empty glass on the floor: more of the vile stuff he had been drinking back home. I was monitoring his pulse when a few pebbles moved outside the tent. Looked up as Ek looked in.

We stared at each other for a long moment. "I knew you'd come," he said finally, without the hint of a smile. "So did Fausto."

"He's not going to make it, is he." Ek didn't answer. Beside me, the zipper rasped. I glanced at a thin man with the face of a hawk. "Dr. Bailey, I presume. My name's Cosima." Louis came in. I didn't shake his hand. "Why'd you lug him all the way out here?"

"We took a helicopter in. Landed in a clearing on top of the mountain. All he had to do was walk down." Louis felt Fausto's forehead. "We almost lost him last night. You do know about his medical condition, don't you?"

I smiled ever so gratefully. "Why don't you explain."

First, Louis told Ek to make coffee. "I became fascinated with this case thirty years ago, when Fausto's mother died. In simple terms, the family goes mad. The first episodes occur around age seventeen and return at random with seizures that precipitate deep psychosis. Then all symptoms may disappear for years. But they always return. I've named it the Kiss syndrome and documented it through three generations. No one has ever survived the fourth recurrence. By then the chemical and electrical disturbances are insuperable." He tested Fausto's pulse and frowned. "He's up to number four."

"What are you doing for him?"

"The first time I treated him with human secretions." Raw material kindly donated by med school cadavers and Morris Morton. Nothing like killing two birds with one music critic. "That didn't work. When he was thirty, I tried hallucinogens."

"Strike two," I smiled. "The seizures returned and he nearly burned to death in the bargain."

"I told him to quit smoking in bed," Louis snapped. "Next time I tried lasers."

"What do you have in mind this time around?" I asked. "Eye of newt?"

"I've spent seventeen years in the rain forest. I know more about plant compounds than anyone on earth. I think I've found a phytochemical that stimulates the vagus. That's the nerve that tells the brain to shut off the seizures. If they can't get started, the whole cycle might be suppressed."

"This stuff?" I sniffed the empty glass. "Then why'd he have a bad night?"

"The supply's low and stale. Ek and I are making fresh distillate now. He needs it immediately. If it works, I've made a major medical discovery."

Patents, riches, Nobel Prize: strike two for the Hippocratic oath. I brushed a fly off Fausto's eyebrow. "When's he going to wake up?"

"He might be out all day. He might smell the coffee and snap to life. It varies."

"He had no signs of a recurrence before you went on your wild goose chase to Washington?"

"Absolutely not! This malady is totally unpredictable. And it wasn't a wild goose chase."

The cicadas suddenly rioted: had their noise been water, the tent would have washed down the hill like a toothpick in a typhoon. *Wake up, husband.* "That catches me up with Fausto," I said. "How about filling me in on yourself. We can begin with your pal Krikor Tunalian."

Louis's eyes went muddy. "I don't know what you're talking about."

"He wired five mil to your Swiss account on July second. Met you in Koko's about a month ago to check on progress. You blew him off and went to Washington with a head full of assassination plots. Got yourself waylaid at the FBI, so Tuna had to help Fausto spirit you out of prison and back in the saddle." I picked a leech off my elbow. "He wants you to make a poison."

"You've been spying on me!" the great doctor snapped. "Who are you?"

"A friend of Polly's. She's been murdered, by the way. Followed you to D.C. and stepped in someone else's cow pie."

"My God! Who killed her?"

"You tell me." I accepted a gourd from Ek. "Has anyone brought you up-to-date on Yvette Tatal?" Louis looked violently at Ek, who averted his eyes. "She ran into a fer-de-lance. I guess it's been classified an accident." Bitter coffee here. "So you see, Louis, your little sideshow with Tuna is the least of my headaches."

He sank to the ground as the enormity of my news hit. A month ago I might have felt sorry for him. Now he was just the last domino in a long, toppling row. "Tell me about Tuna," I repeated.

Louis flecked a beetle off his neck. "He wanted an irreversible poison absorbed through the skin. I'm still working on it. It's not quite ready."

"You got that right. All it does now is reduce grown men to diarrhea factories."

"Since you seem to know everything, perhaps you could tell me what happened to Yvette Tatal."

I reported her death concisely and without a trace of emotion. After Louis called me a liar, Ek went to the cave and returned with a small mesh box. "She tells the truth. I found this on the shelf above Dr. Tatal's body."

Louis flung the box into the corner. "Who did it?"

"A hired killer." I glanced at Ek. "Now dead. Was Tatal working on the poison with you?"

"For God's sake! She was a doctor!"

Fausto shuddered then went still. I kneeled by his ear, whispered his name. He didn't respond. Again I smelled that terrifying odor of spoiled meat. "Get back to your distillery," I told Louis. "I've had enough of you for the moment."

Louis stumbled out of the tent, Ek two steps behind. I swore under my breath before returning to the cot. As I was neatening Fausto's hair, his putty lips edged slowly into a smile. "And you call *me* a troublemaker."

Alive: I forgave everything. "How long have you been listening, you schmuck?"

"I was awake when you came in."

Covered his face with kisses. "How do you feel?"

"Lousy."

"You've got to get to a hospital."

"Won't do any good. Have a little pity on Louis, sweet. He's been trying to save me for thirty years." Fausto patted my hand, felt no ring. "Still married?"

"I'm a covert government agent," I said. "So was Polly. She was supposed to find out what was going on with Louis and Tuna."

Again that cherubic, doomed smile. "I'm perfectly innocent, of course. I only needed Louis to make some more medicine for me."

"You went through all the hassle of a double to get Louis out of prison? Why didn't you just tell Bobby to write a pardon?"

"That's no fun, sweet. And I had a small point to make with Bobby. He needed reminding that all his beloved power was just an illusion. That perhaps he had sold his soul and gained nothing."

Of course these lessons in piety were much easier to pull off when you had limitless disposable income and a healthy disregard for the laws of the land. "The hell with humbling Bobby," I scowled. "You just wanted to see if your scheme would work."

"That too," Fausto admitted. Then he got serious. "I couldn't risk telling Bobby about Louis. Too many nervous advisers in the Oval Office, especially in an election year. The fewer people who knew Louis was in jail, the better. His life was in danger."

"What did he plan to do in Washington? Meet the press?"

"Darling, Louis doesn't often get fits of conscience. When he does, he's not terribly practical. It took him days to buy a Guatemalan passport and get to D.C. First thing he did was call me. I told him to sit still in his office until I got there. Instead he called the FBI. Someone intercepted the call and tried to kidnap him. Fortunately, our girl Rhoby alerted the cops first and Louis ended up in jail. I knew I had to move him out of there quickly, so I enlisted Tuna. Obviously, he was eager that the doctor get back in the saddle."

"Who's Tuna trying to dispose of?"

"Who cares? Some sleazeball who's undercutting him. Try to think of Louis's work as humanitarian."

"He should have been busting his ass on your case, not Tuna's."

"Louis is capable of working on two things at once."

I glanced irritatedly at the cave. "When's he going to have your medicine ready?"

Fausto brought my hand to his mouth. Even now, the slow, exhausted touch of his lips quickened me. "It's a long shot. You know that. God, I love you."

I leaned over his mosquito-nibbled ear. "Cecil tells me you thought I killed Polly."

"I did at first. Then I realized you were looking for her murderer." Large frown. "When did Cecil speak to you?"

"He stayed in Washington to wrap up a few loose ends. Like me. Calm down, he's on my payroll now."

Fausto drifted off for a while. Then he said, "I knew you were more than a Gypsy fiddler the minute you took Polly's seat at Ford's Theatre. When Cecil saw you hanging off her balcony and half the town started breathing up your thigh, I knew you were slightly illegal. A girl after my own heart. Then I heard you play and it was all over." His fingers crawled over mine. "I kept seeing your eyes. Diamonds and ashes."

Great line. I hoped it wasn't another joke. "Brought you something."

Fausto admired his wedding band in the greenish light. "You came all the way through the jungle to give me a ring?"

"No, a bloody nose." I looked impatiently toward the cave. "What the hell's he doing in there?"

"Let him be. I'm ridiculously happy just talking with you." Fausto coughed weakly. "Could you get me a little water, sweet?"

I went into the cave. Barnard's dried flowers still hung on

the wall. Louis and Ek were boiling crud in a beaker. The place reeked of guano, herbs, unwashed human. "Step on it," I said. "He's fading."

When I returned to the tent, Fausto was hemorrhaging water. He drank more and fell asleep. Nothing I could do but fan the flies away and watch massive shudders overtake him every few minutes. The creatures of the forest cawed louder as the temperature rose twenty degrees. Suddenly the sky turned to coal and a typhoon pounded the tent. Just as swiftly, like life, it passed.

Fausto woke with a start. He didn't immediately recognize his surroundings or me. "What day is it?"

I had to think about that. "Thursday."

"No, the date."

"October second."

"Hmm. I don't think I'm going to make my fifty-first birthday."

Great talons of fear crunched my ribs. I took his hand: distract him with mind games. "Don't say that. Who do you think killed Polly?"

"I don't know. Depends on whose dreams she was closest to destroying. And everyone dreams in Washington."

I sighed: lousy answer. Correct but lousy. "Is Louis right about Jojo's dengue?"

"Yes. But we can't figure out how Jojo got infected in the first place."

"What were you doing at the conference?"

"My God! Who's tattling on me?"

"Gretchen. She loved her plane ride home with you and the monkey."

"I was keeping an eye on Polly. Louis didn't know what to make of her."

"Was she in love with him?"

"Love isn't always physical, you know. Not completely." Fausto drifted off again. Then, "Did you sleep with Bobby?"

"Almost."

"I'm sorry to have to set you up like that. I needed the ultimate seductress to divert him while the double went to Lorton. You may have saved my life. Well, prolonged it, in any event." He kissed my hand. "I'm sorry I never got to fuck you properly, Leslie. Serves me right. I should have taken better care of myself. I just didn't care to live until the night I saw you in that little blue dress at Ford's Theatre. By then it was just too late."

Beyond the valley, thunder. Maybe it was the waterfall. "We'll get out of here and throw a huge party. Then I'll tie you to the bedposts and feed you nothing but oysters until you lose a hundred pounds. Then we'll have ten kids. They'll all play instruments and we'll tour the country like the von Trapps. Your dreams of world domination will dissolve in a mountain of dirty diapers."

"Keep talking," Fausto whispered. "I love this."

Louis zipped open the tent flap. "Brought you something, Fausto." He gave the patient a gourd filled with vile brown liquid. "It's a strong dose. You ought to know that there may be side effects. The vagus might overreact. Instead of telling the brain to interrupt seizures, it might signal to begin them."

"That's just great," I snapped. "Seventeen years in the jungle and that's the best you can do? No wonder you never won the Nobel Prize."

"Shhhh." Fausto squeezed my hand. "What if I don't take this?"

"Your seizures will continue. I could always operate, of course. Remove the appropriate brain tissue. But you know the risks of that."

Fausto looked at me. "In a gambling mood?" I didn't answer so he had to refer to Louis. "What are my chances?"

"Fifty-fifty."

"Can't argue with that." Again he looked at me. "It would be a shame not to drink the damn stuff after all that bother. Bottoms up, doll. Thanks for letting me punch out at the top of my game."

Fausto drank. We waited. Nothing happened.

"I think we're over the hump," the doctor finally announced. "You would have had counterindications by now."

"How do you feel?" I asked. "Besides hot."

"Fine."

I stood up. "Great. Let's go back to Washington."

"That's impossible," Louis cried. "Fausto's in no condition to go anywhere without medical supervision."

"Then come back with us. You've got a nice lab in Virginia. You can make gallons of this swill up there."

"You don't understand. I've got to finish Tuna's project. It was part of the deal."

I looked imploringly at Fausto, who merely said, "He's right."

"Then I'm going to Belize City," I said. "Back in two hours. Who's got the keys to the chopper?" Dull stares. "Come on, boys! I haven't got all day!"

"What are you going to do there?" Louis asked suspiciously.

"Figure out who assassinated your brother. I hope you don't mind. Can you come with me, Ek?"

A surplus Blackhawk waited on top of the hill: ah, money. Ten minutes later Ek and I were skimming over the jungle. On all sides, as far as we could see, lay green dense and dark as broccoli, occasionally parted by a slim green river. I counted five rainbows, eight clouds of smoke: deforestation already in high gear. "How have you been?" I shouted at Ek over the *whop whop* of rotor blades.

"Good."

"You were right. Louis came back."

No answer so I didn't push it. We flew in silence to Belize City. The airport was deader than Jonestown. I parked next to Fausto's Piper and paid the landing fees. Inside the terminal I bought an expensive assortment of cheap toys. "Can you take me to Dr. Tatal's clinic?" I asked Ek.

We cabbed to a long building made of whatever construction materials had been available at the time that carpenters had felt like working. Now everything was peeling or rotting. The front doors didn't close: no problem since there was no air-conditioning to conserve and bugs came and went at will through the inch-high gap at the floor. Next to the decayed front steps, perhaps to cushion falls, an overflowing bin of medical waste blistered in the sun. "They fixed it up for the environmental conference," Ek said as we went inside.

Down a grimy corridor to the dengue ward. The smells were indescribably unpleasant. Behind the nurse's desk hung a picture of Paula Marvel and Dr. Tatal, who looked coolly professional in a white tunic. Couldn't say the same for Paula's fussy bows and hat. Schoolgirls in pinafores clustered the two women. "The president's wife visited us," explained the nurse. "The girls sang."

"We'd like to visit Babette and Iris Auclair. We understand they came down with dengue after the conference." Thank you, Tougaw.

"They're in the children's ward." The victims lay in a cubbyhole painted fecal yellow. Poor things looked like voodoo dolls, without the pins: bloodshot eyes, swollen joints . . . breakbone was the correct name for this plague, and they had only mild cases. "Hi girls," I said cheerfully. "My name's Cosima. This is Ek. Which of you is Babette?" The bigger one tried to sit up. I gave her a doll. "How're you feeling?"

"Much better." Ah, that singsong lilt: happy people. "My

sister is coming along, too." The little one smiled with the dignity of a queen.

"I understand you two were at the big conference here."

"Oh yes. We sang for the president's wife."

"I bet she loved it." Paula's best attribute was that beatific smile she wore when bored stiff.

"And I saw the vice president! He gave me a ball!" Babette showed me a hand-sewn mesh ball with ladybug emblems on the outside. "I'll keep it forever."

"Where did he give this to you?"

"Here in the hotel. Iris and I had to wait a long time to get up to the banquet room because only one elevator was working. Then the vice president came out." Babette hugged herself. "I think he's very handsome."

Not anymore, kid. "Did you get a ball, too?" I asked little sister.

"Yes. But the lady took it away. She tried to take Babette's ball too, but Babette wouldn't give it to her."

Something odd here. Vice presidents didn't distribute toys to children only to have grown women snatch them back. "That's not very nice," I said. "Who was this lady?"

"I don't know. She said the balls belonged to her daughter."

Oh God. I passed out the toys to everyone in the room. "Does anyone remember a girl playing the violin here?"

Silence. Maybe they had erased the memory. Or maybe they had all been sleeping, as Gretchen said. Ek and I returned to the nurse, who was sharing a sandwich with two huge flies. "Did a girl visit the hospital a while back? Play the violin?"

"Very short concert," the nurse informed me. "Thank the Lord."

"Could you tell me where?"

"In the room at the end of the hall."

Ek and I walked down an airless corridor. Too quiet here: death was an exhausting opponent. In every room lay two or three demicorpses, mouths open, all exhaling that horrible stench. The gurneys looked like seconds from the Battle of the Somme. I had yet to see one latex glove. Pulled Ek into the last room, which had more windows but no more cross-ventilation than did the hallway. For a moment we stared at the occupants of a dozen beds. Too hot for sheets so their bodies, both wasted and grotesquely swollen, lay in full view. They were all weeping blood from the eyes, nose, ears, fingernails . . . everywhere. The fresh red glowed like nail polish; the old red looked like meat loaf gravy. Humans? Oozing protoplasm. Bendix had Gretchen play *here?*

A doctor entered. He seemed in no particular rush, but none of his patients were going anywhere. "I guess this is the hemorrhagic dengue ward," I said stupidly.

"That's correct. Are you visiting someone?"

Just ghosts. "I think a girl played the violin here recently."

"Just for a few minutes. She and her teacher brought some toys." The doctor indicated a few more mesh balls on a bed table. "The patients were not well enough to appreciate a concert. I told the girl to play for the children instead. But she was not—agreeable to that."

On the way out, I asked the nurse if Dr. Tanqueray Tougaw worked there. "I have never heard that name," she answered.

I could only smile in defeat and leave. Quiet in the streets: sun had driven everyone inside. "Hungry?" I asked Ek.

We went to a café bigger but not tidier than Koko's. Maybe detergents just didn't work in the tropics. Hell, maybe people up north were just too clean. "Glad to see Louis again?" I asked Ek.

His face barely moved as he ate. "I did not know he was working on a poison."

"He was also working on a cure for Fausto. The world needs both."

Ek swallowed a lot of beans before speaking again. "Are you sorry you killed Simon?"

Crap, not Simon again! Then I remembered that Ek wasn't as civilized as the rest of us. "Do you think he was sorry to be killing me? Sorry he succeeded in killing Dr. Tatal? We were just jobs. He was paid for his work."

"What you are saying is someone else is also responsible for killing Dr. Tatal."

"That's right."

Ek put twenty dollars on the table. "Would you kill that person for me? That's all the money I have now but I will earn however much you want."

Ah, damn. "I don't think you understand," I sighed. "There's a big difference between Simon and me." Simon got paid more.

"But what about the person who killed Dr. Tatal? There is no punishment?"

In this life? Forget it. "I'll find who did it. Whether or not I can even the score is beyond my control."

We finished eating in silence. "Why were you asking about Dr. Tougaw?" Ek asked as we were leaving the café.

"You know him?"

"He sells medicines. He has a shop by the wharf."

Ek took me there. Not even the fish were moving in that section of town. Tougaw's place was shut tight. "What are you doing?" Ek whispered, looking around anxiously.

"Opening the door. Just a second." We went inside. The place smelled of roots and herbs and mostly mildew: Tougaw hadn't been here for a while. I turned on the lights. Behind the cash register was a huge picture of the medicine man with Paula Marvel in her Dress of One Dozen Bows. *To Dr. Tougaw*, the inscription read. *With thanks. Paula Marvel.*

"Guess he was at the conference, too," I said, sniffing a few bottles. Gad, was there anyone in Belize who hadn't cashed in on the damn thing?

"He's not a very good doctor," Ek said. "He does not always find the best plants. And he puts spells on people."

No wonder Paula had brought him to Washington. I uncorked a bottle and nearly gagged on the odor of burnt pineapple. "Let's get back to camp."

We had a jagged ride through squalls and hidden thermals rippling over the hills. Fausto was in his tent reading *Macbeth,* borrowed from Barnard's library in the cave. His face looked only slightly less gray than it had this morning. "She was an extraordinary woman," he said, closing the book.

"Lady Macbeth?"

"No, your friend Polly. Terrific botanist. Could have given Louis a real run for his money."

I peeled a mango. "Did you perform any unnatural sex acts with her?"

"No, dear. I deferred to the president. With you I wasn't quite as generous."

"I have a video of her in a bathtub with Marvel." Tiny fib: Fausto would be ripped if I told him Cecil had flouted his house arrest. "It was made at Aurilla's country place. Bobby was given the keys so he'd have a spare bedroom out of town. The upstairs is crawling with cameras." I dropped a piece of mango into Fausto's mouth. "Have you seen the video?"

"No. But it sounds lovely."

"Who would have watched it and then killed Polly? Aurilla and Bendix?"

"Careful. Why should they kill Polly just because she was bathing with Marvel? On the contrary, Aurilla would love to have a tape like that. It would be a huge bargaining chip if the going ever got rough. No, whoever killed Polly was an ally of Bobby's."

"Justine?" I thought a moment. "Forget it. She's too small."

"Size isn't everything, dear. Desire is what counts. Justine's still in love with him. She's fearless after swallowing enough pills."

"Why'd you work with her if she's so unstable?"

"She owes me from way back. The idea of pulling a fast one on Bobby fascinated her."

"But you just said she loved him."

"Hates him in equal measure. Love's a complicated beast. She's been terminally confused over Bobby since the day she laid eyes on him."

"I still can't figure out what she's doing with Duncan."

"It began because she wanted to know about you. Then Duncan's natural charm swept her off her feet. Relax. Duncan's nearing the end of his shelf life. Then he'll be all yours again."

"All right, forget Justine. Do you think Chickering could have killed Polly?"

"She's no friend of Bobby's. She's seen too much since boarding that first bus in Kentucky."

"Paula?"

Fausto paused. "If the First Lady were snuffing Bobby's bimbos, she'd be the worst serial killer in history. But I wouldn't put it past her. Not if she saw a tape of Polly with her husband in a bathtub. Even if Marvel's spin doctors managed to get him off the hook for another relapse, Polly didn't seem the discreet type. She could cost Marvel the election."

Louis came in, covered with muck. He handed Fausto a gourd. "Drink." He turned to me. "Productive trip?"

"I went to the hospital and spoke with two little girls who also came down with dengue after the conference. They ran into Jojo near the hotel elevator."

"*Aedes aegypti* don't breed in elevators," Louis snorted.

"Couldn't a mosquito have been flying around the elevator and bitten the girls after Jojo left?"

"That's pushing it. Anyone else in the elevator would have been bitten as well. If only Jojo and the girls were hit, the mosquitoes would have had to be contained. Controlled. How could that have happened? Did something come into contact with Jojo and the girls alone?"

Ah, Doctor: brilliant questions. No wonder Polly fell for him. "He gave them a ball."

Ek came to life. "It was made of fine mesh. Like the cage holding the fer-de-lance that killed Dr. Tatal." He picked it up from the floor. "See, Cosima."

"He's right." I looked at Louis. "Could someone have put a few mosquitoes inside those balls?"

"Certainly. But in your scenario they would have to be carrying the dengue virus."

"Is that so hard?"

Louis smiled triumphantly: riddle solved. "Xenodiagnosis. Done all the time. You put the female *Aedes aegypti* in a test tube and cover the top with a nylon stocking. Place it on the skin of a dengue victim and let the mosquito bite through the nylon. Then you isolate the mosquito for a few days, feeding it only enough sugar water to stay alive. The virus will move through its digestive system and become concentrated in the salivary glands. The mosquito's now ready for action. With the next bite, she'll pump the dengue virus into her next victim."

Silence in the tent. "Know anyone who's been in a dengue ward lately?" Fausto asked no one in particular. "With nylon stockings and a couple of test tubes?"

How about with mesh balls and a young violinist? *Ace plan, Bendix!* Gretchen distracts everyone with Bach and tantrums while Uncle B puts a few balls laced with mosquitoes on dengue victims too exhausted to play with them. End of concert, Bendix palms a few balls back. Keeps the mosquitoes alive while the virus migrates, then his pal Aurilla steps into an elevator with Jojo. She finds a pretext to hand over a couple of balls, careful to keep her fingers on the decals so the mosquitoes won't bite her. Jojo takes them, gets stung. Stepping out of the elevator, he unwittingly hands toys to Babette and Iris. They're stung, too. Aurilla gets only one ball back without looking like the Wicked Witch. Takes the risk of her life and leaves the second ball behind. Her gamble pays off . . . for a while.

"Stockings and test tubes? I didn't see anyone carrying that around the dengue ward." I tried to look perplexed. "I don't understand why the girls had simple dengue but Jojo went hemorrhagic."

"Simple," Louis replied again. "All his life he took aspirin."

"So what?"

The great doctor tried to be patient. "Step one. Jojo's stung. In two or three days, he aches all over as the simple dengue virus bores holes in his capillaries. That stupid cow Myrna tells him he's under the weather and gets him to take a load of aspirin."

"That's what she said at Aurilla's dinner, didn't she?" Fausto asked me.

"Correct." I thought Fausto hadn't been listening.

"Jojo ate aspirin like M and M's," Louis continued. "Took it for everything. You know what aspirin does to the blood platelets, don't you? It thins them. That means a lot more would escape through the holes in the capillaries than would normally. To make things worse, by now Jojo probably would be running a fever. That would constrict his capillaries even further, increasing his blood pressure. It's like a water main break. You get a situation where the thinned platelets escape the capillaries faster than the capillaries can repair themselves. Full-blown hemorrhagic dengue, and before you know it there's no going back. The victim bleeds beyond recovery." He peered intently at me. "So who's the mastermind behind your plot?"

I scratched an armpit. "Someone who knows Jojo takes aspirin. Myrna, I guess."

Long silence. Fausto quaffed the rest of his drink. "Sounds a little farfetched, sweet. Not only Myrna but the whole story. Those girls play near puddles. They could have been bitten a hundred times in a hundred other places. We also overlook the possibility of Jojo just being near the wrong stinger at the wrong time."

While I was glaring at my husband, Louis stood. "I've got kettles boiling in the cave."

"Aren't you interested in hashing this out?" I cried. "We're talking about your brother, not some dipshit politician."

"Nothing can ever be proven," he retorted. "I've lost weeks of time already. Drink all of that, Fausto. Ek! Come with me!" He stomped out.

I watched the patient lie back on the cot, a big smile on his face. Finally I understood. "You know it was Bendix," I said. "So does Louis. Both of you always knew. And you know I know." Ah, what wonderful games we played! If only we could have kept the body count at zero!

Fausto seemed to be getting his color back. "Do tell me one thing, doll. Who was in the elevator with Jojo?"

"Aurilla."

He whistled. "Brass balls! I would have thought he'd hand off the job to Gretchen. If the girl got sick, so much the better. Don't be angry, love. With Bendix it was just a matter of time. He's been on a direct course for the White House ever since he buried his operas. In a perverse way, it's been inspiring to watch. He'll get away with it, of course."

"You could have stopped him."

"You flatter me. The best I could do was slap his wrists with that hideous sonata. Louis tried to pull the plug by going to Washington and nearly got himself killed." He shut his eyes. "It's a stalemate. The three of us have too many skeletons in our closet."

Wonderful. "Do you think Bendix hit Tatal?"

"Definitely. Bendix knew that the minute Louis found out about his brother's dengue, he'd run to Tatal with a load of questions. She would have nailed Bendix with that visit to the hospital during the conference. Better she was out of the picture."

"Where'd Bendix find Simon?"

"Where everyone else finds him. He's the local contractor for all hired guns. Gets a cut of the action. If I need James to fly my plane, I talk to Simon first." Fausto rolled his head my way. "Did you . . . ah . . ."

"Simon tried to kill me. Nearly succeeded. I think Bendix sicced him on Louis as well as Tatal."

"Bendix had no choice. Louis figured out the dengue problem in ten seconds flat. He just didn't know the mechanics. You gave us that. Smart girl."

I went to the mat, daubed Fausto's forehead with a damp cloth. "Let's go to Paris. Berlin. Any place but Washington."

He pulled me down beside him. "Whatever you want."

Again I heard that enigmatic laughter. Felt a shudder as I realized I had gone through the eye of the needle to the land of the absolutely and defiantly happy: let the gods strike me dead now, while I stood as close as I'd ever get to the sun. "We're flying out tonight. Louis will make you a year's supply of his magic potion. By the way, where's my violin?"

"There's a button in the wall behind my dresser. Press it twice." He touched my eyes. "I was just thinking about the taste of you. Moss and roses. And when you go over the falls . . ." He sighed. "Come lie here with me a minute. God, I want to live forever."

Try twenty years if we were lucky. Two if I kept working for Maxine. I snuggled against a giant, protective bear. I could tolerate infidelity and intemperance, maybe even boredom, as long as a man protected me. Against what, I didn't know. Shadows outside the cave. I was telling Fausto about the music I wanted to play together when I noticed that his fingers had stopped sifting my hair. For a second I thought he had fallen asleep but no, that would have presumed a happy ending, a contented winding down of days, oh Christ he had stopped breathing. I bolted upright. He was staring at me with the frozen horror I had seen twice before. But this time something in his eyes was not entirely human.

"Louis," I screamed, tearing for the cave. "Come here!"

Crash from the tent: Fausto rushed out like a wounded bull and lumbered down the hill. Three times he lost his footing and rolled through the scrub toward that angry water. Twice I caught him but he was a runaway train and each time I managed to grab a branch, our combined weight uprooted it easily as crabgrass. "Fausto!" I shrieked. "Stop!" He fell on top of me, grunting like a hippo. I stepped into a hole, got stuck for just a few seconds while Fausto rampaged into the water.

Dove after him into the frothy green death. *Catch up, Smith. Push him to the side.* I couldn't find him. His head would pop above the surface here, sink, resurface way over there. Sometimes all I saw was a swollen white hand before it cut back beneath the water. Once I almost caught up only to *whop!* hit a rock that could have saved us both and meanwhile that heavy thunder only grew louder. I skidded over a slimy shelf into the first of three whirlpools. *Running out of river.* Swam like a maniac downstream because I saw him slide over the second shelf into the second whirlpool. He had the weight and momentum to flow ahead while I just got sucked back into the undertow but I was gaining on him and last time I had rushed to the edge of this falls a tree had stopped me. It would stop both of us now.

Didn't factor in the rainy season: what had been a foot above water last time was barely breaking the surface now. Movement atop the current: Ek on the submerged trunk. Thickness at his waist: he had tied himself to the tree. Quick as a hawk he dove on top of me, caught me in a viselike hold. We blew forward then, with a violent snap, stopped: his knot held. Tons of water rushed over us. I tried to slither away but Ek was younger, stronger . . . with clearer dreams. As he dragged me backward I saw Fausto's enormous body snag on the trunk just a few feet ahead of us *yes! yes!* then twist ever so slowly ninety degrees starboard. There he floated, suspended for a heart-wrenching second before the current took him. I screamed as he went over the edge.

Ek pulled me onto a smooth rock shelf. I lay facedown, finished forever. Wet the stone with my tears: maybe if I cried long enough, I'd shrivel up and blow away. But the body didn't work like that. It just got more swollen. Finally I rolled over. Ek was staring at the horizon, his Mayan face impassive as the rope heaped at his side.

"I wanted you to live," was all he said.

I pulled a leech off the welt at his waist and flicked it into the water. It went over the falls. Unlike Fausto, it would survive: what a strange world.

Louis came crashing through the brush. He stared a long moment at the two of us. "Fausto's downstream," I said finally. "You failed."

The doctor crumpled to the ground: grieving for the end of his friend or the end of his experiment? "He was responding so well!"

Too well. He had tempted the Furies. "We've got to find him."

"He could be a mile downstream by now. If we don't reach him by nightfall, there will be nothing left."

I stood up and, with great self-control, managed not to fling Louis into the water. "I know you've got more important things to do, but we're going after the body."

I loaded the boys in the Blackhawk and returned to the green river. Waterfall high as Niagara with a fearful clutch of rocks at the bottom: I knew at once that I was a widow. Again. The sun was skimming the horizon when Ek suddenly pointed into the shadows. "There."

We saw Fausto's body wedged between two rocks. I hovered over the whitewater while Ek spun down with the hooks and tied him up like a bale of hay. "Winch," I shouted at Louis, then concentrated on keeping my blades out of the trees. Louis and Ek finally hauled Fausto back inside the cabin. Fiery sunset as I carted my burden over the jungle canopy to the clearing on top of the mountain. Shut down the Blackhawk and stared at the instrument panel: in a few moments I'd have to turn around. *Detach, Smith.* The heat crushed me as I finally faced Fausto's destroyed body. Half his skull was caved in and both legs were broken. Actually, everything was broken: ribs, neck, nose, shoulder . . . his skin alternated between milky white and bright purple. I turned away: perhaps I should have left him to the animals. I would have nightmares about this surreal, humiliated lump for the rest of my life.

Louis inspected the body with a doctor's inquisitive, inhuman care. "Drowned," he pronounced.

From another galaxy I said, "You're going to arrange a proper death certificate. Then you're going to fly the ashes back to Washington. I'm going to be there to pick them up."

"Why not fly them back yourself?"

"You don't understand. I was never here."

Louis laughed harshly. As he laid Fausto's crushed head back on the floor, phlegmy shreds of that wondrous brain clung to his fingers. Louis just wiped them on his khakis. "Besides blackmail, what's your interest in all this?"

"Fausto didn't tell you?" Of course not: I had asked him not to. "I'm his wife. And for the record, we all know Bendix is responsible for the death of your brother and Tatal. You might think about that as you continue your great humanitarian work."

I threw Louis out of the helicopter. While he was moaning on the grass, I gathered my things and stalked into the darkening forest. The cicadas shrieked like air raid sirens, driving me away for good. Ek finally caught up with me. "Was Fausto really your husband?"

"I married him two days ago."

"Does that mean you're going to be rich?"

"That means I'm going to be sad."

"You won't forget your promise about Dr. Tatal?"

Ah, what could I say. This boy had saved my life twice, each time at great risk to his own. He had tied up a body while I dangled him over a raging river. Now I was leaving him behind with Louis, who would pretend I had never happened. "I'll even the score," I promised. "One way or another."

Brushed his cheek then headed east.

Chapter Fourteen

$\mathcal{I}$ RETURNED to Washington. Bought a paper, read that Bobby Marvel would be farting around town vetoing legislation then gracing a campaign rally tonight. Aurilla Perle was in Baltimore at a conference for "concerned lawyers," whatever the hell that was. Way back on page sixteen, a blip about the vice president. He had miraculously stabilized but no one cared because all interest had shifted to his successor. An editorial suggested it was time to declare him legally dead and let Aurilla take a spin at the roulette wheel.

I picked up the Corvette and returned to the hotel. Two messages on the machine in my dirt-free, air-conditioned room with chocolates on the pillow. One, Bendix thanking me for the drinking session. Two, Rhoby Hall still wanting to do lunch, breakfast, midnight snack, anything. No appetite for that so I went shopping. Drove to Silver Spring, where Cecil the impostor was holed up. I found him absorbed in a porno flick. His room reeked of beer and male effluent. "Rise and shine," I said, tossing some clothes on the bed.

"Where have you been?" he said. "I thought you were dead."

Correct. We drove to Aurilla's empty guest house. I took my packages and Cecil upstairs. "Get naked. We're going to play in the bathtub like you and Polly."

His eyes bulged. "How do you know about that?"

"Only one detail will be different. You're not really going to screw me. Wait until I call."

I went into the bathroom. Poised the champagne on the side of the tub and ran water. I stripped and slipped into the suds. Tiddled with the soap and booze before calling, "Bobby!"

Cecil entered on cue with a towel wrapped around his middle. He stared at me exactly as he had with Barnard, then dropped the towel. Great ass and one hell of an erection, twice the size of the first take. Maybe it was all those porno flicks he had been watching. I shook the bottle. As Cecil stepped into the suds, I hosed the swelling with a stream of cold champagne.

"You'll need more than champagne to get me down, darlin'," Cecil said in a voice staggeringly close to Marvel's. He dove on top of me. I got my neck licked, my boobs sucked, then the fake rear hump. All this warm, frothing water brought back pictures of Fausto floating at the edge of the waterfall, twisting serenely starboard . . . *Block it, Smith! Do your job!* Forever later, with a mighty grunt, Cecil was finished. He stepped out of the bath exactly as he had with Barnard, only this time he took the champagne instead of a towel with him. I followed to the bedroom across the hall.

He was guzzling directly from the bottle. "Jesus! Don't ask me to do that again! I'd rather shoot a nun!"

"Shut up and get dressed." I went to the basement. Found the circuit box, killed the electricity. Then I brought Cecil back to the bathroom. "See anything above that cabinet?"

He swore. "That whole scene was taped?"

"You got it." We crossed to the bedroom. "There's another camera. Let's find the VCR." The cables led to a locked closet down the hall. Phone relay: someone had been informed that there had been action out here. I sent Cecil back to the basement while I connected the VCR to a second unit I had bought that afternoon. When he got the power back on, I made a copy of our home movie.

He finished the champagne. "Who's the voyeur?"

"Don't know." Embarrassing.

"Polly knew tape was rolling when she got me in the bathtub?"

"Camera's hard to miss," I answered, packing everything up. "Of course, you had other things on your mind."

He cringed. "Why'd you have me do it again?"

"Same reason she had you do it in the first place. I want someone to come gunning for me. Wrap this job up and go home."

"What's the copy for?"

"Insurance."

He chuckled: no such thing in our business. "Am I done now?"

"Hell no. You're going back to your room and work on elocution."

Maybe he thought that was a new form of torture. "Anything the lady wants."

I drove him back to his hideout for another siege with the adult film channel. Then I went to a pet store and bought an iguana. Called my little friend, who had just returned from school. "Gretchen! I've got something for you. Can I bring it over?"

Another new maid, this one from Indonesia, answered the door. Maybe she and her charge had been fingerpainting with ketchup and tapioca. "I'm here to see Gretchen," I announced.

My playmate came sliding to the front door on the lid of a garbage can, gouging a ten-foot trail on the parquet floor. "Hi Miss Frost!" she cried, springing off. "Did you bring my pet alligator?"

Opened the lid to the long box I was carrying. When the iguana stuck one taloned claw over the edge, the maid retreated with a scream to the kitchen. "Let's go upstairs."

Dumped the box on Gretchen's bed along with a care and feeding book. "You read that and watch your fingers. I'll be right back."

Blew down to the first floor. Aurilla was at her conference in Baltimore, which meant so was Wallace. Had to gamble on Bendix's whereabouts but two to one he was with the team. Aurilla's office was not locked for long. Stuck my head in. No surveillance so I clipped a tiny microphone in a vase of roses on the corner of Aurilla's desk: trite as *Mission Impossible* but they'd get chucked in another day or two and I planned to be in Berlin by then. Charged back upstairs, past the room where Fausto and I had dallied before a concert. I thought I heard his voice and almost looked in.

Gretchen had put reptile and an old peanut-butter sandwich in her bathtub. "I'm going to name him Chopper," she said. "Because he has so many teeth."

I gave Chopper's new mistress a few tips on keeping him alive. Bendix could always eat him if things didn't work out. "Do you miss playing your violin?"

"No. I want a flute now." Gretchen tried to tantalize Chopper with a raisin. "I can do whatever I want. Wallace said Mom's going to be president. I'm going to live in the White House."

Obviously no one had yet told Gretchen she'd be living in Switzerland. I felt a tinge of pity: perhaps I should take her back to Berlin, away from that monstrous mother. But compassion had its limits. "If you ever want to go back to the violin, give me a call, all right?"

"Sure," she sighed with an ennui that made me want to rap her knuckles. With the iguana.

I left. Planted receiver/transmitter beneath Aurilla's mailbox then pulled into a park up the street. Sat in Fausto's Corvette, inhaling his ghost, for hours. Day faded into dusk, then night. Finally my headset clicked on: pickup from Aurilla's office. I pulled my ragged brains back to earth. Heard footsteps and an "Oof" from the chair in the corner. "My feet are killing me," Gretchen's mother bitched. "Wallace, bring some wine."

More footsteps. "Would you like me to massage your calves?" the devoted aide asked. "You've been on your feet all afternoon."

"No! Just get this goddamn thing working before I split a gut! Christ! Bendix! Get in here!" Short pause. "What were you doing up there?"

"Your daughter's acting very strangely," Bendix replied. "The bathroom door is locked. God knows what she's hiding this time."

"Couldn't be anything worse than a monkey," Aurilla retorted. "You and your asinine bribes."

Bendix wisely changed the subject. "Did you get a nibble, Wallace?"

"This afternoon. I just picked up the tape."

"Bobby went out to the cottage? I thought he had business in town all day."

"You know Casanova," Aurilla snorted. "Wallace, what is the problem? I don't have all night for this bullshit."

"Hold on. Here we go."

Silence as they watched Cecil and me cavort in the tub. "That slut," the almost vice president said. "I thought she was fucking Fausto." Fifteen, fifty, ninety seconds went by.

I felt my face burning. *Disinformation, Smith: part of the job.* Finally, in a voice nigh orgasmic with satisfaction, Aurilla said, "We've got the stinker by the balls now."

Which stinker? Fortunately Bendix explained. "Marvel can't talk his way out of two bimbos in a bathtub." Footsteps, more clinking glass. "Bravo, Aurilla. We did it."

"I never had any doubts."

In the background, a loud shriek. "Moooooommmm! Chopper bit me!"

Curses, shuffling, silence. I sat in the dark marveling at Aurilla's ambition and my own stupidity. She knew Bobby too well: dangle a female in front of his nose and he would always come charging. He had fallen for Barnard first. How had Aurilla lured her to the house? Tutor for Gretchen? I had been the convenient violin teacher. I smiled acidly, remembering how Bobby had happened to meet me the first time I had visited. As usual, the Queen had been correct: you don't bump into the president of the United States by accident. Aurilla's plan was simple, perfect, flawlessly executed. Become model senator and presidential favorite. Clear Jojo out of the way with a few mosquito bites. Slide into scoring position. Then sayonara Bobby with a final outbreak of bimbitis. *Balls!* Alas, pride went before a fall: seeing wasn't always believing, Aurilla. And you put the wrong girls in the bathtub.

Through the headphones, seven almost imperceptible plastic clicks. Tape running again. Someone had returned to Aurilla's office to make a phone call. "We've got a problem," Wallace muttered. "Meet me in an hour."

I burst out laughing. Oh God! If only Fausto were here to enjoy this treachery! For a second I saw his round face, that mischievous glint in his eye when the plot thickened: then all went dark and his absence cut through me like a bolt of lightning. I collapsed over the steering wheel as something stole my guts. *Get up, Smith. Return serve.* Rolled the Corvette down Aurilla's street as a Subaru pulled out of her driveway. Followed Wallace to the only cemetery that had seen any action in this campaign and stalked her on foot to the public vault. The earth here felt alive, eager to swallow. Things that went down the maws of that vault never came back. Soon I'd be bringing Fausto here? *No!*

The night was warm, ruffled with winds and the scent of dead leaves. The moon was red. Wallace didn't like waiting near that great dark hole any more than I did. Three cigarettes and a few thousand paces later, a Lexus pulled up to the vault.

Vicky Chickering.

I sighed to an overhead airplane. Shouldn't have been a surprise. I had stumbled on Chickie alone upstairs with Wallace at Aurilla's party. Hadn't given them a second thought because Chickering acted more like pope than pol. Good trick: both Barnard and I had fallen for it. *Someone on Bobby's side,* Fausto had said. As always, he had been several layers of subterfuge ahead of me. Indeed Chickering was on Bobby's side, but that was because she was now and forever on Paula's side. That union went back to bedrock in Kentucky. Whoever threatened Bobby threatened Paula, the diesel behind this presidency. Bobby was only the cow-catcher.

"What the hell's going on?" Chickering demanded.

"He's back in the bathtub. This time with Frost."

"That cunt! Wasn't Fausto enough for her?"

Hey ladies, just doing my job. "Aurilla's got enough ammo to bury Bobby now," Wallace said. "You'd better tell Paula. She's got to deal with the problem same way as last time. We can't afford any loose ends with this bitch, either."

"I'll tell Paula right away." Chickering paced over rumpled graves. "The Frost problem will get fixed soon. You've got to take care of the tapes tonight."

"I'll erase them, but that's dangerous."

"Please, Wally! Your job is nowhere near as dangerous as mine. We've got no choice. Aurilla and Bendix are not going to wait with this."

"Poor Paula," Wallace said after a silence. "Maybe we should just take care of Bobby next time. You know there will always be a next time."

Chickering laughed caustically. "And here I thought Frost was after Rhoby."

"Don't be so sure she's not. The bitch probably goes both ways."

Wishful thinking, Wally. With a fervid embrace, the First Lady's teammates parted. Wallace's Subaru bumped past many headstones out to the real world. Before leaving, Chickering took a ruminative stroll around the chapel, pausing now and then, as if she heard a choir singing inside. I left quickly because that great gaping hole of the public vault just got darker with the passing of night and each time the wind kicked up, I thought I heard it inhaling. Chickering was going to fix me tonight? Let her try.

From the car I called Rhoby Hall at the FBI. "This is Leslie. Sorry I haven't been able to reach you sooner."

"No problem! What've you been up to?"

"The usual. Do you have a lunch break, or whatever it's called on the graveyard shift? We'll grab a bite."

"Sure. But it's at four in the morning."

"That's okay. I'm trying to get back on European time." We arranged to meet at an all-night diner on A Street. "Oh, Rhoby. I wonder if you could help. I met a fellow at Aurilla's party last week. Tanqueray Tougaw. Remember him?"

"Jesus, how could I not? Chickie practically lives with the

guy in our kitchen. They make all kinds of weird stuff for Paula."

"Do you know where he lives? I'll be needing something for my jet lag."

"No idea. Call Chickie. She'd know." Rhoby recited seven digits.

"What's the area code for Annapolis?"

"This number's Washington. She's at the Watergate."

I felt my hair rise. *Watergate?* "I thought you two lived in Annapolis."

"That's my apartment. Chickie lives in town. We switch from place to place depending on the state of our relationship."

True? I couldn't tell anymore. In this town, the worst thing you could do was declare whose side you were on. "Where are you sleeping now?" I asked.

"Her place."

I wandered to the Watergate complex, where I had fished a few keys out of a fountain several lifetimes ago. Stood for a while at the three shallow basins, listening for that low, mysterious laughter that had so entranced me. Moon was round and ripe as a melon, the Potomac burbled like a primeval spring . . . how could that laughter be gone? Another *zzzzt* as Fausto's specter jolted through me and into the next galaxy before I could even raise a hand to stop him. *Finish the job, Smith.* With an effort, I located Chickering's apartment. It was three away from Barnard's.

Drove to the diner on A Street and dozed until four. Rhoby was waiting inside with coffee and crossword. Since our last meeting she had lopped off another few inches of hair but made up for it with shoe leather: tonight's boots laced almost to her crotch. Perhaps the FBI relaxed its dress code for the phone operators. "So did you get Chickie?" Rhoby asked excitedly.

"Sorry. Lost my nerve." Slid into the booth with seats the color of stale blood. "She reminds me of my first-grade teacher. I'm always expecting her to reach into her back pocket and whip out a wooden spoon."

"That's so perfect! The old sow!" Rhoby sounded giddy, under the influence of something. I hoped it wasn't love. "God, it's great to see you! You've been so busy! Tell me about it! I want to know everything!"

Oh, rehearsals, practicing, interviews . . . I made it vague enough that corroboration would be impossible. "How's life at the FBI?"

"Over. I just quit."

I barely swallowed my coffee. "What? Tonight?"

"My adviser didn't want me to leave the building. So I told him to shove it." Rhoby suddenly took my hand. "Let's go dancing."

Our first stop was a lesbian speakeasy on Rhode Island Avenue. Dark, crowded, humid with testosterone: not many lamb chops in this mutton market. Rhoby didn't even let me go to the bathroom alone. I kept her floating in champagne and screwdrivers to celebrate her liberation from the FBI. We danced tit-à-tit until five, when a new band tried to blow out the windows. Next we drove to a raunchier dive on Maryland Avenue, where all the rejects went for one last shot before heading home alone. I had never seen so many deliberately grungy women in my life. But I was an anti-American bitch, incapable of realizing that three-foot-wide asses and rotting tank tops were signs of gay pride rather than evidence of blatant self-indulgence. At least in Berlin the lesbians tried to look like Marlene Dietrich instead of John Belushi.

Rhoby switched from screwdrivers to mai-tais after the third woman came to the table asking for Vicky. "Working,"

Rhoby retorted for the third time. "Just ignore them," she muttered, as if I were offended.

I looked her deep in the eye. "Are you and Chickie having problems?"

"Problems? We're through. Chickie just doesn't know it yet."

"What happened?"

"She started out like a mother but now she's just a jail-keeper. This politics bullshit does a number on her head. She comes home and thinks she's still bossing around the country. Never shuts up about Paula, either. The two of them are twisted. I belong with musicians. At least they're real people. Know what I mean?"

Sure I did. My sympathy was entirely with Chickie, who lusted after both innocence and power. In the great ocean of desire, Rhoby was a rowboat, Paula a nuclear submarine. The sub could surface, enjoy the sun, but the rowboat could never explore the awesome world beneath the waves. Ah Chickie: never fall for the rowboat. One day the wind would carry it away. "You must have some things in common."

"I guess we both like horror movies. But it was the beginning of the end when Chickie gave her piano away."

"Why'd she do that?"

"Paula needed it, of course! One morning it was just gone! An old Mason and Hamlin with the most gorgeous mahogany case. Weighed ten tons. It sat in the corner of her apartment and when the sun came up, it was the most beautiful thing you ever saw. The place looks empty without it."

A thread of ice between the eyes: I blinked a few times but it wouldn't go away. "When did she get rid of it?"

"A few weeks ago. It was our first big fight. Who cares if I wanted the piano? *Her Majesty* comes first." Rhoby's eyes welled at the injustice. "You and Fausto could have played trios at my place."

Again that cold wind. Please God let there be a swirling gray world after this one, full of mist and shadow, where I'd find him again! "Let's dance," I said, getting up. Rhoby clung to me like a wounded child. We were the main act on the floor. Males had never looked me over with such open lechery as these ladies; still, I was flattered. Around seven o'clock I sloshed Rhoby into the car. Sun was high and hot and the sidewalks thronged with briefcase-swinging People Making a Difference. "Whererr you taken me?" Rhoby asked.

"Home. Chickie's probably climbing the walls by now."

"Fuckr! I don't wan go t' Chickie. I wan go home wi you."

"Sorry, I have a rehearsal this morning." I screeched the Corvette into a tiny pocket in traffic. "We can ask Chickie when the piano's coming back."

"Shit onner piano." Rhoby sagged against my shoulder. Made me a little nervous because I didn't want her eyebrow studs catching on my jacket but I guess laceration was half the thrill of body jewelry. Fought my way to the Watergate complex and lugged Rhoby upstairs, making sure the doorman noticed her condition. Chickie's apartment was a nine-second walk from Barnard's: what colossal bad luck.

Rhoby kicked open the door. "Chick! I'm home!"

Chickering, dressed for managing the nation, came running but stopped short at the awful sight before her. Long silence as her flowing tunic slowed to a standstill, then, "What are you doing here?"

"What does it look like?" I cried cheerfully, dragging Rhoby toward the kitchen. One counter was covered with dozens of brown bottles: medicine for Paula. "Any coffee in the house? We've had a long night." Chickie followed at our heels as I propped Rhoby at the table and cleared away a pile of newspapers. "You read these and eat breakfast at the same time? Sheesh."

"Where were you, Rhoby?" she demanded. "I've been calling for hours."

"You can throw that number away," I told her. "Rhoby quit that nowhere desk job." Pushed a steaming cup of coffee under Rhoby's chin. "Drink this, honey."

"You whore," Chickering hissed at me. She turned to her lover. "She's playing with you, Rho. I happen to know your friend here was screwing Bobby Marvel just this afternoon."

I laughed without concern. "What have you been inhaling, Chick Pea? Fumes from Doctor Tougaw's stewpot?"

Rhoby sloshed to a little book near the telephone. She tore out a page. "Therz hiz numr."

"Hey, thanks. Rho tells me you're thinking of opening up a pharmacy, Chick."

She tried an obelisk stare. "Leave. Now."

"See whad I mean 'bout jailkeepr?" Rhoby threw an arm around me. "Chickie shouldv joined the KGB."

"Just don't let her hit me with a wooden spoon!" Rhoby and I giggled hilariously. Then I peered into the living room. "Hey! Didn't you say you had a piano here, Rho? Is it in the bedroom or something?"

"You hearr me," Rhoby pouted. "Iz gone."

"Can you get it back?" I asked Chickering. "I just love those old Mason and Hamlins. I can't believe you'd let something like that out of your sight. They're worth a fortune."

Chickering's face went like a fish. She looked at me with infernal doubt and a thread of fear: did I know everything or was she just paranoid? Ah, Fausto, if only you could see me now! He would not only be amused, he might be able to tell me how to proceed. All I really wanted from Chickering was a clue to the whereabouts of her piano. I wouldn't mind killing her as well: payback for Barnard. I could reach across the table and snap her neck. *Right now.* Or I could sic Cecil on her. He'd love some real action after all this playacting. Hell, maybe I should just take the next plane out of here.

I smiled at Rhoby. "Come on, I'll tuck you in."

Dragged her to the king-size bed in a room painted hideous maroon: maybe that was Chickie's idea of the color of passion. Rhoby didn't resist as I unlaced her boots thigh to ankle and stripped her down to cotton underwear. Pretty body: she'd have no trouble finding another partner. "Why can't you stay?" she whimpered.

"Shhhh." I pulled down the shades. "We'll talk later."

Returned to the kitchen, feigned surprise to see Chickering still lording over the linoleum like Mr. Clean. "Don't you have to get to work, Chickie?"

She puffed up to full width, like a cobra. The sight was impressive, especially if one considered the acres of farmland involved. "I told you to leave Rhoby alone."

"Why? Does she have your name branded on her butt?" I slumped onto a kitchen chair and began rummaging through the little brown bottles. "Did you get all this stuff from Tougaw? Awesome." Removed a cork, sniffed. "Got any aphrodisiacs? Next time you want to screw Rhoby, I suggest you get her to swallow the whole bottle. The poor thing was beginning to hit on me before she passed out back there." Kept sniffing, bending my head far down, exposing plenty of neck. Finally saw Chickie fingering that obnoxious notepad on her chest, remove a stubby pen. Ah, so that's our needle. Unoriginal, but so was Chickering. I bent with renewed interest over the bottle tops. Come on, Chickie! I didn't have all day! "Oh damn. I think I just got my period. Any tampons handy?"

Sudden puff of air and a scream. Not Chickering, Rhoby. "Don't do that!"

I rolled right just as Vicky's hammy fist slammed to the table. Her pen impaled wood instead of neck: sorry, old girl.

You can't have two of us. The table buckled under the combined weight of Rhoby and Chickering. Cups and bottles sprayed all over the kitchen. They toppled right on top of the splintered glass, wrestling with the superhuman savagery of two people who had once been in love. Chickering was big but slow, Rhoby strong but drunk: even match. Blood was everywhere but the combatants didn't slow down. They used fingernails, chairs, pots, plants, and curses that would make a witch tremble. I just dialed 911 and let the good times roll.

Then an awful crack. Rhoby shrieked and went quiet. I was bending over her when I felt a little sting in the shoulder: good move, Chick. Almost at once, a tingling in my throat. My shoulders began to go cold, then my legs. With my last coordinated signals from brain to muscle, I staggered to the living room. As Chickie tackled me from the rear, I saw Rhoby's cello perched innocently against a chair. The corner did look empty without a piano. "You're going to die, bitch," she snarled, whacking my head from side to side, as if it were a punching bag. "Think you can just fuck Bobby and get away with it *whack* well you made a big mistake *whack* Paula's had it up to here *whack* if Aurilla thinks she can walk into the White House *whack* she's got another thing coming *whack* you people are all going to eat shit before Paula and I are done with you *whack*."

After a few dozen shots, Chickering tried to stuff a kitchen towel down my throat. Sorry Chickie: should have done that first, before lockjaw set in. Snarling with fury, she started to pry open my mouth. *Bite hard, Smith.* I tried but she had a pianist's hands. I could feel my jaws giving way when, in surreal slow motion, I saw Rhoby stumble out of the kitchen. Her face was ribboned with blood. She walked calmly to her cello, tightened the eight-inch pin on the bottom. Then she charged.

With a tremendous, hellish twang, the cello rammed

Chickering's back. Chickering blinked as the metal pin entered her heart. Not quite as elegant as a stiletto, but effective nonetheless. "That hurts, Rho," she whispered, thudding to the floor.

Transfixed with horror, Rhoby stared at the mound at her feet. Every second or so blood would drip from the cello pin onto my elbow. "You aright, Les?" she asked finally, trembling. Sure, just a little paralyzed. I managed to gurgle assent. Rhoby dropped the cello and dragged her roommate off me. "I think she's dead. Oh my God! I'm sorry, Chick!" She threw up then passed out.

My body gradually thawed but I didn't move. Chickering might be off my back but I had neglected to ask where she had sent her piano. I was also trying to work out whether, philosophically speaking, I had murdered her. Ah, if only Fausto were here to present arguments for both sides of the question. While I was thinking, two D.C. cops and the Watergate security guard burst in. For a moment they stood in the doorway, taking in the carnage. Then one of the cops rolled Chickering over. First he realized she was dead. Then he realized who she was. A weary look crossed his face as he realized he had stepped into megapoop. Using the code for Special Trouble, he called for reinforcements. His partner slowly hauled me to a sitting position. "You call 911?"

I nodded weakly. "How's Rhoby?"

She groaned as the officer brought her around. Her eyebrow, minus two studs, was in bloody tatters. "Chickie started it," was all she said.

I was helped to the couch. Couldn't take my eyes off Chickering's massive body: Fausto all over again, but in a skirt. I almost threw up. "Is she all right?"

"She's dead," the officer said.

Rhoby screamed and I did throw up: a spontaneous, convincing performance.

The police asked a few opening questions: who lived where, relationship, nature of problem. Soon the place was swarming with federal agents. Rhoby was taken to the hospital for a solo interrogation and a few hundred stitches. I opted for an ice bag and no ambulance. Gave the statement of a very upset acquaintance who had called for help when a domestic quarrel had gotten out of hand. My story would match Rhoby's in all essential details.

"You didn't try to fight back?" the officer asked.

"She had my arms pinned down." No need to drag Tougaw's potion into the fray. They'd deport him. I rubbed my swollen jaw. "Am I going to get in trouble?"

"You do realize who Vicky Chickering is," the detective said.

"She started it," I cried. "Just went berserk. She's the one who should go to jail, not me." What the hell, Bobby could write me a pardon.

The officer closed his laptop with a thud. Give him old-fashioned black-on-black homicide any day of the week. Last thing his career needed was a lesbian love triangle connected straight to the White House. He let me return to the hotel with police guard while he checked my tale against Rhoby's. If I valued my ass, I was not to talk to any reporters. If I went anywhere, I was to notify him first. He'd call this afternoon, using the name Phil.

Returned to my hotel and unfolded a bloody scrap of paper. "Dr. Tougaw? This is Leslie Frost. I wonder if you have any medicine for a sore mouth."

Of course he did. He could come to the hotel and deliver. Half an hour later he was at my door with a huge canvas bag and a broad smile: ah Tougaw, lend me a few of those happy genes. "Leslie Frost! I did not know you were still here!" His smile faded when he saw my jaw.

"I fell." I let him poke around my mouth. "Paula Marvel tells me you're the greatest doctor in Washington."

Tougaw liked that. He said that after the conference she had imported him from Belize to be her personal healer. He had medicines for everything and was treating the First Lady for a number of ailments. In fact, he had just been up with Vicky Chickering last night, replenishing the supply.

I looked impressed. "You make medicine in Vicky's apartment?"

"Oh yes. Vera strong stuff. We boil roots and leaves of special plants in her big pots. We mix it with special oils to make a balm for Mrs. President's arthritis. My secret recipe." Tougaw told me of his illustrious practice in Belize City. He had a large office downtown and people came from all over the country to see him. He now had a list of very famous clients in Washington. So many people were sick here.

I asked him to show me a few of the bottles in his bag. The doctor proudly displayed cures for insect bites. Ladies' cramps. Loose bowels. Sour breath. I kept sniffing until I hit the cork that smelled like burnt pineapple. "What's this?"

Tougaw's gold chains jangled as he grabbed it away. "Leave dat alone! Vera strong medicine! One drop too much and you will be paralyzed!"

"Wow! What's it for?"

"Mrs. Marvel's nervous problems. When she is bad suffrin' I explain that Vicky must give her only two drops in hot water. Neva more."

Never. Not in hot water, anyway. Vicky just went full strength for the injection: poor Barnard. I asked Tougaw if he had anything for insomnia.

He rummaged around the bottles. "Here is some fine sleepin' medicine. Take one teaspoon. You will go right to sleep and have pleasant dreams. When you wake, you will be full of desire. So be careful of the person you will lie down beside."

The stuff smelled like apricot brandy. "What happens if I drink the whole bottle?"

"You will die a happy lady."

What a quack. I paid him and wished him great success with the local sickos. After Tougaw left, I instructed the switchboard to put no calls through except those from Phil. Slept for hours. Midafternoon, I got the call. Phil wanted to see me in my room. I received him in purple silk pajamas that matched my jaw. He was not in uniform and not alone. I was introduced to a robot named Dawson with White House counsel crayoned all over him. "Drink?" I asked, raiding the minibar.

Of course not. First the detective checked the room for bugs. Then he left me alone with Dawson, who smiled with the warmth of a Komodo dragon as he inquired how I was feeling.

"I should be able to get a violin under my chin in another week."

"I'm very glad to hear that." He looked at me for a long moment. I think his pheromones were telling him I was hetero but his head was telling him I must be gay. "Miss Frost," he said finally, "you have become involved in a rather delicate situation that could cause serious political embarrassment. You could suffer personal consequences as well. Manslaughter is a grave offense."

"I didn't kill anyone. All I did was drive a drunk girl home and call 911. Don't look at me if her lover went on a rampage."

Dawson dropped the threats and tried the personal touch. "I'm sure you're aware of Vicky Chickering's relation to Mrs. Marvel. The First Lady is incoherent with grief."

"I'm very sorry to hear that."

"I'm willing to drop criminal charges in exchange for your absolute silence in this matter. In short, you were never at the

Watergate this morning. You never went dancing with Rhoby Hall last night. You will never speak to the press about this incident. Vicky Chickering stumbled and fell as she was leaving for work." Dawson tried to look menacing: tough to pull off wearing a powder blue bow tie. "Understood?"

"No problem."

"Also, you will return to Berlin immediately."

"I'll do my best. How's Rhoby?"

"Resting. She's been instructed not to contact you in any way."

"Thank you. That's the best news I've heard all day."

Uncertain what that meant, Dawson smiled woodenly. "So we're agreed?"

"Absolutely." I walked him to the door.

Dawson shook my hand and left. Things were going to get ugly for a while: Rhoby and I had cavorted in front of a lot of people who could use twenty grand from the *National Enquirer.* I was packing my things when the phone rang.

"This is Paula Marvel. Be downstairs in five minutes."

I hope she didn't plan on strangling me with her own hands now that Chickering was permanently indisposed. The First Lady sat alone in the back of the limousine that her husband usually reserved for his joyrides. She looked blotchy, bloated, and ruthless as an executioner. Today the bows, all seven of them, were red. Brought out the veins in her eyes. I had never seen her smoking before. A long gray cloud swirled over the ice cold cabin with every other exhalation. Skip the hi how are ya. "Tell me how Vicky died," Paula said. "I know it wasn't an accident."

I wanted this conversation as brief and clinical as she did. "Rhoby stabbed her through the back with a cello pin. That's about the size of a major knitting needle. They had been fighting."

"Over what?"

"Me. Chickering thought I was going to run away with her little girl. Ludicrous, of course. I have no interest in women."

"Then what were you doing all over town with Rhoby Hall?"

"Keeping the poor kid company. I had no idea Chickering would be waiting at home with a rolling pin. I've never seen such a cat fight."

"Why didn't you stop it?"

"Because I had been drugged. Paralyzed." Paula flinched. "After she swatted Rhoby around, Chickering injected me with something from her friend Tougaw."

"You didn't say anything to the police about that."

"I can always revise my statement," I retorted. "Now that you're refreshing my memory."

Paula dragged so viciously on her cigarette that it nearly burst into flame. I stared out the window, trying not to inhale, as the limo circled the block. Paula's eyes were moist when she finally whispered, "Did Vicky suffer long?"

"It was over in thirty seconds." A snap of the fingers compared to the slow asphyxiation she had inflicted on Barnard. No justice anywhere. My sympathy for Paula evaporated. "Chickering mentioned you in her dying breath."

"My God! Tell me! What did she say?"

A blast of dirty, humid air hit my face as I cracked open the window. " 'I tried, Paula.' " I turned to the waxen First Lady. "Now what do you think she meant by that? Tried to *kill* me? You wouldn't want her to do that, would you?"

Paula's eyes went cold as she searched for subtext: had I just told her everything or nothing? Unable to fathom my insouciant stare, she said, "What a preposterous suggestion. Why would I want to kill you?" She pressed a fresh cigarette to its smoldering predecessor. I was gratified to see that her hands shook. "Because you're sleeping with my husband?"

"Wrong," I sighed. "I've been fighting off your husband.

He's been on my tail since the night I played in the White House."

"Fighting him off?" Paula echoed sarcastically, blowing fresh carcinogens up my nose. "You've been in a bathtub with him."

Had Paula seen the video or just heard about it? I gambled that Wallace had been as efficient as she was treacherous and had erased it immediately. "Wrong again. I was in the tub when your husband walked in naked. All he did was look at me. Big deal. Tits and ass. I told him to beat it and he did."

"Goddamn animal," Paula seethed, hitting the control on her armrest. My window rolled shut again. "It's on tape."

"Jesus!" I tried to look horrified. "If this gets out, I'll be the laughingstock of Europe!"

"Here's the deal. You never see my husband again, never breathe a word of this affair, and I'll destroy the tape."

"There was no affair, but I'm not going to split hairs. You've got a deal. Better tell hubby yourself, though. He won't take my word for it."

Paula exhaled blithely. I guess after Bobby's first dozen affairs, adultery had lost its sting. "Do you think you're playing some kind of game, Miss Frost? Do you have any idea how dangerous it is to be fooling around with the president?"

Yeah, some. I wanted out of this refrigerator. It had already gone around the block three times. "Don't preach to me, Mrs. Marvel. I didn't screw your husband. But I'll warn my friend Polly Mason. Last I heard, she and Bobby were still a unit. Go lay your guilt trip on her."

Paula coughed on her fumes. "You know Mason?"

"We bump into each other from time to time. I've been calling but can't get an answer at her apartment here. She's probably taking a breather on the Riviera with her Italian count. Bobby can get pretty suffocating, you know."

Seconds dragged into half a minute. Paula knew Barnard would never be coming back. Now that Chickering, who had done the wet work, was gone, could the trail ever be traced back to the First Lady? That depended on how thoroughly Chickering had disposed of the body. *Come on, Paula, crack!* I could feel her brain inching over the craggy moonscape of murder, searching for the loose rocks that could destroy her. Finally, after crushing her last cigarette, she took a card from her purse. Her kewpie mouth curled upward daintily. "Tell Polly to call this number when she returns, would you? I'd like to chat with her."

So Chickering had been thorough: oh God, I'd never find Barnard's body now. For a second I was tempted to blurt who I was, how much I knew. . . . Alas, the Queen would never speak to me again. "I'll do that, Mrs. Marvel," I said.

Paula looked deeply and sincerely into my eyes, as if I were a television camera. "Vicky's death has shocked me tremendously. Please forgive me for being upset."

I wouldn't be forgiving you anything, honey. "I'll be leaving Washington tomorrow. I won't be telling your husband good-bye." Extended my hand. "Thanks for inviting me to the White House."

Where it all started: Paula's glance could have precipitated another ice age. Her cool hand barely touched mine. "Not one word, remember."

I opened the door and reeled back into the light and heat. Bobby had been out of his mind to marry that thing from another planet. I couldn't imagine getting into bed with her. Would she drive straight home and lay down the law? I doubted it: meeting me was enough trauma for one day. If Paula had any of Tougaw's sleeping potions handy, tonight she'd swallow the whole bottle. Tomorrow, after I had left the country, she'd stick it to Bobby.

I drove to Silver Spring and told Cecil he was taking one

last field trip. As the sun slipped out of sight, I brought him to Fausto's and explained what I expected of him tonight. Strange being in this gigantic, empty house again. Something not right here now. *Get out of town, Smith. Don't push your luck.* I laughed out loud. Luck? Mine had disappeared over a waterfall. I went to a button behind Fausto's dresser and pressed it twice. The wood paneling shifted, exposing a small closet. My Strad lay inside on top of a safe. Handy little room: I'd use it later. I fed Cecil and let him make a little noise at the piano as we waited for the phone to ring. At eleven Bobby called: Paula wasn't the only Marvel who wanted to hear my version of Chickering's demise. "Where's Fausto?" he demanded, finally sounding more like president than prom date.

"Out of town."

"I'll be right over. Make sure we're alone." His voice softened. "You all right?"

"Not really."

I dialed a number and handed the phone to Cecil. Wallace answered. "This is President Marvel," Cecil said. "Where's Aurilla?" In the kitchen. Maybe she was making iguana fritters. In any event, she came right to the phone. "Meet me at Fausto's in exactly forty minutes. Come alone." Hung up. "Think she'll bite?"

"I would."

We reviewed our routine then Cecil went upstairs. I turned out the lights in the music room as a three-car parade pulled into the driveway. As always, Secret Service agents circled the house and took positions along the perimeter of the property. Four more came inside and swept the place. No one discovered Cecil, but he was hidden upstairs with the safe and I was Bobby's girlfriend, not a terrorist. Finally satisfied that the coast was clear, another quartet of agents hustled the president to the front door. "Good evening, Mrs.

Kiss," he barked, then noticed my face. "Lord! That old mule had some left hook, didn't she."

"Do you mind if we go upstairs?" I said, shuddering in my purple peignoir. "It's cold out here."

Bobby didn't argue. "Where's your husband?" he asked as we mounted the steps.

"Who knows." I led him into the bedroom. Two agents stayed behind in the hallway. "I expect him back in a day or two." In a box.

Bobby was more impressed by Fausto's massive bed than his oil paintings. Couldn't take his eyes off it, perhaps calculating how large a bacchanalia it could handle. "What's he going to think of this escapade of yours?" he asked, falling onto the mattress.

"He'll laugh. Care for a beer?" I poured a glass and slipped a tiny pill into the bubbles. Forget the jungle swill: this came straight from Maxine's medicine chest. We girls called it Ten-Minute Intermission. Never failed. I handed Bobby his drink and lay next to him on the bed.

As he kissed my bruises, his countenance softened. "Just tell me what happened. Paula's a basket case."

She had been sane enough to see me that afternoon—and not mention it to Bobby. "Remember Chickie's roommate Rhoby? Ever since that concert at Aurilla's she's been calling me. Last night I couldn't sleep so I went to a few bars with her. Chickie went nuts when I brought Rhoby home. Thought I was stealing her wife. First she beat the tar out of Rhoby. Then she started in on me. Fortunately Rhoby stabbed her with her cello pin before she broke my jaw."

Bobby thought it over. "Did you screw her?"

"Rhoby? What for?"

He swallowed a great slug of beer. "Torment, sugar. Pure and simple."

"Torment has its limits. Even for me."

That was the last Bobby heard before plummeting to the pillow. I caught his beer and sprang Cecil from the closet. He dressed in Bobby's clothing: the resemblance was shocking. "Ten minutes," I told him, checking my watch. "Not one second more."

Cecil nodded and switched to Bobby-speak. "Now for a little fun, sugar." He opened the bedroom door a crack. "Time out," I heard him joke to the agents in the hall.

Fortunately Aurilla was a punctual individual. Cecil and a pair of agents were waiting on the front stoop for her as she rolled down the driveway. She didn't get invited into the house. Instead Cecil took her to the porch beneath the bedroom window, where light was dim but acoustics clear. "Is everything all right, Mr. President?" I heard Aurilla ask. "You and the First Lady must have had a terrible day."

"How long have we known each other, Aurilla? Ten years?"

Actually only eight, but she said, "I believe so, sir."

"I always knew you were an ambitious woman," Cecil continued. "But I'm afraid I underestimated the depth of your ambition."

"What do you mean, sir?"

"Oh, let's start with your daughter's recital in a dengue ward in Belize. A couple of mosquitoes in mesh balls. You taking a short elevator ride with Jojo Bailey . . . you get my drift?"

"No sir, I don't know what you're talking about." Aurilla spoke with such conviction that for a second I thought I had imagined everything.

Cecil simply continued. "Then I take you up on your kind offer of a home in the country, little realizing my most private actions would be videotaped."

"Who's been telling you these lies?" Aurilla cried, but her voice was way too high, wrung tight with fear. "I'm absolutely shocked."

"Cut the shit, Aurilla. You're just shocked that I found out before you had a chance to run me out of the presidency," Cecil retorted with awesome calm. He had only been playing this game for three minutes, not thirty years. "I'd ask you why you did it, but the answer is obvious. You're the lowest snake I ever met in my life. Now listen carefully. Tomorrow morning at seven you're going to make an announcement withdrawing your name from consideration for vice president. Make up any damn excuse you want. But you're out of it. Don't contact me in any way. Ever. You're going to drop off both those videotapes here as you leave town for a long vacation. Understand?"

No words as a chorus of crickets serenaded Aurilla's ruin. "I beg you to reconsider, Bobby," she croaked.

"Get out of my sight!" Cecil shouted. Behind me, the president stirred in bed. *Time's up, Cecil! Take your bow and leave!* As if he had heard me, Cecil strode back into the house, leaving Aurilla on the porch. He returned to the bedroom thirty seconds later.

"How'd I do?" he whispered, tearing off his clothes.

"We'll see." In fact, Cecil's performance had been overwhelming. He was dangerous beyond belief, capable of sparking World War III if he ever got serious about impersonating the president. As I shoved him back in the closet, I heard Aurilla's car leave. *Good luck trying to figure out who had betrayed you, sweetheart.*

I replaced Bobby's tainted beer with good stuff and waited for him to come round. Then I picked up exactly where we had left off. "Torment has its limits. Even for me," I repeated. "Sorry about Chickering."

"I'm not, sugar. She was a pain in the ass since she was twelve years old. But she was loyal. Paula's going to have trouble functioning without her."

Paula would bounce back sooner than Bobby thought.

She'd be on the receiving end of a lot of sympathy at Chickie's and Jojo's funerals. Then she could busy herself finding a new vice president. Then she could sift through an army of pit bulls panting to step into Chickie's shoes. Throughout this traumatic period, her personal healer would be at her side, dispensing potions. "Just tell your wife Chickie started it, all right?"

"I've been telling her that all day." Bobby put his beer on the night table. "I just get the feeling there's a piece missing here."

I stayed with him until five o'clock, when he finally gave up trying to get an erection: Maxine's pills had that annoying side effect. Bobby was mortified. Hadn't had this problem in his life but the stress of the day, this whopper bed, the excitement of actually seeing me naked after all the goosing around . . . ah well, some other time. I patted his cheek and walked him downstairs, where the Secret Service agents were just about pickled with boredom. At the front door, near the spot where Fausto had taken me, I kissed Bobby good-bye. "It's been fun."

He seemed bemused. "Good night, ma'am. Take care of yourself."

The presidential party drove home. Bobby wasn't a bad egg. He'd forgive me.

Chapter Fifteen

AFTER BOBBY HAD LEFT, I sprang Cecil from the secret closet. "You nailed it," I told him. "Tell me where to wire the fifty grand."

"You mean I'm done?"

"Class dismissed. You'd better get out of here before the caterers come." Fausto's breakfast ritual had continued in his absence and I wasn't ready to call it off before seeing the death certificate.

"But who killed Polly?"

"Vicky Chickering. Sorry, I've already taken care of her. Aurilla was an accessory, but I'd say you've effectively neutralized her." I started making the bed, smoothing Bobby's wrinkles away. "Good luck with your career. I'd avoid Washington for a while, if I were you."

"Can't leave until I settle with Fausto. He owes me a million bucks."

That frigid wind ruffled the hair at the base of my neck. "He went to Belize. You'll get your money. I promise."

Cecil—Bobby?—shook my hand. "It's been a blast. Will we meet again?"

"Not while you have that face. What are you going to do now?"

"Catch a little sleep. Then get the hell out of here." Cecil's fingers lingered over the bruises on my chin. "You'll keep my secret, won't you?"

"You'll keep mine?"

"Word of honor. I wouldn't want you coming after me with a frying pan." A prim kiss. "Bye, luv. I won't forget you."

In his own twisted way, an honest, hardworking man: if Cecil had any brains, he'd revert to his original face and settle down with a good stockbroker. Outside, dawn was gilding Fausto's trees. Ah, for a man, a pet monkey, the sound of water, the scent of hyacinths, anything alive to keep me company: but I was alone. In this war, I suppose that meant victory.

After the kitchen crew arrived, I got my violin from the closet. Fausto had left a letter inside. I took it to the window and began reading as the first cars piddled down his driveway.

Dearest wife,

You would not be reading this unless the inevitable occurred. It was a long shot, but for a few magical days, because of you, I was immortal. My only regrets are that we met too late and that I have made you a widow again. Be a merry one, would you? I met Finstein the morning after our wedding and told him what to do in case I didn't make it back. In short, you won't be needing pocket money for a while. Lest you think I'm a totally selfless man, I confess that I want to make it extremely hard for you to marry again. I want you to distrust any man who swears he loves you. Forgive me. For the first time in my life, I'm uncontrollably jealous, full of rage and despair at the same time that my heart bursts with a gigantic hope. . . .

Without you I would have departed right on schedule, an empty train. Now I can at least barrel into the long dark tunnel full of freight. God, I feel so young today, so besotted with life! I hear you, smell you, my fingers throb, my mouth aches for your moss and roses. I should never have sent you home. Stage fright at my age . . . how absurd.

After meeting Finstein, I did a rather impulsive thing. If it's any consolation to you, my dear, I'm not totally dead. My frozen sperm awaits your beck and call in a clinic on Wisconsin Avenue. You once told me that you desired nothing. I don't believe that, not anymore. If you would ever like to hold me in your arms again, please avail yourself of it.

If all goes well, Louis and I leave for Belize tonight. I have a hunch you'll come after us with a flogging cane.

Ah Leslie, I pray you never read this! I live—and die—breathing your name.

                                        Love forever,
                                        Fausto

I put my wedding ring back on. Then I went to the dresser with all the pictures on top. Mother and son looked so content, so complete . . . why not try again? Maybe Louis would get his antidote together with the fourth generation of Kisses. I tucked the smallest picture into my case and turned on the tube. Shortly before seven, a bulletin interrupted one of those mindless-as-cornflakes breakfast shows. Flash to a perfectly manicured Aurilla Perle, speaking from the steps of the Capitol. She looked fantastic, triumphant, as if she had just won the Battle of Trafalgar.

"It has been a privilege to have served the nation for the past eight years," she orated to a dozen microphones. "Now it is time to step aside and become, first and foremost, a mother to my daughter Gretchen. I resign my Senate seat, effective immediately, and look forward to private life again. I wish to thank my staff for their devotion and my constituents for their trust." She smiled through the ensuing pandemonium, waiting for the inevitable question.

"What about the vice presidency?" someone shouted. "Are you withdrawing your name from consideration?"

Aurilla's perfect smile augmented. "I will resume the life of a private citizen. Gretchen and I will pray for Jordan Bailey, as we will for President Marvel. Thank you." End of conference.

I watched the instant traffic jam in Fausto's driveway as most of his guests left: Aurilla had reshuffled all their decks. Duncan called from Cleveland. "Justine just ran *out!*" he screamed. "Bobby Marvel called! You could hear him across the room! My mother's *wasted!* She said she would never have voted for him if she knew what kind of language he used!"

"What can I tell you, Duncan. Justine had to get back to Washington."

"This is the last straw! She told me she was leaving him!"

"Get real. They're Siamese twins."

Soon even the caterers left. It was a beautiful morning, full of light and wind. I unlocked the front door. Took my violin to the music room and began practicing scales. I was up to A major when Bendix Kaar stormed in with a small package. "Where's Fausto?" he shouted. "Upstairs? I'll kill the bastard."

"He's out of town. Won't be back for a few days."

Bendix strode up to me. When his eyes got wild, he

looked like a jackal. "And you've been throwing your own parties meanwhile. With AC and DC."

"A girl's got to keep herself amused," I shrugged. "What's the matter with you today?"

"Haven't you been watching the news?"

"No. Am I missing something?"

"God! You're hilarious!" Flung his package on the red divan, apparently not even noticing the bullet hole in the upholstery. "Here are some videos your friend Bobby wanted dropped off here. I wouldn't peek if I were you."

Nothing to see, Bendix: Wallace had erased them. As he was out the door, I called, "Should I tell Fausto to phone when he gets back?"

"Tell Fausto I'm going to catch up with him. His gaming days are over," Bendix shouted, voice shredding. Bad luck: thirty years of work down the tubes, Aurilla would need another ten to rehabilitate herself, and they'd both spend the rest of their lives looking over their shoulders, wondering who knew their secret. Ah, Bendix, maybe you should have stuck to real opera. Washington was nothing but the soaps.

The last I heard of Bendix was a screech of rubber on macadam. Dozed a while on the ruined red divan. Eventually another car squealed to a stop outside the front door. Justine Cortot stomped in. Maybe she had been bitten by a rabid bat in Cleveland. She seemed to be frothing at the mouth. "Where's Fausto?" she shrieked. Gone was the blue-blood accent. "Don't tell me you don't know, you bitch!"

"Out of town. Why is everyone so hyper this morning?"

"Aurilla Perle quit!" she informed me, as if the Japanese had rebombed Pearl Harbor. "She's gone! No one can find her! Bobby's beside himself!" She stamped her foot. "Is she with Fausto? Tell me!"

"Why should she be with Fausto? He doesn't even like

her." I screwed up my face. "Aren't you supposed to be in Cleveland making a good impression on Duncan's mother?"

"Fuck Duncan's mother!" Justine reeled to the bar and downed two inches of vodka. It was the only thing to do when your clever plans to outmaneuver a president, an arms merchant, and a mercenary went down the tubes and all that stood between you and them was a fox named Fausto.

I watched her swallow a small pile of white tablets with another gush of vodka. "What's that? Estrogen?"

"Shut up!" Justine threw herself onto the divan where, just a few days ago, she had perched so nicely with Cecil's head in her lap. Now she looked like a tiny, shriveled mummy. "I've got to find Fausto," she moaned. "He's got to help me."

You find him, you let me know, sister. I played a few more scales. Strange jungle, Washington: the animals herein all thought they would die of old age. "What's the matter?" I asked finally. "Need a loan?"

Justine cackled hysterically, much like Bendix. "Cecil played a trick on me," she raved, rocking her head in her hands. "I knew it knew it knew it. Bastard."

"Who's Cecil?"

She began walking in circles, muttering to herself. "Fucking double-crosser. Damn damn *damn*. Who had what on Aurilla? Who who *who*? Someone big. Bendix won't tell me what happened. Oh my God! Where's Fausto?" A little beep from her pocketbook. Justine fumbled a great deal but finally unearthed her pager. She ran to the phone. "What the *fuck* do you think you're doing?" she screamed. "You think you're being funny? You won't be laughing when I get in front of a dozen microphones." She began to cry. "I need to see you right away. . . . Okay."

"Who was that? Duncan?" I called cheerfully after she had hung up.

"Leave Duncan out of this!"

"Why should I? You dragged him into it."

For a moment Justine's face looked like Chickering's when an eight-inch pin went through her heart. "Why don't you go back where you came from? Screw some Germans for a change! Nothing's been the same around here since you came to the White House! You think Bobby loves you?"

"Jesus, I hope not."

Didn't register. "I set that all up!"

"I know you did. Why, though? Isn't Bobby *your* heart-throb? Oh, sorry. I forgot. You're in love with Duncan now."

Justine frowned, terminally confused. "Fausto!" she screamed, running upstairs. "Where are you, goddamn it!"

As her footsteps rained over my head, I hit redial on the phone. Cecil answered. Bad move, Justine. Should have gone to Bobby. He would have forgiven you.

After she flounced out, I went to sleep in Fausto's bed. If I put my nose deep into the pillow and inhaled, I could still smell him, still feel his tongue between my legs, hear his voice. Alas, he was already fading into a mist of lost dreams.

Later in the afternoon, the phone rang. It was the guy who handled incoming ashes at the airport. I drove down and picked up the remains. My great mound of a husband in that little box? *Bury him and go home, Smith.* Fought my way through tourist traffic to the Congressional Cemetery. As usual, it was devoid of the living except for Old Faithful righting headstones at the bottom of the hill. I walked down to him. "Hi. Got a moment?"

Seeing the box in my hands, he wiped his hands on tattered overalls. "Sure."

We walked to the Kiss plot. It was another clear, gentle evening, fragrant with autumn. A southbound *V* of geese squawked overhead as I stood on Ethel's grave. "What's your name?" I asked.

"Hiram Littlefield."

"I know you're not a preacher, but could you say something?"

He removed his cap. "I am the resurrection and the life." He waited. "Praise God Almighty!"

King of all jungles. I handed over the box. "Scatter that for me, would you?" I whispered.

Hiram tossed Fausto high in the air, in several handfuls. The wind took most of him but a few big pieces hit Ethel's stone and bounced into the flowers. When the box was empty, Hiram repeated, "Praise God Almighty! Amen!"

Ah, what might have been. I would never fill in the final date on Fausto's grave: he wasn't dead yet. Just frozen. Tucked a few bills into Hiram's crusty pocket. "Keep the grass cut for me, would you?"

We walked back to the chapel. The dogwoods surrounding it had already lost their leaves. The heaps of garbage had disappeared. "Trucks came by the other day," Hiram explained. "Some lady senator startin' a committee to put everythin' back in its proper place."

Don't stop righting those headstones, Hiram: your patron saint quit this morning. Then he said, "I told them to start with the chapel. I know for a fact there's an antique piano in the basement. Seen it goin' in with my own eyes just a few weeks ago, before they board the place up. What a waste."

Beyond the hedges, an ambulance wailed toward the hospital, a police cruiser flashed toward the jail. I bade Hiram good night and left the neglected dead. Back to noise, color, mischief: dear life. Traffic crawled past the Jefferson Memorial as if it had been unveiled only yesterday. Got even slower as I neared the airport.

Flag outside the terminal at half-mast. I doubted that was in honor of Vicky Chickering so I joined the somber huddle beneath the nearest television. Jojo Bailey was dead. His heart had finally gotten tired of giving blood and never getting any of it back. I stood through long, reverent footage of his life from Boy Scout to vice president: compared with Jojo, George Washington was just a hack. Tonight, anyway. Next week at this time, Bailey would be just another obstacle for the graveyard lawn mower. The news anchors were already getting tired of acting personally bereaved for an ineffective drunk, especially when there was so much more exciting and unexpected news, like Vicky Chickering's tragic accident, Senator Perle's resignation, and, this just in, Justine Cortot's fall from her Georgetown balcony. She was not expected to live. What a hellish week for the Marvels! No one had seen Paula since yesterday but her doctors, the official ones anyway, reported her to be resting well. As for Bobby, the day had taken its toll. When he'd made his first announcement that morning following Aurilla's resignation, he'd looked numb. Early that afternoon when he'd made his second announcement about Jojo, he'd looked worse. But when he made the last announcement moments ago about Justine Cortot, I felt for him. He had lost his bedrock . . . join the crowd, sugar. Sorry I couldn't be there for you tonight. Soon as Bobby could handle it, Maxine would let him know what had really happened. He'd calm down once he realized what a favor I had done for him.

As I walked to the gate, the wayside televisions puzzled over Justine's mysterious fall. She had been under impossible stress lately and had perhaps developed a dependency on alcohol and chemical relaxants. Flash to a psychologist explaining what normal Americans could do about job-related stress besides topple off balconies. Nice move, Cecil: a man had to protect his investment and Justine had definitely crossed the line from slingshot to loose cannon. Poor Duncan.

I called Maxine. "I found Barnard." Told her where to

look and who was responsible then, time being short, boarded my flight with a load of Germans who had more interest in the booze cart than the sorrows of young Amerika. I didn't look out the window as the plane lifted over the Potomac, a dark thread through a city of splendorous, unnatural light.

Chapter Sixteen

CURTIS PICKED ME UP at the airport in Berlin. Hadn't seen his calm, black face in aeons. I had missed him. He stared for just a second at my swollen jaw, then my eyes: damage assessment. I could have looked worse, all things considered. At least this time I wasn't returning from the field with two dead lovers and a pack of reporters on my tail. For that, I got a long, strong hug. "Good flight?" he asked, taking the violin. "Where's Duncan?"

"Stuck in Cleveland. He should be back tomorrow." In fifty pieces.

Beautiful autumn morning, just nippy enough to warrant fur collars and felt hats. Curtis looked superb in both. As we walked to the car, my manager told me where and with whom I was supposed to be playing in the next few weeks. All orchestra dates, thank God: I wouldn't be needing an accompanist. Neither Duncan nor I was ready for that yet.

Pulling out of the parking lot, Curtis noticed the rock on my left hand. "Souvenir of Washington?"

It wasn't a trophy. "From Fausto. He drowned in Belize four days ago. No one knows yet."

"Sorry." Curtis wedged the M6 into heavy traffic on the

ring road. Instead of conversing, we listened to the radio: even the Germans were trying to figure out why Aurilla Perle had left Washington hours before Jojo finally ceded his job to her. Family reasons? Very few correspondents even knew she had a daughter. Ah well, after the cold war fizzled, no European could figure out American politics. Its only recent constant seemed to be Bobby Marvel's libido. Rumor was he had been wandering again, with a much younger woman. "Tired?" Curtis asked, shutting off the radio before we might hear my name mentioned.

"No. Maxine around?"

"She just left. Back in a day or two."

I inhaled Berlin. It was so much . . . *older* than Washington. More compact, razed more often: rodents here foraged closer to the ground. Dahlem looked like Fausto's neighborhood but not as hilly and my neighbors never threw breakfast parties. Shut my eyes as Curtis parked the M6 next to my Harley in the garage. Home. That's where I had wanted to be. Now that I was here, I wasn't so sure.

He brought my things upstairs and left me alone to pull out the computer and send Maxine a travelogue. When I came down again, he was in the kitchen making apple strudel: my appetite would eventually return. I sat at the table watching his thick, expert fingers at work. They were like Fausto's but a different color. A few people from the papers called, asking if I had been in Washington recently. Curtis would only tell them I had played a concert at the White House then had moved on to New York and no, I had nothing to say about either occasion. I opened mail, practiced, napped, waited: Duncan came barreling in that evening as we were eating supper. I had never seen him look this bad, not even after his comeback recital bombed last spring. If he had bathed recently, it had been in sour milk. He wore a strange outfit that seemed to come half from Justine, half from his mother. "Have you been listening to the news?" he screeched, plopping into a chair.

"Sure. They're expecting riots during the Oktoberfest."

"American news, you horse! Justine's in a coma!" He collapsed over a placemat. "It's my fault! I should have taken her back to Berlin!"

I put an arm around his quivering shoulders. "She had a lot of problems that Berlin wouldn't have solved."

"Oh shut up! You never liked her!" He thunked the table-top with his cast. "I don't believe for one minute she fell. We had too much to look forward to!"

"She was spaced-out, Duncan."

"No! The pager did it! She was terrified of the pager!"

I tried to look mystified. "You mean that guy who called her at six in the morning?"

"He called her all the time! She was supposed to be keeping an eye on him. A secret witness or something. Justine said he was extremely dangerous and all hell would break loose if anyone knew about him. She was a total wreck. We had an awful time in Cleveland. Shit! I *knew* this would happen!"

"Did she tell you his name? What she was doing with him?"

"No. It was for my own protection. I'm going to find out who he is. Then we'll see who falls off whose balcony."

I sighed: another half-assed Lancelot. "I'd be careful, Duncan. You're going to need proof first."

"I've got proof. That morning Justine rushed out of my house to get back to Washington, she dropped her diary. My mother found it wedged in the car seat. She's sending it to me Express Mail."

Curtis slid a dish of strudel in front of the distraught lover. "I'd take a few days to calm down before doing anything rash."

"You don't understand! Justine was all I had! Someone's going to pay for that!"

Correct, Duncan: you were. I filled my dry mouth with apples. "When's your cast coming off?"

"Tomorrow."

"You two can get back to work, then," Curtis said cheerfully.

"How can you be so obtuse? Can't you see I'm in *mourning?*"

"Get a grip, Duncan. Justine's not even dead yet."

My accompanist raged out, slamming many doors. After a moment, Curtis slid Duncan's untouched strudel onto his own plate and began eating it. "Is that diary trouble?"

"Depends on what she wrote. I can't imagine it's going to be a model of clarity." The grandfather clock in the hall struck eight. If Maxine had flown right to Washington after I called her yesterday, she could have hauled that piano out of the chapel in the cemetery by now. She could have had a chat with Wallace and maybe Bobby and be on her way back to Berlin. I wondered if she'd get back in time to intercept that Express Mail package or whether I should start thinking about blowing up the post office: if nothing else, Agent Smith was a thorough girl.

Helped Curtis with the dishes then practiced violin a few hours. The phone rang four times but my housemate wasn't putting any calls through. After the fifth, he came to the music room. "Maxine's on her way."

Already? I didn't know whether that was good news. "How'd she sound?"

"Normal." Curtis delicately cleared his throat. "President Marvel phoned a while ago. I told him you were asleep."

Queen's orders, of course. "How'd *he* sound?"

"Wouldn't know. I'm not as familiar with the man as you are."

Ah Curtis, still protecting me after all these years. He would be crushed to know I had married someone else, however briefly. "Bobby was part of the job," I said, putting away my violin. "The job's over."

I was polishing the chrome on my Harley when I felt the air change in the garage. No forewarning footsteps, no scents, just a dip of the antennae followed by a *whap* of adrenaline: I was in the jungle again, running for my life. Looked up. "Hey."

Maxine straddled my narrow workbench. "Thanks for finding her."

I had only provided directions. Didn't have the stomach for lifting the lid: even Barnard wouldn't have looked good after three weeks in a piano. "If it's any consolation, Chickering almost got me, too. I should have figured it out sooner."

"You were concentrating on Louis," Maxine said diplomatically. "He's back in Belize, I take it."

Saw green, felt tons of water crash on my chest. Kept buffing chrome. "Working on Tuna's poison. He was also working on a cure for Fausto's seizures. That's why the two of them needed him out of jail and back in the saddle."

"They went to a hell of a lot of trouble to do it. The sheer gall of impersonating a president does impress me, though. I suppose that was Fausto's style."

Why play Chopsticks if you could hack *Clair de lune*? "You'd have to be a philosopher to appreciate it."

"Who would have thought Louis and Fausto were just your starting point?" Maxine handed me a fresh chamois cloth. "This job needed a traffic controller. So many 747s going for the same landing strip. But that's Washington."

I buffed the rear fender until it felt hot. "Bendix and Aurilla almost got away with it. I would never have figured out the mosquitoes if they hadn't dragged Gretchen to that dengue ward in Belize. They probably couldn't find a baby-sitter."

"I had a chat with Wallace," the Queen said. "She confessed that she and Chickering moved the piano out of Watergate to the cemetery. On Paula's orders."

"Someone's got to protect that buffoon of a president."

"Wallace and Chickering were old friends. Aurilla knew that when she hired Wallace. She probably thought she'd be getting a direct feed to the First Lady. Never considered that Wallace might be spying in the opposite direction. Which brings us to our next pair of misfits." A short pause. "Did you really have to off Chickering?"

"Pardon me. I was paralyzed, if you recall." Checked the Harley's rearview mirrors. "Rhoby did the dastardly deed."

"After you egged the old girl into a fight. You could have walked out without a scratch."

"Look, you told me to find out who killed Barnard. Did you really expect me to stop there? These cocky Rasputins think they can get away with everything all the time. If it weren't for me, they would have."

"What can I say? Bravo."

At least I hadn't killed anyone on purpose. I just had a special gift for handing the knife to the lunatic with a better grasp of black and white. So was I evil? Couldn't answer that without a philosopher. "No doubt you visited Bobby. How'd he take your horror story?"

"He was stunned, to put it mildly. He had no idea Aurilla was about to screw him. Or that you had no intention of doing so. He wasn't pleased about the double." Maxine sighed. "Which takes us back to Fausto. Bobby wants his head."

"He ain't gonna get it." I swung a leg over the leather pillion. "Fausto's dead."

"Accident?"

"He didn't get back to Belize in time for Louis to make enough fresh medicine. It was a long shot in any case. He was terminally ill when we met." I snapped on my helmet.

"Duncan's back in Berlin. I wouldn't call him refreshed from his road trip. He thinks Cecil pushed Justine off her balcony. He's probably right."

"Duncan knows about Cecil?"

"Not completely. But he might after reading Justine's diary. His mother's sending it from Cleveland. Apparently Justine left it behind in her rush to get back to Bobby."

Maxine considered the implications. "Duncan's a big boy," she said finally. "Let him read it first. Are you aware that Bobby's coming to Berlin in a few weeks?"

"What for?"

"NATO meeting. He likes to look military before elections. You're going to see him. Says he's got a few questions for your ears only." The bench creaked as she slowly left it. Without comment she watched me zip on a black leather jacket. She was probably trying to figure out how, out of seven brilliant and ruthless agents, I could be the only one left. "Did you really marry Fausto?"

"Yes. Any more questions?"

"None that you could answer." Maxine stepped aside as I gunned the Harley into the night.

For a few days, the newspapers went mad. I was reading a hilariously mendacious interview with ex-senator, mother-redux Perle at her new residence in Switzerland when Duncan shuffled in. He looked awful.

"Hey, your cast's off."

Only a dispirited grunt in reply. I brought him to the kitchen, where Curtis was making Wiener schnitzel. "Look who's just in time for lunch."

"What can I get you, Duncan?" Curtis asked, wiping his hands on his apron.

"Beer and a switchblade," Duncan moaned, drooping into

a chair. He drank half the beer in one go. "I've never been so humiliated in my life."

Curtis brought a pile of noodles to the table. "Eat. You'll feel better."

Duncan obliged, but his mood did not improve. My manager and I kept up the small talk until the third bottle of beer. "Say, did you get Justine's diary?" I finally asked. A dismal nod. "Read anything about the pager?"

Duncan burped. "Nope. All she wrote about was Bobby Marvel. She was obsessed with him. They were going to ditch Paula the second he left the White House. Move back to a farm, raise tobacco, ride horses, all that crap. Of course he was the stud of her life. This wasn't a diary. It was a porno fantasy."

"You mean you didn't even get mentioned?"

"A few times. I was Doofus Dunko. My mother was Ma Blimp."

"What a bitch! After all that dancing."

"I should have listened to you. She was beginning to hallucinate at the end. Imagined she was screwing two Bobbys at once. Sick."

"One way of dealing with pressure," Curtis said. "Poor girl. I understand she had a substance abuse problem."

"She had a Bobby problem! Mentioned you a few times, Les."

"Highly complimentary, I'm sure."

"Different ways she'd like to kill you for turning Bobby's head. I had no idea Justine had such a violent imagination. She wasn't too fond of Fausto, either. He's lucky she didn't gas him." Duncan reached for another mound of noodles. "I wish I had never read the thing. At least I would have been left with my delusions of grandeur."

"Can't win 'em all, Duncan. You'll meet someone else."

"I don't think so," he said softly. "Not like her."

"So what are you going to do with the diary?" I asked.

Duncan tossed a small notebook on the table. "Burn it for me, would you, Curt?" He flexed his wrists. "Maybe we could read through some Brahms. See how far out of shape I am."

My pianist followed me to the music room.

I played a dozen concerts. Meanwhile, across the Atlantic, Jojo Bailey got a huge funeral. Chickering's was barely covered, Fausto's never even mentioned. After lying in a coma for weeks, Justine opened her eyes and moaned, "Bobby." He picked a new vice president, this one a vegetarian senator who had recently married an Asian heiress. They'd look great in Jojo's mansion. Meanwhile, a Middle East arms dealer dropped dead in Jerusalem right in the middle of a manicure. No one could figure out what had happened to him.

Maxine called. "Looks like Louis finally earned his five million bucks. He's back in Richmond, at any rate."

Two days later she called again. "Bendix Kaar was found dead this morning. Doctors think he had a heart attack. The cleaning lady found him slumped over his desk." The Queen chuckled. "He had been composing a two-part invention."

Nice going, Louis: a few more hits and that poison might win you the Nobel Peace Prize. "Maybe he died happy," I said. "Poor bastard."

I phoned the café in San Ignacio and said I'd call every day at this time until I got through to Ek. Eventually he was there. "I hear Louis went back to the States," I said. "What are you doing for the winter?"

"I'm a tour guide." Pause. "Easy walks. Nothing like yours."

My insides slid over a bottomless waterfall. "Louis settled your score. The man who killed Dr. Tatal is dead."

"Should I send money?" Ek asked.

"Of course not. Just take care of Louis as best you can."

"Thanks, Cosima."

One innocent soul corrupted, or perhaps civilized: great work, Smith. I spent a lot of time on the Harley chasing dead leaves. A few reporters wouldn't go away because they kept hearing ugly rumors about me dancing in an all-night muffin market on A Street. Fausto's lawyers visited with a pile of papers to sign. They were aghast that I had already scattered his ashes. Their client had married, died, and vanished within a space of three days: was that another of his huge jokes? Wish it were, boys.

I stopped reading newspapers when the NATO conference began wresting headlines from the debacle across the sea. One fine evening I had just blown in from a little Autobahn therapy when the phone rang. Curtis took the call. "Go wash your face," he said. "President Marvel's waiting for you at the embassy."

Traffic wasn't bad for three in the morning. I drove to the new digs near the Friedrichstrasse station. "Leslie Frost," I told the marines guarding America's most valuable human being.

They let the Harley and me inside. I passed the metal detector and another few guards who tried not to look at my black leather legs as I was escorted to a room with heavy curtains and deep chairs. Bobby was inside smoking a cigar. He looked a lot wearier since the last time I had seen him, but he had been stabbed in the back a half dozen times. I knew I didn't look any younger.

We stared across the room for a few seconds, taking in the wreckage. "Welcome to Berlin, sir," I said.

"Smith," he answered, tossing the cigar. "You tricked me." Another long glare, then, "Get your ass over here. Tonight *you* sit on *my* lap."

I obeyed. "Sorry about Aurilla."

"I'm sorry about Fausto." He patted my thigh. "Motherfuckin' weasel. The gall of him, thinking he could just get some clown to impersonate the president of the United States. I still want to tear him in itty bitty pieces."

"He was just trying to get Louis out of jail."

"That was only half the fun, sugar. You know that. Burning my ass was the other half. Where'd that shit impostor go? You have no idea how irritating it is knowing someone's walking around with *my face*."

"He's getting rid of it," I said. "I think."

"He'd better be. You're as bad as both of them, putting me to sleep like a mad dog while your impostor tells Aurilla to pack her bags. I didn't know what hit me the next morning when she resigned. She wouldn't speak one word to me. Simply left town."

"I was just trying to spare you some aggravation."

"The hell you were! You and that faker just wanted to play one last joke! Why didn't you just tell me the truth and let me take care of it?"

I ran a finger over Bobby's unshaven cheek. "The truth, my dear, is that your wife found out you were seeing Polly and had her killed. That's how this whole mess started. I came to Washington to pick up the pieces."

Obviously the Queen had not informed the president of this preludial detail. He was stunned. "Why would Paula do that?"

"For God's sake, think a little."

He did, and sighed. "Oh." He thought some more. "Did she try to kill you, too?"

"Chickering volunteered for that job. It was a little over her head."

His eyes sharpened as he finally understood her sudden death. Bobby's head, overloaded with thought, dropped back to the upholstery. "What a mess. Your boy Fausto was right. I sold my soul for nothing at all. I wish I could start over again, with Justine instead of Paula."

"You wouldn't have ended up in the White House without Paula."

"Wrong, sugar. She wouldn't have ended up there without me." More long, glum thought, ending with a snort. "I think she only deserves one term."

I didn't like the sound of that. "What do you mean?"

"I'm going to leave her. Marry Justine as soon as she leaves the hospital. That should be around Christmas."

"White House divorce. It will be a first," I said unenthusiastically. Poor America!

"Paula will go quietly. She wouldn't want to be convicted of homicide. Besmirch the office of First Lady."

I had to smile: tarnishing office was one area in which Bobby clearly outperformed his wife. "What about your approval ratings?"

"What does a lame duck care? First they'll drop. After I make a few speeches about love and marriage, they'll go through the roof again."

Unfortunately he was right. I played a little with Bobby's tie. Red: probably a gift from his second wife. "I understand Bendix had a heart attack."

"He died of frustration. Aurilla didn't even have the decency to attend his funeral. Although I'm sure she has her hands full with that little abomination of hers. What a perfect punishment." Bobby absently stroked my thighs. "Tell me something. Was I just another job to you?"

"You started out that way." Then all the other tin soldiers melted.

He tugged my head to his shoulder. "The war's over, sugar. We're the only ones left." Survival: what a tired punch line. Ah, Fausto. "Will you stay in touch? I became rather fond of our little talks."

If I ever returned to Washington, I'd be going to a clinic

on Wisconsin Avenue, not the backseat of Bobby's limousine. "Didn't you just say you were marrying Justine?"

"What does that have to do with anything?"

Hopeless. I just couldn't get mad at the guy for nosing through the jungle as best he could. Neither of us could have guessed that the plumed birds like Fausto and Barnard would expire first . . . leaving us bugs behind. "I'll think about it," I said, sliding off his lap.

"Leslie," he whispered, catching my wrist. "Thank you."

For what? Salvaging his presidency? We both knew Aurilla would have been a better leader. But Bobby was a nicer guy, and he had gotten there first. So much for survival of the fittest: morality imposed its own exceptions to the rule. I kissed the top of his head. "Good luck, sir."

Rode until the night ceded to dawn. Chilly outside. The cool air was like a gift, a reminder of civilized life—whatever that was. I crept up to bed but couldn't sleep: Fausto pressing on the heart. He had come and gone much too quickly. Something unfinished there. Perhaps I should defy the gods one more time, reclaim what they had snatched from me in a simmering jungle. Fausto had provided the means to hold him in my arms again: what I had lost in the heat I might yet find in the ice. Wouldn't that be the ultimate flush against a Dealer who always won in the end.

Went to the window. Only a few leaves remained on my trees. It was going to be an early winter. Maybe I should forget saving the world. If statesmen like Marvel were running it, I had nothing to save. The wind lifted, a few more leaves fluttered to the ground. When I closed my eyes, I heard Fausto playing Brahms and, ever so faintly, a woman's low laughter.